OTTO PENZLER PRESENTS
AMERICAN MYSTERY CLASSICS

WALTZ INTO DARKNESS

CORNELL WOOLRICH (1903–1968) is the pen name most often employed by George Hopley-Woolrich, one of America's best crime and noir writers, whose other pseudonyms included George Hopley and William Irish, the moniker under which *Waltz into Darkness* was first published. His novels were among the first to employ the atmosphere, outlook, and impending sense of doom that came to be characterized as noir, and inspired some of the most famous films of the period, including Alfred Hitchcock's *Rear Window*, François Truffaut's *The Bride Wore Black*, *Phantom Lady*, and celebrated B-movies such as *The Leopard Man* and *Black Angel*.

WALLACE STROBY is an award-winning journalist and the author of eight novels, including *Some Die Nameless*, published in 2018, and four titles featuring professional thief Crissa Stone. A native of Long Branch, N.J., he's a lifelong resident of the Jersey Shore.

WALTZ INTO DARKNESS

CORNELL WOOLRICH

Introduction by
WALLACE STROBY

AMERICAN MYSTERY CLASSICS

Penzler Publishers
New York

INTRODUCTION

Love kills.

Nowhere is that truer than in the work of Cornell Woolrich, America's greatest *noir* novelist. And in that work, there is no better example than *Waltz into Darkness*.

First published in 1947, *Waltz* was written under Woolrich's William Irish pseudonym, which he had previously used for his novels *Phantom Lady* and *Deadline at Dawn*. It came near the end of an incredibly prolific period in his creative life—from 1940 to 1950—that saw the publication of eleven classic suspense novels and dozens of short stories.

Woolrich's longest novel, *Waltz* trades his usual Manhattan nightscapes for the gaslight and cobblestones of 1880 New Orleans. All that poor Louis Durand, the novel's ostensible hero, wants is to love, and be loved. Fifteen years earlier, his fiancée died of yellow fever on the night before their wedding. Now an affluent businessman at thirty-seven, Louis is nonetheless lonely, lost, and terrified of growing old alone. He contracts for a mail-order bride from St. Louis, in what he calls "the bargain he had made with love, taking what he could get, in sudden desperate haste, for fear of getting nothing at all."

But when Julia Russell, his bride-to-be, arrives, she looks nothing like the pictures she's sent, and her stories don't match what she's recounted in her letters. Blinded by love and need, Louis accepts her explanations without question, and ignores those first ominous clues that she's not what—or who—she claims to be.

Petite, blond and lovely, Julia (or Bonny, as her real name may or may not be) is nevertheless the most *fatale* of *femmes*. Louis is soon ensnared—helplessly and willingly—in her web. When Julia empties out their joint bank account and flees the city, Louis pursues her across the American South with murder in his heart, only to fall back in love with her after they're reunited in a typically wild Woolrichian coincidence. Driven to desperate ends, Louis finally commits an act in her defense from which there is no return. His fate is sealed.

Despite its uncharacteristic setting and ambitious scope, *Waltz* is vintage Woolrich. Julia/Bonny is another in his series of fascinating female characters—angels bright and dark. Woolrich women could be driven by revenge (*The Bride Wore Black*), unrequited love (*Phantom Lady*) or a quest for justice (*The Black Angel*). Julia/Bonny's primary motivation is greed, but she's a self-made woman as well. She drinks, smokes, and cheats at cards, with no apologies. Louis loves her anyway.

The novel also revisits one of Woolrich's favorite themes and subtexts—the elusiveness of identity. Do we really know this person next to us? Do we really know ourselves? What are we capable of when driven to extremes? His stories are filled with characters being pursued for crimes they didn't commit. Or maybe they did.

On the classic question of free will versus predestination, Louis—and by extension Woolrich—is firmly in the second camp. "It's already too late," Louis admits at one point. "It's been too late since I first met her. It's been too late since the day I was born."

Woolrich's own ill-fated life has become the stuff of legend. The son of a wealthy globe-trotting engineer and a New York socialite, he settled in Manhattan and attended Columbia University (then Columbia College) in the early 1920s. While living with his mother's family in a Harlem brownstone, he began to devote himself to writing. His first novels were Jazz Age society tales patterned on the work of F. Scott Fitzgerald, but he later began submitting mystery stories to the penny-a-word pulp magazines of the day. Following a brief, failed marriage in 1930, he lived with his mother in a series of New York residential hotels until her death in 1957.

An alcoholic and by some accounts (but not all) a closeted

homosexual, Woolrich lived a solitary life, even as his novels and short stories were permeating popular culture. His sturdy suspense-filled plots and visual writing made his work a natural for adaptation to radio, film, and eventually TV. From 1940 to 1954 alone, there were eighteen films based on Woolrich properties. These included high-profile Hollywood fare such as Alfred Hitchcock's 1954 *Rear Window* (based on Woolrich's 1942 novelette "It Had to Be Murder") and B-movie sleepers such as 1949's *The Window* (from the short story "The Boy Cried Murder") and Val Lewton's *The Leopard Man* (based on the novel *Black Alibi*). To date, more than a hundred films and TV shows have been made from his work in a half-dozen languages.

Woolrich himself was no fan of the films based on his books, at least the ones he saw. In a 1947 letter to Columbia professor Mark Van Doren, he claimed to be "ashamed" by Roy William Neill's film version of *The Black Angel*. "It took me two or three days to get over it," he wrote. "All I could keep thinking of in the dark was 'Is *that* what I wasted my whole life at?'" Years after the New York premiere of *Rear Window*, he was still angry at Hitchcock for not inviting him. It's uncertain if he ever saw the film.

Waltz has been filmed twice, first in 1968 as *Mississippi Mermaid*, directed by François Truffaut, who a year earlier had adapted *The Bride Wore Black*. *Mermaid* starred French matinee idol Jean-Paul Belmondo as Louis, and a luminous Catherine Deneuve as Julia, resetting the story on a French island in the Indian Ocean. In 2001, the book was filmed again as *Original Sin*, starring Antonio Banderas and Angelina Jolie, this time relocated to nineteenth-century Cuba.

Like many of Woolrich's novels, *Waltz* feels written from a well of pure emotion. His trademark doomed romanticism haunts every page. Though his style is often idiosyncratic—with a fondness for comma splices, adverbs, and descriptions that run a sentence too long—it's hard not to be swept away by the lushness of his prose. At times, he's also capable of an almost-poetic terseness. As Louis's dream marriage unravels, Woolrich gives it a simple eulogy. "The house was dead. Love was dead. The story was through."

It would be a spoiler to mention too many of the reversals in store, except to say that Woolrich's mastery of suspense is in peak form here. As he does in his best work, he invests the novel with a pervasive undercurrent of dread. The fact that his plots don't always make much sense, or rely too heavily on coincidence, only makes them more effective. This is *noir* so strong it warps reality. The stories unfold with the logic—and inevitability—of a nightmare. His protagonists are haunted and hunted, tripped by fate and trapped by the night.

Woolrich's own already-unhappy life began to spiral after his mother's death. Infirm and alone, he slipped into self-imposed obscurity even as his work continued to generate substantial income. The writer Barry N. Malzberg, who was Woolrich's agent during the last year of his life, remembers him as "a crushed, lonely, and timorous soul, always seeking friendship, finding—because of his naked need—little."

A diabetic, Woolrich eventually lost a leg to gangrene after failing to seek medical attention for an infection. He spent his final months as a recluse, confined to a wheelchair in his one-bedroom apartment at New York City's Sheraton Russell Hotel. It was there he died from a massive stroke on Sept. 25, 1968 at the age of sixty-five. Only a handful of people attended his funeral.

Woolrich's last major attempt at a novel, the posthumously titled *Into the Night*, was unfinished at the time of his death (it was later completed by Edgar Award-winning novelist Lawrence Block, and published in 1987 by The Mysterious Press). Woolrich also left behind chapters of a beautifully written—though likely highly fictionalized—autobiography, *Blues of a Lifetime*. In the chapter "Remington Portable NC69411" (the make of one of his early typewriters), a deeply depressed Woolrich looks back nostalgically—and painfully—on his days as a young writer. He remembers long happy nights on the second floor of the Manhattan brownstone he shared with his mother, grandfather and aunts, crafting his first novel, 1926's *Cover Charge*, in a white-hot rush, writing by hand, reveling in the fierce joy of his art and talent:

"*I was so hooked on it that I couldn't have given it up for love nor money. So every evening after my meal was over I'd sit there, anywhere from nine to eleven-thirty or twelve* . . . *a single lamp lit behind me on a pedestal in the corner* . . . *Every now and again I'd take a breather, lean back to rest my back and ease my neck, and put out even the one light, to facilitate the gathering of new thoughts for the pencil bout to come.*

"*I never forgot those chiaroscuro seances in that second-floor room.* . . . *I like that kid, as I look back at him; it's almost impossible not to like all young things anyway, pups and colts and cubs of all breeds. But I feel dreadfully sorry for him, and above all, I wish and pray, how I wish and how I pray, that he had not been I. He might have had a better destiny, if he hadn't been, he might at least have had a chance to find his happiness.*"

A sad and haunted life, but what beautiful work he left us. Stories of love and obsession, fate and fear, the things that never change. And—most Woolrichian of all—the doom that hovers over us always, waiting for its moment to arrive.

—WALLACE STROBY

WALTZ INTO DARKNESS

"If one should love you with real love
(Such things have been,
Things your fair face knows nothing of
It seems, Faustine) . . ."

SWINBURNE

CHARACTERS THAT APPEAR IN THE STORY

Louis Durand, the man in New Orleans

Tom, who works for him

Aunt Sarah, Tom's sister

Julia Russell, the woman who comes from St. Louis
to marry him

Allan Jardine, his business partner

Simms, a bank manager

Commisioner of Police of New Orleans

Bertha Russell, sister of the woman who comes
to marry Durand

Walter Downs, a private investigator of St. Louis

Colonel Harry Worth, late of the Confederate Army

Bonny, who once was Julia

CHARACTER THAT DOES NOT APPEAR
IN THE STORY

"Billy," a name on a burned scrap of letter, an unseen
figure watching a window, a stealthy knocking at a door.

The soundless music starts. The dancing figures appear, slowly draw together. The waltz begins.

— I —

THE SUN was bright, the sky was blue, the time was May; New Orleans was heaven, and heaven must have been only another New Orleans, it couldn't have been any better.

In his bachelor quarters on St. Charles Street, Louis Durand was getting dressed. Not for the first time that day, for the sun was already high and he'd been up and about for hours; but for the great event of that day. This wasn't just a day, this was *the* day of all days. A day that comes just once to a man, and now had come to him. It had come late, but it had come. It was now. It was today.

He wasn't young any more. Others didn't tell him this, he told himself this. He wasn't old, as men go. But for such a thing as this, he wasn't too young any more. Thirty-seven.

On the wall there was a calendar, the first four leaves peeled back to bare the fifth. At top, center, this was inscribed *May*. Then on each side of this, in slanted, shadow-casting, heavily curlicued numerals, the year-date was gratuitously given the beholder: 1880. Below, within their little boxed squares, the first nineteen numerals had been stroked off with lead pencil. About the twentieth, this time in red crayon, a heavy circle, a bull's-eye, had been traced. Around and around, as though it could not be emphasized enough. And from there on, the numbers were blank; in the future.

He had put on the shirt with starched ruffles that Maman Alphonsine had so lovingly laundered for him, every frill a work of art. It was fastened at the cuffs with garnet studs backed with silver. In the flowing ascot tie that spread downward fanwise from his chin was thrust the customary stickpin that no well-dressed man was ever without, in this case a crescent of diamond splinters tipped by a ruby chip at each end.

A ponderous gold fob hung from his waistcoat pocket on the right side. Linking this to the adjoining pocket on the left, bulky with a massive slab of watch, was a chain of thick gold links, conspicuous across his middle, and meant to be so. For what was a man without a watch? And what was a watch without there being an indication of one?

His flowing, generous shirt, above this tightly encompassing waistcoat, gave him a pouter-pigeon aspect. But there was enough pride in his chest right now to have done that unaided, anyway.

On the bureau, before which he stood using his hairbrush, lay a packet of letters and a daguerreotype.

He put down his brush, and, pausing for a moment in his preparations, took them up one by one and hurriedly glanced through each. The first bore the letter-head: "The Friendly Correspondence Society of St. Louis, Mo.—an Association for Ladies and Gentlemen of High Character," and began in a fine masculine hand:

Dear Sir:
    In reply to your inquiry we are pleased to forward to you the name and address of one of our members, and if you will address yourself to her in person, we feel sure a mutually satisfactory correspondence may be engaged upon—

The next was in an even finer hand, this time feminine: "My dear Mr. Durand:—" And signed: "Y'rs most sincerely, Miss J. Russell."

The next: "Dear Mr. Durand: . . . Sincerely, Miss Julia Russell."

The next: "Dear Louis Durand: . . . Your sincere friend, Julia Russell."

And then: "Dear Louis: . . . Your sincere friend, Julia."

And then: "Dear Louis: . . . Your sincere Julia."

And then: "Louis, dear: . . . Your Julia."

And finally: "Louis, my beloved: . . . Your own impatient Julia."

There was a postscript to this one: "Will Wednesday never come? I count the hours for the boat to sail!"

He put them in order again, patted them tenderly, fondly, into symmetry. He put them into his inside coat pocket, the one that went over his heart.

He took up, now, the small stiff-backed daguerreotype and looked at it long and raptly. The subject was not young. She was not an old woman, certainly, but she was equally certainly no longer a girl. Her features were sharply indented with the approaching emphases of alteration. There was an incisiveness to the mouth that was not yet, but would be presently, sharpness. There was a keen appearance to the eyes that heralded the onset of sunken creases and constrictions about them. Not yet, but presently. The groundwork was being laid. There was a curvature to the nose that presently would become a hook. There was a prominence to the chin that presently would become a jutting-out.

She was not beautiful. She could be called attractive, for she was attractive to him, and attractiveness lies in the eyes of the beholder.

Her dark hair was gathered at the back of the head in a psyche-knot, and a smattering of it, coaxed the other way, fell over her forehead in a fringe, as the fashion had been for some considerable time now. So long a time, in fact, that it was already unnoticeably ceasing to be the fashion.

The only article of apparel allowed to be visible by the limitations of the pose was a black velvet ribbon clasped tightly about her throat, for immediately below that the portrait ended in smouldering brown clouds of photographic nebulae.

So this was the bargain he had made with love, taking what he could get, in sudden desperate haste, for fear of getting nothing at all, of having waited too long, after waiting fifteen years, steadfastly turning his back on it.

That early love, that first love (that he had sworn would be the last) was only a shadowy memory now, a half-remembered name from the past. Marguerite; he could say it and it had no meaning now. As dry and flat as a flower pressed for years between the pages of a book.

A name from someone else's past, not even his. For every seven years we change completely, they say, and there is nothing left of what we were. And so twice over he had become somebody else since then.

Twice-removed he was now from the boy of twenty-two—called Louis Durand as he was, and that their only link—who had knocked upon the house door of his bride-to-be the night before their wedding, stars in his eyes, flowers in his hand. To stand there first with his summons unanswered. And then to see it swing slowly open and two men come out, bearing something dead on a covered litter.

"Stand back. Yellow jack."

He saw the ring on her finger, trailing the ground.

He didn't cry out. He made no sound. He reached down and placed his courtship flowers gently on the death-stretcher as it went by. Then he turned and went away.

Away from love, for fifteen years.

Marguerite, a name. That was all he had left.

He was faithful to that name until he died. For he died too, though more slowly than she had. The boy of twenty-two died into a young man of twenty-nine. Then *he* in turn was still faithful to the name his predecessor had been faithful to, until he too died. The young man of twenty-nine died into an older man of thirty-six.

And suddenly, one day, the cumulative loneliness of fifteen years, held back until now, overwhelmed him, all at one time, inundated him, and he turned this way and that, almost in panic.

Any love, from anywhere, on any terms. Quick, before it was too late! Only not to be alone any longer.

If he'd met someone in a restaurant just then—

Or even if he'd met someone passing on the street—

But he didn't.

His eye fell, instead, on an advertisement in a newspaper. A St. Louis advertisement in a New Orleans newspaper.

You cannot walk away from love.

His contemplation ended. The sound of carriage wheels stopping somewhere just outside caused him to insert the likeness into his money-fold, and pocket that. He went out to the second-story veranda and looked down. The sun suddenly whitened his back like flour as he leaned over the railing, pressing down the smouldering magenta bougainvillea that feathered its edges.

A colored man was coming into the inner courtyard or patio-well through the passageway from the street.

"What took you so long?" Durand called down to him. "Did you get my flowers?" The question was wholly rhetorical, for he could see the cone-shaped parcel, misty pink peering through its wax-wrappings at the top.

"Sure enough did."

"Did you get me a coach?"

"It's here waiting for you now."

"I thought you'd never get back," he went on. "You been gone all of—"

The Negro shook his head in philosophical good nature. "A man in love is a man in a hurry."

"Well, come on up, Tom," was the impatient suggestion. "Don't just stand down there all day."

Humorous grin still unbroken, Tom resumed his progress, passed from sight under the near side of the facade. Several moments later the outermost door of the apartment opened and he had entered behind the owner.

The latter turned, went over to him, seized the bouquet, and pared off its outer filmy trappings, with more nervous haste than painstaking care.

"You going give it to her, or you going tear it to pieces?" the colored man inquired drily.

"Well, I have to see, don't I? Do you think she'll like pink roses and sweet peas, Tom?" There was a plaintive helplessness to the last part of the question, as when one grasps at straws.

"Don't all ladies?"

"I don't know. The only girls I—" He didn't finish it.

"Oh, them," said Tom charitably. "The man said they do," he went on. "The man said that's what they all ask for." He fluffed the lace-paper collar encircling them with proprietary care, restoring its pertness.

Durand was hastily gathering together his remaining accoutrements, meanwhile, preparatory to departure.

"I want to go to the new house first," he said, on a somewhat breathless note.

"You was there only yesterday," Tom pointed out. "If you stay away only one day, you afraid it's going to fly away, I reckon."

"I know, but this is the last chance I'll have to make sure everything's— Did you tell your sister? I want her to be there when we arrive."

"She'll be there."

Durand stopped with his hand to the doorknob, looked around in a comprehensive sweep, and suddenly the tempo of his departure had slackened to almost a full halt.

"This'll be the last time for this place, Tom."

"It was nice and quiet here, Mr. Lou," the servant admitted. "Anyway, the last few years, since you started getting older."

There was a renewed flurry of departure, as if brought on by this implicit warning of the flight of time. "You finish up the packing, see that my things get over there. Don't forget to give the keys back to Madame Tellier before you leave."

He stopped again, doorknob at a full turn now but door still not open.

"What's the matter, Mr. Lou?"

"I'm scared now. I'm afraid she—" He swallowed down his rigid ear-high collar, backed a hand to his brow to blot imperceptible moisture, "—won't like me."

"You look all right to me."

"It's all been by letters so far. It's easy in letters."

"You sent her your picture. She knows what you look like," Tom tried to encourage him.

"A picture is a picture. A live man is a live man."

Tom went over to him where he stood, dejectedly sidewise now to the door, dusted off his coat at the back of his shoulder. "You're not the best-looking man in N'Orleans. But you're not the worst-looking man in N'Orleans either."

"Oh, I don't mean that kind of looks. Our dispositions—"

"Your ages suit each other. You told her yours."

"I took a year off it. I said I was thirty-six. It sounded better."

"You can make her right comfortable, Mr. Lou."

Durand nodded with alacrity at this, as though for the first time he felt himself on safe ground. "She won't be poor."

"Then I wouldn't worry too much about it. When a man's in love, he looks for looks. When a lady's in love, 'scusing me, Mr. Lou, she looks to see how well-off she's going to be."

Durand brightened. "She won't have to scrimp." He raised his head suddenly, as at a new discovery. "Even if I'm not all she might hope for, she'll get used to me."

"You want to—just make sure?" Tom fumbled in his own clothing, yanked at a concealed string somewhere about his chest, produced a rather worn and limp rabbit's foot, a small gilt band encircling it as a mounting. He offered it to him.

"Oh, I don't believe in—" Durand protested sheepishly.

"They ain't a white man willing to say he do," Tom chuckled. "They ain't a white man don't, just the same. Put it in your pocket anyway. Can't do no harm."

Durand stuffed it away guiltily. He consulted his watch, closed it again with a resounding clap.

"I'm late! I don't want to miss the boat!" This time he flung the symbolic door wide and crossed the threshold of his bachelorhood.

"You got the better part of an hour before her stack even climb up in sight 'long the river, I reckon."

But Louis Durand, bridegroom-to-be, hadn't even waited. He was clattering down Madame Tellier's tile-faced stairs outside at a resounding gait. A moment later an excited hail came up through the window from the courtyard below.

Tom strolled to the second-story veranda.

"My hat! Throw it down." Durand was jumping up and down in impatience.

Tom threw it down and retired.

A second later there was another hail, even more agonized.

"My stick! Throw that down too."

That dropped, was seized deftly on the fly. A little puff of sun-colored dust arose from Madame Tellier's none-too-immaculate flagstones.

Tom turned away, shaking his head resignedly.

"A man in love's a man in a hurry, sure enough."

— 2 —

THE COACH drove briskly down St. Louis Street. Durand sat straining forward on the edge of the seat, both hands topping his cane-head and the upper part of his body supported by it. Suddenly he leaned still further forward.

"That one," he exclaimed, pointing excitedly. "That one right there."

"The new one, cunnel?" the coachman marveled admiringly.

"I'm building it myself," Durand let him know with an atavistic burst of boyish pride, sixteen years late. Then he qualified it, "I mean, they're doing it according to my plans. I told them how I wanted it."

The coachman scratched his head. A gesture not meant to indicate perplexity in this instance, but of being overwhelmed by such grandeur. "Sure is pretty," he said.

The house was two stories in height. It was of buff brick, with white trim about the windows and the doorway. It was not large, but it occupied an extremely advantageous position. It sat on a corner plot, so that it faced both ways at once, without obstruction. Moreover, the ground-plot itself extended beyond the house, if not lavishly at least amply, so that it touched none of its neighbors. There was room left for strips of sod in the front, and for a garden in the back.

It was not, of course, strictly presentable yet. There were several small messy piles of broken, discarded bricks left out before it, the sod was not in place, and the window glass was smirched with streaks of paint. But something almost reverent came into the man's face as he looked at it. His lips parted slightly and his eyes softened. He hadn't known there could be such a beautiful house. It was the most beautiful house he had ever seen. It was his.

A questioning flicker from the coachman's whip stirred him from his revery.

"You'll have to wait for me. I'm going down to meet the boat from here, later on."

"Yessuh, take your time, cunnel," the coachman grinned understanding. "A man got to look at his house."

Durand didn't go inside immediately. Instead he prolonged the rapture he was deriving from this by first walking slowly and completely around the two outermost faces of the house. He tested a bit of foundation stone with his cane. He put out his hand and tried one of the shutters, swinging it out, then flattening it back again. He fastidiously speared a small, messy puff-ball of straw with his stick and transported it offside of the walk, leaving a trail of scattered filaments that was worse than the original offender.

He returned at last to the door, his head proudly high. There was a place indicated by pencil marks on the white-painted pinewood where a wrought-iron knocker was to be affixed, but this was not yet in position. He had chosen it himself, making a special trip to the foundry to do so. No effort too great, no detail too small.

Scorning to raise hand to the portal himself, possibly under the conviction that it was not fitting for a man to have to knock at the door of his own house, he tried the knob, found it unlocked, and entered. There was on the inside the distinctive and not unpleasant—and in this case enchanting—aroma a new house has, of freshly planed wood, the astringent turpentine in paint, window putty, and several other less identifiable ingredients.

A virginal staircase, its newly applied maple varnish protected by a strip of brown wrapping paper running down its center, rose at the back of the hall to the floor above. Turning aside, he entered a skeletal parlor, its western window casting squared puddles of gold light upon the floor.

As he stood and looked at it, the room changed. A thick-napped flowered carpet spread over its ascetic floor boards. The lurid red of lazy wood-flames peered forth from the now-blank fireplace under the mantel. A rounded mirror glistened ghostly on the wall above it. A plush sofa, a plush chair, a parlor table, came to life where there was nothing standing now. On the table a lamp with a planet-like milky-white bowl topping its base began to glow softly, then stronger, and stronger. And with its aid, a dark-haired head appeared in one of the chairs, contentedly resting back against the white antimacassar that topped it. And on the table, under the kindly lamp, some sort of a workbasket. A sewing workbasket. A little vaguer than the other details, this.

Then a pail clanked somewhere upstairs, and a tide of effacement flowed across the room, the carpet thinned, the fire dimmed, the lamp went out and with it the dark-haired faceless head, and the room was just as gaunt as it had been before. Rolls of furled wallpaper, a bucket on a trestle, bare floor.

"Who's that down there?" a woman's voice called hollowly through the empty spaces.

He came out into the hall at the foot of the stairs.

"Oh, it you, Mr. Lou. 'Bout ready for you now, I reckon."

The gnarled face of an elderly colored woman, topped by a

dust-kerchief tied bandana-style, was peering down over the up-stairs guardrail.

"Where'd he go, this fellow down here?" he demanded testily. "He should be finishing."

"Went to get more paste, I 'spect. He be back."

"How is it up there?"

"Coming along."

He launched into an unexpected little run, that carried him at a sprightly pace up the stairs. "I want to see the bedroom, mainly," he announced, brushing by her.

"What bridegroom don't?" she chuckled.

He stopped in the doorway, looked back at her rebukingly. "On account of the wallpaper," he took pains to qualify.

"You don't have to 'splain to me, Mr. Lou. I was in this world 'fore you was even born."

He went over to the wall, traced his fingers along it, as though the flowers were tactile, instead of just visual.

"It looks even better up, don't you think?"

"Right pretty," she agreed.

"It was the closest I could get. They had to send all the way to New York for it. See I asked her what her favorite kind was, with-out telling her why I wanted to know." He fumbled in his pock-et, took out a letter, and scanned it carefully. He finally located the passage he wanted, underscored it with his finger. "—and for a bedroom I like pink, but not too bright a pink, with small blue flowers like forget-me-nots." He refolded the letter triumphantly, cocked his head at the walls.

Aunt Sarah was giving only a perfunctory ear. "I got a passel of work to do yet. If you'll 'scuse me, Mr. Lou, I wish you'd get out the way. I got make this bed up first of all." She chuckled again.

"Why do you keep laughing all the time?" he protested. "Don't you do that once she gets here."

"Shucks, no. I got better sense than that, Mr. Lou. Don't you fret your head about it."

He left the room, only to return to the doorway again a moment later. "Think you can get the downstairs curtains up before she gets here? Windows look mighty bare the way they are."

"Just you fetch her, and I have the house ready," the bustling old woman promised, casting up a billowing white sheet like a sail in the wind.

He left again. He came back once more, this time from midstairs.

"Oh, and it'd be nice if you could find some flowers, arrange them here and there. Maybe in the parlor, to greet her when she comes in."

She muttered something that sounded suspiciously like: "She ain't going have much time spend smelling flowers."

"What?" he caught her up, horrified.

She prudently refrained from repetition.

He departed once more. Once more he returned. This time all the way from the foot of the stairs.

"And be sure to leave all the lamps on when you go. I want the place bright and cheery when she first sees it."

"You keep peggin' at me every secon' like that," she chided, but without undue resentment, "and I won't git nothing done. Now go on, scat," she ordered, shaking her apron at him with contemptuous familiarity as though he were seven or seventeen, not thirty-seven. "Ain't nothing git in your way more than a man when he think he helping you fix up a place for somebody."

He gave her a rather hurt look, but he went below again. This time, at last, he didn't come back.

Yet when she descended herself, some full five minutes later, he was still there.

His back was to her. He stood before a table; simply because it happened to be there in the way. His hands were planted flat upon it at each side, and he was leaning slightly forward over it. As if peering intently into vistas of the future, that no one but he could see. As if in contemplation of some small-sized figure coming toward him through its rotary swirls, coming nearer, nearer, growing larger as it neared him, growing toward life-size—

He didn't hear Aunt Sarah come down. He only tore himself away from the entranced prospect, turned, at the first sound of her voice.

"You still here, Mr. Lou? I might have knowed it." She planted her arms akimbo, and surveyed him indulgently. "Just look at that. You sure happy, ain't you? I ain't never seen such a look on nobody's face before."

He sheepishly passed his hand across the lower part of his face, as if it were something external she had reference to. "Does it show that much?" He looked around him uncertainly, as if he still couldn't fully believe that the surroundings were actually there as he saw them. "My own house—" he murmured half-audibly. "My own wife—"

"A man without a wife, he ain't a whole man at all, he's just a shadow walking around without no one to cast him."

His hand rose briefly to his shirt front, touched it questioningly, dropped again. "I keep hearing music. Is there a band playing on the streets somewhere around here?"

"There's a band playing, sure enough," she confirmed, unsmiling. "A special kind of band, for just one person at a time to hear. For just one day. I heard it once. Today's your day for hearing it."

"I'd better be on my way!" He bolted for the door, flung it open, chased down the walk and gave a vault into the waiting carriage that rocked it on its springs.

"To the Canal Street Pier," he sighed with blissful anticipation, "to meet the boat from St. Louis."

— 3 —

THE RIVER was empty, the sky was clear. Both were mirrored in his anxious, waiting eyes. Then a little twirl of smudge appeared, no bigger than if stroked by a man-sized finger against the God-sized sky. It came from where there seemed to be no river, only an embankment; it seemed to hover over dry land, for it was around a turn the river made, before straightening to flow toward New Orleans and the pier. And those assembled on it.

He stood there waiting, others like himself about him. Some so close their elbows all but grazed him. Strangers, men he did not know, had never seen before, would never see again, drawn together for a moment by the arrival of a boat.

He had picked for his standing place a pilehead that protruded above the pier-deck; that was his marker, he stood close beside that, and wouldn't let others preempt it from him, knowing it would play its part in securing the craft. For a while he stood with one leg raised, foot planted squarely upon it. Then he leaned bodily forward over it in anticipation, both hands flattened on it. At one time, briefly, he even sat upon it, but got up again fairly soon, as if with some idea that by remaining on his feet he would hasten the vessel's approach.

The smoke had climbed now, was high in the sky, like dingy black ostrich plumes massed together and struggling to escape from one another. Under its profusion a black that was solid substance, a slender cone, began to rise; a smokestack. Then a second.

"There she is," a roustabout shouted, and the needless, overdue declaration was immediately taken up and repeated by two or three of those about him.

"Yes sir, there she is," they echoed two or three times after him. "There she is, all right."

"There she is," Durand's heart told him softly. But it meant a different she.

The smokestack, like a blunted knife slicing through the earth, cleared the embankment and came out upon the open water bed. A tawny superstructure, that seemed to be indented with a myriad tiny niches in two long even rows, was beneath it, and beneath that, only a thin line at this distance, was the ungainly black hull. The paddles were going, slats turning over as they reached the top of the wheel and fell, shaking off spray into the turgid brown water below that they kept beating upon.

She made the turn and grew larger, prow forward. She was life-sized now, coursing down on the pier as if she meant to smash it asunder. A shrill falsetto wail, infinitely mournful, like the cry of a lost soul in torment, knifed from her, and a plume of white circled the smokestack and vanished to the rear. The *City of New Orleans,* out of St. Louis three days before, was back home again at its namesake-port, its mother-haven.

The sidewheels stopped, and it began to glide, like a paper boat, like a ghost over the water. It turned broadside to the pier, and ran along beside it, its speed seeming swifter now, that it was lengthwise, than it had been before, when it was coming head-on, though the reverse was the truth.

The notched indentations went by like a picket fence, then slower, slower; then stopped at last, then even reversed a little and seemed to lose ground. The water, caught between the hull and pier, went crazy with torment; squirmed and slashed and choked, trying to find its way out. Thinned at last to a crevice-like canal.

No more river, no more sky, nothing but towering superstructure blotting them both out. Someone idling against the upper deck rail waved desultorily. Not to Durand, for it was a man. Not to anyone else in particular, either, most likely. Just a friendly wave of arrival. One of them on the pier took it upon himself to answer it with a like wave, proxying for the rest.

A rope was thrown, and several of the small crowd stepped back to avoid being struck by it. Dockworkers came forward for their brief moment of glory, claimed the rope, deftly lashed it about the pile top directly before Durand. At the opposite end they were doing the same thing. She was in, she was fast.

A trestled gangway was rolled forward, a brief section of lower-deck rail was detached, leaving an opening. The gap between was bridged. A ship's officer came, down, almost before it was fixed in place, took up position close at hand below, to supervise the discharge. The passengers were funnelling along the deck from both directions into and down through the single-file descent-trough.

Durand moved up close beside it until he could rest his hand upon it, as if in mute claim; peered up anxiously into each imminent face as it coursed swiftly downward and past, only inches from his own.

The first passenger off was a man, striding, sample cases in both his hands, some business traveler in haste to leave. A woman next, more slowly, picking her way with care. Gray-haired and spectacled; not she. Another woman next. Not she again; her husband a step behind her, guiding her with hand to her elbow. An entire family next, in hierarchal order of importance.

Then more men, two or three of them in succession this time. Faces just pale ciphers to him, quickly passed over. Then a woman, and for a moment— No, not she; different eyes, a different nose, a different face. A stranger's curt glance, meeting his, then quickly rebuffing it. Another man. Another woman. Red-haired and sandy-browed; not she.

A space then, a pause, a wait.

His heart took premature fright, then recovered. A tapping run along the deck planks, as some laggard made haste to overtake the others. A woman by the small, quick sound of her feet. A flounce of skirts, a face— Not she. A whiff of lilac water, a snub from eyes that had no concern for him, as his had for them, no quest in them, no knowledge. Not she.

And then no more. The gangplank empty. A lull, as when a thing is over.

He stared up, and his face died.

He was gripping the edges of the gangplank with both hands now. He released it at last, crossed around to the other side of it, accosted the officer loitering there, clutched at him anxiously by the sleeve. "No one else?"

The officer turned and relayed the question upward toward the deck in booming hand-cupped shout. "Anyone else?"

Another of the ship's company, perhaps the captain, came to the rail and peered down overside. "All ashore," he called down.

It was like a knell. Durand seemed to find himself alone, in a pool of sudden silence, following it; though all about him there was as much noise going on as ever. But for him, silence. Stunning finality.

"But there must be— There has to—"

"No one else," the captain answered jocularly. "Come up and see for yourself."

Then he turned and left the rail.

Baggage was coming down now.

He waited, hoping against hope.

No one else. Only baggage, the inanimate dregs of the cargo. And at last not even that.

He turned aside at last and drifted back along the pier-length and off it to the solid ground beyond, and on a little while. His face stiffly averted, as if there were greater pain to be found on one side of him than on the other, though that was not true, it was equal all around.

And when he stopped, he didn't know it, nor why he had just when he did. Nor what reason he had for lingering on there at all. The boat had nothing for him, the river had nothing for him. There was nothing there for him. There or anywhere else, now.

Tears filled his eyes, and though there was no one near him, no one to notice, he slowly lowered his head to keep them from being detected.

He stood thus, head lowered, somewhat like a muted mourner at a bier. A bier that no one but he could see.

The ground before his unseeing eyes was blank; biscuit-colored earth basking in the sun. As blank, perhaps, as his life would be from now on.

Then without a sound of approach, the rounded shadow of a small head advanced timorously across it; cast from somewhere behind him, rising upward from below. A neck, two shoulders, followed it. Then the graceful indentation of a waist. Then the whole pattern stopped flowing, stood still.

His dulled eyes took no note of the phenomenon. They were not seeing the ground, nor anything imprinted upon it; they were seeing the St. Louis Street house. They were saying farewell to it. He'd never enter it again, he'd never go back there. He'd turn it over to an agent, and have him sell—

There was the light touch of a hand upon his shoulder. No exacting weight, no compulsive stroke; velvety and gossamer as the alighting of a butterfly. The shadow on the ground had raised a shadow-arm to another shadow—his—linking them for a moment, then dropping it again.

His head came up slowly. Then equally slowly he turned it toward the side from which the touch had come.

A figure swept around before him, as on a turntable, pivoting to claim the center of his eyes; though it was he and not the background that had shifted.

It was diminutive, and yet so perfectly proportioned within its own lesser measurements that, but for the yardstick of comparison offered when the eye deliberately sought out others and placed them against it, it could have seemed of any height at all: of the grandeur of a classical statue or of the minuteness of an exquisite doll.

Her limpid brown eyes came up to the turn of Durand's shoulder. Her face held an exquisite beauty he had never before seen, the beauty of porcelain, but without its cold stillness, and a crumpled rose petal of a mouth.

She was no more than in her early twenties, and though her size might have lent her added youth, the illusion had very little to subtract from the reality. Her skin was that of a young girl, and her eyes were the innocent, trustful eyes of a child.

Tight-spun golden curls clung to her head like a field of daisies, rebelling all but successfully at the conventional coiffure she tried to impose upon them. They took to the ubiquitous psyche-knot at the back only with the aid of forceful pins, and at the front resisted the forehead-fringe altogether, fuming about like topaz sea spray.

She held herself in that forward-inclination that was *de rigueur,* known as the "Grecian bend." Her dress was of the fashion as it then was, and had been for some years. Fitting tightly as a sheath fits a furled umbrella, it had a center panel, drawn and gathered toward the back to give the appearance of an apron or a bib superimposed upon the rest, and at the back puffed into a swollen protuberance of bows and folds, artfully sustained by a wired foundation; this was the stylish bustle, without which a woman's posterior would have appeared indecently sleek. As soon expose the insteps or—reckless thought!—the ankles as allow the sitting-part to remain flat.

A small hat of heliotrope straw, as flat as and no bigger than a man's palm, perched atop the golden curls, roguishly trying to reach down toward one eyebrow, the left, without there being enough of it to do so and still stay atop her head.

Amethyst-splinters twinkled in the tiny holes pierced through the lobes of her miniature and completely uncovered ears, and a slender ribbon of heliotrope velvet girded her throat. A parasol of heliotrope organdy, of scarcely greater diameter than a soup plate and of the consistency of mist, hovered aloft at the end of an elongated stick, like an errant violet halo. Upon the ground to one side of her sat a small gilt birdcage, its lower portion swathed in a flannel cloth, the dome left open to expose its flitting bright-yellow occupant.

He looked at her hand, he looked at his own shoulder, so unsure was he the touch had come from her; so unsure was he as to the reason for such a touch. Slowly his hat came off, was held at questioning height above his scalp.

The compressed mouth curved in winsome smile. "You don't know me, do you, Mr. Durand?"

He shook his head slightly.

The smile notched a dimple; rose to her eyes. "I'm Julia, Louis. May I call you Louis?"

His hat fell from his fingers to the ground, and rolled once about, for the length of half its brim. He bent and retrieved it, but only with his arm and shoulder; his face never once quited hers, as though held to it by an unbreakable magnetic current.

"But no— How can—?"

"Julia Russell," she insisted, still smiling.

"But no— You can't—" he kept dismembering words.

Her brows arched. The smile expired compassionately. "It was unkind of me to do this, wasn't it?"

"But—the picture—dark hair—"

"That was my aunt's I sent instead." She shook her head in belated compunction. She lowered the parasol, closed it with a little plop. With the point of its stick she began to trace cabalistic designs in the dust. She dropped her eyes and watched what she was doing with an air of sadness. "Oh, I shouldn't have, I know that now. But at the time, it didn't seem to matter so much, we hadn't become serious yet. I thought it was just a correspondence. Then many times since, I wanted to send the right one in its place, to tell you— And the longer I waited, the less courage I had. Fearing I'd—I'd lose you altogether in that way. It preyed on my mind more and more, and yet, the closer the time drew— At the very last moment, I was already aboard the boat, and I wanted to turn around and go back. Bertha prevailed upon me to—to continue down here. My sister, you know."

"I know," he nodded, still dazed.

"The last thing she said to me, just before I left, was, 'He'll forgive you. He'll understand you meant no harm.' But during the entire trip down, how bitterly I repented my—my frivolity." Her head all but hung, and she caught at her mouth, gnawing at it with her small white teeth.

"I can't believe—I can't believe—" was all he could keep stammering.

She was an image of lovely penitence, tracing her parasol-stick about on the ground, shyly waiting for forgiveness.

"But so much younger—" he marveled. "So much lovelier even than—"

"That too entered into it," she murmured. "So many men become smitten with just a pretty face. I wanted our feeling to go deeper than that. To last longer. To be more secure. I wanted you to care for me, if you did care, because of—well, the things I wrote you, the sort of mind I displayed, the sort of person I really was, rather than because of a flibbertigibbet's photograph. I thought perhaps if I gave myself every possible disadvantage at the beginning, of appearance and age and so forth, then there would be that much less danger later, of its being just a passing fancy. In other words, I put the obstacles at the beginning, rather than have them at the end."

How sensible she was, he discovered to himself, how level-minded, in addition to all her external attractions. Why, there were the components here of a paragon.

"How many times I tried to write you the truth, you'll never know," she went on contritely. "And each time my courage would fail. I was afraid I would only succeed in alienating you entirely, from a person who, by her own admission, had been guilty of falsehood. I couldn't trust such a thing to cold paper." She gestured charmingly with one hand. "And now you see me, and now you know. The worst."

"The worst," he protested strenuously. "But you," he went on after a moment, still amazed, "but you, knowing all along what I did not know until now, that I was so much—well, considerably, older than you. And yet—"

She dropped her eyes, as if in additional confession. "Perhaps that may have been one of your principal attractions, who knows?

I have, since as far back as I can remember, been capable of—shall I say, romantic feelings, the proper degree of emotion or admiration—only toward men older than myself. Boys of my own age have never interested me. I don't know what to attribute it to. All the women in my family have been like that. My mother was married at fifteen, and my father was at the time well over forty. The mere fact that you *were* thirty-six, was what first—" With maidenly seemliness, she forebore to finish it.

He kept devouring her with his eyes, still incredulous.

"Are you disappointed?" she asked timidly.

"How can you ask that?" he exclaimed.

"Am I forgiven?" was the next faltering question.

"It was a lovely deception," he said with warmth of feeling. "I don't think there's been a lovelier one ever committed."

He smiled, and her smile, still somewhat abashed, answered his own.

"But now I will have to get used to you all over again. Grow to know you all over again. That was a false start," he said cheerfully.

She turned her head aside and mutely half-hid it against her own shoulder. And yet even this gesture, which might have seemed maudlin or revoltingly saccharine in others, she managed to carry off successfully, making it appear no more than a playful parody while at the same time deftly conveying its original intent of rebuked coyness.

He grinned.

She turned her face toward him again. "Are your plans, your, er, intentions, altered?"

"Are yours?"

"I'm here," she said with the utmost simplicity, grave now.

He studied her a moment longer, absorbing her charm. Then suddenly, with new-found daring, he came to a decision. "Would it make you feel better, would it ease your mind of any lingering discomfort," he blurted out, "if I were to make a confession to you on my own part?"

"You?" she said surprised.

"I—I no more told you the entire truth than you told me," he rushed on.

"But—but I see you quite as you said you were, quite as your picture described you—"

"It isn't that, it's something else. I too perhaps felt just as you did, that I wanted you to like me, to accept my offer, solely on the strength of the sort of man I was in myself. For myself alone, in other words."

"But I see that, and I do," she said blankly. "I don't understand."

"You will in a moment," he promised her, almost eagerly. "Now I must confess to you that I'm not a clerk in a coffee-import house." Her face betrayed no sign other than politely interested incomprehension.

"That I *haven't* a thousand dollars put aside, to—to start us off." No sign. No sign of crestfall or of frustrated avarice. He was watching her intently. A slow smile of indulgence, of absolution granted, overspread her features before he had spoken next. *Well* before he had spoken next. He gave it time.

"No, I *own* a coffee-import house, instead."

No sign. Only that slightly forced smile, such as women give in listening to details of a man's business, when it doesn't interest them in the slightest but they are trying to be polite.

"No, I have closer to a hundred thousand dollars."

He waited for her to say something. She didn't. She, on the contrary, seemed to be waiting for him to continue. As if the subject had been so arid, and barren of import, to her, that she did not realize the climax had already been reached.

"Well, that's *my* confession," he said somewhat lamely.

"Oh," she said, as if brought up short. "Oh, was that it? You mean—" She fluttered her hand with vague helplessness. "—about your business, and money matters—" She brought two fingers to her mouth, and crossed it with their tips. Stifling a yawn that, without the gesture of concealment, he would not have detected in the first place. "There are two things I have no head for," she admitted. "One is politics, the other is business, money matters."

"But you do forgive me?" he persisted. Conscious at the same time of a fierce inward joy, that was almost exultation; as when one has encountered a perfection of attitude, at long last, and almost by chance, that was scarcely to be hoped for.

She laughed outright this time, with a glint of mischief, as if he were giving her more credit than was due her. "If you must be forgiven, you're forgiven," she relented. "But since I paid no attention whatever to the passages in your letters that dealt with that, in the first place, why, you're asking forgiveness for a fault I was not aware, until now, of your having committed. Take it, then, though I'm not sure what it's for."

He stared at her with a new intentness, that went deeper than before; as if finding her as utterly charming within as she was at first sight without.

Their shadows were growing longer, and they were all but alone now on the pier. He glanced around him as if reluctantly awakening to their surroundings. "It's getting late, and I'm keeping you standing here," he said in a reminder that was more dutiful than honest, for it might mean their separation, for all he knew.

"You make me forget the time," she admitted, her eyes never leaving his face. "Is that a bad omen or a good? You even make me forget my predicament: half ashore and half still on the boat. I must soon become the one or the other."

"That's soon taken care of," he said, leaning forward eagerly, "if I have your own consent."

"Isn't yours necessary too?" she said archly.

"It's given, it's given." He was almost breathless with haste to convince her.

She was in no hurry, now that he was. "I don't know," she said, lifting the point of her parasol, then dropping it again, then lifting it once more, in an uncertainty that he found excruciating. "If you had not seemed satisfied, if you had looked askance at the deceiver that you found me to be, I intended going back onto the boat and remaining aboard till she set out on the return trip to St. Louis. Don't you think that might still be the wiser—"

"No, don't say that," he urged, alarmed. "Satisfied? I'm the happiest man in New Orleans this evening—I'm the luckiest man in this town—"

She was not, it seemed, to be swayed so easily. "There is still time. Better now than later. Are you quite sure you wouldn't rather have me do that? I won't say a word, I won't complain. I'll understand your feelings perfectly—"

He was gripped by a sudden new fear of losing her. She, whom he hadn't had at all until scarcely half an hour ago.

"But those aren't my feelings! I beg you to believe me! My feelings are quite the opposite. What can I do to convince you? Do *you* want more time? Is it you? Is that what you are trying to say to me?" he insisted with growing anxiety.

She held him for a moment with her eyes, and they were kindly and candid and even, one might have said, somewhat tender. Then she shook her head, very slightly it is true, but with all the firmness of intention that a man might have given the gesture (if he could read it right), and not a girl's facile undependable negation.

"My mind has been made up," she told him, slowly and simply, "since I first stepped onto the boat at St. Louis. Since your letter of proposal came, as a matter of fact, and I wrote you my answer. And I do not lightly undo my mind, once it has been made up. You will find that once you know me better." Then she qualified it: "If you do," and let that find him out with a little unwelcome stab, as it promptly did.

"I'll let this be my answer, then," he said with tremulous impatience. "Here it is." He opened his cardcase, took out the daguerreotype, the one of the other, older woman—her aunt's—minced it with energetic fingers, then let it fall in trifling pieces downward all over the ground. Then showed her both his hands, empty.

"My mind is made up too."

She smiled her acceptance. "Then—?"

"Then let's be on our way. They're waiting for us at the church the past quarter-hour or more. We've delayed here too long."

He tilted his arm akimbo, offered it to her with a smile and a gallant inclination from the waist, that were perhaps, on the surface, meant to appear as badinage, merely a bantering parody, but were in reality more sincerely intended.

"Miss Julia?" he invited.

This was the moment of ultimate romance, its quintessence. The betrothal.

She shifted her parasol to the opposite shoulder. Her hand curled about his arm like a friendly sun-warmed tendril. She gathered up the bottom of her skirt to reticent walking-level.

"Mr. Durand," she accepted, addressing him by surname only, in keeping with the seemly propriety of the still-unmarried young woman that made her drop her eyes fetchingly at the same time.

— 4 —

THE INTERIOR of the Dryades German Methodist Church at sundown. Fulminating orange haze from without blurring its leaded windows into swollen shapelessness; its arched apse disappearing upward into cobwebby blue twilight. Grave, peaceful, empty but for five persons.

Five persons gathered in a solemn little conclave about the pulpit. Four facing it, the fifth occupying it. Four silent, the fifth speaking low. The first two of the four, side by side; the second two flanking them. Outside, barely audible, as if filtered through a heavy screen, the sounds of the city, muffled, dreamy, faraway. The occasional clop of a horse's hoof on cobbles, the creaking protest of a sharply curving wheel, the voice of an itinerant hawker crying his wares, the bark of a dog.

Inside, stately phrases of the marriage service, echoing serenely in the spacious stillness. The Reverend Edward A. Clay the officiant, Louis Durand and Julia Russell the principals. Allan

Jardine and Sophie Tadoussac, housekeeper to the Reverend Clay, the witnesses.

"And do you, Julia Russell, take this man, Louis Durand, to be your lawful wedded husband—

"To cleave to, forsaking all others—

"To love, honor and obey—

"For better or for worse—

"For richer or for poorer—

"In sickness and in health—

"Until death do ye part?"

Silence.

Then like a tiny bell, no bigger than a thimble in all the vastness of that church, but clear and silver-pure—

"I do."

"Now the ring, please. Place it upon the bride's finger."

Durand reaches behind him. Jardine produces it, puts it in his blindly questing hand. Durand brings it to the tapered point of her finger.

There is a momentary awkwardness. Her finger measurement was taken by a string, knotted at the proper place and sent enclosed in a letter. But there must have been an error, either in the knotting or on the jeweler's part. It balks, won't go on.

He tried a second, a third time, clasping her hand tighter. Still it resists.

Quickly she flicks her finger past her lips, returns it to him, edge moistened. The ring goes on, ebbs down it now to base.

"I now pronounce you man and wife."

Then, with a professional smile to encourage the age-old shyness of lovers when on public view, for the greater the secret love, the greater the public shyness: "You may kiss the bride."

Their faces turn slowly toward one another. Their eyes meet. Their heads draw together. The lips of Louis Durand blend with those of Julia, his wife, in sacramental pledge.

— 5 —

ANTOINE'S, rushing all alight toward its nightly rendezvous with midnight; glittering, glowing, mirrored; crowded with celebrants, singing with laughter, sizzling with champagne; sparkling with half-a-thousand jeweled gas flames all over its ceilings and walls, in bowers of crystal; the gayest and best-known restaurant on this side of the ocean; the soul of Paris springing enchanted from the Delta mud.

The wedding table stretched lengthwise along one entire side of it, the guests occupying one side only, so that the outer side might be left clear for their view of the rest of the room—and the rest of the room's view of them.

It was by now eleven and after, a disheveled mass of tortured napkins, sprawled flowers, glassware tinged with repeated refills of red wines and white; champagne and kirsch and little upright thimbles of benedictine for the ladies, no two alike at the same level of consumption. And in the center, dominating the table, a miracle of a cake, snow-white, sugar-spun, rising tier upon tier; badly eaten away by erosion now, so that one entire side was gone. But atop its highest pinnacle, still preserved intact, a little bride and groom in doll form, he in a thumbnail suit of black broadcloth, she with a wisp of tulle streaming from her head.

And opposite them, the two originals, in life-size; sitting shoulder pressed to shoulder, hands secretively clasped below the table, listening to some long-winded speech of eulogy. His head still held upright in polite pretense at attention; her head nestled dreamy-eyed against his shoulder.

He was in suitable evening garb now, and a quick trip to a dress-shop (first at her mention, but then at his insistence) before coming on here had changed her from her costume of arrival to a glorious creation of shimmering white satin, gardenias in her hair and at her throat. On the third finger of her left hand the new gold wedding-band; on the fourth, a solitaire diamond, a husband's wedding gift to his wife, token of an engagement contract fulfilled rather than of one entered into before the event.

And her eyes, like any new wearer's, stray over and over to these new adornments. But whether they go more often to the third finger or to the fourth, who is to detect and who is to say?

Flowers, wine, friendly laughing faces, toasts and wishes of well-being. The beginning of two lives. Or rather, the ending of two, the beginning of one.

"Shall we slip away now?" he whispers to her. "It's getting on to twelve."

"Yes. One more dance together first. Ask them to play again. And then we'll lose ourselves, without coming back to the table."

"As soon as Allan finishes speaking," he assents. "If he's ever going to."

Allan Jardine, his business partner, has become so involved in the mazes of a congratulatory speech that he cannot seem to find his way out of it again. It has been going on for ten minutes; ten minutes that seem like forty.

Jardine's wife, sitting beside him, and present only because of an unguessed but very strenuous domestic tug-of-war, has a dour, disapproving look on her face. Disapproving something, but doing her best to seem amiable, for the sake of her own husband's business interests. Disapproving the good looks of the bride, or her youth, or perhaps the unorthodox circumstances of the preceding courtship. Or perhaps the fact that Durand has married at all, after having waited so many years already, without waiting a few years more for her own underage daughter to grow up. A favorite project which even her own husband has had no inkling of so far. And now will never have.

Durand took out a small card, wrote on it "Play another waltz." Then he folded a currency note around it, motioned to a waiter, handed it to him to be taken to the musicians.

Jardine's wife was surreptitiously tugging at the hem of his coat now, to get him to bring his oration to a conclusion.

"Allan," she hissed. "Enough is enough. This is a wedding-supper, not a rally."

"I'm nearly through," he promised in an aside.

"You're through now," was the edict, delivered with a guillotine-like sweep of her hand.

"And so I give you the two newest apprentices to this great and happy profession of marriage. Julia (May I?" with a bow toward her) "and Louis."

Glasses went up, down again. Jardine at last sat down, mopping his brow. His wife, for her part, fanned herself by hand, holding her mouth open as she did so, as if to get rid of a bad taste.

A chord of music sounded.

Durand and Julia rose; their alacrity would have been highly uncomplimentary if it had not been so understandable.

"Excuse us, we want to dance this together."

And Durand solemnly winked at Jardine, to show him that he must not expect to see them back at their places again.

A fact which Jardine immediately imparted to his wife behind the back of his hand the moment they had left the table. Whereupon she seemed to disapprove that, too, in addition to everything else that she already disapproved about this affair, and took a prudish, astringent sip from her wineglass with a puckered mouth.

The bows of the violinists all rose together, fell together, and they swept into the waltz from *Romeo and Juliet*.

They stood facing one another for a moment, he and she, in the usual formal preliminary. Then she bent to pick up the loop of her furbelowed dress, he opened his arms, and she stepped into his embrace.

The waltz began, the swiftest of all paired dances. Around and around and around, then reversing, and around and around once more, the new way. The tables and the faces swept around them, as if they were standing still in the middle of a whirlpool, and the gaslights flashed by on the walls and ceilings like comets.

She held her neck arched, her head slightly back, looking straight upward into his eyes, as if to say "I am in your hands. Do with me as you will. Where you go, I will go. Where you turn, I will follow."

"Are you happy, Julia?"

"Doesn't my face tell you?"

"Do you regret coming down to New Orleans now?"

"*Is* there any other place but New Orleans now?" she asked with charming intensity.

Around and around and around; alone together, though there was a flurry of other skirts all around them.

"Our life together is going to be like this waltz, Julia. As sleek, as smooth, as harmonious. Never a wrong turn, never a jarring note. Together as close as this. One mind, one heart, one body."

"A waltz for life," she whispered raptly. "A waltz with wings. A waltz never ending. A waltz in the sunlight, a waltz in azure, in gold—and in spotless white."

She closed her eyes, as if in ecstasy.

"Here's the side way out. And no one's watching."

They came to a deft, toe-gliding halt, such as skaters use. They separated, and gave a quick look over at the oblivious wedding party table, half-screened from them by the dancers in between. Then he guided her before him, around palms, and a bronze statuette of a nymph, and a fluted column, out of the main dining room and into a scullery passage, redolent of steamy food and loud with unseen voices somewhere near at hand. She giggled as a small cat, coming their way, stopped to eye them amazed.

He took her by the hand now, and took the lead, and drew her after him, on quick-running joyous little steps, out to an outside alleyway that ran beside the building. And from here they emerged to the street at last. He threw up his arm at a carriage, and a moment later was sitting beside her in it, his arm protectively about her.

"St. Louis Street," he ordered proudly. "I'll show you where to stop,"

And as the bells of St. Louis Cathedral near by began their slow tolling of midnight, Louis Durand and his bride drove rapidly away toward their new home.

— 6 —

THE HOUSE was empty, waiting. Waiting to begin its history, which, for a house, is that of its occupants. Oil lamps had been left lighted, one to a room, by someone, most likely Aunt Sarah, before leaving, their little beaded flames, safe within glass chimneys, winking just high enough to disperse the darkness and cast an amber glow. The same blend of wood shavings, paint, and putty, spiced with a dash of floor varnish, was still in evidence, but to a far lesser degree now, for carpets had been laid over the raw floors, drapes hung athwart the window casings.

Someone had brought flowers into the parlor, not costly store flowers but wildflowers, cheery, colorful, winning none the less; a generous spray of them smothering a widemouthed bowl set on the parlor center table, with spears of pussywillow sticking out all over like the quills of a hedgehog's back.

A clock had even been wound up and started on its course, a new clock on the mantelpiece, imported from France, its face set in a block of green onyx, a little bronze cupid with moth wings clambering up a chain of bronze roses at each side of its centerpiece. Its diligent, newly practised ticking added a note of reassuring, homely tranquility to what otherwise would have been a stony-cold silence.

Everything was ready, all that was lacking were the dwellers.

A house, waiting for a man and his wife to come and claim it.

The resonant, cuplike sound of a horse's hoofs drew near in the stillness outside, came to a halt on a double down-beat. Axles creaked with a shift of weight, then settled again. A human tongue clucked professionally, then the hoofs recommenced, thinned away into silence once more.

There was a slight scrape of leather on paving stone, a mischievous little whisper, like a secret told by one foot to another.

A moment afterward a key turned in the outside of the door.

They stood there revealed in the opening, Durand and she.

Limned amber by the light before them in the house, framed by a panel of night sky sanded with stars behind them and over their heads. They were motionless, as oblivious of what lay before them as of what lay behind them. Face turned to meet face, his arms about her, her hands on his shoulders.

Nothing moved, neither they nor the stars at their back nor the open-doored house waiting to receive them. It was one of those moments never to be captured again. The kiss at the threshold of marriage.

It ended. A moment cannot last beyond itself. They stirred at last and drew apart, and he said softly: "Welcome to your new home, Mrs. Durand. May you find as much happiness here as you bring to it."

"Thank you," she murmured, eyes downcast for a second. "And may you as well."

He lifted her bodily in his arms. She came clear of the ground with a little foamy rustle of skirt bottoms. Moving sideward so that his shoulder might ward off the loose-swinging door, he carried her over the sill and in. Then dipped again and set her back on her feet, in a little froth of lacy hems.

He stepped aside, closed the door, and bolted it.

She was looking around, standing in one place but moving her body in a half-circle from there, to take in everything.

"Like it?" he asked.

He went to a lamp, turned the little wheel, heightening its flame to a yellow stalagmite. Then to another, and another, wherever they had been left. The walls brightened from dull ivory to purest white. The newness of everything became doubly conspicuous.

"Like it?" he beamed, as though the reward for it all lay in hearing her say that.

Her hands were clasped, and elevated upward to height of her face; held that way in a sort of stylized rhapsody.

"Oh, Louis," she breathed. "It's ideal. It's exquisite."

"It's yours," he said, and the way he dropped his voice showed the gratitude he felt at her appreciation.

She moved her hands out to one side of her face now, still clasped, and nestled her cheek against them slantwise. Then across to the other side, and repeated it there.

"Oh, Louis," was all she seemed capable of saying. "Oh, *Louis.*"

They moved around then on a brief tour, from room to room, and he showed her the parlor, the dining room, the others. And for each room she had an expiring "Oh, Louis," until at last, it seemed, breath had left her altogether, and she could only sigh "Oh."

They came back to the hall at last, and he said somewhat diffidently that he would lock up.

"Will you be able to find our room?" he added, as she turned toward the stairs. "Or shall I come up with you?"

She dropped her eyes for a moment before his. "I think I shall know it," she said chastely.

He placed one of the smaller lamps in her hands. "Better take this with you to make sure. She probably left lights up there, but she may not have."

With the light brought close to her like that, raying upward into her face from the glowing core held at about the height of her heart, there was to him something madonna-like about her countenance.

She was like some inexpressibly beautiful image in an old cathedral of Europe come to life before the eyes of a single devotee, rewarded for his faith. A miracle of love.

She rose a step. She rose another. An angel leaving the earthly plane, but turned backward in regretful farewell.

His hand even went out slightly, as if to trace her outline against the air on which he beheld it, and thus prolong her presence.

"Goodbye for a little while," he murmured softly.

"For a little while," she breathed.

Then she turned. The spell was broken. She was just a woman in an evening gown, going up a stair.

The graceful back-draperies of the most beautiful costume-style in a hundred years gently undulated with her climb. Her free hand trailed the banister.

"Keep an eye out for the wallpaper," he said. "That will tell you."

She turned inquiringly, with a look of incomprehension. "How's that?"

"I meant, you'll know it by the wallpaper, when you come to it."

"Oh," she said docilely, but as though she still didn't fully understand.

She reached the top of the stairs and went over their lip, shrinking down toward the floor now as she went on, until her shoulders, then her head, were gone. The ceiling-halo cast by her lamp receded past his ken, down that same illusory incline.

He went into the parlor, first, and then the other downstairs rooms, latching each window that had not already been latched, trying those that had, flinging out the drapes and drawing them sleekly together over each one. Night air was bad, the whole world knew that; it was best kept out of a sleeping house. Then at last blotting out each welcoming lamp, room by room.

In the kitchen Sarah had left a bunch of fine green grapes set out on a platter, as another token of welcome to the two of them. He plucked one off and put it in his mouth, with a half-smile for her thoughtfulness, then put out the light in there too.

The last lamp of all went out, and he moved slowly up the ghost-stairs in the dark, that was already a familiar dark to him though he'd been in this house less than half an hour. The dark of a man's own home is never strange and never fearful.

He found his way toward their own door, in the equal darkness of the upper hall, but guided now by the thread of light stretched taut across its sill.

He stopped a moment, and he stood there.

Then he knocked, in a sort of playful formality.

She must have sensed his mood, by the tenor of the knock alone. There was an answering playful note in her own voice.

"Who knocks?" she inquired with mock gravity.

"Your husband."

"Oh? What does he say?"

"'May I come in?'"

"Tell him he may."

"Who is it invites me to?"

The answer was almost inaudible, but low-voiced as it was, it reached his heart.

"Your wife."

— 7 —

ARRIVING HOME from his office—this was about a week later, ten days at most—he hastened up the stairs to greet her, not having found her in any of the lower-floor rooms when he entered. He was cushioning his tread, to surprise her, to come up unexpectedly behind her and cover her eyes, have her guess who it was. Though how could she fail to know it was he, for who else should it be? But homecoming was still an exquisite novelty, it had to be decked out with all these flourishes and fancies; though it was repeated daily, it still held all the delightful anticipation of a first meeting, each time.

The door of their room was open and she was seated in there, docilely enough, in a fan-backed chair, only the top of her head visible above it, for she was looking away from the entrance. He stood for a moment at the threshold, still undiscovered, caressing her with his eyes. As he watched he could see her hand move, limply turning over the page of some book that was occupying her.

He started over toward her, intent now on bending suddenly down over the back of the chair and pressing his lips to the top of her head, coppery-gilt in the waning sunlight. But as he advanced, and as her hidden form slowly came into view, lengthening into perspective with his own approach, something he saw made him stop again, amazed, almost incredulous.

He changed his purpose now. Moved openly, in a wide circle about the chair, to take it in from the side, and stopped at last before it, with a sort of pained puzzlement discernable on his face.

She had looked up at discovery of him, closed her book with a little throaty exclamation of pleasure.

"Here you are, dear? I didn't hear you come in below."

"Julia," he said, in a tone of blank incomprehension.

"What is it?"

He described her form with a sketchy lengthwise gesture of his hand, and still she didn't understand. He had to put it into words.

"Why, the way you're sitting—"

Her legs were crossed, as only men crossed theirs. One knee reared atop the other in unashamed prominence, the shank of her leg boldly thrust forth, the suspended foot had even been swinging a little, though that had stopped now.

The sheath of her skirt veiled the full rakishness of the position, but shadowy outlines and indentations outlined it only too distinctly even so.

She had been caught in a very real grossness, not to be understood by any later standard of manners, but only when set against its own contemporary code of universal conduct. For a woman to sit like that would have drawn stares anywhere, then, even ostracism and a request that she leave forthwith. No woman, not even the flightiest, sat but with the knees both level and the feet both flat upon the floor, though one might be drawn back behind the other for added grace. Immorality lies not in the nature of an act itself, but in the universality of the accepted tenet which it flouts. Thus a trifling variation of posture can be more shocking, to one era of strictly-maintained behavior, than a very real transgression would be to another and more lax one. The one cannot understand the other, and finds it only a laughable prissiness. Which it was not at the time.

Durand was no more prudish than the next, but he saw something which he had never seen any other woman do. Not even the "young ladies" of Madame Rachel's "Academy," when he visited there during his bachelor days. And this was the wife under his own roof.

"Do you sit that way at other times too?" he queried uneasily.

Subtly, with a sort of dissembling stealth, the offending knees uncoupled, the projecting leg descended beside its mate. Almost without the alteration being detected, she was once more sitting as all ladies sat. Even alone, even before only their own husbands.

"No," she protested virtuously, tipping horrified palms. "Of course not. How should I? I—I was alone in the room, and it must have come about without my thinking."

"But think if it should come about, some time, without your thinking, where others could see you."

"It shan't," she promised, tipping horrified palms at the very thought. "For it never did before, and it never will again."

She dismissed the subject by elevating her face toward him expectantly.

"You haven't kissed me yet."

The incident died out in his eyes, to match its extinction in his mind, in the finding of her lips with his.

— 8 —

ROSY-CHEEKED, dewy-eyed, winsome in the early morning sunlight, in a dressing sack of warm yellow whose hue matched the sunny glow falling about her, she quickly forestalled Aunt Sarah, took the coffee urn from her hand, insisting as she did every day on pouring his cupful herself.

He smiled, flattered, as he did every day when this same thing happened.

Next she took up the small silver tongs, fastened them on a lump of twinkling sugar, carefully carried it past the rim of his cup, and holding it low so that it might not splash, released it.

He beamed.

"So much the sweeter," he murmured confidentially.

She gave her fingertips a brisk little brushing-together, though they had not as a matter of fact touched anything at first hand, placed a kiss at the side of his head, hurried around to her side of the table, and seated herself with a crisp little rustling.

It was like a little girl, he couldn't help thinking, pressing a little boy into playing at house with her. You be the papa, and I'll be the mamma.

Settled in her own chair, she raised her cup, eyes smiling at him to the last over its very rim, until she must drop them to make sure of fitting it exactly to her still incredibly, always incredibly, tiny mouth.

"This is really excellent coffee," she remarked, after a sip.

"It's some of our own. One of the better grades, from the warehouse. I have a small sackful sent home every now and again for Aunt Sarah's use."

"I don't know what I should do without it. It is so invigorating, of a chilly morning. There is nothing I am quite so fond of."

"You mean since you have begun to sample Aunt Sarah's?"

"No, always. All my life I—"

She stopped, seeing him look at her with a sort of sudden, arrested attention. It was like a stone cast into the bubbling conversation, and sinking heavily to the bottom, stilling it.

There was some sort of contagion passed between them. Impossible to give it a name. She seemed to take it from him, seeing it appear on his face, and her own became strained and watchful. It was unease, a sudden chilling of assurance. It was the unpleasant sensation, or feeling of loss, that a worthless iron washer might convey, suddenly detected in a palmful of golden disks.

"But—" he said at last, and didn't go on.

"Yes?" She said with an effort. "Were you going to say something?" And the turn of one hand appeared over the edge of the table before her, almost as if in a bracing motion.

"No, I—" Then he gave himself the lie, went on to say it anyway.

"But in your letter once you said the opposite. Telling me how you went down to a cup of tea in the morning. Nothing but tea would do. You could not abide coffee. 'Heavy, inky drink.' I can still remember your very words."

She lifted her cup again, took a sip. She was unable therefore to speak again until she had removed it out of the way.

"True," she said, speaking rather fast to make up for the restriction, once it had been removed. "But that was because of my sister."

"But your preferences are your own, how could your sister affect them?"

"I was in her house," she explained. "She was the one liked tea, I coffee. But out of consideration for her, in order not to be the means of causing her to drink something she did not like, I pretended I liked it too. I put it in my letter because I sometimes showed her my letters to you before I sent them, and I did not want her to discover my little deception."

"Oh," he grinned, almost with a breath of relief.

She began to laugh. She laughed almost too loudly for the small cause she had. As if in release of stress.

"I wish you could have seen your face just then," she told him. "I didn't know what ailed you for a moment."

She went on laughing.

He laughed with her.

They laughed together, in a burst of fatuous bridal merriment. Aunt Sarah, coming into the room, joined their laughter, knowing as little as either of them what it was about.

— 9 —

HER COMPLEXION was a source of considerable wonderment to him. It seemed capable of the most rapid and unpredictable changes, almost within the twinkling of an eye. These flushes and pallors, if such they were, did not actually occur before his eyes, but within such short spans of time that, for all practical purposes, it amounted to the same thing.

They were not blushes in the ordinary sense, for they did not diminish again within a few moments of their onset, as those would have; once the change had occurred, once her coloring had heightened, it remained that way for hours after, with no immediate counteralteration ensuing.

It was most noticeable in the mornings. On first opening the shutters and turning to behold her, her coloring would be almost camelia-like. And yet, but a few moments later, as she followed in his wake down the stairs and rejoined him at the table, there would be the fresh hue of primroses, of pink carnations, in her cheeks, to set off the blue of her eyes all the more, the gold of her hair, to make her a vision of such loveliness that to look at her was almost past endurance.

In a theatre one night (they were seated in a box) the same transfiguration occurred, between two of the acts of the play, but on this occasion he ascribed it to illness, though if it were, she would not admit it to him. They had arrived late and had therefore entered in the darkness, or at least dimness relieved only by the stage lights. When the gas jets flared high, however, between the acts, she discovered (and seemed quite concerned by it, why he could not make out) that their loge was lined with a tufted damask of a particularly virulent apple-green shade. This, in conjunction with the blazing gas beating full upon her face, gave her a bilious, verdant look.

Many eyes (as always whenever she appeared anywhere with him) were turned upward upon her from the audience, both men and women alike, and more than one pair of opera glasses were centered upon her, as custom allowed them to be.

She shifted about impatiently in her chair for a moment or two, then suddenly rose and, touching him briefly on the wrist, excused herself. "Are you ill?" he asked, rising in the attempt to follow her, but she had already gone.

She returned before the lights had had time to be lowered again, and she was like a different person. The macabre tinge was gone from her countenance; her cheeks now burned with an apricot glow that fought through and mastered the combined efforts of the gaslights and the box-lining and made her beauty emerge triumphant.

The number of pairs of opera glasses tilted her way immediately doubled. Some unaccompanied men even half rose from their seats. A sibilant freshet of admiring comment could be sensed, rather than heard, running through the audience.

"What was it?" he asked anxiously. "Were you unwell? Something at supper, perhaps—?"

"I never felt better in my life!" she said confidently. She sat now, secure, at ease, and just before the lights went down again for the following act, turned to him with a smile, brushed a little nonexistent speck from his shoulder, as if proudly to show the whole world with whom she was, to whom she belonged.

One morning, however, his concern got the better of him. He rose from the table they were seated at, breakfasting, went over to her, and tested her forehead with the back of his hand.

"What do you do that for?" she asked, with unmarred composure, but casting her eyes upward to take in his overhanging hand.

"I wanted to see if you had a temperature."

The feel of her skin, however, was perfectly cool and normal. He returned to his chair.

"I am a little anxious about you, Julia. I'm wondering if I should not have a doctor examine you, just to ease my mind. I have heard of certain—" he hesitated, in order not to alarm her unduly, "—certain ailments of the lung that have no other indication, at an early stage, than these—er—intermittent flushes and high colorings that mount to the cheeks—"

He thought he saw her lips quiver treacherously, but they formed nothing but a small smile of reassurance.

"Oh no, I am in perfectly good health."

"You are as white as a ghost, at times. Then at others— A few moments ago, in our room, you were unduly pale. And now your cheeks are like apples."

She turned her fork over, then turned it back again the way it had been.

"It is the cold water, perhaps," she said. "I apply it to my face with strong pats, and that brings out the color. So you need not worry any longer, there's really nothing to be alarmed at."

"Oh," he exclaimed, vastly relieved. "Is *that* all that causes it? Who would have believed—!"

He turned his head suddenly. Aunt Sarah was standing there motionless, a plate she had forgotten to deliver held in her hand. Her eyes stared at Julia's face with a narrow-lidded scrutiny.

He thought, understanding, that she too must feel concern for the state of her young mistress' health, just as he had, to fix upon her such a speculative stare of secretive appraisal.

— 10 —

COMFORTABLY ENGROSSED in his newspaper, he was vaguely aware of Aunt Sarah somewhere at his back, engaged in a household task known as "wiping." This consisted in running a dustcloth over certain surfaces (when they were equal to or lower than her own height) and flicking it at others (when they were higher). Presently he heard her come to a halt and cluck her tongue enticingly, and surmised by that she must have at last reached the point at which Julia's canary, Dicky Bird, hung suspended in its gilt cage from a bracket protruding close beside the window.

"How my pretty?" she wheedled. "Hunh? Tell Aunt Sarah. How my pretty bird?"

There was a feeble monosyllabic twit from the bird, no more.

"You can do better than that. Come on now, perk up. Lemme hear you sing."

There was a second faltering twit, little better than a squeak.

The old woman gingerly thrust her finger through, apparently with the idea of gently stroking its tiny feathers.

As though that slight impetus were all that were needed, the little yellow tenant promptly fell to the floor of the cage. He huddled there inert, head down, apparently unable to regain the perch he had just lost. He blinked repeatedly, otherwise gave no sign of life.

Aunt Sarah became vociferously alarmed. "Mr. Lou!" she brayed. "Come here, sir! Something the matter with Miss Julia's little old bird. See you can find out what ails her."

Durand, who had been watching her over his shoulder for several minutes past, promptly discarded his newspaper, got up and went over.

By the time he had reached her, Aunt Sarah had already opened the cage wicket, reached a hand in with elephantine caution, and brought the bird out. It made no attempt to flutter, lay there almost inanimately.

They both bent their heads over it, with an intentness that, unintentionally, had a touch of the ludicrous to it.

"Why, it starving. Why, 'pears like it ain't had nothing to eat in days. Nothing left of it under its feathers at all. *Feel* here. Look at that. Seed dish plumb empty. No water neither."

It continued to blink up at them, apparently clinging to its life by a thread.

"Come to think of it, I ain't heard it singing in two, three days now. Not singing right, anyhow."

Durant, reminded by her remark, now recalled that he hadn't either.

"Miss Julia's going to have a fit," the old lady predicted, with an ominous headshake.

"But who's been feeding it, you or she?"

She gave him a look of blank bewilderment. "Why, I—I 'spected she was. She never said nothing to me. She never *told* me to. It b'long to her, I thought maybe she don't want nobody but herself to feed it."

"She must have thought you were," he frowned, puzzled. "But funny she didn't *ask* if you were. I'll hold it in my hand. Go get it some water."

They had it back in the cage, somewhat revived, and were still busy watching it, when Julia came into the room, the long-winded toilette that had been occupying her, apparently at last concluded.

She came toward him, tilted up her face, and kissed him dutifully. "I'm going shopping, Lou dear. Can you spare me for an hour or so?" Then without waiting for the permission, she went on toward the opposite door.

"Oh, by the way, Julia—" he had to call after her, to halt her.

She stopped and turned, sweetly patient. "Yes, dear?"

"We found Dicky Bird nearly dead just now, Aunt Sarah and I."

He thought that would bring her back toward, the cage at least, if only for a brief glance. She remained where she was, apparently begrudging the delay, though brooking it for his sake.

"He going to be all right, honey," Aunt Sarah quickly interjected. "They ain't nothing, man or beast or bird, Aunt Sarah can't nurse back to health. You just watch, he going to be all right."

"Is he?" she said somewhat shortly. There was almost a quirk of annoyance expressed in the way she said it, but that of course, he told himself, was wholly imaginary on his part.

She began to mould her glove to her hand with an air of hauteur. Unnoticeably the subject had changed. "I do hope I don't have a hard time finding a carriage. Always, just when you want them, there's not one to be had—"

Aunt Sarah, among other harmless idiosyncrasies, had a habit of being behindhand in changing subjects, of dwelling on a subject, once current, for several minutes after everyone else had quitted it.

"He be singing again just as good as ever in a day or two, honey." Julia's eyes gave a flick of impatience.

"Sometimes that singing of his can be too much of a good thing," she said tartly. "It's been a blessed relief to—" She moistened her lips correctively, turned her attention to Durand again. "There's a hat I saw in Ottley's window I simply must have. I hope somebody hasn't already taken it away from there. May I?"

He glowed at this flattering deference of seeking his permission. "Of course! Have it by all means, bless your heart."

She gave a gay little flounce toward the door, swept it open. "Ta ta, lovey mine." She blew him a kiss, up the tilted flat of her hand and over the top of it, from the open doorway.

The door closed, and the room dimmed again somewhat.

Aunt Sarah was still standing beside the cage. "I sure enough 'spected she'd come over and take a look at him," she said perplexedly. "Reckon she ain't so fond of him no more."

"She must be. She brought him all the way down from St. Louis with her," Durand answered inattentively, eyes buried in his newspaper once more.

"Maybe she done change, don't care 'bout him no more."

This monologue was for her own benefit, however, not her employer's. He just happened to be there to overhear it.

She left the room.

A moment passed. Several, in fact. Durand's attention remained focused on the printed sheet before him.

Then suddenly he stopped reading.

His eyes left the paper abruptly, stared over its top.

Not at anything in particular, just in abstract thought.

— I I —

HER TRUNK was recalled to his mind one day by the very act of his own sitting on it. It was no longer recognizable at sight for a trunk, it had a gaily printed slip cover over it to disguise it, and stood there over against the wall.

It was a Sunday, and though they did not go to church, they never failed, in common with all other good citizens, to dress up in their Sunday finest and take their Sunday morning promenade; to see and be seen, to bow and nod and perhaps exchange a few amiable words with this one and that of their acquaintances in passing. It was an established custom, the Sunday morning promenade, in all the cities of the land.

He was waiting for her to be ready, and he had sat down upon this nondescript surface without looking to see what it was, satisfied merely that it was level and firm enough to take him.

She was slowed, at the last moment, by difficulties.

"I wore this last week, remember? They'll see it again."

She discarded it.

"And this—I don't know about this—" She curled her lip slightly. "I'm not very taken with it."

She discarded it as well.

"That looks attractive," he offered cheerfully, pointing at random.

She shrugged off his ignorance. "But this is a weekday dress, not a *Sunday* one."

He wondered privately, and with a soundless little chuckle, how one told the first from the second, but refrained from asking her.

She sat down now, still further delaying their start. "I don't know what I'll do. I haven't a thing fit to be seen in." This, taken in conjunction with the fact that the room was already littered with dresses, struck him as so funny that he could no longer control himself, but burst out laughing, and as he did so, swung his arm down against the surface he was sitting on, in a clap of emphasis. He felt, through the covering, the unmistakable shape of a pear-shaped metal trunk lock. And at that moment, he first realized it was her trunk he was sitting upon. The one she had brought from St. Louis. She had never, it suddenly struck him as well, opened it since her arrival.

"What about this?" he asked. And stood up and stripped the cover off. The initialled "J.R.," just below the lock in blood-red paint, stood out conspicuously. "Haven't you anything in here? I should think you would, a trunk this size." And meaning only to be helpful to her, pasted his hand against the top of it in indication.

She was suddenly looking, with an almost taut scrutiny, at one of the dresses, holding it upraised before her. As closely, as arrestedly, as if she were nearsighted or were seeking to find some microscopic flaw in its texture.

"Oh no," she said. "Nothing. Only rags."

"How is it I've never seen you open it? You never have, have you?"

She continued to peer at this thing in her hands. "No," she said. "I never have."

"I should imagine you would unpack. You intend to stay, don't you?" He was trying to be humorous, nothing more.

She didn't answer this time. She blinked her eyes, at the second of the two phrases, but it might have had nothing to do with that; it might simply have occurred simultaneously to it.

"Why not?" he persisted. "Why haven't you?" But with no intent whatever, simply to have an answer.

This time she took note of the question. "I—I can't," she said, somewhat unsurely.

She seemed to intend no further explanation, at least unsolicited, so he asked her: "Why?"

She waited a moment. "It's the—key. It's—ah, missing. I haven't got it. I lost it on the boat."

She had come over to the trunk while she was speaking, and was rather hastily trying to rearrange the slip cover over it, almost as if nettled because it had been disarrayed. Though this might have been an illusion due simply to the nervous quickness of her hands.

"Why didn't you tell me?" he protested heartily, thinking merely he was doing her a service. "I'll have a locksmith come in and make you a new one. It won't take any time at all. Wait a minute, let me look at it—"

He drew the slip cover partly back again, while she almost seemed to be trying to hold it in place in opposition. Again the vivid "J.R." peered forth, but only momentarily.

He thumbed the pear-shaped brass plaque. "That should be easy enough. It's a fairly simple type of lock."

The slip cover, in her hands, swept across it like a curtain a moment later, blotting out lock and initials alike.

"I'll go out and fetch one in right now," he offered, and started forthwith for the door. "He can take the impression, and have the job done by the time we return from our—"

"You can't," she called after him with unexpected harshness of voice, that might simply have been due to the fact of her having to raise it slightly to reach him.

"Why not?" he asked, and stopped where he was.

She let her breath out audibly. "It's Sunday."

He turned in the doorway and came slowly back again, frustrated. "That's true," he admitted. "I forgot."

"I did too, for a moment," she said. And again exhaled deeply. In a way that, though it was probably no more than an expression of annoyance at the delay, might almost have been mistaken for unutterable relief, so misleadingly like it did it sound.

—— 1 2 ——

THE RITE of the bath was in progress, or at least in preparation, somewhere in the background. He could tell by the sounds reaching him, though he was removed from any actual view of what was going on, being two rooms away, in the sitting room attached to their bedroom, engrossed in his newspaper. He could hear buckets of hot water, brought up in relays from the top of the kitchen stove downstairs by Aunt Sarah, being emptied into the tub with a hollow drumlike sound. Then a great stirring-up, so that it would blend properly with the cold water allowed to flow into it in its natural state from the tap. Then the testing, which was done with one carefully pointed foot, and usually followed by abrupt withdrawals and squeals of "Too cold!" or "Too hot!" as well as loud contradictions on the part of the assistant, Aunt Sarah: "No it ain't! Don't be such a baby! Leave it in a minute, how you going to tell, you snatch it back like that? Your husban's sitting right out there; ain't you ashamed to have him know what a scairdy-cat you is?"

"Well, he doesn't have to get in it, I do," came the plaintive answer.

Over and above this watery commotion, and cued by its semi-musical tone, the canary, Dicky Bird, was singing jauntily, from the room midway between, the bedroom.

Aunt Sarah passed through the room where he sat, an empty water-bucket in each hand.

"She sure a pretty little thing," she commented. "White as milk and soft as honey. Got a fo'm like—*unh-umh!*"

His face suddenly suffused with color. It took quite some time for the heightened tide to descend again. He pretended the remark had not been addressed to himself, took no note of it.

She went down the stairs.

The canary's bravura efforts rose to a triumphant, sustained, almost earsplitting trill, then suddenly broke off short. That had been, even he had to admit to himself, quite a considerable amount of noise for so small a bird to emit, just then.

A strange, almost complete silence had succeeded it.

Then the rolling, somehow-undulating sound usually produced by total immersion in a body of water.

After that only an occasional watery ripple.

Aunt Sarah returned, stopped en route to shake out and inspect a fleecy towel, also warmed by courtesy of the kitchen stove, that she was taking in with her. She went on into the bedroom.

"Hullo there," he heard her say, from in there. "How my bird? How my yallo baby?" Suddenly her voice deepened to strident urgency. "Mr. Lou! Mr. Lou!"

He went in running.

"He dead."

"He can't be. He was singing only a minute ago."

"He dead, I tell you! Look here, see for yourself—" She had removed him from the cage, was holding him pillowed on the palm of her hand.

"Maybe he needs water and seed again, like that last—" But the two receptacles were filled; Aunt Sarah had made that her responsibility ever since then.

"It ain't that."

She gave the edge of her hand a slight dip.

Something dropped over the edge of it, hung there suspended, while the body of the bird remained in position.

"His neck's done been broken."

"Maybe he fell off the perch—" Durand tried to suggest inanely, for lack of any other explanation that came to mind.

She scowled at him belligerently.

"They don't fall! What they got wings for?"

He repeated: "But he was singing only a few minutes ago—"

"What he was a few minutes ago and what he is now is two different things!"

"—and no one's been in here. No one but you and Miss Julia—"

In the silence, and incredibly, Julia could be heard in the adjoining bathroom, lightly whistling a bar or two to herself.

Then, as though belatedly realizing how unladylike she was guilty of being, she checked herself, and the water gave a playful little splash for finale.

— 13 —

IT WAS quite by chance that he happened to go through the street in which his former lodgings were. He had no concern with them, would have passed them by with no more than a glance of fond recollection; his errand and his destination lay elsewhere entirely, and it only happened that this was the shortest way to it.

And it was equally by chance that Madame Tellier, his erstwhile landlady, happened to come out and stand for a moment in the entrance just as he was in the act of walking by.

She greeted him effusively, with shrieks of delight that could be heard for doors away in either direction, flung her arms about him like a second mother, asked about his health, his happiness, his enjoyment of married life.

"Oh, but we miss you, Louis! Your old rooms are rented again—to a pair of cold Northerners (I charge them double)—but it's not the same." She creased her rather large nose distastefully. Suddenly she was all alight again, gave her fingers a crackling snap of self-reminder. "I just remembered! I have a letter waiting for you. It's been here several days now, and I haven't seen Tom since it came, to ask where your new address is, or I would have forwarded it. He still comes around now and then to work for me, you know. Wait here, I'll bring it out to you."

She patted him three times in rapid succession on the chest, as if cajoling him to stand patiently as he was for a moment, turned and whisked inside.

He had, he only now recalled rather ruefully, completely over-looked having his mailing address changed from here, his old quarters, to the new house on St. Louis Street, when he made the move. Not that it was vitally important; his business mail all continued to go to the office, as it always had, and of personal correspondence he had never had a great deal, only his courtship letters with Julia, now brought to a happy termination. He would stop by the post office, on his way home, and file the new delivery instructions, if only for the sake of an occasional stray missive such as this.

Meanwhile she had come back with it. "Here! Isn't it good you just happened to come by this way?"

He gave the inscription a brief glance, simply to confirm it, as he took it from her. "Mr. Louis Durand," in spidery penmanship; the three capitals, M, L, and D, standing out in black enlargement, the minuscule letters too finely traced and too diminished in size to make for legibility. However, it was his own name, there could be no mistaking that, so he questioned it no further; thrust it careless-ly into the side pocket of his coat for later reference and promptly forgot about it.

Their leavetaking was as exclamatory and enthusiastic as their greeting had been. She kissed him on the forehead in a sort of ma-ternal benediction, waved him steadily on his way for a distance of the first three or four succeeding house-lengths, even touched her apron to the corner of her eye before at last turning to go inside. She wept easily, this Madame Tellier; wept with only a single glass-ful of wine, or at sight of any once-familiar face. Even those she had once ruthlessly evicted for non-payment of rent.

He accomplished his errand, he returned to his office, he absorbed himself once more in the daily routine of his work.

He discovered the letter a second time only within the last quarter of an hour before leaving to go home, and as equally by accident as it had been thrust upon him in the first place by happening to thrust his hand blindly into his pocket, in search of a pocket handkerchief.

Reminded of its presence, he rested himself for a moment by taking it out, tearing it open, and leaning back to read it. No sooner had his eyes fallen on the introductory words than he stopped again, puzzled.

"My own dearest Julia:"

It was for her, not himself.

He turned to the envelope again, looked at it more closely than he had on the street in presence of Madame Tellier. He saw then what had misled him. The little curl, following the "Mr." so tiny as almost to escape detection, was meant for an "s."

He went back to the paper once more; turned this over, glanced at the bottom of its reverse side.

"Your ever-loving and distressed Bertha."

It was from her sister, in St. Louis.

"'Distressed." The word seemed to cast itself up at him, like a barbed fishhook, catch onto and strain at his attention. He could not pry it off again.

He did not intend to read any further. It was her letter, after all. Somehow the opening words held him trapped, he could not stop once they had seized his eyes with their meaning.

> My own dearest Julia:
> I cannot understand why you treat me thus. Surely I deserve better than this of you. It is three weeks now since you have left me, and in all that time not a word from you. Not so much as the briefest line, to tell me of your safe arrival, whether you met Mr. Durand, whether the marriage has taken place or not. Julia, you were never like this before. What am I to think? Can you not imagine the distracted state of mind this leaves me in—

— 14 —

He waited until after they were through their supper to speak of it, and then only in the mildest, least reproachful way.

He took it out and gave it to her, after they had entered the sitting room from the dining room, and settled themselves there, she across the lamplit table from him. "This came for you today. I opened it by mistake, not noticing. I hope you'll forgive me."

She took the whole envelope first, and studied it a second, this way and that. "Who's it from?" she said.

"Can't you tell?"

Just as he was about to wonder why the script in itself did not tell her that, she had already withdrawn its contents and opened them, and murmured "Oh," so the question never had a chance to form itself in his mind. But whether the "Oh" meant recognition of its sender or merely recognition of the nature of the letter, or even something else quite different, there was no way for him to distinguish.

She read it rather quickly, even hurriedly, her head moving with each line, then back again, in continuous serried little twitchings. Then reached the bottom and had done.

He thought he saw remorse on her face, in its sudden, still abstraction, that held for a moment after.

"She says—" She half-tendered it to him. "Did you read it?"

"Yes, I did," he said, slightly uncomfortable.

She put it back in the envelope, gave the latter two taps where its seam was broken.

He looked at her fondly, to soften the insistence of his appeal. "Write to her, Julia," he urged. "That is not like you at all."

"I will," she promised contritely. "Oh, I will, Louis, without fail." And twisted her hands a little, about themselves, and looked down at them as she did so.

"But why didn't you before now?" he continued gently. "I never asked you, because I felt sure you had."

"Oh, so much has happened—I meant to, time and again I meant to, and each time there was something to take my mind off it. You see, Louis, this has been the beginning of a whole new life for me, these past few weeks, and everything seemed to come at one time—"

"I know," he said. "But you *will* write?" And he took up and lost himself in his newspaper.

"The very first thing," she vowed.

Half an hour went by. She was, now, turning the leaves of a heavy ornamental album, regaling herself with the copperplate engravings, snubbing the text.

He watched her covertly from under lowered lids a moment. Presently he cleared his throat as a reminder.

She took no notice, went ahead, with childlike engrossment.

"You said you would write to your sister."

She looked slightly disconcerted. "I know. But must it be right tonight? Why won't tomorrow do as well?"

"Don't you *want* to write to her?"

"Of course I do, how can you ask that? But why must it be this instant? Will tomorrow make such a difference?"

He put his newspaper aside. "A great deal in time of arrival, I'm afraid. If you write it now, it can go off in the early morning post. If you wait until tomorrow, it will be held over a full day longer; she will have that much more anxiety to endure."

He rose, closed the album for her, since she gave no signs of intending to do this herself. Then he stopped momentarily, looked at her searchingly to ask: "There's no ill-feeling between you, is there? Some quarrel just before you left that you haven't told me about?" And before she could speak, if she had meant to, put the answer in her mouth. "She doesn't write as though there had been."

The lines of her throat, extended for an instant, dropped back again, as if he'd aborted what she'd been about to say.

"How you talk," she murmured. "We're devoted to one another."

"Well, then, come. Why be stubborn? There's no time like the present. And you have nothing to occupy yourself with, that I can see." He took her by both hands and had to draw her to her feet. And though she made no active sign of resistance, he could feel the weight of her body against the direction of his pull.

He had to go to the desk and lower the writing-slab. He had to draw out a sheet of fresh notepaper from the rack, and put it in place for her, slightly tilted of corner.

He had to go back and bring her over, from where she stood, by the hand. Then even when he had her seated, he had to dip the pen and place it in her very fingers. He gave her head a pat. "You are like a stubborn child that doesn't want to do its lessons," he told her humorously.

She tried to smile, but the effect was dubious at best.

"Let me see her letter a moment," she said at last.

He went back to the table, brought it to her. But she seemed only to glance at the very top line of the page, almost as if referring to the mode of address in order to be able to duplicate it. Though he told himself this thought on his part must be purely fanciful. Many people had to have the physical sight of a letter before them to be able to answer it satisfactorily; she might be one of those.

Then turning from it immediately after that one quick look, she wrote on her own blank sheet, "My own dear Bertha:" He could see it form, from over her shoulder. Beyond that she seemed to have no further use for the original, edged it slightly aside and didn't concern herself with it any further.

He let her be. He returned to his own chair, took up his newspaper once more. But the stream of her thoughts did not seem to flow easily. He would hear the scratch of her pen for a few words, then it would stop, die away, there would be a long wait. Then it would scratch for a few jerky words more, then die away again. He glanced over at her once just in time to see her clap her hand harassedly to her forehead and hold it there briefly.

At length he heard her give a great sigh, but one more of short-patienced aversion continuing even after a task has been completed than of relief at its conclusion, and the scratching of the pen had stopped for good. She flung it down, as if annoyed.

"I've done. Do you want to read it?"

"No," he said, "it's between sister and sister, not for a husband to read."

"Very well," she said negligently. She passed her pink tongue around the gummed edge of the envelope, sealed it in. She stood it upright against the inside of the desk, prepared to close the slab over it. "I'll have Aunt Sarah post it for me in the morning."

He had reached for it and picked it up before her hands could forestall him, though they both flew out toward it just a moment too late. She hadn't expected him to be standing there behind her.

He slid it into his inside breast pocket, buttoned his coat over it. "I can do it for you myself," he said. "I leave the house earlier. It'll be that much sooner on its way."

He saw a startled expression, almost of trapped fear, cause her eyes to dodge cornerwise for an instant, but then they evened again so quickly he told himself he must have been mistaken, he must not have seen it at all.

When next he looked she was stroking the edge of her fingers with a bit of chamois penwiper, against potential rather than actual spots, however, and that seemed to be her sole remaining concern at the moment, though she puckered her brows pensively over the task.

— 15 —

THE NEXT morning, he thought she never had looked lovelier, and never had been more loving. All her past gracious endearment was as a coldness compared to the warmth of her consideration now.

She was in lilac watered silk, which had a rippling sheen running down it from whichever side you looked at it. It sighed as she walked, as if itself overcome by her loveliness. She did not stay at table as on other days, she accompanied him to the front door to see him off, her arm linked to his waist, his arm to hers. And as the slanting morning sunlight caught her in its glint, then released her, then caught her again a step further on, playing its mottled game with her all along the hall, he thought he had never seen such a vision of angelic beauty, and was almost awed to think it was his, walking here in his house, here at his side. Had she asked him to lie down and die for her then and there, he would have been glad to do it, and glad of her having asked it, as well.

They stopped. She raised her face from the side of his arm, she took up his hat, she stroked it of dust, she handed it to him.

They kissed.

She prepared his coat, held it spread, helped him on with it.

They kissed.

He opened the door in readiness to go.

They kissed.

She sighed. "I hate to see you go. And now I'll be all alone the rest of the livelong day."

"What will you do with yourself?" he asked in compunction, with the sudden—and only momentary—realization of a male that she too had a day to get through somehow, that she continued to go on during his absence. "Go shopping, I suppose," he suggested indulgently.

Her face brightened for a moment, as though he had read her heart. "Yes—!" Then it dimmed again. "No—" she said, forlorn. Instantly his attention was held fast. "Why not? What's the matter?"

"Oh, nothing—" She turned her head away, she didn't want to tell him.

He took the point of her chin and turned it back again. "Julia, I want to know. Tell me. What is it?" He touched her shoulder.

She tried to smile, wanly. Her eyes looked out the door.

He had to guess finally.

"Is it money?"

He guessed right.

Not an eyelash moved, but somehow she told him. Certainly not with her tongue.

He gasped, half in laughter. "Oh, my poor foolish little Julia—!" Instantly his coat flew open, his hand reached within. "Why, you only have to ask, don't you know that—?"

This time there could be no mistaking the answer. "No—! No—! *No!*" She was almost vehement about it, albeit in a pouty, petulant child's sort of way. She even tapped her toe for emphasis. "I don't like to *ask* for it. It isn't nice. I don't care if you are my own husband. It still isn't nice. I was brought up that way, I can't change." He was smiling at her. He found her adorable. But still he didn't understand her, which was no detraction to the first two factors. "Then what *do* you want?"

She gave him a typically feminine answer. "I don't know." And raised her eyes thoughtfully, as if trying to scan the problem in her own mind, find a solution somehow.

"But you do want to go shopping, don't you? I can see you do by your look. And yet you don't want me to give you the money for it."

"Isn't there some other way?" she appealed to him helplessly, as if willing to extricate herself from her own scruples, if only she could be shown how without foregoing them.

"I could slip it under your plate, unasked, for you to find at breakfast," he smirked.

She saw no humor in the suggestion, shook her head absently, still busy pondering the problem, finger to tooth edge. Suddenly she brightened, looked at him. "Couldn't I have a little account of my own—? Like you have, only— Oh, just a *little* one, tiny—small—" Then she decided against that, before he could leap to give his consent, as he had been about to.

"No, that'd be too much bother, just for hats and gloves and things—" About to fall into disheartened perplexity again, she recovered, once more lighted up as a new variant occurred to her. "Or better still, couldn't I just share yours with you?" She spread out her hands in triumphant discovery. "That'd be simpler yet. Just call it ours instead. It's there already."

He crouched his shoulders down low. He slapped his thigh sharply. "By George! Will that make you happy? Is that all it will take? God bless your trusting little heart! We'll do it!"

She flew into his arms like a shot, with a squeal for a firing-report. "Oh, Lou, I'll feel so *big,* so important! Can I, really? And can I even write my own checks, like you do?"

To love someone, is to give, and to want to give more still, no questions asked. To stop and think, then that is not to love, any more.

"Your own checks, in your own handwriting, in your own purse. I'll meet you at the bank at eleven. Will that time suit you?"

She only pressed her cheek to his.

"Will you know how to find it?"

She only pressed her cheek to his again, around on the other side of his face.

She allowed him to precede her there, as was her womanly prerogative. But once he had arrived, she kept him waiting no more than the fractional part of a minute. In fact so precipitately did she enter, on his very heels, that it could almost have been thought she had been waiting at some nearby vantage point simply to allow him first entry before starting forward in turn.

She accosted him before he had little more than cleared the vestibule.

"Louis," she said, placing her hand confidentially atop his wrist to detain him a moment, and drawing him a step aside, "I have been thinking about this since you left the house. I am not sure I—I want you to do this after all. You may think me one of these presuming wives who— Had we not better let things be as they are—?"

He patted her arresting wrist. "Not another word, Julia," he said with fine masculine authority. "I want it so."

He was now sure that the idea was his own, had been from its very inception.

She deferred to his dictate as it was a wife's place to do, with a seemly little obeisance of her head. She linked her arm in his and accompanied him with slow-moving elegance across the bank floor toward its farther end, where the bank manager had emerged and stood waiting to greet them with courtly consideration behind a low wooden partition banister set with amphora-shaped uprights erected three-square about his private office door. He was a moon-faced gentleman, the roundness of his face emphasized by the circular fringe of carefully waved, iron-gray whiskers that surrounded it, the lips and sides of the cheeks clean-shaven. The gold chain across his plaid vest front must have been composed of the thickest links in all New Orleans, a veritable anchor.

Even he, the establishment's head, visibly swelled like a pouter-pigeon at sight of Julia advancing toward him. The pride she afforded Durand, in escorting her, in itself, would have made the entire proceeding worth while had there been no other reason.

She had donned, for this unwonted invasion of the precincts of commerce and finance, azure crinoline, that filled the arid air with whispers, midget pink velvet buttons in symmetrical rows studding its jerking, pink ruching sprouting at her throat and wrists; a crushed bonnet of azure velvet low over one eye like a tinted compress to relieve a headache, ribbons of pink tying it under her chin, a dwarf veil sprinkled with pink dots like confetti hanging only as low as the underlashes of her eyes. Her steps were as tiny and tapping as though she were on stilts, and her spine was held in the forward-curved bow of the Grecian bend almost to a point where it defied Nature's plan that the human figure hold itself upright on the hip sockets, without falling over forward out of sheer unbalance.

Never had a bustle floated so airily, swaying so languorously, over a bank floor before. Her passage created a sensation behind the tellers' cagelike windows lining both sides of the way. Pair upon pair of eyes beneath their green eyeshades were lifted from dry, stuffy figures and accounts to gaze dreamily after her. The personnel of banking establishments at that time was exclusively male, the clientele almost equally so. Though a discreetly curtained-off little nook, as rigidly segregated as a harem anteroom, bearing over it the placard "Ladies' Window," was reserved for the use of the occasional females (widows and the like) who were forced to come in person to see to their money matters, having no one else to attend to these grubby transactions for them. At least they were spared the ignominy of having to rub elbows with men in the line, or stand exposed to all eyes while money was publicly handed to them. They could curtain themselves off and be dealt with by a special teller reserved for their use alone, and always a good deal gentler and older than the rest.

There was no definite stigma attached to banks, for women; unlike saloons, and certain types of theatrical performance where tights were worn, and almost all forms of athletic contest, such as boxing matches and ball games. It was just that they were to be spared the soilage implicit in the handling of money, which was still largely a masculine commodity and therefore an indelicate one for them.

Durand and his breath-taking (but properly escorted) wife stopped before the whiskered bank manager, and he swung open a little hinged gate in the banister-rail for their passage.

Durand said, "May I present Mr. Simms to you, my dear? A good friend of mine."

Mr. Simms said with a gallant inclination, "I am inclined to doubt that, or you would not have delayed this for so long."

She cast her eyes fetchingly at him, certainly not in flirtation, for that would have been discreditable to Durand, but at least in a sort of beguiling playfulness.

"I am surprised," she said, and allowed that to stand alone, the better to make her point with what followed.

"How so?" Simms asked uncertainly.

She gave the compliment to Durand, to be passed on by him, instead of directly, face to face. "I had thought until now all bank managers were old and rather forbidding looking."

Mr. Simms' vest buttons had never had a greater strain put upon them, not even after Sunday meals.

She said next, looking about her with ingenuous interest, "I have never been in a bank before. What a superb marble floor."

"We *are* rather proud of that," Mr. Simms conceded.

They entered the office. They seated themselves, Mr. Simms seeing to her chair himself.

They chatted for several moments on a purely social plane, business still having the grace to conceal itself behind a preliminary screen of sociability, even where men alone were involved. (Always providing they were of an equal level.) To come too bluntly to the point without a little pleasant garnishing first was considered bad mannered. But year by year the garnishing was growing less.

At last Durand remarked, "Well, we mustn't take too much of Mr. Simms' time, I know he's a busy man."

The point had now arrived.

"In what way can I be of service to you?" Simms inquired.

"I should like to arrange," said Durand, "for my wife to have full use of my account here, along with myself."

"Oh, really," she murmured disclaimingly, upping one hand. "He insists—"

"Quite simple," said Simms. "We merely change the account from a single one, as it now stands, to a joint account, to be participated in by both." He sought out papers on his desk, selected two. "And to do that all I have to do is ask you both for your signatures, just once each. You on this authorization form. And you, my dear, on this blank form card, just as a record of your signature, so that it will be known to us and we may honor it."

Durand was already signing, forehead inclined.

Simms edged forward another paper tentatively, asked him: "Did you wish this on both accounts, the savings as well as the checking, or merely the one?"

"It may as well be both alike, and have done with it, while we're about it," Durand answered unhesitatingly. He wasn't a grudging gift-giver, and any other answer, it seemed to him, would have been an ungracious one.

"Lou," she protested, but he silenced her with his hand.

Simms was already offering her the inked pen for her convenience. She hesitated, which at least robbed the act of seemingly undue precipitation. "How shall I sign? Do I use my own Christian name, or—?"

"Perhaps your full marriage name might be best. 'Mrs. Louis Durand.' And then you'll remember to repeat that exactly each time you draw a check."

"I shall try," she said obediently.

He blotted solicitously for her.

"Is that all?" she asked, wide-eyed.

"That's quite all there is to it, my dear."

"Oh, that wasn't so bad, was it?" She looked about her in delighted relief, almost like a child who has been dreading a visit to the dentist only to find nothing painful has befallen her.

The two men exchanged a look of condescending masculine superiority, in the face of such inexperience. Their instincts made them like women to be that way.

Simms saw them off from the door of his office with an amount of protocol equal to that with which he had greeted them.

Again the bustle floated in such airy elegance above that workaday bank floor as bustle never had before. Save this same one on its way in. Again the sentimental calflike eyes of cooped-up clerks and tellers and accountants rose from their work to follow her in escapist longings, and an unheard sigh of romantic dejection seemed to go up from all of them alike. It was like the sheen of a rainbow trailing its way through a murky bog, presently to fade out. But while it passed, it was a lovely thing.

"He was nice, wasn't he?" she confided to Durand.

"Not a bad sort," he agreed with more masculine restraint.

"May I ask him to dinner?" she suggested deferentially.

He turned and called back, "Mrs. Durand would like you to dine with us soon. I'll send you a note."

Simms bowed elaborately, from where he stood, with unconcealed gratification.

He stood for several moments after they had gone out into the street, thoughtfully cajoling his own whiskers and envying Durand for having such a paragon of a wife.

— 16 —

THE LETTER was on his desk when he returned to the office from his noonday meal. It must have come in late, therefore, been delayed somehow in delivery, for the rest of his mail for that day had already been on hand awaiting his attention when he first came in at nine.

It was already well on toward three by now. The noonday meal of a typical New Orleans businessman, then, was no hurried snack snatched on the run, there then back again. It was a leisurely affair with due regard for the amenities. He went to his favorite restaurant. He seated himself in state. He ordered with care and amplitude. Friends and acquaintances were greeted, or often joined him at table. Business was discussed, sometimes even transacted. He lingered over his coffee, his cigar, his brandy. Finally, in his own good time, refreshed, restored, ready for the second half of the day's efforts, he went back to his place of work. It was a process that consumed anywhere from two to three hours.

Thus it was midafternoon before, returning to his desk, he found the letter there lying on his blotting-pad.

Twice he started to open it, and twice was interrupted. He took it up, finally, and prepared to spare it a moment of his full attention.

The postmark was St. Louis again. Whether spurred by that or not, he recognized the handwriting, from the time before. From her sister again.

But this time there could be no mistake. It was addressed to him directly. Intentionally so. "Louis Durand, Esq." To be delivered here, at his place of business.

He slit it along the top with a letter opener and plucked it out of its covering, puzzled. He swung himself sideward in his chair and gave it his attention.

If dried ink on paper can be said to scream, it screamed up at him.

Mr. Durand!

I can stand this no longer! I demand that you give me an explanation! I demand that you give me word of my sister without delay!

I am writing to you direct as a last resource. If you do not inform me immediately of my sister's whereabouts, satisfy me that she is safe and sound, and have her communicate with me herself at once to confirm this, and to enlighten me as to the cause of this strange silence, I shall go to the police and seek redress of them.

I have in my hand a letter, in answer to the one I last sent her, purporting to be from her, and signed by her name. It is not from my sister. It is written by someone else. *It is in the handwriting of a stranger,—an unknown person—*

— 17 —

HOW LONG he sat and stared at it he did not know. Time lost its meaning. Reading over and over the same words. "The handwriting of an unknown person. Of an unknown person. An unknown person." Until they became like a whirring buzz saw slashing his brain in two.

Then suddenly hypnosis ended, panic began. He flung himself out of his swivel-backed chair, so that it fell over behind him with a loud clatter. He crushed the letter into his pocket, in such stabbing haste as if it were living fire and burned his fingers at touch.

He ran for the door, forgetting his hat. Then ran back for it, then ran for the door a second time. In it he collided with his office boy, drawn to the entryway just then by the sound the chair had made. He flung him almost bodily aside, gripping him by both shoulders at once; fled on, calling back "Tell Jardine to take over, I've gone home for the day!"

In the street, he slashed his upraised arm every which way at once, before, behind him, sideward, like a man combatting unseen gnats, hoping to draw a coach out of the surrounding emptiness. And when at last he had, after a moment that seemed an hour of agonized waiting, he had run along beside it, was in before it had stopped; standing upright in the middle of it like a latter-day charioteer, leaning over the driver's shoulder in the crazed intensity of giving him the address.

"St. Louis Street, and quickly! I must get there without delay!"

The wheel spokes blurred into solid disks of motion, New Orleans' streets began to stream backward around him, quivering, like scenes pictured on running water.

He struck his own flank, as if he were the horse. "Quicker, coachman! Will you never get there?"

"We're practically flying now, sir. We apt to run down somebody."

"Then run down somebody and be damned! Only get me there!"

He jumped from the carriage as he had entered it, slapped coins from his backward-reaching palm into the driver's forward-reaching one, ran for his own door as if he meant to hurl himself bodily against it and crash it down.

Aunt Sarah opened it with surprising immediacy. She must have been right there in the front hall, on the other side of it.

"Is she in?" he flung into her face. "Is she here in the house?"

"Who?" She drew back, frightened by the violence of the question. But then answered it, for it could refer to only one person. "Miss Julia? She been gone all afternoon. She tole me she going shopping, she be back in no time. That was 'bout one o'clock, I reckon. She ain't come back since."

"My God!" he intoned dismally. "I was afraid of that. Damn that letter for not coming an hour earlier!"

Then he saw that a young girl was huddled there waiting on a backless seat against the wall. Frugally dressed, a large boxed parcel held in her lap. She was shrinking timidly back, her wan face coloring painfully as a result of the recent expletive he had used.

"Who's this?" he demanded, lowering his voice.

"Young lady from the dressmaker's, sent over to have Miss Julia try on a dress they making for her. She say she tole her to be here at three. She been waiting a couple hours now."

Then she didn't intend to remain away today, in the ordinary course of events, flashed through his mind. And her doing so now proves—

"When was this appointment made?" he challenged the girl, causing her to cower still further.

"Some—some days ago," she faltered. "I believe last week, sir." He ran up the stairs full tilt, oblivious of appearances, hearing behind him Aunt Sarah's tactful whisper, "You better go now, honey. Some kind of trouble coming up; you call back some other day."

He stood there in their bedroom, breathing hard from the violence of his ascent but otherwise immobile for a moment, looking about in mute helplessness. His eye fell on the trunk. The trunk that had never been opened. Draped deceptively, but he knew it now, since that Sunday, for what it was. He wrenched off the slip cover, and the initials came to view again. "J.R.," in paint the color of fresh blood.

He turned, bolted out again, ran down the stairs once more. Only part of the way this time, stopping halfway to the bottom.

The young apprentice was at the door now, in the act of departing; turning over to Aunt Sarah the boxed parcel. "Tell Mrs. Durand I'm—I'm sorry to have misunderstood, and I'll come back tomorrow afternoon at the same time, if that's convenient."

"Run out and fetch me a locksmith!" he called out from midstairs, shattering their low-voiced parting interview like an explosive shell. The timid emissary whisked from sight, and Aunt Sarah tried to close the door on her with one hand and at the same time come away from it in fulfillment of his order.

Then he changed his mind again before she could carry out the errand. "No, wait! That would take too long. Bring me a hammer and a chisel. Have we those?"

"I reckon so." She scurried for the back.

When she'd handed them to him, he sped upward from sight

again. He dropped to his knees, launched himself at the trunk with vicious energy, his mouth a white scar; he inserted the chisel in the crevice about the lock, began to pound at it mercilessly. In a moment or two the lock had sprung open, dangled there half-severed from its recent mounting.

The fall of the hammer and chisel made a dull clank in the new stillness of the room, like a funereal knell.

He plucked down the side-latchpieces, unbuckled the ancient leather strap that had bound it about the middle, rose and heaved as he rose, and the slightly domed lid came up and swung rearward with a shudder.

There was an exhalation of mothballs, as if an active breath had blown in his face.

It was the trunk of a neat, a fastidious, a prissy person. Symmetrical stacks of belongings, each one not so much as a hairsbreadth out of line and the crevices between artfully stopped with handkerchiefs and such slighter articles, so that the various mounds could not become displaced in transit.

The top tray held only intimate undergarments, of both day- and night-wear; all of them utilitarian rather than beautiful. Yellow flannel nightrobes, flannel petticoats, thick woollen articles of covering with drawstrings whose nature he did not try to discover.

In a moment his hands had ravaged it beyond recognition.

He shifted the upper section aside, and found neatly spread layers of dresses beneath that. Of a more sober nature than any she had bought since coming here; browns and grays, with prim little rounded white collars, black alpacas, an occasional staid plaid of dark blue or green, no brighter hue.

He picked the topmost one out at random, then added a second one.

He stood there, full length like that, between them, helplessly holding one up in each hand, looking from one to the other.

Suddenly his gaze caught his own reflection, in the full-length mirrored panel facing her wardrobe door. He stepped out more fully from behind the trunk, looked again. Something struck his eye as being wrong. He couldn't tell what it was.

He drew a step back with the two trophies, to gain added perspective. Then suddenly, at the shift, it exploded into recognition. There was too much of each dress. He was holding his hands, the hands that held them, at his own shoulder level. They fell away straight to the floor, and, touching it, even folded over in excess.

In memory he saw her stand beside him again, in the mirror. She appeared there for a moment, in brief recapture. The top of her head just rising over the turn of his shoulder: when her hair was up.

He dropped the two wraithlike rags, almost in fright. Stepped to the wardrobe, flung both panels of it wide, with two hands at once. Empty; a naked wooden bar running barren across its upper part. A little puff of ghostly violet scent, and that was all.

This discovery was anticlimactic to the one that had just preceded it, somehow. His real fright lay in the dresses that were here, and not the dresses that were gone.

He ran out again to the stairs, and bending to be seen from below, called to Aunt Sarah, until she had come running in renewed terror. "Yes sir! Yes sir!"

"That girl. What did she leave here? Was that something of Mrs. Durand's?"

"New dress they running up for her."

"Bring it here. Hand it up to me, quick!"

He ran back to the room with it, burst the cardboard open, rifled it out. Gay, sprightly; heliotrope ribbons at its waist. His eye took no note of that.

He retrieved the one from the trunk he had dropped to the floor. He flattened it on the bed, smoothing it out like a paper pattern, spreading the sleeves, drawing down the skirt to its full length.

Then he superimposed the new one, the one just delivered, atop it. Then stood back and looked, already knowing.

At no point did the one match the other. The sleeves were longer, by a full cuff-length. The bosom was fuller, spilling out in an excess curve at either side when rendered two dimensional. The waist was almost half again as wide. The wearer of the one could not have entered the other. And most glaring of all the skirt of one reached in a wide band of continuation far below, broad inches below, where the other had ended.

There was only one length for all skirts, even he knew that; floor-length. There was no such thing as a skirt other than floor-length. Any variation in length was not due to fashion, it was due to the height of the wearer.

And in this undersized, topmost one there still twinkled the pins of her living measurements as he had known her, taken from her very body less than a week ago, waiting for the final sewing.

The clothes from St. Louis—

The color slowly drained from his face, and there was a strange sort of fear in his heart that he'd never known before. He'd already known when he came into this house, a while ago; but now, in this moment, he'd proved it, and there was no longer any escaping from the proof.

The clothes from St. Louis were the clothes of someone else.

— 18 —

IT WAS dark now, the town had dropped into night. The town, the world, his mind, were hanging suspended in bottomless night. It was dark outside in the streets and it was dark in here in the room where he stood.

There was no eye to pierce the darkness where he stood; he was alone, unseen, unguessed-at. He was something motionless standing within a black-lined box. And if it breathed, that was a secret between God and itself. That, and the pain he felt in breathing, and a few other things.

Then at last pale light approached, rising from below, ascending the stairs outside. As it rose, it strengthened, until at last its focus came into view: a lighted lamp dancing restlessly from a wire hoop, held by Aunt Sarah as she climbed toward the upper floor. It paled her figure into a ghost. A ghost with a dark face, but with a sifting of flour outlining its seams.

She came up to the level at last, and turned toward his room; the lamp exploded into a permanent dazzle that filled the doorway, burgeoning in and finding him out.

She halted there and looked at him.

He was standing, utterly, devastatingly motionless. The light fell upon the pile of dresses strewed on the bed, tumbled to the floor. It flushed color into them as it revealed them, like a syringe filled with dye. Blue, green, maroon, dusty pink, they became. It flushed color into him too, the colors a waxen image has, dressed to the last detail like a live man. So clever it could almost fool you; the way those things are supposed to do in waxworks. Verisimilitude without animation.

He was like one struck dead. Upright on his feet, but dead. He could see her, for his eyes were on her face; gravely gazing on her face, that part of the body which the eye habitually seeks when it looks on someone. He could hear her, for when she whispered half-frightenedly: "Mr. Lou, what is it? What is it, Mr. Lou?"; he answered her, he spoke, his voice came.

"She's not coming back," he whispered in return.

"You been in here all this time like this, without a light?"

"She's not coming back."

"How much longer I'm going to have to wait for supper? I can't keep that chicken much more."

"She's not coming back."

"Mr. Lou, you're not hearing me, you're not heeding."

That was all he could keep saying. "She's not coming back." All the thousands of words were forgotten, the thousands it had taken him fifteen years to learn, and only four remained of his whole mother tongue: "She's not coming back."

She ventured into the room, bringing the lamp with her, and the light eddied and fluxed, before it had settled again. She set it down upon the table. She wrung her hands, and knotted parts of her dress in them, as if not knowing what to do with them.

At last she took a small part of her own skirt and wiped sadly at the edge of the table with it, from old habit, as if thinking she were dusting it. That was the only help she could give him, the only ease she could bring him: to dust an edge of the table in his room. But pity takes many forms, and it has no need of words.

And it was as though she had brought warmth into the room; warmth at least sufficient to thaw him, to melt the glacial casque that held him rigid. Just by being there, another human being, near him.

Then slowly he started to come back to life. The dead started to come back to life. It wasn't pleasurable to watch. Rebirth after death. The death of the heart.

Death-throes in reverse. Coming after the terminal blow, not before. When the heart dies, it should stay dead. It should be given the coup de grace, struck still once and for all, not allowed to agonize.

His knees broke their locked rigidity, and he dropped down at half-height beside the bed. His arms reached out across it, clawing in torment.

And one of the dresses stirred, as if under its own impulse; rippled in serpentine haste across the bed top, and was sucked up into the maelstrom of his grief; his head falling prone upon it, his face burrowing into it in ghastly parody of kisses once given, that could never be given again, for there was no one there to give them to. Only the empty cocoon he pleaded with now.

"Julia. Julia. Be merciful."

The old woman's hand started toward his palsied shoulder in solace, then held itself suspended barely clear of touch.

"Hush, Mr. Lou," she said with guttural intensity. "Hush, poor man."

She raised her outstretched hand then, held it poised at greater height, up over his oblivious, gnawing head.

"May the Lawd have mercy on you. May He take pity on you.

You weeping, but you ain't got nothing to weep for. You mourning, but you mourning for something you never had."

He rolled his head sideward, and looked up at her with sudden frightened intentness.

As if kindled into anger now by sight of his wasted grief, as if vindictive with long-delayed revelation, she went to the bureau that had been Julia's. She threw open a drawer of it with such righteous violence that the whole cabinet shook and quivered.

She plunged her hand in, unerringly striking toward a hiding place she knew of from some past discovery. Then held it toward him in speechless portent. Within it was rimmed a dusty cake, a pastille, of cheek rouge.

She threw it down, anathema.

Again her hand burrowed into secretive recesses of the drawer. She held up, this time, a cluster of slender, spindly cigars.

She showed him, flung them from her.

Her hands went up overhead, quivered there aloft, vibrant with doom and malediction, calling the blind skies to witness.

She intoned in a blood-curdling voice, like some Old Testament prophetess calling down apocalyptic judgment.

"They's been a bad woman living in your house! They's been a stranger sleeping in your bed!"

— 19 —

HATLESS, COATLESS, hair awry, just as the discovery had found him in his room moments before, he was running like someone demented through the quiet, night-lidded streets now, unable to find a coach and too crazed to stand still and wait for one in any one given place. Onward, ever onward, toward an address that had fortuitously recurred to him just now, when he needed it most. The house of the banker Simms, halfway across New Orleans. He would have run the whole distance on foot, to get there, if necessary.

But luckily, as he came to a four-way crossing, a gaslit post brooding over it in sulphuric yellow-green, he spied a carriage just ahead, returning idle from some recent hire, screaming after it and without waiting for it to come back and get him, ran down the roadway after it full tilt; floundered into it and choked out Simms' address.

At the banker's house he rang the bell like fury.

A colored servant led him in, showing an offended mien at his impetuosity.

"He's at supper, sir," she said disapprovingly. "If you'll have the patience to seat yourself just a few minutes and wait till he gets through—"

"No matter," he panted. "This can't wait! Ask him to come out here a moment—"

The banker came out into the hall, brow beetling with annoyance, still chewing food and with a napkin still trussed about his collar. When he saw who it was his face cleared.

"Mr. Durand!" he said heartily. "What brings you here at such an hour? Will you come in and join us at table?" Then noting his distracted appearance more closely as he came nearer, "You're all upset— What's the matter, man? Bring him some brandy, Becky. A chair—"

Durand swept a curt hand offside in refusal of the offered restoratives. "My money—" he gasped out.

"What is it, Mr. Durand? What of your money?"

"Is it there—? Has it been touched—? When you closed at three, what was my balance on your ledgers—?"

"I don't understand you, Mr. Durand. No one can touch your money. It's safeguarded. No one but yourself and your wife—"

He caught an inkling of something from the agonized expression that had flitted across Durand's face just then.

"You mean—?" he breathed, appalled.

"I have to know— Now, tonight— For the love of God, Mr.

Simms, do something for me, help me— Don't keep me waiting like this—"

The banker wrenched off his napkin, cast it from him, in sign his meal was ended for that evening at least. "My chief teller," he said in quick-formed decision. "My chief teller would know. That would be quicker than going to the bank; we'd have to open up and go over the day's transactions—"

"Where can I find him?" Durand was already on his way toward the door and out again.

"No, no, I'll go with you. Wait for me just a second—" Simms hurriedly snatched at his hat and a silken throat muffler. "What is it, what has happened, Mr. Durand?"

"I'm afraid to say, until I find out," Durand said desolately. "I'm afraid even to think—"

Simms had to stop first and secure his teller's home address; then they hurriedly left, climbed back into the same carriage that had brought Durand, and were driven to a frugal little squeezed-in house on Dumaine Street.

Simms got out, deterred Durand with a kindly intended gesture of his hand, evidently hoping to spare him as much as possible.

"Suppose you wait here. I'll go in and talk to him."

He went inside to be gone perhaps ten minutes at the most. To Durand it seemed he had been left out there the whole night.

At last the door opened and Simms had reappeared. Durand leaped, as though a spring had been released, to meet him, trying to read his face for the tidings as he went toward him. It looked none too sanguine.

"What is it? For God's sake, tell me!"

"Steady, Mr. Durand, steady." Simms put a supporting arm about him just below the turn of the shoulders. "You had thirty thousand, fifty-one dollars, forty cents in your check-cashing account and twenty thousand ten in your savings account this morning when we opened for business—"

"I know that! I know that already! That isn't what I want to know—"

The teller had followed Simms out. The manager gestured to him surreptitiously, handing over to him the unwelcome responsibility of answering the question.

"Your wife appeared at five minutes of three to make a last-minute withdrawal," the teller said.

"Your balance at closing-time was fifty-one dollars, forty cents in the one account, ten dollars in the other. To have closed them both out entirely, your own signature would have been necessary."

— 20 —

THE ROOM was a still life. It might have been something painted on a canvas, that was then stood upright to dry; life-size, identical to life in every shading and every trifling detail, yet an artful simulation and not the original itself.

A window haloed by setting sunlight, as if there were a brush fire burning just outside of it, kindling, with its glare, the ceiling and the opposite wall. The carpeting on the floor undulant and ridged in places, as if misplaced by someone's lurching footsteps, or even an actual bodily fall or two, and then allowed to remain that way thereafter. A dark stain, crab-shaped, marring it in one spot, as if a considerable quantity of some heavy-bodied liquid had been overturned upon it.

Dank bed, that had once made a bridegroom blush; that would have made any fastidious person blush now, looking as if it had been untended for days. Graying linen receding from its skeleton on one side, overhanging it to trail the floor on the other. A single shoe, man's shoe, abandoned there beside it; as though the original impulse that had caused it to be removed, or else had caused its mate to be donned, had ebbed and faded before it could be carried to completion.

Forget-me-nots on pink wallpaper; wallpaper that had come

from New York, wallpaper that had been asked for in a letter; "not too pink." There was a place where the plaster backing showed through in rabid scars; as if someone had taken a pair of shears and gouged at them in a rage, trying to obliterate as many as possible.

In the center of the still life a table. And on the table three immobile things. A reeking tumbler, mucous with endless refilling, and a bottle of brandy, and an inert head, crown-side up, matted hair bristling from it. Its nerveless body on an off-balance chair at tableside, one hand gripping the neck of the bottle in relentless possessiveness.

A tap at the door, but with no accompanying sound of approach, as though someone had been standing there for a long time, listening, trying to gain courage.

No answer, nothing moved.

Again a tap. A voice added to it this time.

"Mr. Lou. Mr. Lou, turn the key."

No answer. The head rolled a little, exposing a jawline pricked with bluish hair follicles.

Once more a tap.

"Mr. Lou, turn the key. It's been two days now."

The head broke contact with the table top, elevated itself a little, eyes still closed. "What are days?" it said blurredly. "I've forgotten. Oh—those things that come between the nights. Those empty things."

The knob on the door turned sterilely. "Lemme in. Lemme just fraishen up your bed."

"It's just for me alone now. Let it be."

"Don't you want a light, at least? It getting dark. Lemme change the lamp in there for you."

"What can it show me? What's there to see? There's only me in here now. Me, and—"

He tilted the brandy bottle over the tumbler. Nothing came out. He held it perpendicular. Nothing still.

He rose from his chair, swung the bottle back to launch it at the wall. Then he stayed his arm, lowered it, shuffled to the door on one shoe, turned the key at last.

He thrust the bottle at her.

"Get me another of these," he barked. "That's all I want. That's the best the world can do for me now. I don't want your lamps and your broths and your tidying of beds."

But she was brave in the cause of housekeeping cleanliness, this old, spare, colored woman. She sidled in past him before he could stop her, put down the fresh lamp beside the one that had exhausted its fuel, in a moment was pulling and tucking at the bedraggled bed linen, casting an occasional furtive glance toward him, to see if he meant to stop her or not.

She finished, made haste to get out of the room again, coursing the long way around, by the wall, in order not to come too close to him. The door safely in her hand again, she turned and looked at him, where he stood, bottle neck riveted to hand.

And he looked at her.

Suddenly a tremor of unutterable longing seemed to course through him. His rasping bitter voice of a moment ago became gentle. He put out his hand toward her, as if pleading with her to stay, now, to listen to him speak of *her*, the absent. To speak of *her* with him.

"Do you remember how she used to sit there cleaning her nails, with a stick tipped with cotton? I can see her now," he said brokenly. "And then she would hold her fingers up, like this, all spread out, and quirk her head, to one side and to the other, looking at them to see if they would do."

Aunt Sarah didn't answer.

"Do you remember her in that green dress, with stripes of lavender? I can see her now, with the sunlight coming from behind her, breeze stirring her gown, standing there on the Canal Street dock. A little wispy parasol open over her."

Aunt Sarah made no reply.

"Do you remember that way she had, of turning in the doorway, each time she was about to leave, and bending her fingers backward, as if she were calling you *to* her, and saying 'Ta ta!'?"

The old woman's taciturnity burst its floodgates at last, as if she were unable to endure hearing any more. The whites of her eyes dilated righteously and her withered lips drew back from her teeth. She flung up her hand at him, as if enjoining him to silence.

"God must have been angry with you the day He first let you look into that woman's face!"

He stumbled over to the wall, pressed his face against it, arms straight up over his head as if he were trying to claw his way upward toward the ceiling. His voice seemed to come from his stomach, through rolling drums of smothered agony—that were the weeping of a grown man.

"I want her back again. I want her back. I'll never rest until I find her."

"What you want her back again for?" she demanded.

He turned slowly.

"To kill her," he said through his clenched teeth.

He pushed away from the wall, and lurched soddenly to the bed. He overturned an edge of the mattress, and reached below it, and drew something out. Then he slowly raised it, held it in strangulated grip to show her; a bone-handled, steel-barreled pistol.

"With this," he whispered.

— 21 —

THE AUDIENCE was streaming out of the Tivoli Theatre, on Royal Street. Gas flames in the jets on the foyer walls and in the ceiling overhead flickered fitfully with the swirl of its crowded passage. The play had been most enjoyable, an adaptation from the French called *Papa's Little Mischief*, and every animated conversation bore evidence to that.

Once on the sidewalk, the solid mass of people began to disintegrate: the balcony-sitters to walk off in varying directions, the box-holders and orchestra occupants to clamber by twos, and sometimes fours, into successive carriages as they drew up in turn before the theatre entrance, summoned by the colored doorman.

The man lurking back from sight against the shadowy wall, where the brightness failed to reach, was unnoticed, though many passed close enough to touch him.

The crowd drained off at last. The brightness dimmed, as an attendant began to put out the gaslights one by one, with a long, upward-reaching stick that turned their keys.

Only a few laggards were left now, still awaiting their turn at carriage stop. There was no haste, and politeness and deference were the rule.

"After you."

"No, after you, sir. Yours is the next."

And then at last one final couple remain, and are about to enter their carriage. The woman short, and in a lace head-scarf that, drawn close against the insalubrious night air, effectively mists her head and mouth and chin.

Her escort leaves her side for a moment, to see what the delay is in locating their carriage, and suddenly, from out of nowhere, a man is beside her, peering at her closely. She turns her head away, draws the scarf even closer, and edges a step or two aside in trepidation.

He is bending forward now, craning openly, so that he is all but crouched under her lace-blurred face, staring intently up into it.

She gives a cry of alarm and cowers back.

"Julia?" he whispers questioningly.

She turns in fright the other way, giving him her back.

He comes around before her again.

"Madam, will you lower your scarf?"

"Let me be, or I'll call for help."

He reaches up and flings it aside.

A pair of terrified blue eyes, stranger's eyes, are staring taut at him, aghast.

Her escort comes back at a run, raises his stick threateningly. "Here, sir!" Brings it down once or twice, then discarding it as unsatisfactory, strikes out savagely with his unaided arm.

Durand goes staggering back and sprawls upon the sidewalk.

He makes no move to resist, nor to rise again and retaliate. He lies there extended, on the point of one elbow, passive, spent, dejected. The wild look dies out of his face.

"Forgive me," he sighs. "I thought you were—someone else."

"Come away, Dan. The man must be a little mad."

"No, I'm not mad, madam," he answers her with frigid dignity. "I'm perfectly sane. Too sane."

— 22 —

IN THE front parlor of Madame Jessica's house on Toulouse Street, there was a vivacious evening party going on. Madame Jessica's parlor was both expansive and expensively furnished. The furniture was ivory-white, touched with gold, in the Empire style; the upholstery was crimson damask brocade. Brussels carpeting covered the parquetry floor, and the flickering gas tongues above, in nests of crystal, were like an aurora borealis.

A glossy haired young man sat at the rosewood piano, running over Chopin's "Minute Waltz" with a light but competent touch. One couple were slowly pivoting about in the center of the room, but more absorbed in one another's conversation than in dancing.

Two others were on the sofa together, sipping champagne and engaged in sprightly chat. Still a third couple stood together, near the door, likewise lost to their surroundings. Always two by two. The young ladies were all in evening dress. The men were not, but at least all were well groomed and gentlemanly in aspect.

All was decorum, all was elegance and propriety. Madame was strict that way. No voices too loud, no laughter too blaring. None left the room without excusing themselves to the rest of the company.

A colored maid, whose duty it was to announce new arrivals, opened one of the two opposite pairs of parlor-doors and announced: "Mr. Smith." No one smiled, or appeared to pay any attention.

Durand came in, and Madame Jessica crossed the room to greet him cordially in person, arm extended, her sequins winking as she went.

"Good evening, sir. How nice of you to come to see us. May I introduce you to someone?"

"Yes," Durand said quietly.

Madame fluttered her willow fan, put a finger to the corner of her mouth, surveyed the room speculatively, like a good hostess seeking to pair off only those among her guests with the greatest affinity.

"Miss Margot is taken up for the moment—" she said, eying the sofa in passing. "How about Miss Fleurette? She's unescorted." She indicated the opposite pair of doors, leading deeper into the house, which had partially and unobtrusively drawn apart. A tall brunette was standing there, as if casually, in passing by.

"No."

Madame did something with her fan, and the brunette turned and disappeared. A more buxom, titian-haired young woman took her place in the opening.

"Miss Roseanne, then?" Madame suggested enticingly.

He shook his head.

Madame flickered her fan and the opening fell empty.

"You're difficult to please, sir," she said with an uncertain smile. "Is that—all? Is there—no one else?"

"Not quite. There's our Miss Juliette. I believe she's having a tete-a-tete. If you'd care to wait a few minutes—"

He sat down alone, in a large chair in the corner.

"May I send you over some refreshments?" Madame asked, bending attentively over him.

He opened his money-fold, passed some money to her.

"Champagne for everyone else. Don't send any over to me."

A colored butler moved among the guests, refilling glasses. The other young men turned, one by one, saluted with their glasses, and bowed an acknowledgement to him. He gravely bowed in return.

Madame must have been favorably impressed, she evidently decided to hasten Miss Juliette's arrival, in some unknown behind-the-scenes manner.

She came back presently to promise: "She'll be down directly. I've sent up word there's a young man down here asking for her."

She left him, then returned to say: "Here she is now. Isn't she just *lovely?* Everyone's simply mad about her, I declare!"

He saw her in the doorway. She stood for a moment, looking around, trying to identify him.

She was blonde.

She was beautiful.

She was about seventeen.

She was someone else.

Madame bustled over, led her forward through the room, an arm affectionately about her waist.

"Right this way, honey. May I present—"

She gasped. The beautiful creature's eyes opened wide, at the first rebuff she had ever received in her short but crowded life. A puzzled silence momentarily fell upon the animated room.

His chair was empty. The adjacent door, the door leading out, was just closing.

— 23 —

MARDI GRAS. A city gone mad. A fever that seizes the town every year, on the last Tuesday before Ash Wednesday. "Fat Tuesday." Over and over, for fifty-three years now, since 1827, when the first such celebration started spontaneously, no one knows how. A last fling before the austerities of Lent begin, as though the world of human frailty were ending, never to renew itself. Bacchanalia before recantation, as if to give penance a good hearty cause.

There is no night and there is no day. The lurid glare of flambeaux and of lanterns along Canal and Royal and the other downtown streets makes ruddy sunlight at midnight; and in the daytime the shops are closed, nothing is bought and nothing is sold. Nothing but joy, and that's to be had free. For eight years past, the day has already been a legal holiday, and since that same year, 1872, the Legislature has sanctioned the wearing of masks on the streets this one day.

There is always music sounding somewhere, near or far; as the strains of one street band fade away, in one direction, the strains of another approach, from somewhere else. There are always shouts and laughter to be heard, though they may be out of sight for a moment, around some corner or behind the open windows of some house. Though there may be a lull, along some given street, at some given moment, the Mardi Gras is going on just as surely somewhere else just then; it never stops.

It was during such a momentary lull that the motionless figure stood in a doorway sheltered beneath a gallery, along upper Canal Street. The air was still hazy and pungent with smoky pitch-fumes, the ground was littered with confetti, paper serpentines, shredded balloon skins looking like oddly colored fruit-peelings, a crushed tin horn or two; even a woman's slipper with the heel broken off. The feet of an inebriate protruded perpendicularly from a doorway, the rest of him hidden inside it. Someone had tossed a wreath of flowers, as a funereal offering is placed at the foot of a bier, and deftly looped it about his upturned toes.

But this other figure, in its own particular doorway, was sober, erect. It had donned a papier-mache false face, out of concession to the carnival spirit; otherwise it was in ordinary men's suiting. The false face was grotesque, a frozen grimace of unholy glee, doubly grotesque in conjunction with the wearied, forlorn, spent posture of the figure beneath it.

A distant din that had been threatening for several moments suddenly burst into full volume, as it came around a corner, and a long chain, a snake dance, of celebrants came wriggling into view, each member gripping waist or shoulders of the person before him. The Mardi Gras was back; the pause, the breathing space, was over.

Torches came with them, and kettle drums and cymbals. The street lighted up again, as though it had caught fire. Wavering gi-ant-size shadows slithered across the orange faces of the buildings. At once people came back to the windows again on either side of the way. Confetti once more began to snow down, turning rain-bow-hued as it drifted through varying zones of light; pink, laven-der, pale green.

The central procession, the backbone, of dancers was flanked by detached auxiliaries on both sides, singly and in couples, trios, quartettes, who went along with it without being integrated into it. The chain was lengthening every moment, picking up strays, though no one could tell where it was going, and no one cared. Its head had already turned a second corner and passed from sight, before its tail had finished coming around the first. The original lockstep it had probably started with had long been discarded be-cause of its unwieldy length, and now it was a potpourri. Some were doing a cakewalk, prancing with knees raised high before them, others simply shuffling along barely raising feet from the ground, still others jigging, cavorting and kicking up their heels from side to side, like jack-in-the-boxes.

The false face kept switching feverishly, to and fro, forward and back, while the body beneath it remained fixed; centering its ogling eyes on each second successive figure as it passed, following that a moment or two, then dropping that to go back and take up the next but one. The women only, skipping over the clowns, the pirates, the Spanish smugglers, interspersed between.

Ogling, bulging, white-painted eyes, that promised buffoonery and horseplay, ludicrous flirtation and comic impassionment. Anything, but not latent death.

Many saw it, and some waved, and some called out in gay invitation, and one or two threw flowers that hit it on the nose. Roman empresses, harem beauties, gypsies, Crusaders' ladies in dunce caps. And a nursemaid in starched apron wheeling a full-grown man before her in a baby's perambulator, his hairy legs dragging out at the sides of it and occasionally taking steps of their own.

Then suddenly the comic popeyes remained fixed, the whole false face and the neck supporting it craned forward, unbearably intent, taut.

She wore a domino-suit, a shapeless bifurcated garb fastened only at the wrists, the ankles and the neck. A cowl covered her head. She wore an eye-mask of light blue silk, but beneath it her mouth was like an unopened bud.

She was no more than five feet two or three, and her step was dainty and graceful. She was not in the cavalcade, she was part of the footloose flotsam coursing along beside it. She was on the far side of it from him, it was between the two of them. She was passing from man to man, dancing a few steps in the arms of each, then quitting him and on to someone else. Thus progressing, with not a step, not a turn, wasted uncompanioned. She was a sprite of sheer gayety.

Just then her hood was dislodged, thrown back for a moment, and before she could recover and hastily return it, he had glimpsed the golden hair topping the blue mask.

He threw up his arm and shouted "Julia!" He launched himself from the door niche and three times dashed himself against the impeding chain, trying to get through to her side, and three times was thrown back by its unexpected resiliency.

"*No one* breaks through us," they told him mockingly. "Go all the way back to the end, and around, if you must cross over."

Suddenly she seemed to become aware of him. She halted for a moment and was looking straight across at him. Or seemed to be. He heard the high-pitched bleat of her laughter, in all that din, at sight of his comic face. She flung her arm out at him derisively. Then turned and went on again.

He plunged into the maelstrom, and like a drowning man trying to keep his head above water, was engulfed, swept every way but the way he wanted to go.

At last a Viking in a horned helmet, one of the links in the impeding chain, took pity on him.

"He sees someone he likes," he shouted jocularly. "It's Mardi Gras, after all. Let him through." And with brawny arms raised like a drawbridge for a moment, let him duck under them to the other side.

She was still intermittently in sight, but far down ahead. Like a light blue cork bobbing in a littered sea.

"Julia!"

She turned fully this time, but whether at sound of the name or simply because of the strength of his voice could not have been determined.

He saw her crouch slightly, as if taunting him to a mock chase. A chase in which there was no terror, only playfulness, coquetry, a deliberate incitement to pursuit. A moment later she had fled away deftly, slipping easily in and out because of her small size. But looking back every now and again.

It was obvious she didn't know who he was, but thought him simply an anonymous pursuer from out of the Mardi Gras, someone to have sport with. Once when he thought he had lost her altogether, and would have had she willed it so, for she purposely halted aside in a doorway and remained there waiting for him to single her out once more. Then when he had done so, and there could be no mistake, she drew out her clown-like suit wide at the sides, dipped him a mocking curtsey, and sped on again.

At last, with one more backward look at him, as if to say: "Enough of this. I've set a high enough price on your approaching me. Now have your way with me, whatever it is to be," she turned aside from the main stream of the revelers and darted down a dimly lighted alley.

He reached its mouth in turn moments later, and could still see the paleness of her light blue garb running ahead in the gloom. He turned and went in. There were no more obstacles here, nothing to keep him back. In a minute or two he had overtaken her, and had her back against the wall, his raised arms, planted against it, a barrier on either side of her.

She couldn't speak. She was too winded. She leaned back against the wall, in expectation of dalliance, the fruits of the chase now to be enjoyed alike by both of them. He could make out the pale blue mask shimmering there before him in the dark. The red and yellow glare of torches was kept to the mouth of this side street, this byway; it couldn't reach in to where they were. It was twilight dim. It was the very place for it—

He tried to lift the mask from her face and she warded him off, shunting her head aside. She tittered a little, and fanned herself limply with her own hand, to create additional air for breath.

"Julia," he panted full into her face. "Julia."

She tittered again.

"Now I've got you."

He looked around where the light was, where the crowd was still streaming by, as if in measurement.

Then his hand fumbled under his clothing and he took out the bone-handled pistol he'd carried with him throughout the Mardi Gras. She didn't see it for a moment, it was held low, below the level of their eyes.

Then he pulled at his own false face, and it fell to the ground.

"Now do you know me, Julia? Now do you see who I am?"

His elbow backed, and the gun went out away from her, to find room. It clicked as he thumbed back the hammerhead.

It came forward again. It found that empty place, where in others a heart was known to be.

Then he ripped ruthlessly at the eye-mask and pared it from her. The hood went back with it, and the blonde hair was revealed. She saw the gun at the same time that he saw her face fully.

"No, doan', mister, doan'—" she whimpered abjectly. "I din' mean no harm. I was jes foolin', jes foolin'—" She tried to grovel to the ground, but the taut closeness of his arms kept her up in spite of herself.

"Why, you're a—you're a—"

"Please, mister, I cain't help it if I doan' match up right—"

There was a sodden futile impact as the bone-handled gun fell beside him to the ground.

— 24 —

THE ROOM was a still life. Forget-me-nots on pink wallpaper in the background. In the foreground a table. On the table a reeking tumbler, an overturned bottle drained to its dregs, a prone head. Nothing moved. Nothing had feeling, or awareness.

A still life entitled "Despair."

— 25 —

THE COMMISSIONER OF POLICE of the city of New Orleans was the average man of his own metier, no more, no less. Fifty-seven years of age, weight two hundred and one pounds, height five feet ten, silver-black hair, now growing bald, caracul-like beard, parted in two, a poor dresser, high principled, but not beyond the point of normalcy, a hard worker, married, obliged to use spectacles only when reading, and subject to a mild form of kidney trouble. Not brilliant, but not dull; the former certainly more of a disqualification in a public civil servant than the latter.

His office, in the Police Headquarters Building, was not particularly prepossessing, but since it was not for social usage but strictly for work, this doubtless was of no great moment. It had a certain fustian atmosphere which was perhaps inescapable in an administrative business office of its type. Ivory wallpaper rapidly turning brown with age (and unevenly so) adhered to the walls, with pockets and bulges where it had warped; it dated at least from the Van Buren administration. A green carpet, faded sickly yellow, covered the floor. A gaslight chandelier of four burners within reversed tulipshaped soapy-iridescent glass cups hung from the ceiling. The commissioner's desk, massed with papers, was placed so that he sat with his back to the window and those he interviewed had the disadvantage of the light in their faces.

His secretary opened the door, closed it at his back, and then announced: "There's a gentleman out here to see you, sir."

The commissioner looked up only briefly from a report he was considering. "About what? Have him state his business," he said in a rumbling deep-welled baritone.

The secretary retired, conferred, returned.

"It's a personal matter, for your ears alone, sir. I suggested he write, but he claims that cannot be done either. He begs you to give him just a moment of your time."

The commissioner sighed unwillingly. "All right. Interrupt us in five minutes, Harris. Make sure of that, now."

The secretary held the door back, motioned permission with two upraised fingers, and an old man entered. A haggard, dejected, beaten old man of thirty-seven.

The secretary withdrew to begin his five-minute count.

The commissioner put aside the report he had been consulting, nodded with impersonal civility. "Good day, sir. Will you be as brief as possible? I have a number of matters here—" He swept an arm rather vaguely past his own desk top.

"I'll try to, sir. I appreciate your giving me your time."

The commissioner liked that. He was favorably impressed so far,

"Will you have a chair, sir?"

He would give him at least his allotted five minutes, if not more. He looked as if he had suffered greatly; yet behind that there was a certain surviving innate dignity visible, conducive to respect rather than mawkish pity.

The visitor sat down in a large black leather chair, lumpy with broken spring-coils.

"Now, sir," prodded the commissioner, to discourage any inclination toward dilatoriness.

"My name is Louis Durand. I was married on May the twentieth, last, to a woman who came from St. Louis and called herself Julia Russell. I had never seen her before. I have the certificate of marriage here with me. On the fifteenth of June last she withdrew fifty thousand dollars from my bank account and disappeared. I have not seen her since. I want a warrant issued for the arrest of this woman. I want her apprehended, brought to trial, and the money returned to me."

The commissioner said nothing for some time. It was obvious that this was not inattention or disinterest, but on the contrary a sudden excessive amount of both. It was equally obvious that he was rephrasing the story, to himself, in his own mind; marshalling it into his own thought-symbols, so to speak; familiarizing himself with it, the better to have it at his command.

"May I see the certificate?" he said at last.

Durand produced, tendered it to him.

He read it carefully, but said nothing further in respect to it. In fact, he asked but two questions more, both widely spaced, but both highly pertinent.

One was: "You said you had never seen her before; how was that?"

Durand explained the nature of the courtship, and added, moreover, that he believed her not to be the woman he had proposed to, but an impostor. He gave the reasons for that belief, but admitted he had no proof.

The commissioner's second and final question, spoken through steeple-joined fingers, was:

"Did she forge your name in order to withdraw the funds?"

Durand shook his head. "She signed her own. I had given her authorization with the bank to do so; given her access to the accounts."

The five minutes' grace had expired. The door opened and young Harris wedged head and one shoulder through, said: "Excuse me, Commissioner, but I have a report here for you to—"

Countermanding his former instructions, the commissioner silenced him with a sweep of his hand.

He addressed Durand with leisurely deliberation, showing that the interview was not being terminated on that account, but for reasons implicit in its own nature. "I would like to talk this matter over with my associates first," he admitted, "before I take any action. It's a curious sort of case, quite unlike anything that's come my way before. If you'll allow me to keep this marriage certificate for the time being, I'll see that it's returned to you. Suppose you come back tomorrow at this same time, Mr. Durand."

And turning, he enjoined his secretary with unmistakable emphasis: "Harris, I'm seeing Mr. Durand tomorrow morning at this same hour. Make sure my appointments allow for it."

"Thank you, Mr. Commissioner," Durand said, rising.

"Don't thank me for anything yet. Let us wait and see first."

— 26 —

"HAVE A CHAIR, Mr. Durand," the commissioner said, after having offered his hand.

Durand did so, waited.

The commissioner collected his words, ranged them in mind, and at last delivered them. "I'm sorry. I find that there's nothing we can do for you. Nothing whatever. And by we, I mean the police department of this city."

"What?" Durand was stunned. His head went back against the spongy black leather of the chair-back. His hat fell from his grasp and his lap, and it was the commissioner who retrieved it for him. He could hardly speak for a moment. "You—you mean a strange woman, a stray, can come along, perpetrate a mock marriage with a man, abscond with fifty thousand dollars of his money—and—and you say you can do nothing about it—?"

"Just a moment," the commissioner said, speaking with patient kindliness. "I understand how you feel, but just a moment." He offered him the certificate of marriage which he had retained from the previous day.

Durand crushed it in his hand, swept it aside in a disgusted fling. "This—this valueless forgery—!"

"The first point which must be made clear before we go any further is this," the commissioner told him. "This is not a counterfeit. That marriage is not a mock one." He underscored his words. "*That woman is legally your wife.*"

Durand's stupefaction this time was even worse than before.

He was aghast. "She is not Julia Russell! That is not her name! If I am married at all, I am married to Julia Russell, whoever and wherever she may be— This is a marriage by proxy, if you will call it that— *But this woman was someone else!*"

"There is where you are wrong." The commissioner told off each word with the heavy thump of a single fingerpad to the desk top. "I have consulted with the officials of the church where it was performed, and I have consulted as well with our own lay experts in jurisprudence. The woman who stood beside you in the church was married to you *in person,* and not by proxy for another. No matter what name she gave, false or true, no matter if she had said she was the daughter of the President of the United States, heaven forbid!—she is your lawfully wedded wife, in civil law and in religious canon; she and only she and she alone. And nothing can make her otherwise. You can have it annulled, of course, on the ground of misrepresentation, but that is another matter—"

"My God!" Durand groaned.

The commissioner rose, went to the water cooler, and drew him a cup of water. He ignored it.

"And the money?" he said at last, exhaustedly. "A woman can rob a man of his life savings, under your very noses, and you cannot help him, you cannot do anything for him? What kind of law is that, that punishes the honest and protects malefactors? A woman can walk into a man's house and—"

"No. Now hold on. That brings us back again to where we were. A woman cannot do that, and remain immune to reprisal. But a *woman,* just any woman at all, did *not* do that, in your case."

"But—"

"*Your wife* did that. And the law cannot touch her for it. You gave her signed permission to do just what she did. Mr. Simms at the bank has shown me the authorization card. Under such circumstances, where a joint account exists, a wife cannot steal from her husband, a husband from his wife."

He glanced sorrowfully around at the window behind him.

"She could pass by this building this very minute, out there in the street, and we could not detain her, we could not put a hand upon her."

Durand let his shoulders slump forward, crushed. "You don't believe me, then," was all he could think of to say. "That there's been some sort of foul play concealed in the background of this. That one woman started from St. Louis to be my wife, and another suddenly appeared here in her place—"

"We believe you, Mr. Durand. We believe you thoroughly. Let me put it this way. We agree with you thoroughly in theory; in practice we cannot lift a hand to help you. It is not that we are unwilling. If we were to make an arrest, we could not hold the person, let alone force restitution of the funds. The whole case is circumstantial. No crime has been proven committed as yet. You went to the dock to meet one woman, you met another in her stead. A substitution in itself is no crime. It may be, how shall I say it, a personal treachery, a form of trickery, but it is no crime recognized by law. My advice to you is—"

Durand smiled witheringly. "Forget the whole thing."

"No, no. Not at all. Go to St. Louis and start working from that end. Get proof that a crime, either of abduction or even something worse, was committed against the true Julia Russell. Now listen to my words carefully. I said *get proof*. A letter in someone else's handwriting is proof only that—it is a letter in someone else's handwriting. Dresses that are too big are only—dresses that are too big. I said *get proof* that a crime was committed. Then take it—" He wagged his forefinger solemnly back and forth, like a pendulum— "not to us, but to whichever are the authorities within whose jurisdiction you have the proof to show it happened. That means, if on the river, to whichever onshore community lies closest to where it happened."

Durand brought his whole fist down despairingly on the commissioner's desk top, like a mallet. "I hadn't realized until now," he said furiously, "there were so many opportunities for a malefactor to commit an offense and escape scot-free! It seems to me it pays to flout the law! Why bother to observe it when—"

"The law as we apply it in this country," the commissioner said forebearingly, "leans backward to protect the innocent. In one or two rare cases, such as your own, it may work an injustice against an honest accuser. In a hundred times a hundred others, it has preserved an innocent person from unjust accusation, false arrest, wrongful trial, and maybe even capital punishment, which cannot be undone once it has taken place. The laws of the Romans, which govern many foreign countries, say a man is guilty until proven innocent. The Anglo-Saxon common law, which governs us here, says a man is innocent until he is proven guilty."

He sighed deeply. "Think that over, Mr. Durand."

"I understand," Durand said at last, raising his head from its wilted, downcast position. "I'm sorry I lost my temper."

"If I had been tricked into marriage," the commissioner told him, "and swindled out of fifty thousand dollars, I would have lost my own temper, and far worse than you just did yours. But that doesn't alter one whit of what I just told you. It still stands as I explained it to you."

Durand rose with wearied deliberation, ran two fingers down the outer sideward crease of each trouser leg to restore them. "I'll go up to St. Louis and start from there," he said with tight-lipped grimness. "Good day," he added briefly.

"Good day," the other echoed.

Durand crossed to the door, swung it inward to go out.

"Durand," the commissioner called out as an afterthought. Durand turned his head to him.

"Don't take the law into your own hands."

Durand paused in the opening, held back his answer for a moment, as though he hadn't heard him.

"I'll try not to," he said finally, and went on out.

— 27 —

THE *City of Baton Rouge* reached the St. Louis dockside at 6 PM, days later. That was Wednesday, the eleventh.

He'd never been in the town before, but where a year ago he would have relished and appreciated all its differences, its novelty: its brisker, more bustling air than languorous New Orleans, its faintly Germanic over-all aspect, impalpable but still very patent to one who came from the French-steeped city down-river; now his heart was too heavy to care or note anything about it, other than that his trip was at an end, and this was the place where it had ended; this was the place that was going to solve the riddle for him, decide his problem, settle his fate.

It was a cloudy day, but even in its cloudiness there was something spruce, tangy, lacking in New Orleans overcasts. There was energy in the air; less of graciousness, considerably more of ugliness.

It was, to him at any rate, the North; the farthest north he'd yet been.

He had Bertha Russell's address ready at hand, of course, but because of the advanced hour, and perhaps also without realizing it because of a latent cowardice, that strove to put off the climactic ordeal for as long as possible, he decided to find himself quarters in a hotel first before setting out to locate and interview this unknown woman upon whom all now depended.

He emerged cityward of the pier shed, was immediately accosted with upraised whips by a small bevy of coachmen gathered hopefully about, and climbed into one of their vehicles at random.

"Find me some kind of a hotel," he said glumly. "Nothing fancy. And not too far into the town."

"Yes sir. The Commercial Travelers' be about right, I reckon. Just a stone's throw from here."

Even the colored people spoke more rapidly up here than at home, he noted with dulled detachment.

The hotel was a dingy, beery, waterfront place, but it served his purpose well enough to be accepted. He was given key and directions and allowed to find his own way to a cheerless bedroom with an almost viewless window, triply blocked by a brick abutment, a film of congealed dust ground into its panes, and a dank curtain, its pores long-since sealed by soilage. But twilight was already blurring the air, and he wouldn't have looked forth even if he could. He hadn't come here to enjoy a view.

He dropped his bag and settled down with heavy despondency in a chair, to chafe his wrists and brood.

He pictured again the scene to come, as he had been doing all day on the boat, and the night before. Heard again the reassuring voice he hoped to hear. "She was always wild, Mr. Durand; our Julia was like that. This isn't the first time she has run away. She will come back to you again, never fear. When you least look for her, she will suddenly return and ask your forgiveness."

He must want it to be that way, he realized, always to shape it so in his imaginings. To be assured that she was the actual Julia; a cheat, a robber, an absconder, but still the person she had represented herself to be. Why, he wondered, why?

Because anonymity meant her loss would be even more complete, more irremediable. Anonymity meant she was gone forever, there was not even a she to hope to find some day, there was nothing left him.

Or was it because the alternative to her still being Julia was something still darker, even worse, the very thought of which sent a shudder coursing through him.

And then he remembered the letter, that Bertha had said was in a stranger's handwriting, and—all his hope was taken away.

He quitted his room presently and went down and tried to eat something in the wholly unprepossessing dining room connected with the hotel, a typical traveling salesman sort of eating place, filled with smoke, noisy with boastful voices, and with not a woman in the place; he ate out of sheer habit and without knowing what it was he ate. Then, sitting there with a cup of viscous, stone-cold coffee untouched before him, he suddenly noted that it was nearing nine on the large, yellowing clockface aloft on the wall, and decided to carry out his errand then and there and have done with it, without waiting for morning. To try to sleep on it would be agonizing, unbearable. He wanted it over, whether for best or worst; he wanted to know at once, he couldn't stand the uncertainty another half-hour.

He went back to his room for a moment, got the sister's two letters, his marriage certificate, and all the other pertinent memoranda of the matter, gathered them into one readily accessible pocket, came down, found a coach, and gave the address.

He couldn't tell much about the house from the outside in the gloom. It seemed large enough. The upper part of its silhouette sloped back, meaning it had a mansard roof. It was in a vicinity of eminent cleanliness and respectability. Trees lined the streets, and the streets were lifeless with the absence within doors, where law-abiding citizens belonged at this hour, of those who dwelt hereabout. An occasional gas lamppost twinkled like a lime-colored glowworm down the vista of trees. A church steeple sliced like a stubby black knife upward against the brickdust-tinted sky, paler than earth because of its luminous low-massed cloud banks.

As for the house itself, orange lamp shine showed through a pair of double windows on the lower floor, the rest were in darkness. Someone, at least, was within.

He got out and fumbled for money.

"Wait for you, sir?" the man asked.

"No," he said reluctantly, "no. I don't know how long I'm going to have to be." And yet he almost hated to see the coach turn about and go off and leave him there cut off, as it were, and helpless to retreat now at the last moment, as he felt sorely tempted to do.

He went over to the door and found a small bone pushbutton, and thumbed it flat.

There was a considerable wait, but he forebore from ringing again.

Then presently, but very gradually, as if kindled by the approach of light from a distance, a fanlight that had been invisible to him until now slowly glowed into alternating bands of dark red and colorless glass.

A woman's voice called through the door, "Who is it, please? What did you wish?"

She lived alone, judging by these characteristic precautions.

"I'd like to speak to Miss Bertha Russell, please," he called back. "It's important."

"Just a moment, please."

He could hear a bolt forced out, then the catch of a finger lock being turned. Then the door opened, and she was standing there surveying him, kerosene lamp held somewhat raised in one hand so that its rays could reach out to and fall upon him for her own satisfaction.

She was about fifty, or very close upon it. She was a tall, large-built woman, but not stout withal; she gave an impression of angularity, rather. Her color was not good; it had a waxlike yellowishness, as of one who has worried and kept indoors for a considerable period. Her hair, coarse and glossy, was in the earlier stages of turning gray. Still dark at the back, it was above the forehead that the first slanting, upward wedges of white had appeared, and the way she wore it emphasized rather than attempted to conceal this: drawn severely back, so tight that it seemed to be pulled-at, and then carelessly wound into a knot. It gave her an aspect of sternness that might not have been wholly justified, though in truth there was little humor or tenderness to be read in her features even by themselves.

She wore a dress of stiff black alpaca, a stringy white crocheted collar closing its throat and fastened by a carnelian brooch.

"Yes" she said on a rising inflection. "I'm Bertha Russell. Do I know you?"

"I'm Louis Durand," he replied gravely. "I've just arrived from New Orleans."

He heard her draw a sharp breath. She stared for a long moment, as if familiarizing herself with him. Then abruptly slanted the door still further inward. "Come in, Mr. Durand," she said. "Come in the house."

She closed the street door behind him. He waited aside, then he once more let her take the lead.

"This way," she said. "The parlor's in here."

He followed her down a dark-floored, rag-carpeted hall, and in at one side. She must have been reading when he interrupted; as she set the lamp down on a center table, a massive, open, gilt-edged book swam into view, a pair of silver-edged spectacles discarded to one side. He recognized it as the Bible. A ribbon of crimson velvet protruded as a bookmark.

"Wait, I'll put on more light."

She lit a second lamp, evening the radius of brightness somewhat, so that it did not all come from one place. The room still remained anything but brilliant.

"Sit down, Mr. Durand."

She sat across the table from him, where she had originally been sitting while still alone. She drew the ribbon marker through the new place in the Bible, closed the heavy cubical volume, moved it slightly aside.

He could see her throbbing with a mixture of excitement and anticipatory fear. It was almost physical, it was so strong an agitation; and yet so strongly quelled.

She clasped her hands with an effort, and placed them against the edge of the table, where the Bible had been until now.

She moistened the bloodless outline of her lips.

"Now what can you tell me? What have you come here to say to me?"

"It's not what I can tell you," he replied. "It's what you can tell me."

She nodded somewhat dourly, as though, while disagreeing with the challenge, she was willing none the less to accept it, for the sake of progressing with the matter.

"Very well, then, I can tell you this much. My sister Julia received a proposal of marriage from you, by letter, on about the fifteenth of April of this year. Do you deny that?"

He brushed away the necessity of a direct answer to that; held silent to let her continue.

"My sister Julia left here on May the eighteenth, to join you in New Orleans." Her eyes bored into his. "That was the last I saw of her. *Since that date I have not heard from her again.*" She drew a long, tightly compressed breath. "I received an answer to one of my letters in a stranger's handwriting. And now you come here alone."

"There is no one down there any longer I could bring."

He saw her eyes widen, but she waited.

"Just a moment," he said. "I think it will save both of us time if we establish one thing before we go any—"

Then suddenly he stopped, without need of completing the sentence. He'd found the answer for himself, looking upward to the wall, past her shoulder. It was incredible that he had failed to see it until now, but his whole attention had been given to her and not to the surroundings, and it was subdued by the marginal shade beyond the lamps.

It was a large photographic portrait, set in a cherry-colored velour frame, of a head nearly life-size. The subject was not young, not a girl. There was an incisiveness to the mouth that promised sharpness. There was a keen appearance to the eyes that heralded creases. She was not beautiful. Dark hair, gathered at the back. . . .

Bertha had risen, was standing slightly aside from it, holding the lamp aloft and backward to it past her own shoulder, so that it was in fullest untramelled pathway of the upsurging glow.

"*That* is Julia. *That* is my sister. There. Before you. What you are looking at now. It's an enlargement taken only two or three years ago."

His voice was a whisper that barely reached her. "Then it was— not she I married."

She hastily put the lamp down, at what it showed her now in the opposite direction. "Mr. Durand!" She half started toward him, as if to support him. "Can I get you something?"

He warded her off with a vague lift of his hand. He could hear his labored breathing sounding in his own ears like a bellows. He sought the chair he had risen from and by his own efforts dropped back into it, half turned to clutch at it and hold it steady as he did so.

He extended his hand and pointed a finger; the finger switching up and down while it waited for his lips to gain speech and catch up to it. "That is the woman whose photograph I received from here. *But that is not the woman I was married to in New Orleans on last May the eighteenth.*"

Her own fright, which was ghastly on her face, was overruled, submerged, by the sight of his, which must have been that much greater to witness.

"I'll get you some wine," she offered hastily.

He raised his hand protestingly. Pulled at his collar to ease it.

"I'll get you some wine," she repeated helplessly.

"No, I'm all right. Don't take the time."

"Have you a photograph, any sort of likeness, of the other person you can show me?" she asked after a moment.

"I have nothing, not a scrap of anything. She somehow even postponed having our bridal photograph taken. It occurs to me now that this oversight may have been intentional."

He smiled bleakly. "I can tell you what she was like, if that will do. I don't need a photograph to remember that. She was blonde. She was small. She was a good deal—I should say somewhat younger than your sister." He faltered to a stop, as if realizing the uselessness of proceeding.

"But Julia?" she persisted, as though he were able to give her the answer. "Where's Julia, then? What's become of her? Where *is* she?" She planted her hands in flat despair on the tabletop, leaned over above them. "I saw her off on that boat."

"I met the boat. It came without her. She wasn't on it."

"You're sure, you're sure?" Her eyes were bright with questioning tears.

"I watched them get off it. All left it. She wasn't among them. She wasn't on it."

She sank back into the chair beyond the table. She planed the edge of her hand flat across the top of her forehead, held her head thus for a moment or two. She did not weep, but her mouth winced flickeringly once or twice.

They both had to face the thing. It was out in the open between them now. Not to be avoided, not to be shunned. It had come to this. It was a question of which of them would first put it into words.

She did.

She let her hand drop. "She was done away with!" she whispered hoarsely. "She met her end on that boat." She shuddered as though some insidious evil presence had come into the room, without need of door or window. "In some way, at someone's hands." She shuddered again, almost as if she had the ague. "Between the time I waved her goodbye that Wednesday afternoon—"

He let his head go down slowly in grim assent. Convinced now at last, understanding the whole thing finally for what it really was. He finished it for her.

"—and the time I stood by the gangplank to greet her that Friday afternoon."

— 28 —

He found Bertha Russell, coated, gloved and bonnetted, a spectral figure in the unrelieved black of full mourning, waiting for him in the open doorway of her house, early as it was, when he drove up shortly before nine the following morning to keep their appointment prearranged the night before. Whatever grief or bitterness had been hers during the unseen hours of the night just gone, she had mastered it now, there were only faint traces of it left behind. Her face was cold and stonelike in its fortitude; there were, however, bluish bruises under her eyes, and the transparent pallor of sleeplessness lay livid upon her features. It was the face of a woman bent upon retribution, who would show no more mercy than had been shown her, whatever the cost to herself.

"Have you breakfasted?" she asked him when he had alighted and come forward to join her.

"I have no wish to," he answered shortly.

She closed the door forthwith and made her way beside him to the carriage; the impression conveyed was that she would have served him food if obliged to, but would have begrudged the time it would have cost them.

"Have you anyone in mind?" he asked as they drove off. She had given an address, unfamiliar to him as all addresses up here were bound to be, on entering the carriage.

"I made inquiries after you left last evening. I have had someone recommended to me. He was well spoken of."

They were driven downtown into the bustling business section, the strange pair that they made, both so tight-lipped, both sitting so stark and straight, with not a word between them. The carriage stopped at last before a distinctly ugly-looking building, of beefy red brick, honeycombed with countless windows in four parallel rows, all with rounded tops. A veritable hive of small individual offices and businesses. Its appearance did not bespeak a very prosperous class of tenantry.

Durand paid off the carriage and accompanied her in. A rather chill musty air, far cooler than that outside on the street, immediately assailed them, as well as a considerable lessening of light, in no wise ameliorated by the bowls of gaslight bracketed at very sparing intervals along its corridors.

She consulted a populous directory-chart on the wall, but without tracing her finger down it, and had quitted it again before he could gain an inkling of whose name she sought.

They had to climb stairs, the building offered no lift. Following her up, first one flight, then a second, at last a third, he received the impression she would have climbed a mountain, Everest itself, to gain her objective. They were, she had told him, ancestrally of Holland-Dutch stock, she and her sister. He had never seen such silent stubbornness expressed in anyone as he did in every move of her hard-pressed laboring body on those stairs. She was more dreadfully inflexible in her stolid purpose than any passionate, quick-gesturing Creole of the Southland could have been. He couldn't help but admire her and, for a moment, he couldn't help but wonder what sort of wife the other one, Julia, would have made him.

At the third landing stage they turned off down endless reaches of arterial passageway, even more poorly lighted than below, and in sections that were not of one level, some higher than others, some lower.

"It doesn't indicate very much prosperity in business, would you say?" he remarked idly, without thinking.

"It bespeaks honesty," she answered shortly, "and that is what I seek."

He regretted having made the observation.

She stopped at the very last door of all but one.

On a shield of blown glass set into its upper-half was painted in rounded formation, to make two matching arcs:

Walter Downs
Private Investigator.

Durand knocked for the two of them, and a rich baritone, throbbing with its own depth, vibrated "Come in." He opened the door, stood aside for Bertha Russell, and then entered behind her.

The light was greater on the inside, by virtue of the street beyond. It was a single room, and even less affluent in aspect than the building that housed it had promised it would be. A large but extremely worn desk divided it nearly in two, with the occupant on one side of it, the visitors—all visitors—on the other. On this other side there were two chairs, no more, one of them a negligible cane-bottomed affair. On the first side there was a small iron safe, its corners rusted, its face left ajar. Not accidentally, for several ledgers which protruded, and an unsorted mass of papers which topped them, seemed to have rendered it incapable of closing.

The man sitting in the midst of this rather unappetizing enclave was in his early forties, Durand's senior by no more than two or three years. His hair was sand colored, and still copious, save for an indented recession over each temple, which heightened his brow and gave his face somewhat of a leonine look. He was, uncommonly enough for his age in life, totally clean-shaven, even on the upper lip. And paradoxically, instead of lending an added youth, this idiosyncrasy on the contrary seemed to increase his look of maturity, so strong were the basic lines of his face and particularly of his mouth. His eyes were blue, and on the surface there was something kindly and humane about them. Yet deeper within there was an occasional glint of something to be caught at times, some tiny blue spark, that hinted at fanaticism. They were at any rate the steadiest Durand had ever met. They were sure of themselves and attentive as those of a judge.

"Am I speaking to Mr. Downs?" he heard Bertha say.

"You are, madam," he rumbled.

There was nothing ingratiating about his manner. Intentionally so, that is. It was as if he were withholding himself from commitment, to see whether the clients met with his approval, rather than he with theirs.

And so Durand was looking for the first time at Walter Downs. Out of a hundred lives that cross a particular one, during its single span, ninety-nine leave no trace, beyond the momentary swirl of their passing. And yet a hundredth may come that will turn it aside, deflect it from its course, alter it so, like a powerful cross-current, that where it was going before and where it goes thereafter are no longer recognizably the same direction.

"There is a chair, madam." He had not risen.

She sat down. Durand remained standing, breaking his posture with a shoulder occasionally against the wall to ease himself.

"I am Bertha Russell and this is Mr. Louis Durand."

He gave Durand a curt nod, no more.

"We have come to you about a matter that concerns both of us."

"Which one of you will speak, then?"

"You speak for the two of us, Mr. Durand. That will be easiest, I think."

Durand, looking down at the floor as if reading the words from it, took a moment to begin. But Downs, who had now altered the position of his head to direct his gaze upon him exclusively, showed no impatience.

The story seemed so old already, so often told. He kept his voice low, left all emphasis out of it.

"I corresponded with this lady's sister, from New Orleans, where I was, to here, where she was. I offered marriage, she accepted. She left here to join me, on May the eighteenth last. Her sister saw her off. She never arrived. Another person altogether joined me in New Orleans when the boat arrived, managed to convince me that she was Miss Russell's sister in spite of the difference in their appearances, and we were married. She stole upward of fifty thousand dollars from me, and disappeared in turn. The police down there inform me that they cannot do anything about it for lack of proof that the original person I proposed marriage to was done away with. The impersonation and the theft are not punishable by law."

Downs said only three words.

"And you want?"

"We want you to obtain proof that a murder was committed. We want you to obtain proof of the murder that we both know must have been committed. We want you to trace and apprehend this woman who was a chief participant in it." He took a deep, hot breath. "We want it punished."

Downs nodded dourly. He looked thoughtfully.

They waited. He remained silent for so long that at last Durand, almost feeling he had forgotten that they were present, cleared his throat as a reminder.

"Will you take this case?"

"I have taken it already," Downs answered with an impatient off-gesture of his hand, as if to say: Don't interrupt me.

Durand and Bertha Russell looked at one another.

"I made up my mind to take it while you were still telling me of it," he went on presently. "It is the kind of a case I like. You are both honest people. As far as you are concerned, sir—" He raised his eyes suddenly to Durand; "You must be. Only an honest man could have been such a fool as you appear to have been."

Durand flushed, but didn't answer.

"And I am a fool, too. I have not had a client in here for over a week before you came to me today. But if I had not liked the case, nevertheless I would not have taken it."

Something about him made Durand believe that.

"I cannot promise you I will succeed in solving it. I can promise you one thing and one only: I will never quit it again until I do solve it."

Durand reached for his money-fold. "If you will be good enough to tell me what the customary—"

"Pay me whatever you care to, to be put down against expenses,"

Downs said almost indifferently. "When they outrun whatever it is, if they should, I'll let you know."

"Just a moment." Bertha Russell interrupted Durand, opening her purse. °

"No, please—I beg you— It's my obligation," he protested.

"This is no matter of parlor gentility!" she said to him almost fiercely. "She was my sister. I am entitled to the right of sharing the expense with you. I demand it. You shall not take that from me."

Downs looked at them both. "I see I was not mistaken," he murmured. "This is a fitting case."

He picked up a copy of that morning's newspaper, first shook it to spread it full, then narrowed it once more to the span of a single perpendicular column. He traced his finger down this, a row of paid commercial advertisements.

"This boat she sailed on from here," he said, "was which one?"

"The *City of New Orleans*," Durand and Bertha Russell said in unison.

"By a coincidence," he said, "here it is down again, for the company's next sailing. Its turn has come about once more, it leaves from here tomorrow, at nine o'clock in the forenoon."

He put the paper down.

"Do you propose remaining here, Mr. Durand?"

"I'm returning to New Orleans at once, now that I've put this matter in your hands," Durand said. Then he added wryly, "My business is there."

"Good," Downs remarked, rising and reaching for his hat. "Then we'll both be sailing together, for I'm going down there now and get my ticket. We will begin by retracing her steps, making the same journey she did, on the same boat, with the same captain and the same crew. Someone may have seen something, someone may remember. Someone must."

— 29 —

THE CABINS of the *City of New Orleans* were small, little better than shoeboxes ranged side by side along the shelves of a shop. The one they shared together seemed even smaller than the rest, perhaps because they were both in it at once. Even to move about and hang their things, they had continually to flatten themselves and swerve aside to avoid grazing and knocking into one another at every step.

Outside in the failing light two soiled ribbons, the lower gray, the upper tan, could be seen unrolling through the window; the Mississippi's bosom and its shore.

"I will help in any way I can," Durand offered. "Just tell me what to do and how to go about it."

"The passengers will not be the same on this trip as on that other," Downs told him. "That would be too much to hope for. Those who will be, are those whose job it is to run the boat and tend it. We will share them between us, from the captain down to the stokers. And if we find out nothing, we are no worse off than before. And if we find out something, no matter what, we are that much better off. So don't be discouraged. This may take months and years, and we are just at the very beginning of it."

"And what is it you—we—try to find out, now, for a beginning?"

"We try to find a witness who saw them *both together;* and by that I do not necessarily mean in one another's company: the true Julia and the false. I mean, both alive and on the boat during one and the same trip, at one and the same time. For the sister is a witness that the true one left on it, and you are a witness that the false one arrived on it. What I am trying to arrive at, by a process of elimination, is when was the true one last seen, when the false one first? I mark that off, as closely as I can get it, against that out there—" he gestured toward the two ribbons, "and that gives

me, roughly, the point during the voyage at which it happened, the
State whose jurisdiction it falls within, and the area in which to
devote myself to searching for the only evidence, *if* any, there will
ever be."

Durand didn't ask him what he meant by that last. Perhaps a
chill sensation running down his back told him only too well.

The captain was named Fletcher. He was deliberate of speech;
the type of man who thinks well before speaking, and thus later
does not have to think ill of what he has spoken. His memory,
by way of his hand, sought refreshment in his luxuriant black
beard.

"Yes," he said at long last, after hearing Downs's exhaustive de-
scription. "Yes, I do recall a little lady such as you describe. The
breeze caught up her skirt just as we were both coming along the
deck from opposite directions. And she quickly held it down with
her hands. But for a moment—" He didn't finish it; his eyes, however, were reminiscently kind. "Then as I passed, I tipped my cap.
She dropped her eyes and would not see me—" he gave a little
chuckle; "yet as she passed, she smiled, and I know the smile was
for me, for there was no one else in sight."

"And now this one," Downs said.

He offered in assistance a small photograph of Julia, supplied
them by Bertha, much similar to the one once owned by Durand.

The captain studied it at length, but with no great relish; and
then after that ruminated a considerable while longer.

"No," he said at last. "No, I've never seen this old mai— this
woman." He handed it back, as if glad to be rid of it.

"You're sure?"

The captain had no more interest in trying to recall, even if he
could have.

"We carry many people, sir, trip after trip, and I cannot be expected to remember all their faces. I am only a man, after all."

"And strange," Downs repeated to Durand later, "are the ways
of men; they see with their pulses and their blood. For the one

whom I could only describe to him by word of mouth, and secondhand at that, he could recall instantly, and will go on recalling probably for the rest of his active life. But the one whose very photograph he had before him, he could not recall at all!"

Durand thumbed the pushbutton in their little cubbyhole, and after an in ordinate length of time, a shambling steward appeared.

"Not you," Durand told him. "Who takes care of the ladies' cabins?"

A stewardess appeared in dilatory turn. He gave her a coin.

"I want to ask you something. See if you can remember. Did you ever come to one of your ladies' cabins, of a morning, and find the bunk undisturbed, no one had been in it?"

She nodded readily. "Sho', lots times. We ain't full up every trip. Sometime' mo'n half my cabin' plumb empty,"

"No, I'll have to ask it another way, then. Did you ever come to one of your ladies' cabins which had had someone in it *first,* and then find the bunk untouched?"

It seemed to present difficulties to her. "You mean nobody slep' in it, but somebody done tuk it just the same?"

"That's it; that's about it."

She wasn't sure; she scratched and strove, but she wasn't sure. He tried to help her. "With somebody's clothes in it, perhaps. With somebody's belongings there for you to see. Surely you could tell by that. But no one had lain in the bunk."

She still wasn't sure.

He tried his trump card. "With a *birdcage* in it, perhaps."

She ignited into recollection, like tinder when the spark strikes it square. "Tha's right, tha's how it was! How you know that? Cab'n with a birdcage in it, and I didn't have to tech the bunk nohow—"

He nodded darkly. "No one had lain in it the night before."

She drew up short. "I di'n say that. The lady fix up her berth herseff befo' I get there; she kine of tidy that way, and used to doing things with her own han's 'thout waiting fo' nobody."

"Who told you that, how do you kn—?"

"She *in* there when I come in. The pretties' little lady I ever done see; blon' like an angel and li'l like a chile."

In the dining saloon, Durand saw, Downs had held back one of his plates even after he had finished with it. At the end of the meal, when all others but the two of them had left the single, long table, Downs called the waiter over and said to him simply: "Watch this. Watch me do this a minute."

Then he took out a pocket handkerchief, spread it flat on the table top. Into it he put a small scrap of lettuce that had decorated his plate as a garnish, folded the corners of the handkerchief over toward the center, like a magician about to cause something to disappear.

"Did you ever see anyone do that, at the end of a meal? Did you?"

"You mean fold up their napkin like—?"

"No, no." Downs had to reopen it to show him the lettuce, then start the process over. "Put a leaf of lettuce in first, to carry away. It's a handkerchief. Think of it as a smaller one, far smaller, a little wisp—"

The waiter nodded now. "I seen a lady do that, one trip. I wondered what she— It wasn't meat or nothin', just a little old—"

Downs held up his finger in admonition. "Now listen carefully. Think well. How many times can you remember seeing her do that? After how many meals?"

"Just once. On'y once. After on'y one meal. That was the on'y time I ever seen her, just at that one meal."

"I can't get the two of them together," Downs said to Durand under his breath afterward. "One ends before the other begins. But it happened sometime during the first night. At suppertime the waiter saw the real one filch a scrap of lettuce for her bird. At eight in the morning the stewardess found a blonde 'like an angel' had already made up her own bunk, in that cabin where the birdcage was."

The first stop, at eight the following morning, Durand found Downs already making his preparations for departure.

"You're getting off here?" he queried in surprise. "So soon? Already?"

Downs nodded. "That boat's first stop this time was the boat's first stop that time too. The same schedule is held to. She was already hours dead and hours in the water by this moment. To go on past here only carries me farther away at every turn of the paddles. Come, walk me to the landing plank."

"If she is anywhere," he said, lowering his voice as they went out on the misty early-morning deck together, "she is back there somewhere, along the stretch we have covered this past night. If she ever floats ashore—or has already, unrecognized or maybe even unseen—it will be back there somewhere. I will go back along the shoreline, hamlet by hamlet, yard by yard, inch by inch; on foot if necessary. First on this side, then on the opposite. And if she is not ashore already, I will wait until she comes ashore."

His face was that of a fanatic, with whom there is no reasoning.

"Back there she is, on the river bottom, in the great wide eddy below Cape Girardeau, and back there I will wait for her."

Durand's blood ran a little cold at the turn of speech.

Downs held out his hand.

"Good luck to you," Durand said, half frightened of the man now.

"And to you," Downs answered. "You will see me again some day, sooner or later. I can't say when, but you will surely see me again some day."

He went down the gangplank. Durand watched his head sink from sight. Then he turned away with an involuntary shiver, the last thing he had heard the other man say repeating itself strangely in his mind:

You will see me again some day. You will surely see me again some day.

— 30 —

THE DEATH of a man is a sad enough thing to watch, but he goes by himself, taking nothing else with him. The death of a house is a sadder thing by far to watch. For so much more goes with it.

On that last day, Durand moved slowly from room to room of the St. Louis Street house. It was already dying before his very eyes; the furniture dismantled, rugs stripped from its floor boards, curtains from its windows, closet doors left gapingly ajar with nothing behind them any more. Its skeleton was peering through. The skeleton that stays on after death, just as in a man's case.

And yet, he realized, he was not so much leaving this place as leaving a part of himself behind in a common grave with it. A part that he could never regain, never recall. He could never hope again as he'd once hoped here. There was nothing to hope for. He could never be as young again as he'd once been here, even though it was a youngness late in coming, at thirty-seven; late in coming and swift in going, just a few brief weeks. He could never love again— not only not as he'd once loved here, but to any degree at all. And that is a form of death in itself. His broken dreams were lying all around; he could almost hear them crunch, like spilled sugar, each time he moved his foot.

He was standing in the doorway of what had been their bedroom, looking across at the wallpaper. The wallpaper that had come from New York—"pink, but not too bright a pink, with small blue flowers, like forget-me-nots"—put up for a bride to see, a bride who had never lived to see it, nor lived even to be a bride.

He closed the door. For no particular reason, for there was nothing to be kept in there any longer. Perhaps the more quickly to shut the room from sight.

And as it closed, a voice seemed to speak through it for a moment, with sudden lifelike clarity in his ears:

"Who is it knocks? . . . Tell him he may."

Then was gone, stilled forever.

He went slowly down the stairs, his knees bending reluctantly over each step, as if they were rusted.

The front door was standing open, and there was a mule and two-wheeled cart out before it, piled high with the effluvia he had donated to Aunt Sarah. She went hurrying past from the back just then, a dented-in gilt birdcage swinging from one hand, a bulky mantel clock hugged in her other. Then, seeing him, and still incredulous of his largesse, she stopped short to ask for additional assurance.

"This too? This yere clock?"

"I told you, everything," he answered impatiently. "Everything but the heavy pieces with four legs. Take it all! Get it out of my sight!"

"I'm sure going to have the grandest cabin in Shrevepo't when I gets back home there."

He looked at her grimly for a moment, but his grimness was not for her.

"That band's not playing today, I notice," he blurted out accusingly.

She understood the reference, remembered it with surprising immediacy.

"Hush, Mr. Lou. Anyone can make a mistake. That was the devil's music."

She went on out to the cart, where a gangling youth, a nephew by remote attribute, loitered in charge of the booty.

"Got everything you want now?" Durand called out after her. "Then I'll lock up."

"Yes sir! Yes *sir!* Couldn't ask for no more." And, apparently, secretly a little dubious, to the end, that Durand might yet change his mind and retract, added in a hasty aside: "Come on, boy! Get this mule started up. What you lingering for?" She clambered up beside him and the cart waddled off. "God bless you, Mr. Lou! God keep you safe!"

"It's a little late for that," thought Durand morosely.

He turned back to the hall for a moment, to retrieve his own hat from the pronged, high-backed rack where he had slung it. And as he detached it, something fell out sideward to the floor from behind it with a little clap. Something that must have been thrust out of sight behind there long ago, and forgotten.

He picked up the slender little stick, and withdrew it, and a little swath of bunched heliotrope came with it at the other end. Limp, bedraggled, but still giving a momentary splash of color to the denuded hall.

Her parasol.

He took it by both ends, and arched his knee to it, and splintered it explosively, not once but again and again, with an inordinate violence that its fragility didn't warrant. Then flung the wisps and splinters away from him with full arm's strength, as far as they would go.

"Get to hell, after your owner," he mumbled savagely. "She's waiting for you to shade her there!"

And slammed the door.

The house was dead. Love was dead. The story was through.

— 31 —

MAY AGAIN. May that keeps coming around, May that never gets any older, May that's just as fair each time. Men grow old and lose their loves, and have no further hope of any new love, but May keeps coming back again. There are always others waiting for it, whose turn is still to come.

May again. May of '81 now. A year since the marriage.

The train from New Orleans came into Biloxi late in the afternoon. The sky was porcelain fresh from the kiln; a little wisp of steam seeping from it here and there, those were clouds. The tree tops were shimmering with delicate new leaf. And in the distance, like a deposit of sapphires, the waters of the Gulf. It was a lovely place to come to, a lovely sight to behold. And he was old and bitter now, too old to care.

He was the last one down from the steps of the railroad coach. He climbed down leadenly, grudgingly, as though it were all one to him whether he alighted here or continued on to the next place. It was. To rest, to forget awhile, that was all he wanted. To let the healing process continue, the scars harden into their ugly crust. New Orleans still reminded him too much. It always would.

A romantic takes his losses hard, and he was a romantic. Only a romantic could have played the role he had, played the fool so letter-perfect. He was one of those men who are born to be the natural prey of women, he was beginning to realize it himself by now; if it hadn't been she, it would have been someone else. If it hadn't been a bad woman, then it would have been what they called a "good" woman. Even one of those would have had him in her power in no time at all. And though the results might have been less catastrophic, that was no consolation to his own innermost pride. His only defense was to stay away from them.

Now that the horse was stolen, the lock was on the stable door. The lock was on, and the key was thrown away, for good and all. But there was nothing it opened to any more.

Amidst all the bustle of holidaymakers down here from the hinterland for a week or two's sojourn, the prattle, the commotion as they formed into little groups, joining with the friends who had come to train side to meet them, he stood there solitary, apart, his bag at his feet.

The eyes of more than one marriageable young damsel in the groups near by were cast speculatively toward him over the shoulder of some relative or friend, probably wondering if he were eligible to be sketched into plans for the immediate future, for what is a holiday without a lot of beaux? Yet whenever they happened to meet his own eyes they hurriedly withdrew again, and not wholly for the sake of seemliness either. It left them with a rather disconcerting sensation, like looking at something you think to be alive

and finding out it is inanimate after all. It was like flirting with a
fence post or water pump until you found out your mistake.

The platform slowly cleared, and he still stood there. The train
from New Orleans started on again, and he half turned, as if to
reenter and ride on with it to wherever the next place was. But he
faced forward again and let the cars go ticking off behind his back,
on their way down the track.

— 32 —

HE SOON fell into the habit of dropping into the bar of one of the
adjacent hotels, the Belleview House, at or around seven each evening for a slowly drunk whiskey punch. Or at most two of them,
never more; for it wasn't the liquor that attracted him, but the lack
of anything to do until it was time for the evening meal. He chose
this particular place because his own hotel had no such establishment, and it was the nearest at hand and the largest of those that
had.

It was a cheery, bustling, buzzing place, this, characteristic of
its kind and of the period. A gentleman's drinking place. And like
all others of its nature, while it was strictly a male preserve, wom-
en were never so pervasively present in thought, spirit, implication
and conversation, as here where they were physically absent. They
permeated the air; they were in every *double entendre,* and wink,
and toast, and bragging innuendo. And here they were as men
wishfully wanted them to be, and as they so seldom were beyond
these portals: uncommonly accommodating. At all times and in
every reminiscence.

Even in allegory they presided. Upon the wall facing the horse-
shoe-shaped mahogany counter, cheery lights blinking at either
side of it—like glass-belled altar lights at the shrine of woman in-
carnate—extended a tremendous oil painting of a reclining fem-

inine form, presumably a goddess. Attended at its head by two winged cupids flying in rotary course, at its feet a cornucopia spilling fruits and flowers. Purple drapery was present, but more in discard than in application; one skein straggling downward across the figure's shoulder, another wisp stretching across its middle. In the background, and never noted by an onlooker since the canvas had first been hung, was an azure sky with puffballs of cottony clouds.

Dominating the place as it did, and shrewdly intended to, it was as a matter of fact the means of Durand's striking up his first acquaintanceship since arriving in Biloxi. The man nearest to him, on the occasion of his second successive visit to the place, alone as he was, was standing there with his eyes raptly fixed on it, and almost humid with a sort of silly, faraway greediness, when Durand happened to idly glance that way and catch the expression.

Durand couldn't resist smiling slightly, but to himself and not the devotee; but the other man, catching the half-formed smile just as it was about to turn away, mistook it for one of esoteric kinship of thought, and promptly returned it, but with an increment of friendly gregariousness that had been lacking in the original.

"Bless 'em!" he remarked fervently, and hoisted his glass toward the composition for Durand to see.

Durand nodded in temperate accord.

Emboldened, the other man raised his voice and invited over the three or four yards that separated them: "Will you join me, sir?"

Durand had no desire to, but to have refused would have been unwarrantedly boorish, so he moved accommodatingly toward his neighbor, and the latter made up the difference from his side.

Their orders were renewed, they saluted one another with them, and swallowed: thus completing the preliminary little ritual.

The other man was in his mid-forties, as far as Durand could judge. He had a good-looking, but rather weak and dissipated face; lines of looseness, rather than age, printed on it, particularly across the forehead. His complexion was extremely pallid; his hair dark, but possibly kept so with the aid of a little shoeblacking here and there; this, however, could only be a matter of conjecture. He was of lesser height than Durand, but of greater girth, albeit in a pillowy, less compact way.

"You alone here, sir?" he demanded.

"Quite alone," Durand answered.

"Shame!" he said explosively. "First time here, then, I take it?"

It was, Durand admitted laconically.

"You'll like it, soon as you get to know the ropes," he promised. "Takes a man a few days, I don't care where it is."

It did, Durand agreed tepidly.

"You stopping at this hotel here?" He cast his thumb joint toward the inner doors leading into the building itself. "I am."

"No, I'm over at the Rogers."

"Should have come to this one. Best one in the place. Kind of slow over there where you are, isn't it?"

He hadn't noticed, Durand said. He didn't expect to remain for very long, anyway.

"Well, maybe you'll change your mind," the other suggested breezily. "Maybe we can get you to change your mind about that," he added, as though vested with a proprietary interest in the resort.

"Maybe," Durand assented, without overmuch enthusiasm. "Now join me," he invited dutifully, noting that his companion's drink was near bottom.

"Honored," said the other man zestfully, making quick to complete its disappearance.

Just as Durand was about to give the order, one of the hotel page boys came through the blown-glass doors leading from the hotel proper, looked about for a moment, then, marking Durand's partner, came up to him, excused himself, and said a word in his ear which Durand failed to catch. Particularly since he did not try to.

"Oh, already?" the other man said. "Glad you told me," and handed the boy a coin. "Be right there."

He turned back to Durand. "I'm called," he said cheerfully.

"We'll have to resume this where we left off, some other evening." He preened himself, touching at his tie, his hair, the fit of his coat shoulders. "Mustn't keep a lady waiting, you know," he added, unable to resist letting Durand know of what nature the summons was.

"By no means," Durand conceded.

"Good evening to you, sir."

"Good evening."

He watched him go. His face was anything but leisurely, even while still in full sight, and at the end he flung apart the doors quite violently, so anxious was he not to be delinquent.

Durand smiled a little to himself, half contemptuously, half in pity, and went back to his drink alone.

— 33 —

THE FOLLOWING evening they met again, he and the other man. The other was already there when Durand entered from the street, so Durand joined him without ceremony, since the etiquette of the bar prescribed that he owed the other a drink, and to have shunned him—as he would have preferred to do—might have seemed on his part an attempt to avoid the obligation.

"Still alone, I see," he greeted Durand.

"Still," Durand said cryptically.

"Well, man, you're slow," he observed critically. "What's hindering you? I should think by this time you'd have any number of—" He didn't complete the phrase, but allowed a soggy wink to do so for him.

Durand smiled wanly and gave their order.

They saluted, they swallowed.

"By the way, let me introduce myself," the other said heartily. "I'm Colonel Harry Worth, late of the Army." The way he said it showed which army he meant; or rather that there was only one *to* be meant.

"I'm Louis Durand," Durand said.

They gripped hands, at the other's initiative.

"Where you from, Durand?"

"New Orleans."

"Oh," nodded the colonel approvingly. "Good place. I've been there some."

Durand didn't ask where he was from. He didn't, his own train of thoughts phrased it to himself, give a damn.

They talked of this and that. Of business conditions (together). Of a little girl in Natchez (the colonel). Of the current administration (together, and with bitterness, as if it were some sort of foreign yoke). Of a little girl in Louisville (the colonel). Of recipes of drinks (together). Of horses, and their breeding and their racing (together). Of a "yellow" girl in Memphis (the colonel, with a resounding slap against his own thigh).

Then just as Worth was about to reorder, again the page came in, accosted him, said that word into his ear.

"Time's up," he said to Durand. He offered him his hand. "A pleasure, Mr. Randall. Be looking forward to the next time."

"Durand," Durand said.

The colonel recoiled with dramatic exaggeration, apologized profusely. "That's right; forgive me. There I go again. Got the worst-all head for names."

"No harm," said Durand indifferently. He had an idea the mistake would continue to repeat itself for as long as their acquaintanceship lasted; a name that is not got right the second time, is not likely to be got right the fourth or the tenth time either. But it mattered to him not the slightest whether this man miscalled him or not, for the man himself mattered even less.

Worth renewed their handclasp, this time under the authentic auspices. Then as he turned to go, he reached downward to the counter, popped a clove into his mouth.

"That's just in case," he said roguishly.

He left rearward, into the hotel. Durand, was standing near the outside of the cafe, toward the street. Several minutes later, turning his head disinterestedly, he was just in time to catch the colonel's passage across the thick, soapy greenish plate glass that fronted the place and bulged convexly somewhat like a bay window.

The thickness of the medium they passed through blurred his outlines somewhat, but Durand could tell it was he. On the far side of him three detached excrescences, over and above those pertaining to his own person, were all that revealed he was escorting a woman. At the height of his shoulder blades the tip of a glycerined feather projected, from a hidden woman's bonnet on the outside, as though a quill or bright-tipped dart were sticking into him.

Then at the small of his back, and extending far beyond his own modest contours, a bustle fluctuated both voluptuously and yet somehow genteelly, ballooning along as its hidden wearer walked at his side. And lastly, down at his heels, as though one of the colonel's socks had loosened and were dragging, a small triangular wedge of skirt hem, an evening train, fluttered along the ground, switching erratically from side to side as it went.

But Durand didn't even allow his tepid glance to linger, to follow them long enough until they had drawn away into perspective sufficient to separate into two persons, instead of the one composite one, superimposed, they now formed.

Again he gave that wearied smile as on the night before. This time his brows went up, much as to say: Each man to his taste.

— 34 —

THE PAGE was later tonight in putting in an appearance. The colonel, therefore, had had one drink more than on their former evenings. This showed itself only in the added warmth of his friendliness, and in a tendency to clap and grip Durand on the upper arm at frequent intervals, in punctuation of almost every second remark he made. Otherwise Worth's speech was clear enough and his train of thought coherent enough.

"My fiancée is a lovely girl, Randall, a lovely girl," he reiterated solemnly, as though unable to impress it sufficiently upon his hearer.

"I'm sure she is," Durand said, as he had twice already. "I'm sure." Having corrected the mistake in nomenclature once for the evening, he no longer took the trouble after that, let Worth have his way about it.

"I tell you, I'm the luckiest man. But you should see her. You don't have to believe *me;* you should just see her for yourself."

"Oh, I do believe you," Durand protested demurely.

"You should have a girl like that" (clap). "You should get yourself a girl like that" (clap, clap).

"We can't all be as lucky," Durand murmured, stropping the edge of one foot restlessly along the brass bar rail.

"Hate to see a fine figure of a man like you mooning around alone" (clap).

"I'm not complaining," Durand said, scouring the bottom of his glass disclaimingly around on the bar-top in interlocked circles, until he had brought it back again around to where it had started from.

"But, dammit, look at me. I have you bettered by ten years, I vow. I don't stand around waiting for them to come to me. You'll never get anyone that way. You have to go out and find one."

"That's right, you do," agreed Durand, with the air of a man pledging to himself: I'll keep up my end of this conversation if it kills me.

The colonel was suddenly assailed by belated misgivings of having transgressed good taste. This time he pinioned Durand fondly by the coat revere, in lieu of a clap. "I'm not being too personal, am I?" he besought. "If I am, just say so, and I'll back out. Wouldn't want you to think that for the world."

"No offense whatever," Durand assured him. Which was literally true. It was like discussing astrology or some other remote subject.

"Reason I take such an interest in you is, I like you. I find your company most enjoyable."

"I can reciprocate the feeling," said Durand gravely, with a brief inclination that seemed to be exerted by the top of his head alone.

"I'd like to have you meet my fiancée. There's a girl."

"I'd be honored," said Durand. He was beginning to wish the nightly page boy would put in an appearance.

"She'll be coming down in a minute or two for me to pick her up." The colonel was suddenly visited with an inspiration. Pride of possession very frequently being synonymous with pride of display. "Why don't you join us for tonight? Love to have you. Come on out with me and I'll introduce you."

"Not tonight," said Durand a little hastily. Grasping at any excuse he could find, he stroked his own jaw line tentatively. "I wasn't expecting— Afraid I'm not presentable."

The colonel cocked his head critically. "Nonsense. You look all right. You're clean shaven."

He bethought himself of a compromise. "Well, just step out the door with me a moment and let me have you meet her, as she comes down. Then we'll go on alone."

Durand was suddenly visited by scruples of delicacy, which came in handy to his purpose. "I don't think she'd thank you for bringing anyone straight out of *here* to be presented to her face to face. It mightn't look right; you know how the ladies are. After all, this is a men's drinking cafe."

"But I come in here every night myself," the colonel said uncertainly.

"But you know her; I'm a stranger to her. It's not the same thing."

Before Worth could make up his mind on this fine point of social etiquette, the habitual bellboy had come in and delivered his summons.

"Your lady's down, sir."

The colonel put a coin in his gloved hand, drained his drink.

"Tell you what. I have a better idea. Suppose we make it a foursome. I'll have my fiancée bring someone along for you. She must know some of the unattached young ladies around here by now. That'll make it more comfortable for you. How about tomorrow night? Nothing on for then, have you?"

"Not a thing," said Durand, satisfied with having gained his reprieve for the present at least, and toying with the thought of sending his excuses sometime during the course of the following day as the best way of getting out of it. Any further reluctance at the moment, he realized, would have veered over into offense, even where such a thick-skinned individual as Worth was concerned, and it was none of his intent to offend the man gratuitously.

"Fine!" said Worth, beaming. "That's an engagement, then. I'll tell you what's just the place for it. There's a little supper establishment called The Grotto. Open late. Not *fast*, you understand. Just good and lively. They have music there, and very good wine. We go there often, Miss Castle and I. Instead of meeting here at the hotel, where there are a lot of old fogies around ready to gossip, you join us there. I'll bring the two young ladies with me."

"Excellent," said Durand.

The colonel rubbed his hands together gleefully, evidently former facets of his life not having yet died out as completely as he himself might have wished to believe.

"I'll engage a private alcove. They have them there, curtained off from prying eyes. Look for us, you'll find us in one of them."

He tapped Durand on the chest with his index finger. "And don't forget, the invitation's mine."

"I dispute you there," Durand said.

"We'll quarrel over that when the time comes. Tomorrow night, then. Understood?"

"Tomorrow night. Understood."

Worth went hurrying toward the page who stood waiting for him just within the doors, evidently having received literal instructions to *bring* him with him, on the part of one who knew the colonel well.

Suddenly he turned, came hastening back, rose on tiptoe, and whispered hoarsely into Durand's ear: "I forgot to ask you. Blonde or brunette?"

Her image crossed Durand's mind for a minute. "Brunette," he said succinctly, and a flicker of pain crinkled his eyes momentarily.

The colonel dug an elbow into his ribs with ribald camaraderie.

— 35 —

SOMEHOW, the next day, he was too lackadaisical about the engagement even to send his perfunctory regrets in time, and so before he knew it, it was evening, the appointment had become confirmed if only by default, and it was too late to extricate himself from it without being guilty of the grossest rudeness, which would not have been the case had he canceled it a few hours earlier.

He'd lain down on his bed, fully dressed, late in the afternoon for a short nap, and when he awoke the time set was already imminent, and there was nothing left to do now but fulfill the engagement.

He sighed and grimaced privately to his mirror, but then commenced the necessary preparations none the less, stirring his brush vigorously within his thick crockery mug until foam swelled up and beaded driblets of it ran down the sides. He could remain a half-hour, he promised himself, as a token of participation, then arrange to have himself called away by one of the waiters with a decoy message, and leave. Making sure to pay his share of the entertainment before he did, so they wouldn't think that the motive. They would be offended, he supposed, but less than if he were not to appear at all.

Fortified by this intention, shaved and cleanly shirted, he shrugged on his coat, thumbed open his money-fold to see that it was sufficiently well filled, and glumly set forth. No celebrant ever started out with poorer grace or longer face to join what was meant to be a pleasure party. He was swearing softly under his breath as he closed the door of his room behind him: at the overgregarious colonel for inveigling him into this; at the unknown he was expected to pay court to for the mere fact that she was a woman and so could force him into a position where he was obliged to; and at himself, first and foremost, for not having had the bluntness to refuse point-blank the night before when the invitation had first been put to him.

Some vapid, simpering heifer; everyone's leavings. He could imagine the colonel's taste in women, judging by the man himself.

A ten-minute walk, in this caustic frame of mind, and unmellowed to the very end by the spangled brocade of starred sky hanging over him, had brought him to his destination.

The Grotto was a long, narrow, cabinlike, single-story structure, flimsy and unprepossessing on the outside like many another ephemeral holiday resort catering-place. Gas and oil light rayed forth from every crack and seam of it, tinted rose and blue by some peculiarity of shading on the inside. The interior, due to some depression in the ground, was somewhat lower than the walks outside, so that he had to descend a short flight of entry steps once he had been bowed in by the colored door-flunkey. The main dining room itself, seen from their top, was a disordered litter of white-clothed table tops, heads studding them in circular formation, and each one set with a rose or blue-shaded table lamp, an innovation borrowed from Europe, which dimmed the glare, usual in such places, to a twilight softness and created a suggestion of illicit revelry and clandestine romance. It gave the place the appearance of a field of blinking fireflies.

A pompous dining steward, with wide-spreading frizzed sideburns, clasping a bill-of-fare slantwise like a painter holding a palette, greeted him at the foot of the stairs.

"Are you alone, sir? May I show you to a table?".

"No, I was to join a party," Durand said. "Colonel Worth and friends. In one of the private booths. Which way are they?"

"Oh, straight to the back, sir. At the far end of the room. You are expected. They are in the first one on the right."

He made his way down the long central lane of clearance to the rear, like someone wresting his way through a brawl, auditory and olfactory, if not combative. Through cellular entities or zones of disparate food odors, that remained isolated, each in its little nucleus, refusing to mingle; now lobster, now charcoaled steak, now soggy linen and spilled wine. Through dismembered snatches of conversation and laughter that likewise remained compartmentalized, each within its own little circular area.

"When he's with me he says one thing, and when he's with the next girl he says another. Oh, I've heard all about you, never you mind!"

"—an administration that's the ruination of this country! And I don't care who hears me, I'm entitled to my opinion!"

"—and now I come to the best part of the story. This is the part that will delight you—"

At the back, the room narrowed to a single serving passage leading to the kitchen. Lining each side of this, however, were openings leading into the little private alcoves or dining nooks Worth had mentioned. All alike discreetly curtained-off from view, although otherwise they were doorless. The nearest one on either side, however, was not strictly parallel to the passage but placed slantwise to it, cutting off the corner.

As he fixed his eyes upon the one to the right, marking that for his eventual destination, though still a little distance short of it, with the last bank of tables projecting somewhat between, the protective curtain gashed back at one side and a waiter came out backward, in the act of withdrawal but lingering a moment half-in half-out to allow the completion of some instruction being given him. He held the curtain, for that moment, away from the wall in a sort of diamond-shaped aperture, with one hand.

Durand's foot, striking ground, never moved on again, never took him a space nearer.

It was as if a cameo of purest line, of clearest design, were in that opening, held there for Durand to see, a cameo of dazzling clarity, presented against a dark velvet mounting.

On one side, fluctuating with utterance of orders to the waiter, was a slice of the lumpy profile of the colonel. At the other, facing back toward him, was a slice of the smooth-turned profile of an unknown, dark of hair and dark of eye.

Midway between the two, facing outward, bust-length, white as alabaster, dazzling as marble, regal as a diminutive Juno, beautiful as a blonde Venus or the Helen of the Trojans, were the face and throat and bared shoulders and half-bared bosom that he would never forget, that he could never forget, brought as if by magic transmutation back from out his dreams into the living substance again.

Julia.

He could even see the light on her hair, in moving golden sheen. Even see the passing glint, as of crystal, as her eyes moved.

Julia, the killer. The destroyer of his heart.

That she failed to see him out there was incredible. All but the pupils of her eyes alone were bearing straight toward him. They must have been deflected, unnoticeable at that distance, toward one or the other of her table companions, to miss striking him.

The waiter dropped his restraining hand, the curtainside swept to the wall, the cameo was blotted out.

He stood there as stunned, as blasted, as robbed of his powers of motion, as though that white, searing glimpse—there, then gone again—had been a flash of lightning which had struck too close and fused him to the ground. All its effects lacked was to cause him to fall flat in front of everybody, then and there.

Then a waiter, hurrying obliviously by, jarred against him, and that set him into motion at last; as one ball strikes another on a billiard table, starting it off.

He was going back the other way, the way he'd come, now, unsteadily, jostling into tables and the backs of chairs that lined his route, past momentarily upturned, questioning faces, past a blurred succession of table lamps like worthless beacons that only confused and failed to guide him straight through their midst.

He reached the other end of the raucous place, and the same steward as before came solicitously to his side.

"Did you fail to find your party, sir?"

"I—I've changed my mind." He took out his money-fold, crushed an incredible ten-dollar bill into the man's hand. "I haven't been here asking for them. You didn't see me."

He stumbled up the steps and out, lurching as though he'd filled himself with wine in those few minutes. Wine of hate, ferment of the grapes of wrath.

— 36 —

HE HAD at first no very clear concept of what he meant to do. The black fog of hate that filled his mind clouded all plans and purposes. Instinct alone had kept him from rushing in through those curtains, not calculation.

Alone. Alone he must have her, where no onlookers could save her. He wanted no hot-mouthed denunciation, quickly over. What was one more denunciation to her? Her path must have been strewn with them already. He wanted no public wrangle, in which her coolness and composure would inevitably have the better of him. "I've never seen this man before. He must be mad!" One thing and one alone he wanted, one thing alone he'd have. He wanted her death. He wanted the few moments just ahead of it to be between the two of them alone.

He stood for a while outside their hotel, hers and Worth's, to calm himself, to compose himself. Stood with his back to it, looking out to seaward. And as he stood, motionless, inscrutable of attitude in all else, over and over and over again he brought his hand down upon the wooden railing. At stated intervals, like a pestle, pulverizing his intentions, grinding them fine.

Then it slackened, then it stopped. He was ready.

He turned abruptly and went into the brightly lighted lobby of the place, purposefully yet not too hurriedly. He went undeviatingly toward the desk, stopped before it, drummed his fingernails upon its white-veined black marble top to hasten the clerk's attention.

Then when he had it: "I'm a friend of Colonel Worth's. I've just left him and his party at the Grotto."

"Yes, sir. Can I be of service?"

"One of the young ladies with us—I believe she's stopping here— found the evening chillier than she expected it to be. She's sent me back for her scarf. She explained to me where it's to be found. May I be allowed to go up and fetch it for her?"

The clerk was professionally cautious. "Could you describe her to me?"

"She's blonde, and a rather small little person."

The clerk's doubts vanished. "Oh, that's the colonel's fiancée, Miss Castle. In Room Two-six. I'll have a bellboy take you up immediately, sir."

He jarred a bell, handed over a key with the requisite instructions.

Durand was taken up to the second floor, in a ponderous latticework elevator, its shaft transparent on all sides. He noted that a staircase coiled around this on the outside, rising as it rose, attaining the same destination at last. He noted that, well and grimly.

They went down a hall. There was a brief delay as the bellboy fitted key to door and tried it. Then as the door opened, the most curious sensation that he had ever had swept over Durand. It was as though he were near her all over again. It was as though she had just this moment stepped out of the room on the far side as he entered it on the near. She was present to every faculty but vision. Her perfume still lay ghostly on the air. He could feel her at the ends of all his pores. A discarded taffeta garment flung over the back of a chair rustled again as she moved, in memory, in his ears.

It whipped his hate so, it steeled him to his purpose. He made no false step, wasted not a move. He went about it as one stalks an enemy.

The bellboy had remained deferentially beside the open door, allowing him to enter alone. He remained, however, in a position from which he could watch what Durand was about.

"She must be mistaken," Durand said plausibly, for the other's benefit but as if speaking to himself. "I don't see it over the chair." He raised the taffeta underslip, replaced it again. "It must be in one of these bureau drawers." He opened one, closed it again. Then a second.

The bellboy was watching him now with the slightly anxious air of a hen having its nest searched for eggs.

"Women never know where they leave things, did you ever notice?" Durand said to him in man-to-man confidence.

The boy grinned, flattered at being included into a stage of experience which he had not yet reached of his own efforts.

Durand, secretly desperate, at length discovered something in the third drawer, withdrew a length of flimsy heliotrope voile, sufficient at least for the purposes of his visit if nothing else.

"This, I guess," he said, concealing a relieved smile at his good fortune.

He closed the drawer, came back toward the door, stuffing it into his side pocket.

The boy's eyes, inevitably, were on his prodding hand. His were on the edge of the door, turned inward so that it faced him. It had, above the latch-tongue, a small rounded depression. A plunger, controlling the lock. Just as his own room door, in the other build-ing, had. He had counted on that.

Before the boy was aware of it, Durand had relieved him of the duty of reclosing the door; grasping it by its edge, not its knob, di-rectly over the plunger, and drawing it closed after the two of them.

He had, while doing so, changed the plunger, pressing it in, leav-ing the door off-lock and simply on-latch no matter whether a key was used or not.

He then allowed the boy to complete his appointed task of turn-ing the key, extracting it and once that was done, distracted him from testing it further by having a silver half-dollar extended in his hand for him.

They went down together, the boy all smiles and congenitally unable to harbor suspicion of anyone who tipped so lavishly. Du-rand smiling a little too, a very little.

He nodded his thanks to the clerk as he went by, tapped his pocket to show him that he had secured what he'd come for.

There wasn't a glint of pity in the stars over him as he came out into the open night and his face dimmed to its secretive shade. There wasn't a breath of tenderness in the humid salt breeze that came in from the Gulf. He'd have her alone, and no one should save her. He'd have her death, and nothing else would do.

— 37 —

HE WENT from there to his own room, unlocked his traveling bag, and took out the pistol. The same pistol that one night in New Orleans he'd told Aunt Sarah he would kill her with. And now, it seemed, the time was near, was very near. He cracked it open, though he knew already it was fully charged; and found that it was. Then he sheathed it in the inside pocket of his coat, which was deep and took it up to the turn of the butt and held it securely.

He looked down and noted the heliotrope scarf dangling from his side pocket, and in a sudden access of hate he ripped it out and flung it on the floor. Then he ground his heel into the middle of it, and kicked it away from him, like something unclean, unfit to touch. His face was putrefied with the hate that reeks from an unburied love.

He tweaked out the gaslight, and the greenish-yellow cast of the room turned to moonlight tarnished with lampblack. He stood there in it for a moment, half-man, half-shadow, as if gathering purpose. Then he moved, the half of him that was man became shadow, the half that was shadow became man, as the window beams rippled at his passage. There was a flicker of citron from the lighted hall outside, as he opened the door, closed it after him.

He went up the stairs to the second floor without meeting anybody, and the hubbub of voices from the several public parlors on the main floor grew fainter the farther he ascended. Until at last there was silence. He quitted the staircase at the second, and followed the corridor along which the page had led him before, with its flower-scrolled red carpeting and walnut-dark doors. Here for the first time he nearly met mischance. A lady coming out of her room caught him midway along it, too far advanced to turn back. Her eyes rested on him for an instant only, then she passed him with discreetly downcast gaze, as befitted their distinction of gender, and the rustle of her multi-layered skirts sighed its way along the passage. He gave her time to turn and pass from sight at the far end, stopping for a moment opposite a door that was not his destination, as if about to go in there. Then swiftly going on and making for the door he had in mind, he cast a quick precautionary look about him, seized the knob, gave it a rapid turn, and was in. He closed it after him.

There were the same low night lights burning as before, and she wasn't back yet. Her presence was in the air, he thought, in faded sachet and in the warm, quilted voluptuousness the closed-for-hours room breathed. He couldn't have come any nearer to her than this; only her person itself was absent. Her aura was in here with him, and seeming to twine ghost-arms about his neck from behind. He squared his shoulders, as if to free them, and twisted his neck within his collar.

He stood at the window for a while, safely slantwise out of sight, staring ugly-faced at the moonlight, his face pitted like a smallpox victim's by the pores of the lacework curtain. Below him there was the sloping white shed of the veranda roof, like a tilted snowbank. Beyond that, the smooth black lawns of the hotel grounds. And off in the distance, coruscating like a swarm of fireflies, the waters of the inlet. Overhead the moon was round and hard as a medicinal lozenge. And, to him, as unpalatable.

Turning away abruptly at last, he retired deeper into the room, and selecting a chair at random, sank into it to wait. Shadow, the way he happened to be sitting, covered the upper part of his face, running across it in an even line, like a mask. A mask inscrutable and grim and without compunction.

He waited from then on without a move, and the night seemed to wait with him, like an abetting conspirator eager to see ill done.

Once toward the end he took out his watch and looked at it, dipping its face out into the moonlight. Nearly a quarter after twelve. He had been in here three full hours. They'd stayed the evening out without him at the supper pavilion. He clapped the watch closed, and it resounded bombastically there in the stillness.

Suddenly, as if in derisive answer, he heard her laugh, somewhere far in the distance. Perhaps coming up in the lift. He would have known it for hers even if he hadn't seen her in the alcove at the restaurant earlier tonight. He would, he felt sure, have known it for hers even if he hadn't known she was here in Biloxi at all. The heart remembers.

— 38 —

HE JUMPED up quickly and looked around. Strangely enough, for all the length of time he'd been in the room, he'd made no plans for concealment, he had to improvise them now. He saw the screen there, and chose that. It was the quickest and most obvious method of effacing himself, and she was already nearing the door, for he could hear her voice now, merrily saying something, close at hand in the hallway.

He spread the screen a little more, squaring its panels, so that it made a sort of hollow pilaster protruding from the wall, and got in behind there. He could maintain his own height, he found, and still not risk having the top of his head show. He could see through the perforated, lacelike, scrolled woodwork at the top, his eyes came up to there.

The door opened, and she had arrived.

Two figures came in, not one; and advancing only a step or two beyond the doorway, almost instantly blended into one, stood there locked in ravenous embrace in the semishadow of the little foyer. A gossamer piquancy of breath-borne champagne or brandy reached him, admixed with a little perfume. His heart drowned in it.

There was no motion, just the rustle of pressed garments.

Again her laugh sounded, but muffled, furtive, now; lower now that it was close at hand than it had been when at a distance outside.

He recognized the colonel's voice, in a thick whisper. "I've been waiting for this all evening. My li'l girl, you are, my li'l girl."

The rustling strengthened to active resistance.

"Harry, that's enough now. I must wear this dress again. Leave me at least a shred of it."

"I'll buy you another. I'll buy you ten."

She broke away at last, light from the hallway came between their figures; but the embrace was still locked about her like a barrel-hoop. Durand could see her pushing the colonel's arms perpendicularly downward, unable to pry them open in the usual direction. At last they severed.

"But I like this one. Don't be so destructive. I never saw such a man. Let me put the lights up. We mustn't stand here like this."

"I like it better as it is."

"I've no doubt!" she said pertly. "But up they go just the same."

She entered the room itself now, and went to the night light, and it flared from a spark to a sunburst at her touch. And as the light bathed her, washing away all indistinctness of outline and of feature, she glowed there before him in full life once more, after a year and a month and a day. No longer just a cameo glimpsed through a parted curtain, a disembodied laugh down a hallway, a silhouette against an open door; she was whole, she was real, she was *she*. She broke into bloom. In all her glory and her ignominy; in all her beauty and all her treachery; in all her preciousness and all her worthlessness.

And an old wound in Durand's heart opened and began to bleed all over again.

She threw down her fan, she threw down her shoulder scarf; she drew off the one glove she had retained and added that to the one she had carried loose, and threw them both down. She was in garnet satin, stiff and crisp as starch, and picked with scrolls and traceries of twinkling jet. She took up a little powder-pad and touched it to the tip of her nose, but in habit rather than in actual application. And her courtier stood there and watched her every move, idolizing her, beseeching her, with his greedy smoking eyes.

She turned to him at last, offhandedly, over one shoulder. "Wasn't it too bad about poor Florrie? What do you suppose became of the young man you arranged to have her meet?"

"Oh, blast him!" Worth said truculently. "Forgot, maybe. He's no gentleman. If I run into him again, I'll cut him dead."

She was seeing to her hair now. Touching it a bit, without disturbing it too much. Gracefully crouching a trifle so that the top of the mirror frame could encompass it comfortably. "What was he like?" she asked idly. "Did he seem well-to-do? Would we—would Florrie, I mean—have liked him, do you think?"

"I hardly know him. Name was Randall or something. I've never seen him spend more than fifty cents at a time for a whiskey punch."

"Oh," she said on a dropping inflection, and stopped with her hair, as if losing interest in it.

She turned and moved toward him suddenly, hand extended in parting gesture. "Well, thank you for a congenial evening, Harry. Like all your evenings it was most delectable."

He took the hand but kept it within his two.

"Mayn't I stay just a little while longer? I'll behave. I'll just sit here and watch you."

"Watch me!" she exclaimed archly. "Watch me do what? Not what you'd like to, I warn you." She pushed him slightly, at the shoulder, to keep the distance between them even.

Then her smile faded, and she seemed to become thoughtful, ruefully sober for a moment.

"Wasn't it too bad about poor Florrie, though?" she repeated, as though discovering some remaining value in the remark that had not been fully extracted the first time.

"Yes, I suppose so," he agreed vaguely.

"She took such pains with her appearance. I had to lend her the money for the dress."

Instantly he released her. "Oh, here. Let me. Why didn't you tell me this sooner?" He busied himself within his coat, took out his money-fold, opened and busied himself with that.

She darted a quick glance down at it, then the rest of the time, until he had finished, looked dreamily past him to the rear of the room.

He put something in her hand.

"Oh, and while I think of it—" he said.

He fumbled additionally with the pocketbook, put something further into her uncooperative, yet unresistant, hand.

"For the hotel bill," he said. "For the sake of appearance, it's better if you attend to it yourself."

She circled, swept her back toward him. Yet scarcely in offense or disdain, for she said to him teasingly: "Now don't look. At least, not over my left shoulder."

The folds of garnet satin swept up at her side for a moment, revealing the long shapely glint of smoky black silk. Worth, up on the toes of his feet to gain height, was peering hungrily over her right shoulder. She turned her face toward him for a moment, gave him a roguish look, winked one eye, and the folds of her dress cascaded to the floor again, with a soft little plop.

Worth made a sudden convulsive move, and they had blended into one again, this time in full light of mid-room, not in the shadow of the vestibule.

Durand felt something heavy in his hand. Looked down and saw that he'd taken the pistol out. "I'll kill both of them," stencilled itself in white-hot lettering across his mind.

"And now—?" Worth said, lips blurred against her neck and shoulder. "Are you going to be kind—?"

Durand could see her head avert itself from his; smiling benevolently, yet avert itself. She twisted to face the door, and in turning, managed to get him to turn likewise; then somehow succeeded in leading him toward it, her face and shoulders still caught in his endless kiss. "No—" she said temperately, at intervals. "No— No— I *am* kind to you, Harry. No more kind than I've always been to you, no less— Now that's a good boy—"

Durand gave a sigh of relief, put the gun away.

She was standing just within the gap of the door now, alone at last, her arm extended to the outside. Worth must have been kissing it repeatedly, the length of time she maintained it that way.

All he could hear was a subdued murmur of reluctant parting.

She withdrew her arm with effort, pressed the door closed.

He saw her face clearly as she came back into the full light. All the playfulness, coquetry, were wiped off it as with a sponge. It was shrewd and calculating, and a trifle pinched, as if with the long wearing of a mask.

"God Almighty!" he heard her groan wearily, and saw her strike herself a glancing blow against the temple.

She went first and looked out the window, as he had earlier; stood there motionless by it some time. Then when she'd had her fill of whatever thoughts the sight from there had managed to instill in her, she turned away suddenly, almost with abrupt impatience, causing her skirts to swirl and hiss out in the silence. She came back to the dresser, fetched out a drawer. No powdering at her nose, no primping at her hair, now. She had no look to spare for the mirror.

She withdrew the money from her stocking-top and flung it in, with a turn of the wrist that was almost derisive. But not of the money itself, possibly; of its source.

Reaching into some hiding place she had in there, she took out one of those same slender cigars Aunt Sarah had showed him in the St. Louis Street house in New Orleans.

To him there was something repugnant, almost obscene, in the sight of her bending to the lamp chimney with it until it had kindled, holding it tight-bitten, smoke sluicing from her miniature nostrils, as from a man's.

In a sickening phantasmagoric illusion, that lasted but a moment, she appeared to him as a fuming, horned devil, in her ruddy longtailed dress.

She set the cigar down, presently, in a hairpin tray, and seated herself by the mirror. She unfastened her hair and it came tumbling down in a molasses-colored cascade to the small of her back. Then she opened a vent in her dress at the side, separating a number of hooks from their eyes, but without unfastening or removing it farther than that. Leaving a gap through which her tightly laced side swelled and subsided again at each breath.

She took out the money now she had cast in only a moment before, but took out far more than she had flung in, and counted it over with close attention. Then she put it into a small lacquered casket, of the type used to hold jewels, and locked that, and gave it a commending little thump on its lid with her knuckles, as if in pleased finality.

She reclosed the drawer, stood up, moved over to the desk, took down its lid and seated herself at it. She drew out a sheet of note-paper from the rack. Took up a pen and dipped it, and squaring her other arm above the surface to be written on, began to write.

Durand moved out from behind the screen and slowly walked across the carpet toward her. It gave his tread no sound, though he wasn't trying for silence. He advanced undetected, until he was standing behind her, and could look down over her shoulder.

"Dear Billy," the paper said. "I—"

The pen had stopped, and she was nibbling for a moment at its end.

He put out his hand and let it come lightly to rest on her shoulder. Left it there, but lightly, lightly, as she had once put her hand to *his* shoulder, lightly, on the quayside at New Orleans; lightly, but crushing his life.

Her fright was the fright of guilt, and not innocence. Even before she could have known who it was. For she didn't turn to look, as the innocent of heart would have. She held her head rigidly as it was, turned the other way, neck taut with suspense. She was *afraid* to look. There must have been such guilt strewn behind her in her life, that *anyone's* sudden touch, in the stillness of the night, in the solitude of her room, she must have known could bode no good.

Her one hand dropped the pen lifelessly. Her other clawed secretively at the sheet of notepaper, sucking it up, causing it to disappear. Then dropping it, crumpled, over the desk side.

Still she didn't move; the sleek taffy-colored head held still, like something an axe was about to fall on.

Her eyes had found him in the mirror by now. It was over to the left of her, and when he looked at it himself, he could see, in the reflection of her talcum-white face, the pupils darkening the far corners of her eyes, giving her an ugly unnatural appearance, as though she had black eyeballs.

"Don't be afraid to look around, Julia," he said ironically. "It's only me. No one important. Merely me."

Suddenly she turned, so swiftly that the transplacement of the silken back of her head by the plaster-white cast of her face was almost like that of an apparition.

"You act as though you don't remember me," he said softly. "Surely you haven't forgotten me, Julia. *Me* of all people."

"How'd you know I was here?" she demanded granularly.

"I didn't. I was the other man who was to have met you at the restaurant party tonight."

"How'd you get in here?"

"Through the door."

She had risen now, defensively, and was trying to reverse the desk chair to get it between them, reedy as it was, but there was no room to allow for its insertion.

He took it from her and set it to rest with his hand.

"How is it you don't order me from your room, Julia? How is it you don't threaten to scream for help? Or all those other things they usually do?"

She said, summoning up a sort of desperate tractabilfty, that he couldn't help but admire for an instant, "This is a matter that has to be settled between us, without screams or ordering you from the room." She stroked one arm, shiveringly, all the way up to the top. "Let's get it over with as soon as we can."

"It's taken *me* better than a year," he said. "*You* won't grudge a few added minutes, I hope?"

She didn't answer.

"Were you going to marry the colonel, Julia? That would have been bigamous."

She shrugged irritably. "Oh, he's just a fool. I'm not accountable for him. The whole world is full of fools." And in this phrase, at least, there was unmistakable sincerity.

"And the biggest of them all is the one you're looking at right now, Julia."

He kicked the crumpled tossball of notepaper leniently with the toe of his foot, moving it a little. But gently, as if it held somebody else's wracked hopes.

"Who's Billy?"

"Oh, no one in particular. A chance acquaintance. A fellow I met somewhere." She flung out her hand, still with nervous irritability, as if causing the person to disappear from her ken in that way.

"The world must be full of Billys for you. Billys and Lous and Colonel Worths."

"Is it?" she said. "No, there was only one Lou. It may be a little late to say it now. But I didn't marry the Billys and the Colonel Worths. I married Lou."

"You acted it," he agreed mordantly.

"Well, it's late," she said. "What's the good now?"

"We agree on that, at least."

She went over to the lamp, and thoughtfully spanned her hand against it, so that her flesh glowed translucent brick-red, and watched that effect for a while. Then she turned toward him.

"What is it, Lou? What are your plans for me?"

His hand rose slowly to that part of his coat which covered where the gun was resting against him. Remained there a moment. Then crept around to the inside and found it, by the handle. Then drew it out, so slowly, so slowly, the bone handle, the nickelled chambers and fluted barrel seemed never to stop coming, like something pulled on an endless train.

"I came here to kill you, Julia."

A single glance was all she gave it. Just enough to identify it, to see that he had the means to do it on his person. Then after that, her eyes were for his alone, never left them from then on. Knowing where the signal would lie: in his eyes and not on the gun. Knowing where the only place to appeal lay: in his eyes.

She looked at him for a long time, as if measuring his ability to do it: what he'd said. What she saw there, only she could have told. Whether full purpose, hopeless to deflect, or half-purpose, waiting only to be crumbled.

He didn't point it, he didn't raise it to her; he simply held it, on the flat side, muzzle offside. But his face was white with the long pain she'd given him, and whatever she'd read in his look, still all that was needed was a turn of his hand.

Perhaps she was a gambler, and instinctively liked the odds, they appealed to her, whetted her; she hated to bet on a sure thing. Or perhaps the reverse: she was no gambler, she only banked upon a certainty, never anything else, in men or in cards; and this was a certainty now, though he didn't know it himself yet. Or perhaps, again it was solely vanity, self-esteem, that prompted her, and she must put her power over him to the test, even though to lose meant to die. Perhaps, even, if she were to lose, she would want to die, vanity being the thing it is.

She smiled at him. But in brittle challenge, not in anything else.

She suddenly wrenched at the shoulder of her dress, tore it down. Then pulled at it, farther down and still farther down, withdrawing her arm from the bedraggled loop it now made, until at last the whiteness of her side was revealed all but to the waist. On the left, the side of the heart. Moving toward him all the while, closer step by step. White as milk and pliable as China silk, flesh flexing as she walked.

Then halted as the cold gun touched her, holding her ravaged dress-bodice clear and looked deep into his eyes.

"All right, Lou," she whispered.

He withdrew the gun from between them.

She came a step closer with its removal.

"Don't hesitate, Lou," she breathed. "I'm waiting."

His heel edged backward, carrying him a hair's breadth off. He stuffed the gun into his side pocket, to be rid of it, hastily, fumblingly, careless how he did so, leaving the hilt projecting.

"Cover yourself up, Julia," he said. "You're all exposed."

And there was the answer. If she'd been a gambler, she'd won. If she'd been no gambler, she'd read his eyes right the first time. If it was vanity that had led her to the brink of destruction, it had triumphed, it was intact, undamaged.

She gave no sign. Not even of having triumphed; which is the way of the triumphant when they are clever as well. His face was bedewed with accumulated moisture, as though it were he who had taken the risk.

She drew her clothes upward again, never to where they had originally been but at least in partial restoration.

"Then if you won't kill me, what *do* you want of me?"

"To take you back to New Orleans and hand you over to the police." As if uneasy at their close confrontation, he sundered it, shifted aside. "Get yourself ready," he said over his shoulder.

Suddenly his head inclined, to stare downward at his own chest, as if in involuntary astonishment. Her arms had crept downward past his shoulders, soft as white ribbons, and were trying to join together before him in supplicating embrace. He could feel the softness of her hair as it came to rest against him just below the nape of his neck.

He parted them, flung them off, sending her backward from him. "Get yourself ready," he said grimly.

"If it's the money, wait—I have some here, I'll give it to you. And if it's not enough, I'll make it up—I swear I will—"

"Not for that. You were my wife, in law, and there was no crime committed, in law."

"Then for what?"

"To answer what became of Julia Russell. The real one. You're not Julia Russell and you never were. Do you pretend you are?"

She didn't answer. He thought he could detect more real fright now than at the time of the gun. Her eyes were wider, more strained, at any rate.

She quitted the drawer she had thrown open and been crouched beside, where the money was, and came toward him.

"To tell them what you did with her," he said. "And there's a name for that. Would you like to hear it?"

"No, no!" she protested, and even held her palms fronted toward him as she came close, but whether her protest was for the thought he had suggested, or for the very sound itself of the word he had threatened to utter, he could not tell. Almost, it seemed, the latter.

"Mur—" he began.

And then her palms had found his mouth and stopped it, terrifiedly. "No, no! Lou, don't say that! I had nothing to do with it. I don't *know* what became of her. Only listen to me, hear me; Lou, you must listen to me!"

He tried to cast her off as he had before, but this time she clung, she would not be rejected. Though his arms flung her, she came back upon them again, carried by them.

"Listen to what? More lies? Our whole marriage was a lie. Every word you spoke to me, every breath you drew, in all that time was a lie. You'll tell them to the police, not to me any longer. I want no more of them!"

That word, just as the one she'd stifled before, seemed to have a particular terror for her. She quailed, and gave a little inchoate moan, the first sound of weakness she'd made yet. Or if it was artifice, calculation pretending to be weakness for its effect upon him, it succeeded by that much, for he took it to be weakness, and thus its purpose was gained.

Still clinging in desperation to the wings of his coat, she dropped to her knees before him, grovelling in posture of utmost supplication the human figure is capable of.

"No, no, the truth this time!" she sobbed drily. "Only the truth, and nothing else! If you'll only listen to me, let me speak—"

He stopped trying to rid himself of her at last, and stood there stolid.

"Would you know it?" he said contemptuously.

But she'd gained her hearing.

Her arms dropped from him, and she turned her head away for a moment and backed her hand to her own mouth. Whether in hurried search of inspiration, or whether steeling herself for the honest unburdening about to come, he could not tell.

"There's no train a while yet," he said grudgingly. "And I can't take you to the railroad station as you are now and keep you dawdling about there with me half the night—so speak if you want to." He dropped back into a chair, pulled at his collar as if exhausted by the emotional stress they had both just been through. "It will do you no good. I warn you before you begin, the outcome will be the same. *You are coming back to New Orleans with me to face justice.* And all your tears and all your kneeling and all your pleas are thrown away!"

Without rising, she inched toward him, crept as it were, on her very knees, so that the distance between them was again lessened, and she was at his very feet, penitent, abject, her hands to the arm of the chair he was in.

"It wasn't I. I didn't do it. *He* must have done something to her, for I never saw her again. But what it was, I don't know. I didn't see it done. He only came to me afterward and said she'd had a mishap, and I was afraid to question him any further than—"

"He?" he said sardonically.

"The man I was with. The man on the boat I was with."

"Your paramour," he said tonelessly, and tried not to let her see him swallow the bitter lump that knobbed his throat.

"No!" she said strenuously. "No, he wasn't! You can believe it if you choose, but from first to last he wasn't. It was purely a working arrangement. And no one else ever was either, before him. I've learned to care for myself since I've been about in the world, and whether I've done things that were right, or done things that were wrong, I've been no man's but yours, Lou. No man's, until I married you."

He wondered why he felt so much lighter than a moment ago,

and warned himself sternly he mustn't; and in spite of that, did anyway.

"Julia," he drawled reproachfully, as if in utter disbelief. "You ask me to believe that? Julia, Julia."

"Don't call me Julia," she murmured remorsefully. "That isn't my name."

"Have you a name?"

She moistened her lips. "Bonny," she admitted. "Bonny Castle."

He gave a nod of agreement that was a jeer in pantomime. "To the colonel, Bonny. To me, Julia. To Billy, something else. To the next man, something else again." He turned his face from her in disgust, then looked back again. "Is that what you were christened? Is that your baptismal name?"

"No," she said. "I was never christened. I never had a baptismal name."

"Everyone has a name, I thought."

"I never had even that. You need a mother and father to give you that. A wash basket on a doorstep can't give you that. Now do you understand?"

"Then where is it from?"

"It's from a postal picture card," she said, and some old defiance and rancor still alive in her made her head go up higher a moment. "A postal picture card from Scotland that came to the foundling home, one day when I was twelve. I picked it up and stole a look. And on the face of it there was the prettiest scene I'd ever seen, of ivy-covered walls and a blue lake. And it said 'Bonny Castle.' I didn't know what it meant, but I took that for my name. They'd called me Josie in the foundling home until then. I hated it. Anyway, it was no more my rightful name than this was. I've kept to this one ever since, so it's rightfully mine by length of usage if nothing else. What difference do a few drops of holy water sprinkled on your head make? Go on, laugh if you will," she consented bleakly.

"I no longer know how," he said in glum parenthesis. "You saw to that. How long were you there, at this institution?"

"Until I was fifteen, I think. Or close onto it. I've never had an exact birthday, you see. That's another thing I've done without. I made one up for myself, at one time; just as the name. I chose St. Valentine's Day, because it was so festive. But then I tired of it after a while, and no longer kept up with it."

He gazed at her without speaking.

She sighed weariedly, to draw fresh breath for continuation. "Anyway, I ran away from there when I was fifteen. They accused me of stealing something, and they beat me for it. They'd accused me before, and they'd beaten me before. But at thirteen I knew no better than to endure it, at fifteen I no longer would. I climbed over the wall at night. Some of the other girls helped me, but they lacked the courage to come with me." And then she said with an odd, speculative sort of detachment, as though she were speaking of someone else: "That's one thing I've never been, at least: a coward."

"You've never been a coward," he assented, but as though finding small cause for satisfaction in the estimate.

"It was up in Pennsylvania," she went on. "It was bitterly cold. I remember trudging the roadside for hours, until at last a drayman gave me a ride in his wagon—"

"You're from the North?" he said. "I hadn't known. You don't speak as they do up there."

"North, South," she shrugged. "It's all one. I speak as they do wherever I've been last, until I come to a new place."

And always lies, he thought; never the truth.

"I came to Philadelphia. An old woman took me in for a while, an old witch. She found me ready to drop on the cobbles. I thought she was kind at first, but she wasn't. After she'd fed and rested me for a few days, she put me into the clothes of a younger child—I was small, you see—and took me with her to shop in the stores. She said 'Watch me,' and showed me how to filch things from the counters without being detected. I ran away from her too, finally."

"But not without having done it yourself, first." He watched her closely to see if she'd labor with the answer.

She didn't stop for breath. "Not without having done it myself, first. She would only give me food when I had."

"And then what happened?"

"I worked a little, as a scrub girl, a slavey; I worked in a bakery kitchen, helping to make the rolls; I even worked as a laundress' helper. I was homeless more often than I had a place to sleep." She averted her head for a moment, so that her neck drew into a taut line. "Mostly, I can no longer remember those days. What's more, I don't want to."

She probably sold herself on the streets, he thought, and his heart sickened at the suggestion, as though she were in actuality someone to cherish.

With an almost uncanny clairvoyance, she said just then: "There was one way I could have got along, but I wouldn't take it."

Lies, he vowed, lies; but his heart sang wildly.

"I ran in horror from a woman one night who had coaxed me into stopping in her house for a cup of tea."

"Admirable," he said drily.

"Oh, don't give me credit for goodness," she said, with a sudden little flare of candor. "Give me credit for perversity, rather. I hated every human being in the world, at times, in those days, for what I was going through; man, woman, and child. I would give no one what they wanted of me, because no one would give me what I wanted of them."

He looked downward mutely, trapped at last into credulity, however brief; this time even of the mind as well as the heart.

"Well, I'd best be brief. It's what happened on the river you want to know of, mainly. I fell in with a troupe of traveling actors, joined up with them. They didn't even play in regular theatres. They had no money to afford them. They went about and pitched tents. And from there I fell in with a man who was a professional gambler on the river boats. The girl who had been his partner before then had quitted him to marry a plantation owner—or so he told me—and he was looking for someone to take her place. He offered me a share of his profits, if I would join with him." She waved her hand. "And it was but a different form of acting, after all. With quarters preferable to the ones I'd been used to." She stopped.

"He was the one," she told him.

"What was his name, what was he called?" he said with a sudden access of interest.

"What does it matter? His name was false, like mine was. On every trip it changed. It had to, as a precaution. Once it was Mc-Lamin. Once it was Rideau. I doubt that I ever knew his real one, in all the time we were together. I doubt that he did himself, any more. He's gone now. Don't ask me to remember."

She's trying to protect him, he thought. "You must have called him something."

She gave a smile of sour reminiscence. " 'Brother dear.' So that others could hear me. That was part of my role. We traveled as brother and sister. I insisted on that. We each had our own cabin."

"And he agreed." It wasn't a question, it was a statement of disbelief.

"At first he objected. His former partner, it seems—well, that's neither here nor there. I pointed out to him that it was better even for his own purposes that way, and when I had made him see that, he agreed readily enough. Business came first with him, always. He had a sweetheart in every river town, he could forego one more. You see, I acted as the—attraction, the magnet, for him. My part was to drop my handkerchief on the deck, or collide with someone in a narrow passageway, or even lose my bearings and have to seek directions of someone. There is no harm in gentlemen striking up a respectful acquaintance with a man's unmarried sister. Whereas had I been thought his wife—or something else—they would have been deterred. Then, as propriety dictated, I would introduce my brother to them at the earliest opportunity. And the game would take place soon afterward."

"You played?"

"Never. Only a shameless hussy would play cards with men."

"You were present, though."

"I replenished their drinks. Flirted a little, to keep them in good humor. I sided with them against my own brother when there was a dispute."

"You signalled."

Her shoulders tipped slightly, in philosophic resignation. "That's what I was there for."

His arms were folded, in the attitude of one passing grim judgment—or rather having already irrevocably passed it—whom none of the pleas, the importunities, of the suppliant could any longer sway. He tapped his fingers restlessly against the sides of his own arms.

"And what of Julia? The other Julia, the actual one?"

"I've come to that now," she murmured acquiescently. She drew deep breath to see her through the cumulative part of her recital. "We used to go down about once a month, never more often. It wouldn't have been prudent. Stop a while, and then go up again. We left St. Louis the eighteenth of May the last time, on the *City of New Orleans.*"

"As she did."

She nodded. "The first night out something went wrong. He met his match at last. I don't know how it came about. It could not have been sheer luck on the prospect's part, for he had too many sure ways of curing that. It must have been that he'd finally come across someone who had even better tricks than his own up his sleeve. I couldn't see the man's cards; he seemed to play from memory, keeping them turned inward to one another face to face. And all my messages to show the suits, by fondling necklace, bracelet, earring, finger ring, were worthless, I couldn't send them. The game kept on for half the night, and my partner lost steadily, until at last he had nothing left to play with any longer. And since, in these games, the players were always travelers and strangers to one another, nothing but actual money was ever used, so the loss was real."

"The cheaters cheated," he commented.

"But long before that, hours earlier, the man had already asked me to leave the two of them to themselves. Pointedly, but in such a polite way that there was nothing I could do but obey, or risk bringing to the point of open accusation the certainty that it was obvious he already felt about me. He pretended he was unused to playing in the presence of ladies, and wished to remove his coat and waistcoat, and the instant permission I gave him to do so, he rejected, so I had to go. My partner tried to forbid it by every urgent signal at his command, but there was no further use in my remaining there, so I went. We'd fallen into our own trap, I'm afraid.

"Loitering on deck, beside the rail, a woman, unaccompanied like myself, presently stopped beside me and struck up a conversation. I was not used to chatting with other women, there was no meat in it for my purpose, so at first I gave her only half an ear.

"She was a fool. Within the space of minutes she was telling me all her business, unsolicited. Who she was, where she was bound, what her purpose in going there was. She was too trustful, she had no experience of the outside world. Especially the world of the river boats, and the people you meet on them.

"I tried to shake her off at first, but without succeeding. She attached herself to me, followed me around. It was as though she were starving for a confidante, had to have someone to pour out her heart to, she was brimming so full of romantic anticipations. She gave me your name, and, stopping by a lighted doorway, insisted on taking out and showing me the picture you had sent her, and even reading passages from the last letter or two you had sent her, as though they were Holy Gospel.

"At last, just when I was beginning to feel I could bear no more of it without revealing my true feelings by a burst of temper that would have startled her into silence once and for all, she discovered the—for her—lateness of the hour and fled in the direction of her own cabin like a tardy child, turning all the way to wave back at me, she was so taken by me.

"We had a bitter quarrel later that night, he and I. He accused me of neglecting our 'business.' Unwisely, in self-defense, I told him about her. That she was on her way, sight unseen, to marry a man worth one hundred thousand dollars, who—"

He straightened alertly. "How could she know that?" he said sharply. "I only told the 'you' that was supposed to be she after you'd once arrived and were standing on the dock beside me."

She laughed humorlessly. "She'd investigated, long before she'd ever left St. Louis. I may have fooled you in the greater way, but she fooled you just as surely in the lesser."

He held silent for a long moment, almost as if finding in this new revelation of feminine guile some amelioration of her own.

Presently, unurged, as if gauging to a nicety the length of time he should be allowed for contemplation, of what she knew him to be contemplating, she proceeded.

"I saw him look at me when I told him that. He broke off our quarrel then and there, and left me, and paced the deck for a while. I can only tell you what happened as it happened. I did not know then its meaning as it was happening. Looking back, I can give it meaning now. I couldn't have then. You must believe me. You must, Lou."

She clasped her hands, and brought them close before his face, and wrung them supplicatingly.

"I must? By what compulsion?"

"This is the truth I'm telling tonight. Every word the truth, if never before, if never again."

If never before, if never again, he caught himself gullibly repeating after her, unheard in his own mind.

"I went out again to find him, to ask him if he intended to recoup his losses any more that night; if he'd have any further need of me, or if I could shut my door and go to sleep. I found him motionless, in deep thought, against the rail. The moon was down and the river was getting dark. We were still coasting the lower Missouri shore, I think we were to clear it before dawn. I scarcely knew him for sure until I was at his elbow, he was so indistinct in the gloom.

"He said to me in a whisper, 'Knock on her door and invite her out for a walk on deck with you.'

"I said, 'But it's late, she may have already retired. She's unused to hours such as we keep.'

"'Do as I tell you!' he ordered me fiercely. 'Or I'll put some compliance into you with my fists. Find some way of bringing her out here, you'll know how. Tell her you are lonely and want company. Or tell her there are some lights coming presently on the shore that are not to be missed, that she must see. If she is as innocent as you say, any excuse should do.'

"And he gave me a push that nearly sent me face down to the deck boards."

"You went?"

"I went. What could I do? Why should I suffer for a stranger? What stranger had ever suffered for me?"

He didn't answer that.

"I went to her door and I knocked, and when she called out, startled, to ask who it was, I remember answering in honeyed tones to reassure her, 'It's your new little friend, Miss Charlotte.'"

"You had that name upon the boat?"

"For that voyage. She opened at once, so great was her trust in me. She had not yet removed her clothes, but told me she had been about to do so. If only she already had!"

"You're merciful now in retrospect," he let her know. "You weren't at the time."

She didn't flinch. "I delivered my invitation. I complained of a headache, and refusing all the remedies she instantly put herself out to offer me, said I preferred to let the fresh air cure it, and would she walk with me a while, because of the lateness of the hour.

"I remember I was strangely uneasy, as to what his intentions might be—oh, I knew he boded her no good, but I didn't dare allow myself to believe he meant her any actual bodily harm; some intricate blackmailing scheme, at most, I thought, to be brought to bear on her later, once she was married to you—and even as I spoke, I kept hoping she would refuse me, and I could give him that for an excuse. But she seemed to have become inordinately fond of me. Before I could ask her twice she had already accepted, her face all alight with pleasure at my seeking her out. She hurriedly put a shawl about her for warmth, and closed the door after her, and came away with me."

His interest had been trapped in spite of himself. "You are telling the truth, Julia? You are telling the truth?" he said with bated breath.

"Bonny," she murmured deprecatingly.

"You are telling the truth? You did not know, actually, what the intent was?"

"Why do I kneel here at your feet like this? Why are there tears of regret in my eyes? Look at them well. What shall I say to you, what shall I do? Shall I take an oath on it? Fetch a Bible. Open it before me. Hold its pages to my heart as I speak."

He had never seen her cry before. He wondered if she ever had. She cried as one unused to crying, who leashes it, stifles it, not knowing what it is, rather than one who has many times before made use of it for her own ends, and hence knows it is an advantage and lets it flow untrammelled, even abets it.

He waved aside the suggestion that his own skepticism had produced. "And then? And then?" he pressed her.

"We walked the full length of the deck three times, in harmonious intimacy, as women will together." She stopped for a moment.

"What is it?"

"Something I just remembered. And wish I had not. *Her arm was about my waist* as we walked. Mine was not about hers, at least, but hers was about me. She chattered again about you, endlessly about you. It was always you, only you."

She drew a breath, as if again feeling the tension of that night, that promenade upon the lonely, darkened deck.

"Nothing happened. He did not accost us. At every shadow I had been ready to stifle a scream, but none of them was he. At last

I had no further excuse to keep her out there with me. She asked me how my headache was, and I said it was gone. And she couldn't have dreamed the relief with which I told her so.

"I took her back to her door. She turned to me a moment, I remember, and even kissed my hand in fond good night, she was so taken with me. She said 'I'm so glad we've met, Charlotte. I've never really had a woman friend of my very own. You must come and see me and my—' and then she faltered prettily—'my new husband, visit with us, as soon as we're settled. I shall want new friends badly in my new life.' And then she opened her door and went in. Unharmed, untouched. I even heard her bolt it fast after her on the inside.

"And that was the last I ever saw of her."

She came to a full halt, as if knowing this was the time for it, to gain fullest the effect she wished to achieve.

"No more than that you participated?" he said slowly.

"No more than that I participated. No more than that I took part in it, whatever it was.

"I have thought of it since then," she resumed presently. "I see now what it was, what it must have been. I didn't at the time, or I would never have left her. I had thought he meant to accost her on the deck in some way; brutalize her into some predicament from which she could only extricate herself later by payment of money, or even steal some memento from her to be redeemed later in the same way, to preserve your trust in her and her own good name. It even occurred to me, as I made my way back to my own cabin alone, he might have changed his mind entirely, discarded the whole intention, whatever it had been. I'd known him to do that before, after a scheme was already under way, and without notifying me until afterward."

She shook her head sombrely. "No, he hadn't.

"He must have inserted himself in the cabin while she was gone from it with me, and lain in wait there on the inside. He wanted the opportunity, that was why he had me stroll the deck with her."

"But later—he never told you in so many words what happened in there, inside that cabin of hers?"

She shook her head firmly. "He never told me in so many words. Nor could I draw it out of him. He had no moments of confidence, no moments of weakness, especially not with women. The way in which he told me of it was not meant to be believed; I knew that, and he knew that as well. It was just a catch phrase, to gloss over a thing, to have done with it as quickly as possible. And yet that is the only way in which he would tell me of it, from first to last. And I must be content with that, that was all I got."

"And what was that?"

"This is the way in which he told me of it, word for word. He came and knocked surreptitiously upon my door, and woke me, about an hour before daylight, when the whole boat was still asleep. He was fully dressed, but whether newly so or still from the night before, I don't know. He had a single scratch on his forehead, over the eyebrow. A very small one, not more than a half-inch mark. And that was all.

"He came in, closed the door carefully, and said to me very business-like and terse in manner, 'Get dressed, I want you for something. Your lady friend of last night had an accident awhile ago and fell from the boat in the dark. She never came up again.' And then he flung my various things at me, stockings and such, one by one, to hurry me along. That was all he told me, then or ever again, that she'd had an accident and fallen from the boat in the dark."

"But you knew?"

"How could I help but know? I told him I knew. He even so much as agreed I might know, admitted I might know. But his answer for that was 'What are you going to do about it?'

"I told him that wasn't in our bargain. 'Card-games are one thing, this another.'

"He carefully took off his ring first, so it wouldn't mar my skin, and he gave me the back of his hand several times, until my head swam, and, as he put it, 'it had taken a little of the religion out of me.' He threatened me. He said if I accused him, he would accuse me in turn. That we would both be jailed for it alike. And I had been seen with her, and he hadn't. That it would serve neither one of us any good, and undo the two of us alike. He also threatened, finally, that he would kill me himself if necessary, as the quickest way of stopping my mouth, if I tried to get anyone's ear.

"Then when he saw he had me sufficiently cowed and intimidated to listen, he reasoned with me. 'She's gone now beyond recall,' he pointed out, 'nothing you can do will bring her back up over the side, and there's a hundred thousand dollars waiting for you when you step off this boat in New Orleans tomorrow.'

"He swung back the door for me, and I adjusted my clothing, and followed him out.

"He took my baggage, the little I had, into his cabin and blended it with his. And hers we removed, between us, from her cabin to mine, to take the place of my own. Not forgetting that caged bird of hers. He took from his pocket her letters from you, and the photograph you had sent her, and I put them in my own pocketbook. And then we bided our time and waited.

"In the confusion of docking and disembarking she was not missed. No passenger remembered her, they were all busy with their own concerns. And each baggage-handler, if he noted her empty cabin at all, must have thought some other baggage-handler had taken charge of her and her belongings. We left the boat separately, he at the very beginning, I almost at the last. And that was not noticed either.

"I saw you standing there, and knew you from your photograph, and when at last the dock had cleared, I approached and stopped there by you. And there's the story, Lou."

She stopped, and settled back upon her own upturned heels, and her hands fell lifeless to her lap, as if incapable of further gesture. She seemed to wait thus, inert, deflated, for the verdict, for his judgment to be passed upon her. Everything about her sloped downward, shoulders, head, and even the curve of her back; only one thing turned upward: her eyes, fixed beseechingly upon his graven face.

"Not quite," he said. "Not quite. And what of What's-his-name? What was the further plan?"

"He said he would send word to me when enough time had passed. And when I heard from him, I was to—"

"Do as you did."

She shook her head determinedly. "Not as I did. As it seemed to you I did, maybe. I met him once for a few moments, in secret, when I was out on one of my shopping tours without you—that part was by prearrangement—and I told him there was no need for him to count on me any longer, he must abandon the scheme, I could no longer prevail on myself to carry it out."

"Why did you have a change of heart?"

"Why must you be told that now?"

"Why shouldn't I be?"

"It would be breath wasted. It wouldn't be believed."

"Let me be the judge."

"Very well then, if you must be told," she said almost defiantly. "I told him I could no longer contemplate doing what it had been intended for me to do. I told him I'd fallen in love with my own husband."

It was like a rainbow suddenly glistening in all its striped glory across dismal gray skies. He told himself it was an illusion, just as surely as its counterpart, the actual rainbow, is an illusion in Nature. But it wouldn't dim, it wouldn't waver; there it beamed, the sign of hope, the sign heralding sunshine to come.

She had gone on without interruption, but the grateful shock of that previous remark, still flooding over him in benign warmth, had caused him to lose the sense of a part of her words.

"—laughed and said I no more knew what love was than the man in the moon. Then he turned vengeful and told me I was lying and simply trying to keep the whole of the stake for myself alone."

I'd fallen in love, kept going through his head, dimming the sound of her voice. It was like a counterpoint that intrudes upon the basic melody and all but effaces it.

"I tried to buy him off. I said he could have the money, all I could lay my hands on, almost as much as he might have expected in the first place, if he would only quit New Orleans, let me be. Yes, I offered to *rob* my own husband, endanger the very thing I was trying to hold onto, if he would only let me be, let me stay as I was, happy for the first time in my life."

Happy for the first time in her life, the paean swelled through his mind. She was really happy with me.

"If he would only have accepted the bribe, I had in mind some desperate excuse to you—that my purse had been snatched in a crowd, that I'd dropped the money in the street, after drawing it from the bank; that my 'sister' had suddenly fallen ill and was without means, and I'd sent it to her in St. Louis—oh, anything, anything at all, no matter how thin, how paltry, so long as it was less discreditable than the reality. Yes, I would have risked your displeasure, your disapproval, even worse than that, your very real suspicion, if only I was allowed to keep you for myself as I wanted to, to go on with you."

To go on with you. He could remember the warmth of her kisses now, the unbridled gaiety of her smiles. What actress could have played such a part, morning, noon, and night? Even actresses play but an hour or two of an evening, have a respite the rest of the time. It must have been sincere reality. He could remember the look in her eyes when he took leave of her that last day; a sort of lingering, reluctant melancholy. (But had it been there then, or was he putting it in now?)

"That wouldn't satisfy him, wouldn't do. He wanted *all* of it, not part. And, I suppose, there was truly no solution. No matter how large a sum I would have given him, he would still have thought I was keeping far more than that myself. He trusted no one—I heard it said of him, in a quarrel once—not even himself.

"Taking me at my word, that I loved you, he discovered he had a more powerful threat to hold over me now. And no sooner had he discovered it, than he brought it into play. That he would reveal my imposture to you himself, anonymously, in a letter, if I refused to carry out our deal. He wouldn't have his money, maybe, but neither should I have what I wanted. We'd both be fugitives alike, and back where we started from. 'And if you intercept my letter,' he warned, 'that won't help you any. I'll go to him myself and make the accusation to his face. Let him know you're not only not who you claimed, but were my sweetheart all those years to boot.' Which wasn't true," she added rather rapidly in an aside. "'We'll see how long he'll keep you with him then.'

"And as I left him that day," she went on. "I knew it was no use, no matter what I did. I knew I was surely going to lose you, one way or another.

"I passed a sleepless night. The letter came, all right. I'd known it would. He was as good as his word, in all things like that; and only in things like that. I seized it. I was waiting there by the door when the post came. I tore it open and read it. I can still remember how it went. 'The woman you have there in your house with you is not the woman you take her to be, but someone of another name, and another man's sweetheart as well. I am that man, and so I know what I am saying. Keep a close watch upon your money, Mr. Durand. If you disbelieve me, watch her face closely when you say to her without warning, "Bonny, come here to me," and see how it pales.' And it was signed, 'A friend.'

"I destroyed it, but I knew the postponement I'd gained was only for a day or two. He'd send another. Or he'd come himself. Or he'd take me unaware sometime when I was out alone, and I'd be found lying there with a knife-hilt in my side. I knew him well; he never forgave anyone who crossed him." She tried to smile, and failed in the attempt. "My doll house had come tumbling down all about my ears.

"So I made my decision, and I fled."

"To him."

"No," she said dully, almost as if this detail were a matter of indifference, now, this long after. "I took the money, yes. But I fled from him just as surely as I deserted you. That small satisfaction was all I had out of it: he hadn't gained his way. The rest was ashes. All my happiness lay behind me. I remember thinking at the time, we formed a triangle, we three, a strange one. You were love, and he was death—and I was the mid-point between the two.

"I fled as far away as I could. I took the northbound boat and kept from sight until it had left New Orleans an hour behind. I went to Memphis first, and then to Louisville, and at last to Cincinnati, and stayed there hidden for some time. I was in fear for my life for a while. I knew he would have surely killed me had he found me. And then one day, in Cincy, I heard a report from someone who had once known us both slightly when we were together, that he had lost his life in a shooting affray in a gaming house in Cairo. So the danger was past. But it was too late by that time to undo what had been done. I couldn't return to you any more."

And the look she gave him was of a poignancy that would have melted stone.

"I made my way back South again, now that it was safe to do so, and only a few weeks ago met this Colonel Worth, and now I'm as you find me. And that's my story, Lou."

She waited, and the silence, now that she was through speaking, seemed to prolong itself into eternity.

He was looking at her steadfastly, but uttered not a word. But behind that calm, reflective, judicious front he maintained so stoically, there was an unguessed turmoil, raging, a chaos, of credulity and disbelief, accusation and refutation, pro and con, to and fro, and around and around and around like a whirlpool.

She took your money, none the less; why, if she "loved" you so? She was about to face the world alone for years to come, she knew only too well how hard it is for a woman alone to get along in the world, she'd had that lesson from before. Can you blame her?

How do you know she didn't cheat the two of you alike; that what it was, was nothing more than what he accused her of, of running off and keeping the entire booty for herself, without dividing it with him? A double betrayal, instead of a single.

At least she is innocent of Julia's death, you heard that. How do you know even that? The living, the survivor, is here to tell *her* side of the tale to you, but the dead, the victim, is not here to tell you hers. It might be a different story.

You loved her then, you do not question yourself on that. Why then do you doubt her when she says she loved you then? Is she not as capable of love as you? And who are you to say who is to feel love, and who is not? Love is like a magnet, that attracts its like. She must have loved you, for your love to be drawn to her. Just as you must have loved her—and you know you did—for her love to be drawn to you. Without one love, there cannot be another. There must be love on both sides, for the current to complete itself.

"Aren't you going to say something to me, Lou?"

"What is there to say?"

"I can't tell you that. It must come from you."

"Must it?" he said drily. "And if there is nothing there to give you, no answer?"

"Nothing, Lou?" Her voice took on a singsong timbre. "Nothing?" It became a lulling incantation. "Not even a word?" Her face rose subtly nearer to his. "Not even—this much?" He had seen pictures, once, somewhere, of India, of cobras rising from their huddles to the charmer's tune. And like one of those, so sleekly, so unguessably, she had crept upward upon him before he knew it; but this was the serpent charming the master, not the master the serpent. "Not even—this?"

Suddenly he was caught fast, entwined with her as with some treacherous tropic plant. Lips of fire were fused with his. He seemed to breathe flame, draw it down his windpipe into his breast, where the dry tinder of his loneliness, of his long lack of her, was kindled by it into raging flame, that pyred upward, sending back her kiss with insane fury.

He struggled to his feet, and she rose with him, they were so interlocked. He flung her off with all the violence he would have used against another man in full-bodied combat; it was needed, nothing less would have torn her off.

She staggered, toppled, fell down prone, one arm alone, thrust out behind her, keeping one shoulder and her head upward a little from the floor.

And lying there, all rumpled and abased, yet somehow she had on her face the glint of victory, on her lips a secretive smile of triumph. As though she knew who had won the contest, who had lost. She lolled there at her ease, too sure of herself even to take the trouble to rise. It was he who wallowed, from chair back to chair back, stifling, blinded, like something maimed; his ears pounding to his own blood, clawing at his collar, as if the ghosts of her arms were still there, strangling him.

He stood over her at last, clenched hand upraised above his head, as if in threat to strike her down a second time should she try to rise. "Get yourself ready!" he roared at her. "Get your things! Not that nor anything else will change it! I'm taking you back to New Orleans!"

She sidled away from him a little along the floor, as if to put herself beyond his reach, though her smirk denied her fear; then gathered herself together, rose with an innate grace that nothing could take from her, not even such violent downfall.

She seemed humbled, docile to his bidding, seemed resigned; all but that knowing smile, that gave it the lie. She made no further importunity. She swept back her hair, a lock of which had tumbled forward with her fall. Her shoulders hinted at a shrug. Her hands gave an empty slap at her sides, recoiled again, as if in fatalistic acceptance.

He turned his back on her abruptly, as he saw her hands go to the fastenings at the side of her waist, already partly sundered.

"I'll wait out here in this little entryway," he said tautly, and strode for it.

"Do so," she agreed ironically. "It *is* some time now that we have been apart."

He sat down on a little backless wall-bench that lined the place, just within the outer apartment door.

She came slowly over after him and slowly swung the second door around, the one between them, leaving it just short of closure.

"My windows are on the second floor," she reassured him, still with that overtone of irony. "And there is no ladder outside them. I am not likely to try to escape."

He bowed his head suddenly, as sharply as if his neck had fractured, and pressed his two clenched hands tight against his forehead, through the center of which a vein stood out like whipcord, pulsing and throbbing with a congestion of love battling hate and hate battling love, that he alone could have told was going on, so still he crouched.

So they remained, on opposite sides of a door that was not closed. The victor and the vanquished. But on which side was which?

A drawer ticked open, scraped closed again, behind the door. A whiff of fresh essence drifted out and found him, as if skimmed off the top of a field of the first flowers of spring. The light peering through from the other side dimmed somewhat, as if one or more of its contributing agents had been eliminated.

Suddenly he turned his head, finding the door had already been standing open a second or two before his discovery of it. She was standing there in the inviting new breadth of its opening, one arm to door, one arm to frame. The foaming laces that cascaded down her were transparent as haze against the light bearing directly on her from the room at her back. Her silhouette was that of a biped.

Her eyes were dreamy-lidded, her half-smile a recaptured memory of forgotten things.

"Come in, Lou," she murmured indulgently, as if to a stubborn little boy who has put himself beyond the pale. "Put out the light there by you and come into your wife's room."

— 39 —

A sound at the door awoke Durand. It was a delicate sort of tapping, a coaxing pit-pat, as if with one fingernail.

As his eyes opened he found himself in a room he had difficulty recalling from the night before. The cooling silvery-green of low-burning night lights was no longer there. Ladders of fuming Gulf Coast sunlight came slanting through the slits of the blinds, and formed a pattern of stripes across the bed and across the floor. And above this, there was a reflected brightness, as if everything had been newly whitewashed; a gleaming transparency.

It was simply that it was day in a place that he had last seen when it was night.

He thought he was alone at first. He backed a hand to his drugged eyes, to keep out some of the overacute brilliancy. "Where am I?"

Then he saw her. Her cloverleaf mouth smiled back at him, indirectly, via the surface of the mirror she sat before. Her hand sought her bosom, and she let it linger there a moment, one finger pointing upward, one inward as if toward her heart. "With me," she answered. "Where you belong."

There was something fragilely charming, he thought, in the evanescent little gesture while it lasted. And he watched it wistfully and hated to see it end, the hand drop back as it had been. It had been so unstudied. With me; finger unconsciously to her heart.

The stuttering little tap came again. There was something coy about it that irritated him. He turned his head and frowned over that way. "Who's that?" he asked sternly, but of her, not the door.

She shaped her mouth to a soundless symbol of laughter; then she stilled it further, though it hadn't come at all, by spoking her fingers over it, fanwise. "A suitor, I'm afraid. The colonel. I know him by his tap."

Durand, his face growing blacker by the minute, was at the bedside now, struggling into trousers with a sort of cavorting hop, to and fro.

The tapping had accosted them a third time.

He cut his thumb slashingly backhand toward the door, in pantomime to have her answer it temporizingly while he got ready.

"Yes?" she said sweetly.

"It's Harry, my dear," came through the door. "Good morning. Am I too early."

"No, too late," growled Durand surlily. "I'll attend to 'Harry, my dear' in a moment!" he vowed to her in an undertone.

She was in stitches by now, head prone on the dressing table, hands clasped across the back of her neck, palpitating with smothered laughter.

"In a minute," she said half-strangled.

"Don't hurry yourself, my dear," the cooing answer came back. "You know I'll wait all morning for you, if necessary. To wait outside your door for you to come out is the pleasantest thing I know of. There is only one thing pleasanter, and that would be—"

The door sliced back and he found himself confronted by Durand, feet unshod, hair awry, and in nothing but trousers and undershirt.

To make it worse, his face had been bearing down close against the door, to make himself the better heard. He found his nose almost pressed into Durand's coarse-spun barley-colored underwear, at about the height of Durand's chest.

His head went up a notch at a time, like something worked on a pulley, until it was level with Durand's own. And for each notch he had a strangulated exclamation, like a winded grunt. Followed by a convulsive swallowing. "Unh—? Anh—? Unh—?"

"Well, sir?" Durand rapped out.

Worth's hand executed helpless curlycues, little corkscrew waves, trying to point behind Durand but unable to do so.

"You're—in *there?* You're—not *dressed?*"

"Will you kindly mind your business, sir?" Durand said sternly.

The colonel raised both arms now overhead, fists clenched, in some sort of approaching denunciation. Then they faltered, froze that way, finally crumbled. His eyes were suddenly fixed on Durand's right shoulder. They dilated until they threatened to pop from his head.

Durand could feel her arm glide caressingly downward over his shoulder, and then her hand tipped up to fondle his chin, while she herself remained out of sight behind him. He looked down to where Worth was staring at it, and it was the one with the wedding band, their old wedding band, on it.

It rose, was stroking and petting Durand's cheek now, letting the puffy gold circlet flash and wink conspicuously. It gave the slack of his cheek a fond little pinch, then spread the two fingers that had just executed it wide apart, in what might have been construed as a jaunty salute.

"I—I—I didn't know!" Worth managed to gasp out asthmatically, as if with his last breath.

"You do now, sir!" Durand said severely. "And what brings you to my wife's door, may I ask?"

The colonel was backing away along the passage now, brushing the wall now at this side, now at that, but incapable apparently of turning around once and for all and tearing his eyes off the hypnotic spectacle of Durand and the affectionate straying hand.

"I—I beg your pardon!" he succeeded in panting at last, from a safe distance.

"I beg yours!" Durand rejoined with grim inflexibility.

The colonel turned at last and fled, or rather wallowed drunkenly, away.

The detached hand suddenly went up in air, bent its fingers inward, and flipped them once or twice.

"Ta ta," her voice called out gaily, "lovey mine!"

— 40 —

ARMS CLOSE-KNIT about one another's waists, leaning almost avidly from the open window of her room, shimmering in unison with laughter, they watched the streaming debacle of the colonel's luggage, poured forth from under the veranda shed, followed by its owner's hurried, trotting departure. The colonel could not seem to climb into his waiting coach quickly enough and be gone from this scene of ego-shrivelling discomfiture with enough haste; he all but hopped in on one leg, like an ungainly crane in waddling earthbound flight, and the whole buggy rocked with his plunge.

It was not his own private conscience that spurred him on, conjecturably, it was public ridicule. The story had obviously spread like wildfire about the establishment, in the inexplicable way of such things at seashore resorts, though neither Durand nor she had breathed a word to living soul. It was as though the tale were water and the hotel a sponge; it was as though the keyholes themselves had found tongues for their perpendicular slitted mouths and whispered it. Strollers entering or leaving, at this moment, as he was going, stopped and turned to stare at the spectacle he made in flight, with either outright smiles visible upon their faces, or tactfully sheltering hands to mouths, which betrayed the fact that there were smiles beneath them to conceal.

The colonel fled, within a sheltering turret of his own massed luggage piled high on the seat, the plumage of his male pride as badly frizzled as feathers in a flame. The yellow wheel spokes sluiced into solidified disks, a spurt of dust haze arose, the roadway was empty, the colonel was gone.

She had even wanted to wave, this time with her handkerchief, as she had waved at the door an hour or so before, but Durand, some remnants of masculine fellow-feeling stirring in him, held her hand back, quenched the gesture, though laughing all the same. They turned from the window, still chuckling, arms still tight about one another in new-found possession. They had been cruel just now, though they hadn't intended it, their only thought had been their own amusement. Yet what is cruelty but the giving of pain in the taking of pleasure?

"Oh, dear!" she exhaled, breathless. She parted from him, drooped exhausted over the back of a chair. "That man. He wasn't cut out to be a romantic lover. Yet always that is the type that tries hardest to play the role. I wonder why?"

"Am I?" he asked her, curious to hear what she would say.

She turned her eyes toward him, lidded them inexpressibly. "Oh, Louis," she said in bated whisper. "Can you ask *me* that? You're the perfect example. With the blushes of a boy—look at you now. The arms of a tiger. And a heart as easily broken as a woman's."

The tiger part was the only one that appealed to him; he decided the other two were wholly her own imaginings.

He exercised them once again, briefly but heartily, as any man would after such prompting.

"We'll have to go soon ourselves," he reminded her presently.

"Why?" she asked, as if willing enough but failing quite to understand the need to do so.

Then thinking she had found the answer for herself, gave it to him without waiting. "Oh, because of what's happened. Yes, it's true; I was seen with him constantly all these past—"

"No," he said, "that isn't what I meant. It's that—business on the boat. I told you last night, I went to a private investigator in St. Louis, and so far as I know he's still engaged upon it."

"There's no warrant out, is there?"

"No, but I think it's better for us to stay out of his way. I'd rather not have him accost us, or even learn where we are to be found."

"He has no police power, has he?" she asked with quick, brittle interest.

"Not so far as I know. I don't know what he can do or can't do, and I've no wish to find out. The police in New Orleans told me you were immune, but that was at that time, before he took hand in it. Your immunity may expire from one minute to the next, when least we expect it, while he's still around and about. It's safer for us not to place ourselves too close at hand, under their thumbs. Don't you see, we can't go back to New Orleans now."

"No," she agreed without emotion, "we can't."

"And it's better for us not to linger here too long either. Word travels quickly. You cannot help drawing the admiration of all eyes wherever you appear. You're no drab wallflower. Besides, my own presence here is well known; I made no secret I was coming here, and they'd know where to reach me—"

"Will you—be able to?"

He knew what she meant.

"I have enough for now. And I can get in touch with Jardine, if need should arise."

She raised her hand and snapped her fingers close before her face. "Very well, we'll go," she said gaily. "We'll be on our way before the sun goes down. Where shall it be? You name it."

He pocketed one hand, spread the other palm up. "How about one of the northern cities? They're large, they can swallow us whole, we'll never be noticed. Baltimore, Philadelphia, even New York—" He saw her chew the corner of her underlip in sudden distaste.

"Not the North," she said, with a distant look in her eyes. "It's cold and gray and ugly, and it snows—"

He wondered what Damoclean sword of retribution, from out of the past, hung over her suspended there.

"We'll stay down here, then," he said, without hesitation. "It's closer to them, and we'll have to keep moving about more often. But I want to please you. What about Mobile or Birmingham, then; those are large enough towns to lose ourselves in."

She made her choice with a pert little nod. "Mobile for now. I'll begin to pack at once."

She stopped again in a moment, holding some article in her hands, and drew close to him once more. "How different this is from last night. Do you remember? Then it was an arrest. Now it is a honeymoon."

"The beginning of a new life. Everything new. New plans, new hopes, new dreams. A new destination. A new you. A new I."

She crept into his arms, looked up at him, her very soul in her eyes. "Do you forgive? Do you take me back?"

"I never met you before last night. There *is* no past. This is our real wedding day."

The "tiger-arms" showed their stripes, went around her once more.

"My Lou," she sobbed ecstatically.

"My Jul—"

"Careful, there," she warned, with finger upright to his lips.

"My Bonny."

— 41 —

MOBILE, THEN.

They went to the finest hotel there, and like the bride and groom they were in everything but count of time, they took its finest suite, its bridal suite. Chamber and sitting room, height of luxury, lace curtains over the windows, maroon drapes, Turkish carpeting thick on the floors, and even that seldom-met-with innovation, a private bath of their own that no one else had access to, complete with clawlegged tub enamelled in light green.

Bellhops danced attendance on them from morning to night, and all eyes were on them every time they came and went through the public rooms below. The petite blonde, always so dainty, so exquisitely dressed, with the tall dark man beside her, eyes for no one else. "That romantic pair from—" Nobody knew just where, but everybody knew who was meant.

More than one sigh of benevolent regret swept after them.

"I declare, it makes me feel a little younger just to look at them."

"It makes *me* feel a little sad. Because we all know that it cain't last. They're bound to lose it 'fore long."

"But they've had it."

"Yes, they've had it."

Every sprightly supper resort in town knew them, every gay and brightly lighted gathering place, every theatre, public ball, entertainment, minstrelsy. Every time the violins played, somewhere, anywhere, she was in his arms there, turning in the endless, fevered spirals of the waltz. Every time the moon was full, she was in his arms there, somewhere, in a halted carriage, heads close together, sweetness of magnolia all around, gazing up at it with dreamy, wondering eyes.

But they were right, the musers and the sighers and the cast-asides in the hotel lobby. It lasts such a short time. It comes but once, and goes, and then it never comes again. Even to the upright, to the blessed, it never comes again. And how much less likely, to the hunted and the doomed.

But this was their moment of it now, this was their time for it, their share: Durand and his Julia. (Julia, for love's first thought is its lasting one, love's first name for itself, is its true one.) The sunburst of their happiness. The brief blaze of their noon.

Mobile, then, in the flood tide of their romance; and all was rapture, all was love.

— 42 —

WITHOUT RAISING her eyes, she smiled covertly, showing she was well aware that his gaze was lingering on her, there in the little sitting room outside their bedroom. Studying her like an elusive lesson; a lesson that seems simple enough at first glance, but is never to be fully learned, though the student goes back to it again and again.

"What are you thinking?" she teased, keeping her eyes still downcast.

"Of you."

She took that for granted. "I know. But what, of me?"

He sat down beside her, at the foot of the chaise longue, tilted his knee, hugged it, and cast his eyes upon her more speculatively than ever. Shaking his head a little, as if in wonderment himself, that this should be so.

"I used to want what they call a good wife. That was the only kind I ever thought I'd have. A proper little thing who'd sit demurely, working a needle through a hoop, both feet planted on the floor. Head submissively lowered to her task, who'd look up when I spoke and 'Aye' and 'Nay' me. But now I don't. Now I only want a wife like you. With yesterday's leftover dye still on her cheeks. With the tip of her bent knee poked brazenly through her dressing gown. With cigar ashes on the floor about her. Jeering at a man in their most private moments, egging him on, then ridiculing him, rather than swooning limp into his arms." He shook his head, more helplessly than ever. "Bonny, Bonny, what have you done to me? Though I still know you should be like that, like those others are, I don't want anyone like that any more. I've forgotten there are any. I only want you; bad as you are, heartless as you are, exactly as you are, I only want you."

Her tarnished golden laughter welled up, showered down upon the two of them like counterfeit coins.

"Lou, you're so gullible. There aren't two kinds of women; there never were, there never will be. Only one kind of woman, one kind of man— And both of them, alike, not much good." Her laughter had stopped; her face was tired and wise, and there was a little flicker of bitterness, as she said the last.

"Lou," she repeated, "you're so—unaware."

"Are you sure that's the word you had in mind?"

"Innocent," she agreed.

"Innocent?" he parried wryly.

"A woman's innocence is like snow on a hot stove; it's gone at the first touch. But when a man is innocent, he can have had ten wives, and he's as innocent at the end of them all as he was at the beginning. He never learns."

He shivered feverishly. "I know you drive me mad. At least I've learned that much."

She threw herself backward on the couch, her head hanging over so that she was looking behind her toward the ceiling, in a sort of floundering luxuriance. She extended her arms widely upward in a greedy, grasping, ecstatic V. Her voice was a dreamy chant of longing.

"Lou, buy me a new dress. All white satin and Chantilly lace. Lou, buy me a great big emerald for my pinkey. Buy me diamond drops for my ears. Take me out in a carriage to twelve o'clock supper at some lobster palace. I want to look at the chandelier lights through the layers of colored liqueurs in a pousse cafe. I want to feel champagne trickle down my throat while the violins play gypsy music. I want to live, I want to live, I want to live! The time is so short, and I won't get a second turn—"

Then, as her fear of infinity, her mistrust that Providence would look out for her if left to its own blind course—for it was that at bottom, that and nothing else—were caught by him in turn, and he was kindled into a like fear and defiance of their fate, he bent swiftly toward her, his lips found hers, and her litany of despair was stilled.

Until, presently, she sighed: "No, don't take me anywhere— You're here, I'm here— The champagne, the music are right here with us— Everything's here— No need to look elsewhere—"

And her arms dropped, closed over him like the trap they were.

— 43 —

PRESENTLY THEY quitted their suite in the hotel and rented a house. An entire house, for their own. A house with an upstairs and down.

It was at her suggestion. And it was she who engaged the agent, accompanied him to view the several prospects he had to offer, and made the final selection. An "elegant" (that was her word for it) though rather gingerbready affair on one of the quieter residential streets, tree flanked. Then all he had to do was sign the necessary papers, and with but a coaxing smile or two from her, he did so, with the air of a man fondly indulging a child in her latest whim. A whim that, he suspects, tomorrow she will have tired of; but that, while it remains valid, today, he has not the heart to refuse her.

It seemed to fill some long-felt, deep-seated, longing on her part: a house of one's own; to be—more than merely an expression of great wealth—an expression of *legitimate* great wealth; to be the ultimate in stability, in *belonging,* in caste. It was as if her catalogue of values ran thus: jewels and fine clothes, any fly-by-night may have them from her sweetheart; even a lawfully wedded husband, any sweetheart may be made into one if you cared to take the pains; but a house of your own, then indeed you had reached the summit, then indeed you were socially impregnable, then indeed you were a great lady. Or (pitiful parenthesis) as you fondly imagined one to be.

"It's so much grander," she said. She sighed wistfully. "It makes me feel like a really married woman."

He laughed indulgently. "What had you felt like until now, madame?"

"Oh, it is useless to tell this to a man!" she said with a little spurt of playful indignation.

And it was, in truth, for each of them had the instincts of their own kind.

Even when he tried, half-teasingly, and only when the arrangement had already been entered into, to warn her and point out the
disadvantages, she would have none of it.

"But who'll cook for us? A house takes looking after. You're
taking on a great many cares."

She threw up her hands. "Well, then I'll have servants, like
the other ladies who have houses of their own. You'll see; leave
that to me."

A colored woman appeared, and lasted five days. There was
some question of a missing trinket. Then after her stormy discharge and departure, which filled the lower floor with noise for
some fifteen minutes, Bonny came to him presently and admitted
she had unearthed the valuable in a place she had forgotten having
put it.

"Why didn't you search first, and then accuse her afterward?"
he pointed out, as gently as he could. "That is what any other lady,
mistress of her own house, would have done."

"Oh, would she?" She seemed at a loss. "I did not think of that."

"You must not tyrannize over them," he tried to instruct her.
"You must be firm and gentle at the same time. Otherwise you
show that you are not used to having servants of your own."

The second one lasted three days. There was less commotion,
but there were tears this time. On Bonny's part.

"I tried being gentle," she came to him and reported, "and she
paid no heed to any of my orders. I don't seem to know how to
handle them. If I am severe, they walk out. If I am kind, they do
not do their work."

"There is an art to it," he consoled her. "You will acquire it presently."

"No," she said. "There is something about me. They look at me
and sneer. They do not *respect* me. They will take more from another woman, and be docile; they will take nothing from me, and still
be impudent. Is this not my own house? Am I not your wife? What
is it about me?"

He could not answer that, for he saw her with the eyes of

love, and he could not tell what eyes they saw her with, nor see with theirs.

"No," she said in answer to his suggestion, "no more servants. I've had enough of them. Let me do it. I can try, I can manage."

A meal followed that was a complete fiasco. The eggs broke in the water meant to boil them, and a sort of milky stew resulted, neither to be eaten nor to be drunk. The coffee had the pallor of tea without any of its virtues, and on second try became a muddy abomination that filled their mouths with grit. The toast was tinctured with the cologne that she so liberally applied to her hands.

He uttered not a word of reproach. He stood up and discarded his napkin. "Come," he said, "we're going back to the hotel for our meals."

She hastened to get her things, as if overjoyed herself at this solution.

And on their way over he said, "Now aren't you sorry?" with a twinkle in his eye.

But on this point, at least, she was steadfast. "No," she said. "Even if we have to eat elsewhere, at least I still have my own house. I would not change that for anything." And she repeated what she'd said before. "I want to feel like a really married woman. I want to feel like all the rest do. I want to know what it feels like."

She couldn't, it seemed, quite get used to the idea that she was legally married to him, and all this was hers by right and not by conquest.

— 44 —

INCREASINGLY UNCOMFORTABLE, and extremely bored in addition, feeling that all eyes were on him, he paced back and forth in the modiste's anteroom, and at every turn seemed to come into collision with some hurrying young girl carrying fresh bolts of goods into a curtained recess behind which Bonny had disappeared an interminable length of time previously. These flying supernumeraries always came out again empty handed; judging by the quantity of material that he had already seen go in the alcove, with none ever taken out again, it should have been filled to ceiling height by this time.

He could hear her voice at intervals, topping the rustles of unwound fabric lengths and carefully chosen phrases of professional inducement.

"I cannot decide! The more you bring in to show me, the harder it becomes to settle on one. No, leave that, I may come back to it."

Suddenly the curtains parted, gripped by restraining hands just below the breach, so that it could not spread downward, and her head, no more, peered through.

"Lou, am I taking dreadfully long? I just remembered you, out there."

"Long, but not dreadfully," he answered gallantly.

"What are you doing with yourself?" she asked, as if he were a small boy left for a risky moment to his own devices.

"Getting in everyone's way, I'm afraid," he admitted.

There was a chorus of polite feminine laughter, both from before and behind the secretive curtain, as though he had said something very funny indeed.

"Poor thing," she said contritely. Her head turned to someone behind her. The grip on the curtain slit slid slightly downward for a moment, and the turn of an unclad shoulder was revealed, a tape-like strip of white ribbon its only covering. "Haven't you any magazines or something for him to look over, pass the time with?"

"Only pattern magazines, I'm afraid, madam."

"No, thank you," he said very definitely.

"It's so hard on *them*," she said patronizingly, still in conversation with someone behind her. Then back to him once more. "Why don't you leave and then call back for me again?" she suggested generously. "That way you needn't suffer so, and I can put my whole mind to this."

"How soon shall I come back?"

"I won't be through for another hour yet at the very least. We haven't even got past the choice of a material yet. Then will come the selection of a pattern, and the cutting, and the taking of the over-all measurements—"

"Unh," he groaned facetiously, and another courtier-like laugh went up.

"You had best give me a full hour and a half, I shall need that much. Or if you tire in the meantime, go straight back to the house, and I'll follow you there."

He took up his hat with alacrity, glad to make his escape.

Her bodyless face, formed its lips into a pout.

"Aren't you going to say goodbye to me?"

She touched her lips to show him what she meant, closed her eyes expectantly.

"In front of all these people?"

"Oh dear, how you talk! One would think you weren't my husband at all. I assure you it's perfectly proper, in such a case."

Again a chorus of flattery-forced laughter went up, almost as if on cue. She seemed to make quite an *opera bouffe* entertainment of the making of a new dress, taking the part of main luminary surrounded by a doting, submissive chorus. There should have been music, he couldn't help reflecting, and a tiered audience surrounding her on three sides.

He stepped over to the curtains, coloring slightly, pecked at her lips, turned, and got out of the place.

Strangely, in spite of his embarrassment, he had a flattered, self-important feeling at the same time; he wondered how she had been able to give him that, and whether she had known she was doing it when she did. And secretly decided that she had.

She knew every cause, she knew every effect, she knew how to achieve them. Everything she did, she knew she did.

There must have been other times, in other modistes' fitting rooms, when the man waiting was not legally obligated to shoulder the expense she was incurring, that this glow of self-esteem had had an intrinsic value of its—

He put that thought hurriedly from mind, and set out to enjoy the afternoon sunlight, and the blue Gulf reaching to the horizon, and the crowd of strollers drifting along the shoreline promenade. He mingled with them for a while, taking his place in the leisurely moving outermost stream, then turned at the end of the structure and came back with them, but now a part of the inside stream going in the opposite direction.

The slow baking warmth of the sun was pleasant on his shoulders and his back, and occasionally a little salty breeze would come, just enough to temper it. Clouds that were thick and unshadowed as egg white broke the monotony of the sky, and on everyone's face there was a smile—as there must have been on his, he at last realized, for what he was seeing was the unthinking answer to his own smile, offered by face after face in passing; without purpose or premeditation, without knowing they were doing it, simply in shared contentment.

He had money enough now for a long while to come, and she loved him—she had shown it by inducing him to kiss her in front of a shopful of girls. What more was there to wish for?

The world was a good world.

A little boy's harlequin-sectioned ball glanced against his leg in rolling, and the child himself clung to it for a moment in the act of unsteady retrieval. Durand stopped where he was and reached down and tousled still further the already tousled cornsilk thatch.

"Does your mother let you take a penny from a strange man?"

The youngster looked up, open-mouthed with that infantile stupefaction that greets every act of the grown world. "I 'on't know."

"Well, take this to show her then and find out."

He went on again without waiting.

The world was a good world indeed.

After two complete circuits of the walking space provided, he stopped at last by the wooden rail flanking it, and rested his elbows on it, and stood in contemplation with his back to the slow-moving ambulators he had just been a member of.

He had been at rest that way for perhaps two or three minutes, no more, when he became conscious of that rather curiously compelling sensation that is received when someone's eyes are fixed on one steadfastly, from behind.

There was no time to be warned. The impulse was to turn and seek out the cause, and before he could check it he had done so.

He found himself staring full into the face of Downs, the St. Louis investigator, just as Downs was now staring full into his.

He was within two or three paces of Durand, almost close enough to have reached out and touched him had he willed. His whole body was still held in the act of an arrested footfall, the one at which recognition had struck; one leg out behind him, heel clear of ground. Shoulders still forward, the way in which he had been going; head alone oblique, frozen that way at first sight of Durand.

Durand had a sickening impression that had he kept his own place in the belt line of promenaders, they might have gone on circling after one another the rest of the afternoon, equidistant, never drawing any closer, they might have remained unaware of one another. For Downs must have been fairly close behind him, to come upon him this quickly after, and so they would both likely have been on the same side of the promenade at any given time. But by falling out of line and coming to a halt, he had allowed Downs to overtake him, single him out. Where everyone is at rest, a moving figure is quickly noted. But where everyone is moving, it is the motionless figure that is the more conspicuous.

"Durand," Downs said with a curious matter-of-factness.

Durand tried to match it: nodded temperately, said, "You, eh?" Try not to show any fear of him, he kept cautioning himself, try not to show any fear. Forget that she is in such terrible proximity at this very moment, or you will betray that to him by the very act of trying not to. Don't look over that way, where the shop is. Keep your eyes off it. Above all, move him around, circle him around the other way so that his back is to it. If she should happen suddenly to emerge—

"Are you alone here?" Downs asked. The question was idly turned, but following it, for a long moment, his eyes seemed to bore into Durand's, until the latter could scarcely endure it.

"Certainly," he said somewhat testily.

Downs lazily reared one palm in protest. "No offense," he drawled. "You seem to resent my asking."

"Can you give me any reason why I should take offense at such a question?" He realized he was speaking too quickly, almost on the verge of sputtering.

"If you cannot, then I cannot," Downs said with feigned amiability.

Durand gave the railing a slick smack of quittance, moved in away from it, drifted in an idle saunter past Downs and to the rear of him, closed up to the railing again, and came to rest against it on a negligent elbow. Downs automatically pivoted to face him where he now was.

"And what brings you here, in turn?" Durand said, when the adjustment had been completed.

Downs smiled with special meaning. Special meaning he, Durand, was intended to share, whether he would or not. "What brings me anywhere?" he countered. "Not a holiday, rest assured."

"Oh," was all Durand could think to say to that. A very small, limp "oh."

In the modiste shop entrance, in the middle distance, but still close enough at hand to be only too visible, a lengthwise streamer of color suddenly peered forth, as some woman, about to leave, lingered there half-in half-out in protracted farewell, probably talking to someone behind her. Durand's heart thrust hard against the cavern of his chest for a moment, like a pointed rock. Then the figure came out: tall, in blue; someone else.

His attention swerved back to Downs, to overtake what he had been about to miss. "I had heard reports," the latter was saying, "of a flashy blonde who has been creating a stir down here with some man. They even got back to New Orleans."

Durand shrugged, a little jerkily. The point of his elbow slipped a trifle on the rail top, and he had to readjust it. "There are blondes wherever there are women."

What fools we've been, he thought bitterly. Lingering on here week after week; we might have known—

"This was a flashy blonde, almost silver in her lightness," Downs took pains to elaborate, eyes on him intent and unmoving. "A fast woman, I understand."

"Someone has fooled you."

"I don't think anyone has fooled *me,*" Downs emphasized, "because: this was not intended for *my* ears at all in the first place. They just happened to overhear it, to pick it up." He waited a moment. "Have you happened to note any such pair? You have been down here longer than I, I take it."

Durand looked down at the planks underfoot. "I have been cured of blondes," he murmured grudgingly.

"A relapse can occur," Downs said drily.

How did he mean that? thought Durand, startled. But—don't quarrel with it, or you will make it worse.

He took out his watch. "I must go."

"Where are you staying?"

Durand thumbed back across his shoulder, misleadingly. "Down that way."

"I'll walk back with you to your stopping place, wherever it is," Downs offered.

He wants to find out where it is; I'll never lose him! thought Durand, harassed.

"I'm a little pressed for time," he managed to get out.

Downs smiled calmingly. "I never force myself on a man." Then he added pointedly, "That is, in sociability."

"Which way are you going?" Durand asked suddenly, seeing that he was about to turn and go back the other way, toward and past the modiste's. She might emerge just as he neared there—

He took Downs by the arm all at once, pressing him. As insistent now as he had been reluctant a moment ago. "Come with me, anyway. Can I offer you a schooner of beer?"

Downs glanced overhead. "The sun *is* warm," he accepted. "Your own face, for instance, is quite moist." There was something faintly satiric in the way he said it, Durand thought.

They walked along side by side. At every pace Durand told himself: I've drawn him a step farther away from her. She is that much safer.

"Here's a place; let's try this," he said presently.

"I was just going to suggest it myself," Downs observed. Again there was that overtone of satire to be detected.

They went in and seated themselves at a small wicker table.

"Two Pilseners," Durand told the mustachioed, striped-shirted waiter. Then before he could withdraw again. "Where is the closet?"

"Straight back."

Durand rose. "Excuse me for a moment." Downs nodded, ironically it seemed to him.

Durand left him seated there, went out through the spring door. He found himself in a passage. Ignoring the intermediate door to the side, he followed it to the rear, let himself out at the back of the place. He began to run like one possessed. He *was* possessed; possessed with the thought of saving her.

— 45 —

He ran back and forth like mad between the gaping wardrobe and the uplidded trunk, empty-armed on each trip to, half-smothered under masses of her dresses on each trip fro. He dropped them into it in any old way, so that long before the potential capacity of trunk was exhausted, its actual capacity was filled and overflowing. This was no time for a painstaking job of packing. This was get out fast, run for their lives.

He heard her come in at the street door, and before she had even had time to quit the entryway, he called down to her sight-unseen from above, in wild urgency: "Bonny!" And then again, "Bonny! Come up here quick! Hurry! I have something to tell you!"

She delayed for some reason. Perhaps over the feminine trait of removing her bonnet or disposing of her parcels before doing anything further, even at a moment of crisis.

Half mad with his own haste, he rushed recklessly out of the room, ran down to get her. And then halfway to the bottom of the stairs he stopped short, as if his legs had been gripped by a brake; and stood still, stock still and yet trembling, and died a little.

The figure back to door, back to just-reclosed door, equally stock still, was Downs.

Neither of them moved. The discovery came, the discovery went, the discovery was long past. Just two icy still men endlessly looking at one another. From stairs to door. From door to stairs. One of them bleakly smiling now in ultimate vindication. One of them ashen-faced, stricken to death.

One of them sighed deeply at last. Then the other sighed too, as if in answer. Two sighs in the intense silence. Two different sighs. A sigh of despair, a sigh of completion.

"You called her just now," Downs said slowly. "You called her by name. Thinking it was her. So she *is* here with you."

Durand had turned partly sidewise, was gripping the rail with both hands and bent slightly over it, as if able to support himself by that means alone. He shook his head. First slowly. Then at each repetition, faster, faster; until he was beating the stubborn air with it. "No," he said. "No. No. No."

"Mr. Durand, I have good ears. I heard you."

Ostrichlike, terrified, craven, trying to hide his head in the sands of his own mesmeric denial. As though to keep saying No, if persisted in long enough, would ward off the danger. Using the word as a sort of talisman.

"No. No. *No!*"

"Mr. Durand, let's be men at least. You called her name, you hollered it down here."

"No. No." He took a toppling step, that brought him down a stair lower. Then another. But seeming to *slide* his body downward along the slanted rail rather than move his legs, so hard and fast did he cling to it. Like an inebriate; which he was. An inebriate of fright. "Someone else. Woman that comes in to do my cleaning. Her name sounds like that—" He didn't know what he was saying any more.

"Very well," Downs said drily. "I'll take the woman that comes in to do your cleaning, the woman whose name sounds so much the same. I'm not hard to please."

They were suddenly wary, watchful of one another; both pairs of eyes slanting first far over to this side, then far over to that, in a sort of synchronization of wordless guile. Physical movement followed, also in complete unison.

Durand broke from the stairs, Downs broke from the doorback. Their two diagonal rushes brought them together before the mirrored, antlered hatrack cabinet against the wall, with its armed seat that was also the lid of a storage box. Durand tried to hold it down, Downs to pry it up. Downs' arm treacherously thrust in and out again, came up with the two long heliotrope streamers depending from a straw garden hat. The tip of one had been protruding, caught fast by the lid on its last closing; a fleck of color, a fingernail's worth of color, in all that vast ground-floor area of house.

("But why do you like it so?" he had once asked her.

"*I* don't know. It's my color, and anyone who knows me *knows* it's my color. Wherever I am, there's bound to be some of it around.")

Downs let it fall back again into the box. "The costume for the woman who comes here to do your work," he remarked. And then, looking his disgust and complete forfeiture of respect at Durand, he murmured something in a swallowed voice that sounded like, "God help you, in love with a—!"

"Downs, listen, I want to talk to you—!" The words tumbled over one another in their eagerness to be out. He was so breathless he could hardly articulate. He took him by the lapels, a hand to each, held him close in a sort of pleading stricture. "Come inside here, come in the next room, let me talk to you—!"

"You and I have nothing to talk about. All my talking is for—"

Durand moved insistently backward, drawing him after him by that close coat lock, until he had him in there past the threshold where he wanted him to be. Then let him go, and Downs stayed there where he'd brought him.

"Downs, listen— Wait a minute, there's some brandy here, let me pour you a drink."

"I keep my drinking for saloons."

"Downs, listen— She's not here, you're making a terrible mistake—" Then quickly stilling his presumed contradiction by a fanwise rotation of the hand; "—but that isn't what I want to talk to you about. It's simply this. I—I've changed my mind. I want to drop the matter. I want the proceedings to stop."

Downs repeated with ironic absence of inflection, "You want to drop the matter. You want the proceedings to stop."

"I have that right, I have that choice. It was my complaint originally."

"As a matter of fact, that's only partly true. You were cocomplainant along with Miss Bertha Russell. But let's say for the sake of argument, it *was* your sole complaint originally. Then what?" His brows went up. "*And* what?"

"But if I withdraw the complaint, if I cancel it—?"

"You have no control over me," Downs said stonily. He slung one hip astride the arm of a chair he was standing beside, settled himself as if to wait. "You can rescind your complaint. All well and good. You can cease payment of any further fees to me. And as a matter of fact, your original retainer to me expired months ago. But you can't compel me to quit the case. Is that plain enough to you? As the old saying goes, this is a free country. And I'm a free agent. If I happen to want to continue on my own account until I bring the assignment to a satisfactory conclusion—and it happens that I do—there's nothing you can do about it. I'm no longer working for you, I'm working for my own conscience."

Appalled, Durand began to tremble all over. "But that's persecution—" he quavered.

"That's being conscientious, I'd call it, though it's not for me to say so," Downs said with a frosty smile.

"But you're not a public police official— You have no right—"

"Fully as much right as I had in the first place, when I took up the assignment on *your* behalf. The only difference being that now I'll turn my findings over to them direct, when I'm ready, instead of through you."

Durand, his feet clogging, had stumbled around and to the far side of the large bulky table desk present in the room, pacing his way along its edge with both hands, as if in momentary danger of collapse.

"Now wait— Now listen to me—" he panted, and fumbled with excruciating anxiety in the pockets of his waistcoat, one after the other, not finding the right one immediately. He brought out a key, turned it in the wood, pulled out a drawer. A moment later a compact ironbound box had appeared atop the desk, its lid standing up. He grubbed within it, came back toward Downs with both hands extended, paper money choking them.

"There's twenty thousand dollars here. Downs, open your hand. Downs, hold it a minute; just hold it a minute."

Downs' hands had retreated into his trouser pockets at his approach; there was nothing there to deposit the offering in.

Downs shook his head with indolent stubbornness. "Not a minute, not an hour, not for keeps." He switched his head commandingly. "Take it back where you got it, Durand."

"Just *hold* it for me," Durand persisted childishly. "Just hang onto it a moment, that's all I'm asking—"

Downs stared at him imperturbably. "You've got the wrong man, Durand. That's your misfortune. The one wrong man out of twenty. Or maybe even out of a hundred. I took the case professionally in the beginning, for a money payment. I'm on it for my own satisfaction now. I not only won't take any further money to stay on it, but no amount of money could make me quit it any more. And don't ask me why, because I can't answer you. I'm a curious johnny, that's all. You made a mistake, Durand, when you came to me in St. Louis. You should have gone to somebody else. You picked the one private investigator in the whole country, maybe, that once he starts out on something can't leave off again, not even if he wants to. Sometimes I wonder what it is myself, I wish I knew. Maybe I'm a fanatic. I want that woman, not for you any more, but for my own satisfaction." He drew his hands out of his pockets at last, but only to fold his arms flintily across his chest and lean back still farther against the chair he was propped against.

"I'm staying here until she comes in. And I'm taking her back with me."

Durand was back beside the money box again, hands bedded atop its replaced contents, pressing down on it in strained futility.

Downs must have seen him glance speculatively toward the doorway. He read his mind.

"And if you go out of here, to try to meet her on the outside and Warn her off, I'm going right along with you."

"You can't forbid me to leave my own house," Durand said despairingly.

"I didn't say that. And you can't prevent me from walking

along beside you. Or just a step or two behind you. The streets are public."

Durand pressed the back of his hand to his forehead, held it there a moment, as though there were some light overhead that was too strong in his eyes. "Downs, I can raise another thirty thousand in New Orleans. Inside twenty-four hours. Go with me there, keep me in sight every step of the way; you have my promise. Fifty thousand dollars, just to let us alone. Just to forget you ever heard of—"

"Save your breath, I made my speech on that," Downs said contemptuously.

Durand clenched a fist, shook it, not threateningly, but imploringly, at him. "Why do you have to blacken her name, ruin her life? What good—?"

Downs' mouth shaped a laugh, but no sound came. "Blacken the name of that wanton? Ruin the life of that murdering trollop?"

The impact left physical traces across Durand's face, blanching it in livid streaks across the mouth and eyes, yet he ignored it. "She didn't do anything. The whole thing's circumstantial. She just happened to be on the same boat, that's all. So were dozens of others. *You* can't say for certain what happened to Julia Russell. No one can, no one knows. She just disappeared. She may have met with an accident. People have. Or she may still be alive at this very hour. She may have run off with someone else she met on the boat. All Bonny is guilty of, was passing herself off on me under another name, in the very beginning. And if *I* forgive her for that, as I have long ago—"

Downs suddenly left his semirecumbent position on the chair arm. He was on his feet, facing him alertly, eyes glittering now.

"Here's something you don't seem to know yet, Mr. Durand. And I think you may as well know it now, as later. You're going to soon enough, anyway. There *isn't* just a disappearance involved any longer. And I *can* say for certain just what happened to Julia Russell! I can now, if I couldn't the last time you saw me!"

He was leaning slightly forward in his intensity, in his zeal; that zeal of which he had spoken himself a few minutes earlier.

"A body drifted ashore out of the eddies at Cape Girardeau on the tenth of this month. You can get white, Mr. Durand; you have reason. A body that had been murdered, thrown into the water dead. There was no water in the lungs. I took Bertha Russell down to look at it. And badly decomposed as it was, she identified it. As that of Julia Russell, her sister. Triply fortified, even though there was no face left any more. By twin moles high on the inner side of the left thigh. That no other human being ever saw since early childhood, practically. By the uncommon fact that both end-teeth on both jaws, all four in other words, bore gold crowns. And lastly by the fact that her side bore peculiar scars in a straight line, from the teeth of a garden rake; again from her childhood. The rake had been rusty and the punctures had had to be cauterized by a hot iron."

He stopped for lack of breath, and there was a moment of silence. Durand was standing there, head bowed, looking downward before himself. Perhaps to the floor in implicit capitulation, perhaps to the outthrust drawer from which the strongbox had come. He was breathing with difficulty; his chest rose and fell with visible labor at each intake and expulsion.

"Do the official police know about this?" he asked finally, without raising his head.

"Not yet, but they will when I get her back there with me."

"You'll never get her back there with you, Downs. She's not going to leave this house. *And neither are you*"

Now his head came up. And with it the pistol his hand had fallen upon, long ago, long before this.

Shock slashed across Downs's face; it mirrored fear, collapse, panic, for a moment each, in turn; all the usual and only-human reactions. But then he curbed them, and after that he bore himself well.

He spoke for his life, but his voice was steady and reasonable, and after the first abortive step back, he held his ground sturdily.

Nor did he cringe and bunch his shoulders defensively, but held himself tautly erect. He did not try to disguise his fear, but he mastered it, which is the greater bravery of the two.

"Don't do anything like that. Keep your head, man. You're still not involved. There's nothing punishable as yet in your taking up with this woman. The crime was committed before you met her. You were not a party to it. You've been foolish but not criminal so far— Don't, Durand— Stop and think before it's too late. For your own sake, while there's still time, put that down. Put it back where you got it."

Durand, for the first time during the entire interview, seemed to be addressing, not the investigator, but someone else. But who it was, no one could have said. He didn't know himself. "It's already too late. It's been too late since I first met her. It's been too late since the day I was born. It's been too late since God first created this world!"

He looked down, to avoid seeing Downs's face. He looked down at his own finger, curled about the trigger. Watching it with a sort of detached curiosity, as though it were not a part of him. Watching as if to see what it would do.

"Bonny," he sobbed brokenly, as though pleading with her to let him go.

The detonation stunned him briefly, and smoke drew a transient merciful curtain between the two of them. But that thinned again and was wafted aside long before it could do any good.

Then he looked up and met the face he hadn't wanted to.

Downs was still up, strangely.

There was in his face such unutterable, poignant rebuke that, to have had to look at it a second time during a single lifetime would have cost Durand his reason, he had a feeling then.

A hushed word hovered about them in the sudden new stillness of the room, like a sigh of penitence. Somebody had breathed "Brother," and later Durand had the strange feeling it had been he.

Downs's legs gave abruptly, and he went with a crash. More violently, for the delay, than if he had fallen at once. And lay there dead. Dead beyond mistaking, with his eyes open but viscid opaque matter, with his lips rubbery and slightly unsealed.

The things he did then, Durand, he was slow in coming to, as though it were he and not Downs who was now in timeless eternity; and even as he did them, though he saw himself doing them, he was unaware of doing them. As though they were the acts of his hands and his body, and not of his brain.

He remembered sitting for a while on a chair, on the outermost edge of a chair, like someone uneasy, about to rise again at any moment, but yet who fails to do so. He only saw that he had been sitting when he finally did stand and quit the chair. He'd been holding the pistol in his hand the whole time, and tapping its muzzle against the cap of his knee.

He went over to the desk and returned it to where he'd taken it from. Then he noted the cash box still standing there on top the desk, with its lid up and some escaped bank notes lying about it. These he returned to it, and then closed and locked it, and then he put it away too. Then he locked the drawer and pocketed the key.

Yes, he thought dazedly, I can repair everything but one thing. There is one thing I cannot return to, what it was before. And he swayed, shuddering, for a moment against the corner of the desk, as if the thought were a strong cold wind assailing him and threatening to overbalance him.

The situation seemed timeless, as if he were going to stay in here forever with this dead man. This dead thing that had been a man; dressed like a man, but not a man any longer. He felt no immediate urge to get out of the room; instinct told him it was better to be here, behind its concealing walls, than elsewhere. But he wanted not to have to look at what lay on the floor any longer. He wanted his eyes not to have to keep returning to it every other moment.

Downs lay upon an oblong rug, and he lay transverse upon it, so that one upper corner protruded far out past his shoulder, one lower far down below his foot. There was in this violation of symmetry, too, an irritant that continually inflamed his nerves every time his gaze fell upon the high relief offered by the floor.

He went over at last and dropped down by the dead face, and, folding over the margin of rug, covered it, as with a thick, woolly winding sheet. Then noting in himself symptoms of relief or at least amelioration, shifted rapidly down by the feet of the corpse—without standing, by working his upended feet along under his body—and turned over that corner, swathing the feet and lower legs. All that lay revealed now was a truncated torso.

Suddenly, inspired, he turned the body over, and the rug with it. And then a second time, and the rug still with it. It was gone now, completely hidden, disappeared within a cocoon of roughspun rugback. But he did it still once more, and the rug had become a long, hollow cylinder. No more than a rolled rug; nothing about it to amaze or attest or accuse.

But it was in the way. It blocked passage in or out of the doorway.

He scrambled downward upon all fours and began to roll it across the room, toward the base of the opposite wall. It rolled lumpily and a little erratically, guided by the weight of its own fill rather than his manipulations. He had to stop and straighten, and move ahead of it to get a chair out of the way.

Then, tired, when he had returned to it, he no longer got down and used his hands to it. He remained erect and planted his foot against it and prodded it forward in that way, until at last he had it close up against the wall base, and as unobtrusive as it would ever be.

A small mother-of-pearl collar button had jumped out of it en route and lay there behind it on the floor. He picked that up, and returned to it, and tossed it in freehand at one of the openings; but no longer sure which one of the two it was, whether at head or at feet.

Exhausted now, he staggered back across the room, and found the wall nearest the door-opening, the farthest one from it, and sank back deflated against that, letting it support him at shoulders and at rump. And just remained that way, inert.

He was still there like that when she came in.

Her arrival now was anticlimax. He could give it no import any longer. He was drained of nervous energy. He turned listlessly at the sound of her entrance, back beyond sight in the hall. A moment later she had arrived abreast of him, was standing looking into the room, busied in taking a glove off one hand.

A little flirt of violet scent seemed to reach him; but perhaps more imagined by the sight of her, recalled to memory from former times, than actually inhaled now.

She turned her head and saw him there, propped upright, splayed hands at a loss.

Her puckered mouth ejaculated a note of laughter. "Lou! What are you doing there like that? Flat up against—"

He didn't speak.

Her gaze swept the room in general, seeking for the answer.

He saw her glance halt at the transverse dust patch coating the floor. The rug's ghost, so to speak.

"What happened to the rug?"

"There's someone in it. There's a man's body in it." Even as he said it, it struck him how curious that sounded. There's someone in it. As though there were some miniature living being dwelling in it.

But what other way was there to say it?

He turned his head to indicate it. She turned hers in accompaniment, and thus located it. A rounded shadow secretively nestling along the base of the wall; easy for the eye to miss, the legs of chairs distracting it.

"Don't go over—" he started to say. But she had already started swiftly for it. He didn't finish the injunction, more from lack of energy than because she had already disobeyed it.

He saw her crouch down by the oval, stovepipe-like opening, her skirts puddling about her. She put her face close and peered. Then she thrust her arm in, to feel blindly if there was indeed something in there. He saw her grasp it by its edges next, as if to partially unroll it, or at least stretch the aperture.

"Don't—" he said sickly. "Don't open it again."

She straightened and came back toward him again. There was an alertness in her face, a sort of wary shrewdness, but that was all; no horror and no fear, no pallor of shock. She even seemed to have gained vitality, as if this were—not a moral catastrophe—but a test to put her on her mettle.

"Who did it? You?" she demanded in a brisk whisper.

"It's Downs," he said.

Her eyes were on him with bright insistency; there was a single-minded intentness to them that almost amounted to avidity; insistency on knowing, on being told. Hard practicality. But no emotional dilution whatever.

"He came here to get you."

He wouldn't have gone ahead. His head dipped in conclusion. But she urged the continuation from him by putting hand to his chin and tipping it up again.

"He found out you were here."

She nodded now, rapidly. The explanation sufficed, that seemed to mean; she accepted it, she understood it. The act, the consequence stemming from it, was a normal one. None other could have been expected. None other could have been desired. A nod or two of her head spoke to him, saying these things.

She gripped his upper arm tight. He hadn't known she possessed so much strength, so much burning heat, in her fingers. He had the curious impression it was a form of commendation.

There was an intimacy tincturing her next remark, a rapport, none of their love passages had ever had before.

"What'd you do it with? What'd you take?"

"The gun there," he said. "The one in the desk."

She turned and looked at the rug. And while she stood turned thus, she struck him lightly on the chest with the back of her hand. And the only thing he could read in the gesture was rakish camaraderie, a sort of flippant, unspoken bond.

Then she looked back at him, and looked him in the face long and well. Lazily half smiling the while, as if discovering in the familiar outlines of his face, for the first time, some new qualities, to be appreciated, to be admired.

"You need a drink," she said with brittle decisiveness. "I do too. Wait a minute, I'll get us one."

He watched her go to it, and pour from the decanter twice, and put the glass stopper back in, and give it a little twist as if it were a knob.

He felt as if he were venturing into a strange new world. Which had had its well-established customs all along, but which he was only now encountering for the first time. That was what you did after you took a life; you took a drink next. He hadn't known that, it wouldn't have occurred to him, but for her. He felt like a novice in the presence of a practised hand.

She put one of the two glasses into his hand, and continuing to clasp that same hand about the wrist, as if in token of affection, poked her other hand wildly, vertically, up into the air.

"Now you're a man after my own heart," she said with glittering fervor. "Now you're worth taking up with. Now you're *my* kind of man."

She smote his uncertain glass with hers, and her head went back, and she pitched the liquor in through those demure lips, that scarcely seemed able to open at all.

"Here's to us," she said. "To you. To me. To the two of us. Drink up, my lovey. A short life and an exciting one."

She cast her drained glass against the wall and it sprayed into fragments.

He hesitated a moment, then, as if hurrying to overtake her, lest he be left all alone, drained his own and sent it after hers.

— 46 —

THE EYE, falling upon them unwarned half an hour later, would have mistaken them for a pretty picture of domesticity; discussing some problem of meeting household expense, perhaps, or of planning the refurnishing of a room.

He sat now, legs outspread, head lolling back, in a chair with arms, and she sat perched on one of the arms of it, close beside him, her hand occasionally straying absently to his hair, as they mulled and talked it over.

He had been holding a glass, a succeeding one, in his hand. She took it away from him at last and placed it on the table. "No more of that just now," she admonished, and patted him on the head. "You must keep your head clear for this."

"It's hopeless, Bonny," he said wanly.

"It's nothing of the sort." Again she patted him on the head. "I've been—"

She didn't finish it, but somehow he guessed what she'd been about to say. I've been in situations like this before. He wondered where, he wondered when. He wondered who had done it, who she'd been with at the time.

"To run flying out of here," she resumed, as if taking up a discussion that had been allowed to lapse some little time before, "would be the most foolhardy thing people in—our position— could do." As if hearing her from a great distance, he was amazed at how prim, how mincing, her words sounded; as if she were a pretty young schoolmistress patiently instructing a not-very-bright pupil in his lesson. She should have had some embroidery on her lap, and her eyes downcast to it as she spoke, to match her tone of voice.

"We can't *stay*, Bonny," he faltered. "What are we going to do? How can we *stay*?" And hid his eyes for a moment behind his own hand. "It's already an hour."

"How long was it before I came home?" she asked with an almost scientific detachment.

"I don't know. It seemed like a long time—" He started up rebelliously from the chair. "We could have been far from here, already. We should have been!"

She pressed him gently but firmly back.

"We're not staying," she calmed him. "But we're not rushing off helter-skelter either, at the drop of a hat. Don't you know what that would mean? In a few hours at most, someone would have found it out, be on our heels."

"Well, they will anyway!"

"No they won't. Not if we play our cards right. We'll go in our own good time. But that comes last of all, when we're good and ready for it. The first thing is—" she hooked her thumb negligently across the room, "—*that* has to be got out of the way."

"Taken outside the house?" he suggested dubiously.

She gnawed her lips reflectively. "Wait, let me think a minute." At last she shook her head, said slowly: "No, not outside— We'd be seen. Almost certainly."

"Then—?"

"Somewhere inside," she said, with a slight motion of her shoulders, as though that were to be understood, went without saying. The idea horrified him. "Right here in the house—?"

"Of course. It's a lot safer. In fact, it's the only thing for us to do. We're here alone, just the two of us; no servants. We can take all the time we need—"

"Ugh," he groaned.

She was pondering again, worrying her lip; she seemed to have no time for emotion. She frightened him almost as much as the fact they were trying to conceal.

"One of the fireplaces?" he faltered. "There are two large ones down on this floor—"

She shook her head. "That would only be a matter of days."

"A closet?"

"Worse. A matter of hours." She stretched her foot out and

tapped down her heel a couple of times. Then she nodded, as if she were at last nearing a satisfactory decision. "One of the floors."

"They're hardwood. It would be noticed the minute anyone came into the room."

"The cellar. What's the floor of that like?"

He couldn't recall having seen it; had never been down there, to his knowledge.

She quitted the chair abruptly. The period of incubation had ended, the period of action had begun. "Wait a minute. I'll go down take a look." From the doorway, without turning her head, she warned: "Don't take any more of those drinks while I'm gone."

She came running back, squinting shrewdly. "Hard dirt. That'll do."

She had to think for the two of them. She pulled at him briskly by the shoulder. "Come on, let's get it down there awhile. It's better than leaving it up here until we're ready. Someone may come to the door in the meantime."

He went over to it and stopped, trying to quell the nausea assailing his stomach.

She had to think of everything. "Hadn't you better take your coat off? It'll hamper you."

She took it from him and draped it carefully over a chair back, so that it would not wrinkle. She even brushed a little at one of the sleeves for a moment, before letting it be.

He wondered how such a commonplace, everyday act, her helping him off with his coat, could seem so grisly to him, making him quail to his marrow.

He took it up by its middle, the furled rug, packed it underarm, clasping it overarm with his other. One end, where the feet presumably were, of necessity slanted and dragged on the floor, of its own weight. The other end, where the head was, he managed to keep upward.

He advanced a few paces, draggingly. Suddenly the weight had eased, the lower end had lost its restraining drag on the floor. He looked, and she was holding that for him, helping him.

"No, for God's sake, no!" he said sickly. "Not you—"

"Oh, don't be a fool, Louis," she answered impatiently. "It's a lot quicker this way!" Then she added, with somewhat less asperity, "It's just a rug to me. I can't *see* anything."

They traveled with it out of the room, and along the cellarward passage to its back. Then had to stop and set it down, while he opened the door. Then in through there, and down the stairs, to cellar bottom. Then set it down once more, for good.

He was breathing hard. He passed his hand over his forehead.

"Heavy," she agreed. She blew out her breath, with a slight smile.

All the little things she did horrified him so. His blood almost turned cold at that.

They picked a place for it against the wall. She used the sharp toe of her shoe to test several, kicking and prodding at them, before settling on it. "I think this is about the best. It's a little less compact here."

He picked up a piece of rotting, discarded timber, broke it over his upthrust knee to obtain a sharp point.

"You're not going to do it with that, are you? It would take you the live-long night!" There was almost a hint of risibility in her voice, inconceivable as that was to him.

He drove it into the hard-packed floor, and it promptly broke a second time, proving its worthlessness.

"It'll take a shovel," she said. "Nothing else will do."

"There's none down here."

"There's none anywhere in the house. We'll have to bring one in." She started up the steps. He remained standing there. She turned at their top and beckoned him. "I'll go out and get it," she said. "You're kind of shaky yet, I can see that. Don't stay down there while I'm gone, it'll make you worse. Wait upstairs for me."

He followed her up, closed the cellar door after him.

She put on her poke bonnet, threw a shawl over her shoulders, as if it were the merest domestic errand she were going upon.

"Do you think it's prudent?" he said.

"People buy shovels, you know. There need be no harm in that. It's all in the way you carry it off."

She went toward the outside door, and he trailed behind her.

She turned to him there. "Keep your courage up, honey." She held his chin fast, kissed him on the lips.

He'd never known a kiss could be such a gruesome thing before.

"Stay up here, away from it," she counselled. "And don't go back to that liquor." She was like a conscientious mother giving a small boy last minute injunctions, putting him on his good behavior, before leaving him to himself.

The door closed, and he watched her for a moment through its pane. Saw her go down the front walk, just like any bustling little matron on a housewifely errand. She was even diligently stroking her mittens on as she turned up the road and went from sight.

He was left alone with his dead.

He sought the nearest room at hand, not the one in which it had happened, and collapsed into a chair, and huddled there inert, his face pressed inward against its back, and waited for her to return.

It seemed hours before she did. And it must, in truth, have been the better part of one.

She brought it in with her. She was carrying it openly—but then how else was she to have carried it? Its bit was wrapped in brown paper, tied with a string. The stick protruded unconcealed.

"Was I long?"

"Forever," he groaned.

"I deliberately went out of my way," she explained. "I didn't want to buy it too near here, where we're known by sight."

"It was a mistake to get it at all, don't you think?"

She gave him a confident smirk. "Not in the way I did it. I did not ask to buy a shovel at all. It was his advice that I buy one. What I asked was what implement he could suggest my using to cultivate in the space behind our house, whether a spade or a rake. I was dubious of a shovel; it took all his persuasion to convince me." She wagged her head cocksurely.

And she could stand there and dicker; he thought, incredulous.

He took it from her.

"Shall I come down with you?" she offered, carefully removing her bonnet with both hands, replacing the pins in it, and setting it down meticulously so that its shape would not suffer.

"No," he said in a stifled voice. To have had her watch him would have been an added horror, for some reason, that he could not have borne. "I'll let you know when—I've done."

She gave him helpful last minute instructions. "Mark it off first. You know, how long and how wide you'll want it. With the tip of the shovel. That'll keep you from doing more work than is needful."

His silent answer to this was the reflex of retching.

He closed the door after him, went down the steps.

The lamp was still burning where they'd left it before.

He turned it up higher. Then that was too bright, it showed him too much; he quickly moderated it a little.

He'd never dug a grave before.

He marked it off first, as she'd told him. He drove the shovel into the marked-off space and left it, standing upright of its own weight. He rolled his shirt sleeves up out of the way.

Then he took up the shovel and began.

The digging part was not so bad. *It* was behind him, out of sight, while he was at it. Horror, though it did not disappear altogether, was kept to a minimum. It might have been just a necessary trench or pit he was digging.

But then when he was through—

It took him some moments to work himself up to the necessary pitch of resoluteness. Then suddenly he walked rapidly over to it, from the far side of the cellar, where he'd withdrawn and kept his back to it in the interim.

He dragged the rug over, placed it even with the waiting cavity's edge. Then, taking a restraining hold along its exposed flap, he pushed the rounded part from him. It unrolled and emptied itself into the trough, with no more than a sodden thump. Then he drew it up. It came back to him again facilely unweighted. An arm flung up for a moment, but quickly dropped back again.

He avoided looking into it. He stepped around it to the other side, where the mound of disinterred fill was, and, holding his face averted, began to push and scrape that down into it with the back of the shovel.

Then when at last he had to look, to see how far he had progressed, the worst was over. There was no longer any face down there to confront him. There was just a fragmentary midsection seeming to float there on the surface, as it were; peering through the surrounding film of earth.

Then that went, presently.

"And all God's work has come to this," passed through his mind.

He had to tramp and stamp on it, at the end, to firm it down. That part was bad too.

He kept it up far longer than was needful. As if to keep what lay under from ever coming out again. He almost seemed to be doing a jig of fear and despair, unable to quit of his own volition.

He looked up suddenly.

She was standing there at head of the steps watching him.

"How did you know just when?" he panted, haggard.

"I came down twice to see how far along you were. I went back again without disturbing you. I thought perhaps you'd best be left alone." She looked at him inscrutably. "I didn't think you'd be able to go through with it to the finish. But you did, didn't you?"

Whether that was praise or not, he couldn't tell.

He kicked the shovel out of his path, tottered up the steps toward her.

He fell before he'd quite reached her. Or rather, let himself fall. He lay there, extended on the step, face buried in one arm, and sobbed a little.

She bent over toward him. Her hand came down upon his shoulder, consolingly.

"There, now. It's over. It's done. There's nothing more to worry about."

"I've killed a man," he said smotheredly. "I've killed a man. God has forbidden that."

She gave a curt, humorless snuff of laughter. "Soldiers in a battle kill them by the tens and never give it a second thought. They even give them medals for it."

She plucked at him by the arm, until he had found his feet again, stood beside her.

"Come, let's get out of here."

She stepped down there a moment to get the lamp, which he had forgotten, bring it with her, put it out. Then she closed the door after the two of them. She brushed her fingertips off fastidiously, against each other; no doubt from having touched the lamp. Or perhaps—

She put her arm comfortingly about his waist, as she rejoined him. "Come upstairs to bed. You're worn out. It's nearly ten o'clock, did you know that? You've been down there four full hours."

"You mean—?" He didn't think he'd heard her aright. "Sleep here in this same house tonight?"

She cast up her hand, as if at the nonsense of such a qualm. "It's late. What trains are there any more? And even if there were, people don't bolt out suddenly in the middle of the night. That *would* give them something to—"

"But *knowing*, as we do, Bonny. Knowing all the time, you and I both, what lies—"

"Don't be childish. Just put it from your mind. It's all the way down in the cellar. We're—all the way up in the bedroom."

She tugged at him until she got him to climb beside her.

"You're like a little boy who's afraid of the dark," she mocked. He said nothing more.

In the lamplit bedroom he watched her covertly, while apathetically, with numbed motions, drawing off his own things. There was no difference to be detected in the bustling routine with which she prepared herself for retirement, from any other night. Again certain under-layers of garments billowed up over her head in as much armless commotion as ever. Again the petticoats dropped to the floor and she stepped aside from them, one after the other. Again her unbound hair was trapped first on the inside of her high-collar flannel gown, then freed and brought to the outside, with a little backward shake. Every move was normal, unforced.

She even sat to the mirror and stroked her hair with the brush.

He lay back and closed his eyes, with a weazened sickish feeling.

They didn't say goodnight to one another. She perhaps thought he was already asleep, or was a little offended at his excess of morality. He was glad of that, at least. Glad she didn't try to kiss him. He had a curious sensation for a moment or two, that if she had tried, he would have, involuntarily, reared up, run for the window, and hurled himself through it.

She turned their bedside lamp and the room dimmed indigo.

He lay there motionless, as rigid, as extended, as what he had put into the trough down below in the cellar awhile ago.

Not only couldn't he sleep, he was afraid to sleep. He wouldn't have let himself if he could have. He was fearful of meeting the man he had just slain, should he drift across the border.

She too was sleepless, however, in spite of all her insouciance. He heard her turning about a number of times. Presently she gave a foreshortened sigh of impatience. Then he heard the bed frame jar slightly as she propped herself up on her arm.

He could somehow tell, in another moment, that she was leaning over toward him. The direction of her breath, perhaps, coming toward him.

Her silken whisper reached him.

"Awake, Lou?"

He kept his eyes closed.

He heard her get up, the rustle as she put something over her. Heard her take up the lamp, tread softly from the room with it, unlighted. Then outside the door, left ajar, the slowly burgeoning glow as she lit it. Then this receded as she bore it down the stairs with her.

His breath started to quicken. Was she leaving him? Was she about to commit some act of disloyalty, of betrayal, in the depths of night? Terrified, he suddenly burst the frozen mould that had encased him, started up himself, flung something on, crept cautiously out into the hall.

He could see the light from below peering wanly up the stairs. He could hear a faint sound now and again, as she moved softly about.

He felt his way down the stairs, step by step, his breath erratic, and rearward toward where the light was coming from. Then stepped up to the doorway at last and confronted her.

She was seated at the table, in the lamplight, holding a chicken-joint in her hand and busily gnawing at it.

"I was hungry, Lou," she said sheepishly. "I didn't have any supper." And then, putting her hand to the vacant chair beside her and swiveling it out invitingly, "Join me?"

— 47 —

THE GENTLE but insistently repeated pressure of her small hand on his shoulder, rubbed sleep threadbare, wore it away. He started upward spasmodically.

Then it came back. Then he remembered. Like a waiting knife it struck and found him.

"I'm going to get the tickets, Lou. Lou, wake up, it's after ten. I'm going to get the tickets. For us, at the station. I've done all the packing, while you were lying there. I've left out your one suit, everything else is put away—Lou, wake up, clear your eyes. Can't you understand me? I'm going to get the tickets. What about money?"

"Over there," he murmured vacantly, eyes turned inward on yesterday. "Back pocket, on the left side—"

She had it in a moment, as though she'd already known, but only wanted his cognizance to her taking it.

"Where will I get them for? Where do you want us to go?"

"I don't know—" he said blurredly, shading his eyes. "I can't tell you that—"

She gave her head a little toss of impatience at his sluggishness. "I'll go by the trains, then. Whichever one is leaving soonest, we'll take."

She came to him and, bending, gave him a hurried little peck of parting. The fragrance of her violet toilet water swirled about him. "Be careful," he said dismally. "It may be dangerous."

"We have time. There's no danger yet. How can there be? It's not even known." She gave him a shrug of assurance. "If we go about it right, there may never be danger."

The froufrou of her skirts crossed the floor. She opened the door. She turned there. She bent the fingers of her hand as if beckoning him to her.

"Ta ta," she said. "Lovey mine."

— 48 —

SHE SEEMED to be gone the whole morning. How could it take that long just to buy tickets for a train? he asked himself over and over again, sweating agony. How? How? Even if you bought them twice over, three times over?

He was pacing endlessly back and forth, holding tightly clasped between his two hands, as if afraid to lose it, a cup of the coffee she had left for him warming on the stove. But the plume of steam that had at first, with a sort of rippling sluggishness, traced his course behind him on the air, had long since thinned and vanished. He took a hurried swallow every so often, but dipping his mouth nervously down into the cup, held low as it was, rather than raising it to his lips. He wasn't aware of its taste, or of its degree of warmth, or even what it was.

She wasn't coming back, that was it. She'd abandoned him, boarded a train by herself, left him to meet the consequences of his own act as best he might. Sweat would start out anew at the thought, sweat that hurt like blood, though it was only the dew of fear. Then he would remember that she had intentionally awakened him before leaving, that she would have carefully avoided that above all had desertion been her purpose, and he'd breathe again and his misgivings would abate somewhat. Only to return again presently, stronger than ever, as if on a wicked punishing spiral.

He was in the midst of this inner turmoil, when suddenly, on the outside, crisis confronted him, and he was alone to face it.

There was a knocking at the door that he knew could not possibly be hers, and when he peered from one of the sideward frontal windows, cloaking his face with the edge of the drape, there was a coach and coachman standing waiting empty out before the house for someone.

The rapping came again. And when he drew nearer, through the inside of the house, and stole a frightened look out from mid-hall toward the glass curtain veiling the upper part of the door, there were the filmy shadowed busts of a man and a woman imprinted on it, standing waiting on the threshold.

Side by side, in chiaroscuro; the cone of a man's tophat, the slanting line of a woman's bonnet brim.

The knocking repeated itself, and seemed to trap his voice into issuing forth, against every intent of his own to use it. "Who's there?" Too late he tried to stem it, to recall it, but it was already gone.

"Dollard," a man's voice answered, deeply resonant.

He didn't know the name, couldn't identify it.

Unmanned, he quailed there.

The voice came again. "May I speak with you a minute, Mr. Durand?"

So the voice knew him at least. It was no mistake, it was he that was wanted.

He would have been incapable of further movement, even after having revealed himself, had they let him be.

But his name came again. "Mr. Durand." And then the knocking, puzzled now and questioning. And then his name again. "Mr. Durand. Hello! Mr. Durand?"

He was drawn to it as if in a trancelike condition, and unbolted, and drew it back.

They flamed instantly into full color, from the pewter silhouettes they had been, and into full stature, from the shoulder busts.

The woman was dark haired, sallow skinned, rather thin of face but pretty none the less; wearing a costume of grape velveteen, adorned with black frogs across the bodice like a hussar's jacket. The man was florid of face, with a copper walrus mustache drooping over the corners of his mouth, a cane handle riding over the crook of his arm, and a shirt front with small blue forget-me-nots patterned all over it.

He raised his hat to Durand, in deference to his companion, and revealed the crown of his head to be somewhat bald, and also somewhat sunburned.

Durand didn't recognize him for a minute.

"I'm Dollard, the agent from whom you rented the house."

He waited, ready to smile at the expected acknowledgement, but there was none.

"Mrs. Durand tells me you are unexpectedly called away and the house will be available."

She had been there then. She had even thought of that.

"Oh," he said stupidly. "Oh. Oh, yes. Of course."

Dollard gave him a somewhat quizzical look, as if unable to understand his lack of immediate comprehension. "That *is* correct, isn't it?"

"Yes," he said, realizing he'd already blundered copiously in the moment or two since he'd appeared at the door.

"Have I your permission to show this possible client through the house?"

"Now?" he murmured aghast. He could almost feel his chest pucker, as if closing up for lack of oxygen.

Dollard seemed to miss the intonation, having suddenly remembered his best business manners. "Oh, forgive me. Mrs. Thayer, may I present Mr. Durand?"

He saw the young woman glance at the forgotten coffee cup his hand still clung to, as if it were some kind of a chalice with mystic powers to save him. "I'm afraid we may have come at an unfortunate time," she suggested deprecatingly. "We're disturbing Mr. Durand. Should we not perhaps come back at another time, Mr. Dollard?"

The agent had already deftly inserted himself on the inside, however, and since he refused to return to her, she had to follow somewhat hesitantly to where he was, even in the act of speaking.

"I know how upset everything is when a move is contemplated; the packing and all," she apologized.

"I'm sure Mr. Durand doesn't mind," Dollard said. "We won't be very long." And since he had unobtrusively managed to close the door after the three of them by this time, the fact was already an accomplished one.

They moved down the hall parallel to one another, the young woman in the middle; Dollard striding with heavy-footed assurance, Durand all but tottering.

"This is the hall. Notice how spacious it is." Dollard swept his arm up, like an opera tenor on a high note.

"The light is quite good too," agreed the young woman.

Dollard tapped his cane. "The finest hardwood parquetry. You don't always find it."

They advanced after the momentary halt.

"Now, in here is the parlor," Dollard proclaimed grandly, again with a sweep.

"Is the furniture yours, Mr. Durand?" she asked.

Dollard's answer overrode whatever one he might have brought himself to make, sparing him the necessity. "The furniture goes with the house," he stated flatly.

She nodded her head approvingly. "This is quite a nice room. Yes, it's quite nice."

She had already turned her shoulder to it, about to lead them on elsewhere, and Dollard had turned in accord with her. When suddenly, as if only now struck by something he had already observed a moment ago, he looked back, pointed unexpectedly with his cane.

"Shouldn't there be a rug here?"

The dust patch was suddenly the most conspicuous thing in the room. In the house, in the whole world. It glowed livid, as if limned with phosphorus. To Durand, at least, it almost appeared incandescent, and he felt sure they must see it that way too. He could feel his face bleaching and drawing taut over the cheekbones, as if the slack of his skin were being pulled at the back of his head by some cruel hand.

"Where?" he managed to utter.

Dollard's cane tapped down twice, for irritated emphasis. "Here. Here."

"Oh," Durand said pitifully, crumbling phrases in a play for time. "Oh, there—Oh, yes—I think you're—I'd have to ask my—" Then suddenly he'd regained command of himself, and his tone was firm, though still brittle. "It was removed to be beaten out. I remember now."

"Then it's outdoors?" Dollard queried, as though not wholly pleased. Without waiting to be answered, he crossed to one of the windows, lowered his head to avoid the interplay of the curtains, and swept his gaze about. "No, I fail to see it there." He turned his head back to Durand, as if uneasily asking reassurance.

The latter's eyelids, which had closed for a moment over some inner illness of his own, went up again in time to meet the agent's boring glance.

"It's safe," he said. "It's somewhere about the house. Just where, I couldn't exactly—"

"It was quite valuable," Dollard said. "I trust it hasn't been stolen. It will have to be accounted for, of course."

"It will be," Durand breathed almost inaudibly.

The young woman shifted her foot slightly, in forebearing reminder that she was being detained; this instantly succeeded in recalling his present duties to Dollard, and he dropped the topic.

He hastened back to her, and tipped two fingers to her elbow in courtly guidance. "Shall we continue, Mrs. Thayer? Next I would like you to see the upstairs."

They ascended in single file, she in the lead, Durand at the rear. They ascended slowly, and he seemed to feel each footfall imprinted on his heart, as though it were that they were treading upon. The rustle and hiss of her multiple skirts was like the sound of volatile water rushing down a wooden trough, though it flowed the other way, upward instead of down.

"You will notice the excellent light that is obtained throughout this house," Dollard preened himself, as soon as they were on level flooring once more. He hooked his thumbs to the armholes of his waistcoat, allowed his fingers to trip contentedly against his chest. "In here, an extra little sitting room for the lady of the house. To do her sewing, perhaps." He smiled benevolently, winked at Durand behind her back, as though to show him he knew women, knew what pleased them.

He was in fine fettle today, apparently; enjoying every moment of his often-performed duties. Durand remembered enjoyment, an academic word from the vague past; remembered the word, but not its sensation. His wrists felt as cold as though tight coils of wire were cutting into their flesh, had long since stopped all circulation.

At their bedroom door she balked, chastely withdrew the tentative foot she had put forward, as soon as she had identified it for what it was.

"And this room has a most desirable outlook," Dollard orated heedlessly. "If you will be good enough to go in—"

Her eyes widened in dignified, gravely offered reproach. "Mr. Dollard!" she reminded him firmly. "There is a *bed* in there. And my husband is not accompanying me."

"Oh, your pardon! Of course!" he protested elaborately, with recessive genuflections. "Mr. Durand?"

The two men delicately withdrew all the way up-hall to the stairhead, to wait for her, and with the impurity of mixed company thus removed, she proceeded to enter the room and inspect it at her leisure.

"A real lady," Dollard commented admiringly under his breath, punctiliously looking the other way so that even his eyes could not seem to follow her on her unchaperoned expedition.

Durand's hand lay draggingly on his collar, forgotten there since he had last tried to ease his throat some moments ago.

She came out again very shortly. Her color was a trifle higher than when she had gone in, since the bed had not been made up, but she had no comment to offer.

They descended again, in the same order in which they had gone up. Her undulating hand left the railing at the bottom, and she turned to Dollard.

"Have you shown me everything?"

"I believe so." Perhaps judging her to be not yet wholly convinced of the house's desirability, he groped for additional inducements to display to her, turned his head this way and that. "All but the cellar—"

Durand could feel a sharp contraction go through his middle, almost like a cramp. He resisted the instinctive urge to clutch at himself and bend forward.

Their eyes were not on him, fortunately; they were looking back there toward where its door was, Dollard's gaze having led her own to it.

"It is quite a large and commodious one. Let me show you. It will only take a moment—"

They turned and paced toward it.

Durand, clinging for a necessary moment to the newel post

of the banister, released it again and took a faulty step after them.

His mind was suddenly spinning, casting off excuses for delaying them like sparks from a whirring whetstone. Rats, say there are rats; she will be afraid—Cobwebs, dust; she may harm her clothes—

"There is no light," he said hoarsely. "You will not be able to see anything. I'm afraid Mrs. Thayer may hurt herself—"

His tone was both too abrupt and too raucous for the intimate little elbow passage that now confined them all. Both turned their heads in surprise at the intensity of voice he had used, as though they were at a far greater distance. But then immediately, they seemed to take no further notice of the aberration, beyond that.

"No light in your cellar?" said Dollard with pouting dissatisfaction. "You should have a light in your cellar. What do you do when you wish to go down there yourself?" And glancing about him in mounting peevishness at thus being balked, his gaze suddenly struck the lamp which had been put down close by the doorframe by one of the two of them, Bonny or himself—Durand could no longer remember which it was—on coming up the night before.

Again he died inwardly, as he'd been dying at successive intervals for the past half-hour or more. He'd chosen the wrong preventative: it should have been rats or dust.

"No light, you said?" Dollard exclaimed, brows peaked. "Why, here's a lamp right here. What's this?"

All he could stammer in a smothered voice was: "My wife must have set it there— There was none last time— I remember complaining—"

Dollard had already picked it up, hoisted the chimney. He struck a match to it, recapped it, and it glowered yellow; to Durand like the fuming, imprisoned apparition of a baleful genie, called into being to destroy him.

He thought, Shall I turn and run from the house? Shall I turn and run out through the door? Why do I stand here like this, looking over their shoulders, waiting for them to—? And badly as he wanted to turn and flee, he found he couldn't; his feet seemed to have adhered to the floor, he found he couldn't lift them.

Dollard had opened the cellarway door. He stepped through onto the small stage that topped the stairs, and then downward a step or two. A pale yellow wash from the lamp, like something alive, lapped treacherously ahead of him, down the rest of the steps, and over the flooring, and even up the cellar walls, but growing fainter and dimmer the greater its distance from him, until it finally lost all power to reveal.

He went down a step or two more, and stretching out his arm straight before him, slowly circled it around, so that it kindled all sides of the place, even if only transiently.

"There are built-in tubs," he said, "for the family's washing, and a water boiler that can be heated by wood to supply you with—"

He descended farther. He was now all but at the foot of the stairs. Mrs. Thayer had come out onto the stage above, was holding her skirts tipped from the ground as a precaution. Durand, his own breath roaring and drumming in his ears, was gripping the doorframe with both hands, one above the other, head and shoulders thrust forward around it.

Dollard extended his hand upward in her direction. "Would you care to come down farther?"

"I believe I can see it from here," Mrs. Thayer said.

To accommodate her, he reversed the lamp, swinging it back again the other way. As its reflected gleam coursed past the place, an oblong darker than the rest of the flooring, a patch, a four-square stain or shadow, seemed to shoot out into its path, then recede again as the heart of the glow swept past. It was as sudden as though it had moved of its own accord; as mobile, due to the coursing-past of the lamp, as a darkling mat suddenly whisked out, then snatched back again. There, then gone again.

It sent a shock through him that congested his heart and threatened to burst it. And yet they seemed not to have seen it, or if they had, not to have known it for what it was. Their eyes hadn't been seeking it as his had, perhaps.

2

1

224122

2224 CORNELL WOOLRICH

Dollard suddenly hoisted the lamp upward, so that it evened with his head, and peered forward. A little over from the place, though, not quite at it.

"Why, isn't that the rug from the upstairs room we were just speaking of?" He quitted the bottom steps, crossed toward it.

Again that deeper-tinted strip sidled forward, this time under his very feet. He stopped directly atop it, both feet planted on it, bending forward slightly toward the other object nearby that had his attention. "How does it come to be down here? Do you beat out your rugs in the cellar, Mr. Durand?"

Durand didn't utter a sound. He couldn't recall if there had been any blood marks on the rug. All he could think of was that.

Mrs. Thayer tactfully came to his aid.

"I do that myself at times. When it's raining outdoors one has to. In any case I'm sure Mr. Durand doesn't attend to that *himself*, in person." She smiled pacifyingly from one to the other of them.

"One can wait until after it's stopped raining," Dollard grumbled thickly in his throat. "Besides, it hasn't rained all week long, that I can recall—" But he didn't pursue the stricture any further for the present.

A second later Durand was watching him stoop to recover the rug in his arms, lift it furled as it was, and turn toward the stairs bearing it with him crosswise in front of him, to return it to where it belonged. He perhaps wanted to avoid contaminating it further by spreading it open on the dusty cellar floor.

But the light would be better upstairs. And Durand's breath was hot against the roof of his mouth, like something issuing from a brick oven. He couldn't have formed words even if he'd had any to produce. They drew back one on each side to give Dollard passage, Mrs. Thayer with a graceful little retraction, Durand with a vertiginous stagger that fortunately seemed to escape their notice, or if not, to be ascribed to no more than a masculine maladroitness in maneuvering in confined spaces.

Then they turned and followed the rug-bearer back to the rear sitting room, Durand paying his way with hand to wall, unseen, like a lame man.

"That could have waited, Mr. Dollard," the young matron said.

"I know, but I wanted you to see this room at its best."

Dollard gave the unsecured edge of the rug a fine upward fling, let it fall, paid it out, shuffling backward to give it its full spread on the floor.

Something flew out as he did so. Something small, indeterminate. The eye could catch its leap, but not make out what it was. The wooden flooring offside clicked with its relapse.

Dollard stooped and pinched with two fingers at a place where there was nothing to be seen. At least not from where the other two people in the room stood. Then he straightened with it, whatever it was, came toward Durand with it.

"This is yours, I presume," he said, looking him straight in the eye. "One of your collar buttons, Mr. Durand."

He thrust it with a little peck, point first, into Durand's reluctantly receptive palm, and the latter closed his fingers over it. It was warm yet from Dollard's hand, but to Durand it seemed to be warm yet from Downs's throat. It felt like the nail of a crucifix going straight through the flesh of his palm, and he almost expected to see a drop of blood come stealing through the tight crevice of his fingers.

"Mr. Thayer is always dropping them about our house," put in the friendly Mrs. Thayer, in an effort to salve what she took to be his mortification at this public exposure, in her presence, of one of the necessary fastenings of his intimate apparel. Thinking that men were like women in that respect, and that if some safety pin or other similar clasp had been lost from her own undergarb, she too might very well have had that look of consternation on her face and confusedly sought support from the back of a chair, as she saw him do now.

"Hnh!" grunted Dollard, as if to say: I don't, only a sloven does.

But he returned to the rug, smoothing out its ripples now with strokes of his foot.

Durand thrust the token deep into his pocket. A burning sensation, coming through his clothes, stayed with it. He beheld them swayingly through thick-lensed, fear-strained eyes. He wondered if, to them, he appeared to sway, as they did to him. Apparently not, for their expressions showed no sudden attention nor undue concern whenever they were momentarily cast his way.

"I think I've shown you everything," Dollard said at last.

"Yes, I think you have," his prospective client agreed.

They sauntered now toward the front door, Durand like a wraith faltering beside them. He had the door at last to cling to, and any see-saw vagary of balance could be ascribed to the flux of its hinges.

Mrs. Thayer turned toward him, smiled. "Thank you very much; I hope we haven't disturbed you."

"Good day," said Dollard, with an economy of urbanity that, from his point of view, it would have been a waste to use on people who were about to cease being lessees of the property.

He escorted her down to the carriage, helped her in, talking assiduously the while in an effort to persuade her into concluding the transaction. He was just about to step in after her and drive off with her—to Durand's unutterable relief—when suddenly Bonny appeared, walking rapidly along the sidewalk, and turned in toward the house, glancing back toward them as she did so.

Durand widened the door, to admit her and close it after her, but she stopped there, blocking it.

"For God's sake," he said exhaustedly, "get in here—I'm half-dead."

"Just a moment," she said, immovable. "He can't rent this place unless we sign a release. Did you give him the keys yet?"

"No."

"Good," she said crisply. To his horror, she raised her arm and beckoned Dollard back. She even called out his name. "Mr. Dollard! Just a moment, if you will!"

"Don't call him back," pleaded Durand. "Let him go, let him go. What are you thinking of?"

"I know what I'm doing," she said firmly.

Durand, aghast, saw the agent reluctantly descend, come back toward them again. He chafed his hands propitiously. "I think I have the transaction concluded," he confided. "And at a considerably better figure. Her mind is all but made up."

The remark brought a shrewd glint of calculation into Bonny's eyes, Durand saw.

"Yes?" she said dulcetly. "But there are a couple of things you've forgotten, aren't there? The keys, and the signed release."

Dollard fumbled hastily for his pocket. "Oh, so I have. But I have the form right here on me, and if you'll give me the keys now, that will save me a trip back for them later—" He glanced around at the waiting carriage. He was as anxious to be off, or nearly so, as Durand was anxious to have him be.

Bonny, however, seemed to be in no hurry. She intercepted the paper, which Dollard had been extending toward Durand, and consulted it herself. She studiously ignored the mute, frantic appeal in Durand's dilated eyes. He mopped furtively at his forehead.

She raised her head; then with no sign of returning the paper to Dollard, tapped it questioningly against her arched pulse.

"And what of the unused portion of our rental fee? I see no mention here—"

"The unused—? I don't understand you."

She retained the paper against his tentatively extended hand seeking to reclaim it. "The rental for this month has already been paid."

"Naturally."

"But today is only the tenth. What of the three weeks we relinquish?"

"You forfeit that. I cannot return it to you once it has been paid."

"Very well," she said waspishly. "But then neither can you rent it to anyone else until after the thirtieth of the month. You had best go and tell the lady that, and spare her a disappointment."

Dollard's mouth dropped slack, astounded. "But you are not

going to be here! You leave today. It was you yourself who came to me this morning to tell me so." He glanced helplessly at the carriage, where the waiting Mrs. Thayer was beginning to show ladylike signs of impatience. She looked over at him inquiringly, she coughed pantomimically—unheard at that distance—into the hollow of her hand. "Come, be reasonable, madam. You said your-self—"

Bonny was adamant. There was even a small smile etched into the corner of her mouth. Her eyes, as if guessing the surreptitious, agonized signs Durand was trying to convey to her from behind the turn of the agent's shoulder, refused to look across at him. "You be reasonable, Mr. Dollard. My husband and I are not going to make you a present of the greater part of a month's rental. Our departure can very well be postponed in such a case. Either you return it to us, or we stay until the first of the new month."

She deliberately turned and entered the hallway. She stopped before the mirror. In full view of Dollard, she raised hands to her bonnet, removed it. She adjusted her hair, to make sure it was not disturbed.

"Close the door, dear," she said to Durand. "And then come upstairs and help me unpack our things. Good day, sir," she added pointedly to Dollard.

The agent looked apprehensively at the carriage, to gauge how much longer he might dare keep it waiting. Then to her; she was now moving toward the stairs, as if about to ascend them. Then, more quickly, to the carriage. Then, more quickly still, to her once more. The carriage, at least, was standing still, but she wasn't.

At last he blundered into the house after her, past the—by this time—almost audibly moaning Durand. "Just a moment!" he ca-pitulated. "Very well; seventy-five dollars by the month. I will give you the amount for the last two weeks. Thirty-seven, fifty."

Bonny turned, gave him a granite smile, shook her head. Then she continued, put her foot to the bottommost step, her hand to the newel-post. "Today is not the fifteenth of the month. Today is the tenth. We have had the use of this house for only one third of the time paid for. Therefore there is two thirds coming to us. Fifty dollars."

"Madam!" said Dollard, striking hand to his scalp, forgetful that there was no longer hair there to ruffle.

"Sir!" she echoed ironically.

A shadow darkened the open doorway behind the three of them and the coachman had appeared in it. "Excuse me, sir, but the lady says she can't wait any longer—"

"Here," said Dollard bitterly, grubbing money from his billfold, "Fifty dollars. Let me get out of here before you demand payment for having *lived* in the house at all!"

"Sign the paper, dearest," she said sweetly. "And give Mr. Dollard his keys. We must not detain him any longer."

Durand got the door closed behind the fuming figure. Then he all but collapsed against it on the inside. "How could you do it, knowing all the time what's lying under the very floor we—?" he gagged, tearing at his collar. "What have you for nerves, what have you for heart?"

She was standing on the stairs, triumphantly counting over the cabbagehead of money she held bunched in her hand. "Ah, but *he* didn't know; and that's where the difference lay. You never played poker, did you, Lou?"

— 49 —

SHE LED the way down the railroad car aisle, he following, the railroad porter struggling along in the rear with their hand baggage, three or four pieces on each arm. She had the jaunty little stride of one who has been on trains a great deal, enjoys traveling, and knows just how to go about getting the most out of it.

"No, not there," she called back, when Durand had stopped tentatively beside one of the padded green-plush double seats.

"Down here, on this side. You'll get the sun on you, on that side."

They moved on obediently to her bidding.

She stood by, supervising with attentive look, piece by piece, the disposing of their luggage to the rack overhead. Intervening once to counsel: "Put that lighter one on top of the other; the other one will crush it if you don't."

Then when he had finished: "Draw up the shade a little higher." Durand gave her a quickly cautioning glance over the porter's bent back, implying they should not make themselves too conspicuous.

"Nonsense," she answered it aloud. "Draw it up a little more, porter. There, that will do." Then gestured benevolently toward Durand, to have him tip the man for his trouble.

She sidled into the seat, when it had been sufficiently readied, drawing out her skirts sideward and settling them about her comfortably. Durand inserted himself beside her, his face pale and strained, as though he were sitting on spikes.

She turned her head and began to survey the scene outside the window with enjoyable interest, bending the back of her hand to support her chin.

"How soon do they start?" she asked presently.

He didn't answer.

She must have been able to view his reflection on the pane of glass. Without turning her head, she said slurringly out of the corner of her mouth: "Don't take on so. People will think you are ill."

"I am," he shuddered, blowing into his hands as if to warm them. "I am."

Her little lace-mittened hand suddenly reached across his body, below cover of the seat top before them. "Take my hand, hold it for a moment. We'll be out of here before you know."

"Merciful God," he whispered, with furtively downcast eyes, "why don't they start, what are they waiting for?"

"Read something," she suggested in a low voice, "take your mind off it."

Read something, he thought despairingly, read something! He could not have joined the letters of a single word together to make sense.

A locomotive bell began to peal, somewhere up front, and then a steam whistle blew in shrill warning.

"There," she said reassuringly. "Now!"

There was a sudden preliminary jar, that set aquiver the row of oil lamps dangling from the deep-set trough bisecting the car ceiling, then a secondary, lesser one; then the train stuttered into creaking motion. The fixed scene outside became fluid, began to slip slowly onward past the limits of their window pane, while a new one continually flowed into it, without a break, at the opposite side. She released his hand, turned her full attention to it, as enthralled as a child.

"I love to be on the go," she remarked. "Anywhere, I don't care where it is."

A butcher made his way slowly down the aisle, basket over arm, crying his wares to add to the noisy confusion of grinding wheels, creaking woodwork, and hum of blended voices that filled the car.

"Here you are, ladies and gentlemen. Mineral water, fresh fruit, all kinds of delicious sweets for yourselves or your children. Caramellos, gumdrops, licorice lozenges. It'll be a long, dusty ride. Here you are. Here you are."

She suddenly whisked her head around from the window that had absorbed her until now. "Lou," she said vivaciously, "buy me an orange, I'm thirsty. I love to suck an orange whenever I'm riding on a train."

The vendor stopped at his reluctant signal.

She leaned across him, pawing, rummaging, in the basket. "No, that one over there. It's plumper."

Durand hoisted himself sideward on the seat, to be able to reach into his pocket and draw up some coins.

The butcher took one and moved on.

Suddenly he stared, stricken, at the residue he had been left holding. Downs's collar button lay within the palm of his hand.

"Oh, God!" he moaned, and cast it furtively under the seat they were on.

— 50 —

ANOTHER HOTEL room, in another place. And yet the same. The hotel had a different name, that was all. The scene its windows looked out upon had a different name, that was all.

But they were the same two, in the same hotel room. The same two people, the same two runaways.

This, he realized, watching her broodingly, was what their life was going to be like from now on. Another hotel room, and then another, and still another. But always the same. Another town, and then another, and still another. Onward, and onward, and onward— to nowhere. Until some day they would come to their last hotel room, in their last town. And then—

A short life and an exciting one, she had toasted that night back in Mobile. She had it wrong. A short life and a dull one, she should have said. No pattern of security can ever be so wearyingly repetitious as the pattern of the refugee without a refuge. No monotony of Law-abidance can ever compare to the monotony of crime. He had found that out by now.

She was sitting there in a square of orange-gold sunlight by the window, one leg crossed atop the other, head bent intently to her task. Which was that of tapering her nails with an emery board.

Her arms were bare to the shoulders, and the numerous all-white garments she wore were not meant to be seen by other eyes than his. The moulded cuirass of the corset was visible in its entirety, from underarms to well below the hips. And over this only the thinnest film of cambric, an in-between garment, neither under-nor over-, known as the "corset-cover" (he had learned), fell short at the unwonted height of her lower calf.

Her hair was unbound and fell loose, clothing her back in rippling finespun tawny-gold, but at the same time giving the top of her head an oddly flat aspect, ordinarily seen only on young schoolgirls. The bangs alone remained in evidence, of the customary coiffure.

One of the spikelike cigars was burning untouched on the dresser edge near her.

She felt his long-maintained, speculative look, and raised her eyes, and gave him that compressed, heart-shaped smile that was the only design her lips could fall into when expressing a smile.

"Cheer up, Lou," she said. "Cheer up, lovey."

She hitched her head pertly to indicate the scene beyond the sun-flooded window. "I like it here. It's pretty here. And they dress up to kill. I'm glad we came."

"Don't sit so close to the window. You can be seen."

She gave him an incredulous look. "Why, no one knows us here."

"I don't mean *that*. You're in your underthings."

"Oh," she said. Then, as if still not wholly able to comprehend his punctiliousness on this point, "But they can only see my back. Not one can see my face, tell *whose* back it is." She moved her chair a trifle, condescendingly, with a smile as if she were doing it simply to please him.

She went back to her nails for a complacent stroke or two.

"Don't you—think of it sometimes?" he couldn't resist blurting out. "Doesn't it weigh upon you?"

"What?" she said blankly, again looking up. "Oh—that, back there."

"That's what I mean," he said. "If I could only forget it, as you do."

"I don't forget it. It's just that I don't brood about it."

"But the very act of remembering at all, isn't that the same as brooding?"

"No," she said, flipping her hands outward in surprise. "Let me show you." She tapped the rim of her teeth, as if in search of an illustration. "Say I buy a new hat. Well, once it's bought, it's bought, and there's no more to it. I *remember* I bought the hat; it's not that I forget I've bought it. But I don't necessarily brood about it, dwell on it, every minute of the live-long day." She pounded one clenched hand into the hollow of the other. "I don't keep saying over and over: 'I've bought a hat,' 'I've bought a hat,' 'I've bought a hat.' Do you see?"

He was looking at her with a stunned expression. "You—you compare what happened that day at Mobile with buying a new hat?" he stammered.

She laughed. "No. Now you're twisting it around; making me out worse than I am. I know it's not punishable to buy a new hat, and the other thing is. I know you don't have to be afraid of anyone finding out you've bought a new hat, and you do of anyone finding out you've done the other thing. But that was just given for an example. You can remember a thing perfectly well, but you don't have to worry about it all the time, let it darken your life. That's all I mean."

But he was speechless; he still couldn't get past that horrendous illustration of hers.

She rose and moved over toward him slowly; stood at last, and looked down, and let her hand come to rest on his shoulder, with almost a patronizing air. Certainly not one of overweening admiration.

"Do you want to know what the trouble is, Lou? I'll tell you. The difference between you and me is *not* that I'm any less afraid than you of its being found out; I'm just as afraid. It's that you let your conscience bully you about it, and I don't. You make it a matter of good or bad, wrong or right; you know, like children's Sunday school lessons: going to heaven or going to hell. With me it's just something that happened, and there's no more to be said. You keep wishing you could go back and have it over again, so that you wouldn't have done it. That's where the trouble comes in. It's that your own conscience is nagging you. That's what's ailing you."

She saw that she'd shocked him. She shrugged a little, and tamed away. She took up a muslin petticoat that lay in wait folded over the side of the bed, flung it out so that its folds opened circularly, stepped into it, and fastened it about her waist. The grotesque shortness of her attire disappeared, and her extremities were once more normally covered to the floor.

"Take my advice, and learn to look at it my way, Lou," she went on. "You'll find it a lot simpler. It's not something good, and it's not something bad; it's—" here she made him the concession of dropping her voice a trifle, "—just something you have to be careful about, that's all."

She took up a second petticoat, this one of taffeta bordered with lace, and donned that over the first.

He was appalled at the slow, frightening discovery he was in the process of making: which was that she had no moral sense at all. She was, in a very actual meaning of the word, a complete savage.

"Shall we go for a little stroll?" she suggested. "It's an ideal day for it."

He nodded, lips parted, unable to articulate.

She was now turning this way and that before the glass, holding up a succession of outer costumes at shoulder level to judge of their desirability. "Which shall I wear? The blue? The fawn? Or this plaid?" She made a little pouting grimace. "I've worn them all two or three times now apiece. People will begin to know them. Lou, fetch out that money box of yours before we go, that's a good boy. I really think it's time you were buying me a new dress."

No moral sense at all.

— 5 1 —

THE DISCOVERY was catastrophically sudden, though it shouldn't have been. One moment, they were affluent, he could afford to give her anything she wanted. The next, they were destitute, they could scarcely meet the cost of the immediate evening's pleasure they had contemplated.

It shouldn't have been as unforeseen as all that, he had to admit to himself; shouldn't have taken them unaware like that. There had been no theft, save at his own hands; nothing like that. But there had been no replenishment either. A vanishing point was bound to be reached eventually. It had been imminent for some time, if he'd only taken the trouble to make inventory. But he hadn't; perhaps he'd been afraid to, afraid in his own mind of the too-exact knowledge that he would have derived from such a summing up: the certainty of termination. Afraid of the chill that would have been cast upon their feasting, the shadow that would have dimmed their wine. There was always tomorrow, tomorrow, to make reckoning. And tomorrow, there was always tomorrow still. And meanwhile the music swelled, and the waltz whirled ever faster, giving no pause for breath.

He'd delved in each time, in haste, in negligence, without counting what was over. So long as there was something left, that was all that mattered. Something that would take care of the next time. And now that next time was the last time, and there was no next time beyond.

They'd been about to go out for the evening, swirls of sachet fanning out behind her like an invisible white peacock's tail spread in flaunting gorgeousness, an electric tide of departure crackling about them, she stuffing frothy laced handkerchief within the collar of her gloves, he lingering behind a moment to pluck out gas jet after gas jet. She was sibilant in tangerine taffeta, flounced with bands of brown sealskin, orange willow plumes snaking like live tentacles upon her hat. She was already in the open doorway, thirsting to be gone, waiting a moment to allow him to overtake her and close the door after them, and grudging that moment's wait.

"Have you enough money with you, lovey?" she asked companionably. And somehow made it sound entrancingly domestic; a wife being solicitous of her husband's welfare, much as if she'd said "Are you warmly enough dressed?" or "Have you brought the latch key with you?"; though its ends were not domestic at all, but quite the reverse.

He consulted his money-fold.

"No, glad you reminded me," he said. "I'll have to get some more. I'll only be a moment, I won't keep you."

"I don't mind," she assented graciously. "When you enter late, everyone has a better chance to take in what you're wearing."

She was still there by the door, idly tapping the furled sticks of her small dress-fan, secured by silken loop about her wrist, upon the opposite recipient palm, when he returned from the bedroom where he had gone.

When she saw him coming, she dipped her knees a graceful trifle, caught higher the spreading bottom of her dress, and reached behind her to grasp the doorknob, prepared to go, this time offering to close the door for him instead of him for her.

Then she saw his gait had changed, was hesitant, expiring, not as it had been when he went briskly in.

"What is it? Something wrong?"

He was holding two single bank notes in his hand, half extending them before him, as though not knowing what to do with them.

"This is all that's left. This is all there is," he said stupidly.

"You mean it's missing, been taken?"

"No, we've used it all. We must have, but I didn't know it. I could see it growing slimmer, but—I should have looked more closely. Each time I'd just reach in and— There always seemed to be some over. I didn't know until this moment that—this was all it was—" He raised it helplessly, lowered it again.

He stood there without moving, looking at her now, not it, as if she could give him the answer he could not find for himself. She returned his look, but she said nothing. There was silence between them.

Her lips had parted, but in some sort of inward appraisal; they said no word. A little breath came through, in a soft, wordless "Oh" of understanding.

Her hand left the doorknob at last, and dropped down to its own level, against her side, with a little inert slap of frustration.

"What shall we do?" she said.

He didn't answer.

"Does that mean we—can't go now?"

He looked at her, still without answering. Surveyed her entire person, from head to toe. Saw how beautifully she'd arrayed herself, how perfect in every detail the finished artistic picture she was offering for presentation. Or rather, had intended to offer, if given opportunity.

Suddenly he swerved, reached purposefully—and defiantly— for his hat.

"I'll ask for credit. We've spent enough by now, wherever it is we've gone; they should give us that."

It was now she who didn't move, remained poised there by the door. She looked thoughtfully downward at nothing there was to be seen. At last she shook her head slightly, a smile without mirth influencing her lips. "No," she said. "It's not the same. It would cast a pall, now, just knowing. And then they treat you with less respect, when you ask them. Or they commence to hound you within a few days, and you're twice as badly off as before."

She came away from the door. She closed it at last, but now before, and not behind, her. And she gave it a sort of fling away from her, in doing so; let it carry itself to its proper junction. He tried to make out if there was ill temper lurking in the gesture, and couldn't tell for sure. It might have been nothing more than jaunty disregard, an attempt to show him she didn't care whether she stayed or went. But even if there *was* no ill temper in it, the thought of ill temper was in his mind. So it had already appeared on the scene, in a way.

He watched her return, with indolent gait, to the seat before the mirror that she had occupied for the better part of an hour only just now. But now she gave her back to the glass, not her face. Now the former process was reversed. Now she rid herself, one by one, with limp gesture, of the accessories she had so zestfully attached to herself only a brief while ago. Her gloves fell, stringy, over her shoulder on the dressing table. Her untried fan atop them a moment later, its stylized, beguiling usage never given a chance to go into effect. Off came the tiny hat with orange willow feathers, she pitched it from her broadside (but not with violence, with philosophic riddance), and it fell upon the seat of a nearby chair. The plume tendrils fluctuated above it for a moment, like ocean-bottom vegetation stirring in deep water, then settled down over it.

"You may as well turn up the gas jets again," she said dully, "as long as we're staying in."

She raised her feet, heels upward, one by one, and taking them from behind, plucked off the bronze satin slippers with their spool-shaped Louis XV heels, full three inches in length, a daring height but pardonable because of her own stature. And let them fall as they would, and set her stockinged soles back on the floor as they were.

And last of all, undoing some certain something behind her, she allowed her dress to widen and fall of its own looseness, but only down to her seated waist, and sat that way, half-in and half-out of it, in perfect disarray. Almost as if to make a point of it.

It did something to him, to watch her undo that completed work of art she had so deftly and so painstakingly achieved. More than any spoken reproaches could have, it implicitly rebuked him.

Hands grounded in pockets, he looked down at the floor and felt small and humbled.

She took off the string of pearls that had clasped her throat and, allowing them to drizzle together, tossed them in air as if weighing them and finding them wanting, caught them in her palm.

"Will these help? You can have them if they will."

His face whitened, as if with some deep inward incision. "Bonny!" he commanded her tautly. "Don't ever say anything like that to me again."

"I meant nothing by it," she said placatingly. "You paid better than a hundred for them, didn't you? I only thought—"

"When I buy you a thing, it's yours."

They were silent for a while, their lines of gaze in opposite directions. He looking toward the window, and the impersonal, aloof evening outside. She toward the door, and (perhaps) the beckoning evening outside that.

She lit a cigar after a while. Then said in immediate compunction, "Oh, I forgot. You don't like me to do that." And turned to discard it.

"Don't put it out," he said absently. "Finish it if you like."

She extinguished it nevertheless.

Turning back, she reared one knee high before her, clasped her hands about it, settled comfortably backward. Then instantly, and again with contrition, she dissolved the pose once more. "Oh, I forgot. You don't like me to do that either."

"That was before, when you were supposed to be Julia," he said. "It's different now."

Suddenly he looked at her with redoubled closeness, as if wondering belatedly if this was some new indirect way of chiding him: reminding him of his past criticism of *her* faults. Her face seemed plotless enough, however. She didn't even seem to see him looking at her. The edges of her trivial mouth were curved upward in placid contentment.

"I'm sorry, Bonny," he said at last.

She returned her attention to him, from wherever it had strayed. "I don't mind," she said evenly. "I've had this happen to me before. For you, it's your first time; that makes it hard."

"You haven't had any supper," he said presently. "And it's near-ing eight."

"That's right," she agreed cheerfully. "We can still eat. Can't we?"

Again he wondered if that was an indirect jibe; again it seemed to be only in his mind. But at least it *was* there in his mind; it must have come from somewhere.

She got up and went over to the wall and took down the pneu-matic speaking-tube. She blew through the orifice and a whistling sound went traveling far downward, to its destination below.

"Will you send up a waiter," she said. "We're in Suite 12."

When the man had arrived, she ordered, taking precedence over Durand.

"Bring us something *small*," she said. "We're not very hungry. A mutton chop apiece would do very nicely. No soup, no sweet—"

Again Durand's eyes sought out her face to see if that was meant for him, that ironic emphasis. But hers were not to be met.

"Will that be all, madam?"

"And, oh yes, one thing more. Bring us up a deck of cards, along with the tray. We're staying in this evening."

"What'd you want those for?" Durand asked, as soon as the door had closed.

She turned to him and smiled quite sweetly. "To play double solitaire," she said. "I'll teach you the game. There's nothing like it for passing the time."

His reaction didn't come at once. It was slow, it didn't material-ize for some four or five minutes.

Then suddenly he picked up a bisque ornament from the center table and heaved it with all his strength, mouth knotted, and shat-tered it against the wall opposite him.

She must have been used to violence. She scarcely turned a hair, her eyelids barely rose enough to let her see what it had been.

"They'll charge us for that, Lou. We can't afford it now."

"I'm going to New Orleans tomorrow," he said, thick-voiced

with truculence. "I'm taking the first train out. You wait for me here. I'll have money for you again, you'll see. I'll raise it from Jardine."

Her eyes were wider open now, but whether any deeper with concern, could not have been told. "No!" she said aghast. "You can't go *near* there. You mustn't. We're wanted. They'll catch you."

"Rather that than go on here this way, living like a dog."

Now she smiled a real smile, beaming-bright; no sweet pale copy like a stencil on her lips. "That's my Lou," she purred, velvet smooth, her voice velvet warm. "That was the right answer. I love a man that takes chances."

— 52 —

JARDINE LIVED on Esplanade Avenue. Durand remembered the house well. He'd had dinner with them there on many a Sunday night during his bachelor days, and been honorary "uncle" to Jardine's little girl Marie.

The house had not changed. It was not houses that changed, he reflected ruefully, it was men. It was still honest, amiable, open of countenance. He might have been standing before it again back two or three years ago, with a little bag of bonbons in his hand for Marie. But he wasn't.

He stood there after he'd knocked, and kept holding his handkerchief to his nose, as if he were suffering from a bad head cold. It was to hide as much of his features as possible, however. And even while doing so, it occurred to him how futile such precautions were. Anyone who knew him by sight at all, would know him as well from the back, without seeing his face.

Before the door had opened he had already given up the attempt, lowered and pocketed the handkerchief.

They still had the same colored woman he remembered, Nelly, to open their door.

At sight of him her face lit up and her palms backed to shoulders.

"Well, lookit who's here! Well, I declare! Why, Mr. Lou! You *sure* a stranger!"

He smiled sheepishly, glanced uneasily down the street.

"Is Mr. Allan back from his office yet?"

"Why, no sir. But come in anyway. He'll be along right smart. Miss Gusta, she's home. And young Miss Marie. They'll both be mighty pleased to see you, I know."

He went in past the threshold, then faltered there. "Nelly, don't—don't tell them I'm calling—just yet; I have to see Mr. Allan on business first. Just let me wait down here somewhere until he comes home, without saying anything—" He caught himself winding the brim of his hat around in his hands, like a suppliant, and quickly stopped it.

Nelly's face dropped reproachfully.

"You don't want me to tell Miss Gusta you drap in?"

"Not just yet. I have to see Mr. Allan alone first."

"Well, come in the parlor, sir, and make yourself comf'table. I light the lamp." Her effusiveness was gone. She was a little cooler now. "Take your hat?"

"No, thanks; I'll keep it."

"You wants anything while you waiting, you just ring for me, Mr. Lou."

"I'll be all right."

She gave him a backward glance from the doorway, then she went out.

He was on thin ice, he realized. Any one of them, even Jardine himself, might have heard about it, could denounce his presence here, effect his immediate arrest. He was at their mercy; he was putting his trust where he had no certainty it could be put. Friendship? Yes, for an ordinary man, of their own kind. But friendship for a man branded a murderer? Those were two different matters, not the same thing at all.

He could hear a well-remembered woman's voice call down ringingly from somewhere above-stairs: "Who was that, Nelly?"

And at the momentary hesitation on Nelly's part, he involuntarily tightened his grip on his still nervously circling hat brim, held it arrested a moment.

"Gentleman to see Mr. Jardine on business."

"Did he wait?"

Nelly adroitly got around the problem of telling an outright lie. "I told him he not in yet."

The upstairs voice, still audible but no longer in as high a key, as if now pitched to someone else on the same floor with her, was heard to remark: "How strange to come here instead of to your papa's office." After which it withdrew, and there was no further colloquy.

Durand sat there in the glowing effulgence of the parlor, staring as if spellbound at a small handpainted periwinkle on the surface of the lamp globe, which seemed to hang suspended between himself and the white sheen that came translucently through all around it.

This is home, he thought. Nothing ever happens here, nothing bad. You come home to it with impunity, you go out again with immunity, you turn your face openly toward the world. And murder—human death brought about by the act of human hands—that is something in the Bible, in the history books, something done by the captains and the kings of old. In the passages that you perhaps skip over, when you are reading aloud to your children. Cortez and the Borgias and the Medici; poinards and poisons, long ago and faraway. But not in the full light of nineteenth-century day, in your own personal life.

This should be my home, he thought. I mean, my home should be like this man's. Why was I robbed of this? What did I do that was wrong?

Again the woman's voice came, upstairs, calling with pleasant firmness from one room to the next: "Marie. Your hair, dear, and your hands. It's getting near the time for Papa to come home."

And a younger, higher voice in answer: "Yes, Mamma. Shall I wear a ribbon in my hair tonight? Papa likes me to."

And below, sensuously drifting from the back somewhere, intermittent whiffs of rice and greens and savory frying fat.

This was all I wanted, he thought. Why have I lost it? Why was it taken from me? All other men have it. How did I offend? *Who* did I offend?

Jardine's key clicked in the door, and he swung around alertly in his chair, to face the open doorway, to be ready when he should appear beyond it, on his way through.

There was the tap of his stick going down to rest, and a little drumlike thump as his hat found a prong on the rack.

Then he appeared, facing stairward toward his family, unbuttoning the thigh-length mustard-colored coat he wore.

"Allan," Durand said in a circumspect voice, "I have to talk to you. Can you give me a few minutes? I mean before—before the family?"

Jardine turned abruptly, and saw him there for the first time. He came striding in, outstretched arm first, to shake his hand, but his face had already been sobered, made anxious, by Durand's opening remark.

"What are you *doing* here like this? When did you come back? Does Auguste know you're here? Why do they leave you sitting alone like this?"

"I asked Nelly not to say anything. I must talk to you alone first."

Jardine pulled a velour tape ending in a thin brass ring. Then went back to the open doorway, looked out, and when she had come in answer to the summons, said with a bruffness that betokened his uneasiness: "Hold supper a few minutes, Nelly."

"Yes sir. Only I hope you two gentlemen'll bear in mind it don't git no tastier with holding."

Jardine spread out his arms and drew together the two sliding

doors that sealed off the parlor. Then he came back and stood looking at Durand questioningly.

"Look, Allan, I don't know how to begin—"

Jardine shook his head, as if in dissatisfaction at the condition
he found him in. "Would a drink help, Lou?"

"Yes, I think it would."

Jardine poured them, and they each drank.

Again he stood there, looking down at him in the chair.

"There's something wrong, Lou."

"Very much so."

"Where did you go? Where've you been all this time? Not a
word to me. I haven't known whether you're dead or alive—"

Durand stemmed the flow of questions with a half-hearted lift
of his hand.

"I'm with her again," he said after a moment. "I can't come back
to New Orleans. Don't ask me why. That isn't what I came here
about." Then he added, "Haven't you seen anything in the papers,
that would explain it to you?"

"No," Jardine said, mystified. "I don't know what you mean."

Hasn't he, Durand wondered. Doesn't he really know? Is he
telling the truth? Or is he too delicate, too considerate, to tell
me— Jardine consulted his glass, drained the last drop, said: "I
don't want to know anything you don't want to tell me, Lou. Each
man's life is his own."

Downs's was his own too, passed through Durand's mind;
until I—

"Well, then we'll come to the point that brings me here," he
said, with a briskness he was far from feeling. He turned around
in the chair to face him once more. "Allan, how much would the
business bring as it stands today? I mean, what would be a fair
price for it, if someone were to come along and—"

Jardine's face paled. "You're thinking of selling, Lou?"

"I'm thinking of selling, Allan, yes. To you, if you'll buy out my
share from me. Will you? Can you?"

Jardine seemed incapable of answering immediately. He started walking slowly back and forth, on a short straight course beside the chair Durand sat in. He clasped his arms. Then presently he locked hands over his two rear pockets, and let the skirt of his coat flounce down over them.

"You may as well know this now, before we go any further," Durand added. "I can't sell to anyone else *but* you. I can't put in an appearance to do so. I can't approach anyone else. The lawyer will have to come here to your house. The whole thing will have to be done quietly."

"At least wait a day or two," Jardine urged. "Think it over—"

"I *haven't* a day or two in which to wait!" Durand slowly wagged his head from side to side in exasperated impatience. "Can't you understand? Must I tell you openly?"

In a moment more, he cautioned himself, it will be too late; once I have told him, I will be completely at his mercy. What I am asking him to buy from me, would go to him by default anyway; all he would have to do is step over to that bellpull over there—

But he went ahead and told him anyway, with scarcely the pause required by the warning thought to deliver its admonition.

"I'm a fugitive, Allan. I'm outside the law. I've lost all my rights of citizenship."

Jardine stopped his pacing, stunned. "Great God!" he breathed slowly.

Durand slapped at his own thigh, with a sort of angry despair. "It's got to be right tonight. Right now. It can't wait. *I* can't. I'm taking a risk even staying in the town that long—"

Jardine bent toward him, took him by the shoulders, gripped hard. "You're throwing away your whole future, your whole life's work—I can't let you—"

"I have no future, Allan. Not a very long one. And my life's work, I'm afraid, is behind me, anyway, whether I sell or not."

He let his wrists dangle limp, down between his legs, in a cowed attitude. "What are we going to do, Allan?" he murmured abjectly. "Are you going to help me?"

There was a tapping at the door. Then a childish voice: "Papa.

Mamma wants to know if you're going to be much longer. The duck's getting awfully dry. Nelly can't do a thing with it."

"Soon, dear, soon," Jardine called over his shoulder.

"Go in to your family," Durand urged. "I'm spoiling your supper. I'll sit in here and wait."

"I couldn't eat with this on my mind," Jardine said. He bent to him once more, as if in renewed effort to extract the confidence from him that he sought. "Look, Lou. We've known each other since you were twenty-three and I was twenty-eight. Since we were clerks together in the shipping department of old man Morel, perched on adjoining stools, slaving away. We got our promotions together. When he wanted to promote you, you spoke for me. When he wanted to promote me, I spoke for you. Finally, when we were ready, we pooled our resources and entered into business together. Our own import house. On a shoestring at first, even with the help of the money Auguste had brought to me in marriage. And you remember those early days."

"I remember, Allan."

"But we didn't care. We said we'd rather work for ourselves, and fail, than work for another man, and prosper. And we worked for ourselves—and prospered. But there are things in this business of ours, today, that cannot be taken out again. There is sweat, and worry, and the high hopes of two young fellows, and the prime years of their lives. Now you come to me and want to *buy* these things from me, want me to *sell* them to you, as if they were sackfuls of our green beans from Colombia— How can I, even if I wanted to? How can I set a price?"

"You can tell what the business is worth, in cold cash, that is on our books. And give me half, in exchange for a quit-claim, a deed of sale, whatever the necessary paper is. Forget I am Durand. I am just anybody, I am a stranger who happens to have a fifty per cent interest. Give its approximate value back to me in money, that is all I ask you." He gestured violently. "Don't you see, Allan? I can no longer participate in the business, I can no longer play any part in it. I can't *be* here to do so, I can't *stay* here."

"But why? There isn't anything you can have done—"

"There is. There's one thing."

Jardine was waiting, looking at him fixedly.

"Once I tell you, Allan, I'm at your mercy. You needn't give me a cent, and my half of the business goes to you, eventually, anyway— by default."

But he was at his mercy anyway, he realized ruefully, whether he told him or not.

Jardine bridled a little, straightened up. "Lou, I don't take that kindly. We're friends—"

"Friendship stops short at what I'm about to tell you. There are no friends beyond a certain point. The law even forbids it, punishes it."

The tapping came again. "Mamma's getting put out. She says she's going to sit down without you, Papa. It was a special duck—"

And on that homespun domestic note, Durand blurted out, as if already past the point at which he could any longer stop himself:

"Allan, I've done murder. I can't stay here past tonight. I have to have money."

And dropped his head into his upturned, sheltering hands, as though the hangman's noose had already snapped his neck.

"Papa?" came questioningly through the door.

"Wait, child, wait," Jardine said sickly, his face white as a sheet.

There was a ghastly silence.

"I knew it would come to this," Jardine said at last, dropping his voice. "She was bad for you from the first. Auguste sensed it on the very day of your marriage, she told me so herself; women are quicker that way—"

He was pouring himself a drink, as though it were his crime. "You met her— You found her— You lost your head—" He brought one to Durand. "But you're not to be blamed. Any man— Let me find you a good lawyer, Lou. There isn't a court in the state—"

Durand looked up at him and gave a pathetic smile.

"You don't understand, Allan. It isn't—she. It's the very man I engaged to find her and arrest her. He did find her, and to save her I—"

Jardine, doubly horrified now, for at least in his earlier concern there had been, noticeably, a glint of vengeful satisfaction, recoiled a step.

"I'm with her again," Durand admitted. And in an almost inaudible whisper, as if he were telling it to his conscience and not to the other man in the room with him, "I love her more than my life itself."

"Papa," accosted them with frightening proximity, in a piping treble, "Mamma said I shouldn't leave this door until you come out of there!" The doorknob twisted, then unwound.

Jardine stood for a long moment, looking not so much at his friend as at some scene he alone could see.

His arm reached out slowly at last and fell heavily, dejectedly, but with unspoken loyalty, upon Durand's shoulder.

"I'll see that you get your half of the business' assets, Lou," he said. "And now—we mustn't keep Auguste waiting any longer. Keep a stiff upper lip. Come in and have supper with us."

Durand rose and crushed Jardine's hand almost shatteringly for a moment, between both of his. Then, as if ashamed of this involuntary display of emotion, hastily released it again.

Jardine opened the door, bent down to kiss someone who remained unseen, through the guarded opening. "Run in, dear. We're coming."

Durand braced himself for the ordeal to come, straightened his shoulders, jerked at the wings of his coat, adjusted his collar. Then he moved after his host.

"You won't tell them, Allan?"

Jardine drew the door back and stood aside to let him go through first. "There are certain things a man doesn't take in to his supper-table with him, Lou." And he slung his arm about his friend's shoulder and walked beside him, loyally beside him, in to where his family waited.

— 53 —

AT DAWN he was already up, from a sleepless, worried bed, and dressed and pacing the floor of his shabby, hidden-away hotel room. Waiting for Jardine to come with the money—

("I can't get you the money before morning, Lou. I haven't it here in the house; I'll have to draw it from the bank. Can you wait?"

"I'll have to. I'm at the Palmetto Hotel. Under the name of Castle. Room Sixty. Bring it to me there. Or as much of it as you can, I cannot wait for a complete inventory.")

—fearing more and more with the passing of each wracking hour that he wouldn't. Until, as the hour for the banks to open came and went, and the morning drew on, fear had become certainty and certainty had become conviction. And he knew that to wait on was only to invite the inevitable betrayal to overtake him, trap him where he was.

A hundred times he unlocked the door and listened in the dingy corridor outside, then went back and locked himself in again. Nothing, no one. He wasn't coming. Only a quixotic fool would have expected him to.

Again it occurred to him how completely at the mercy of his former partner he had put himself. All he had to do was bring the police with him instead of the money, and there was an end to it. Why should he give up thousands of hard-earned dollars? And money, Durand reminded himself, did strange things to people. Turned them even against their own flesh and blood, why not an outsider?

Bonny's remark came back to him. "And we're none of us very much good, the best of us, men or women alike." She knew. She was wise in the ways of the world, wiser by far than he. She would never have put herself in such a false position.

No friend should be put to such a test. A man without the law no longer had a claim, no longer had a right to expect—

There was a subdued knock, and he shrank back against the wall. "Here they come now to arrest me," flashed through his mind. "He's put them onto me—"

He didn't move. The knock came again.

Then Jardine's whispered voice. "Lou. Are you in there? It's all right. It's me."

He'd brought them with him; he'd led them here in person.

With a sort of bitter defiance, because he could no longer escape, because he'd waited too long, he went to the door and unlocked it. Then took his hands from it and let it be.

There was a moment's wait, then it opened of itself, and Jardine came in, alone. He closed and relocked it behind him. He was holding a small satchel.

He carried it to the table, set it down.

All he said, matter of factly and with utter simplicity, was: "Here is the money, Lou. I'm sorry I'm so late."

Durand couldn't answer for a moment, turned away, overcome.

"What's the matter, Lou? Why, your eyes—!" Jardine looked at him as though he couldn't understand what was amiss with him.

Durand knuckled at them sheepishly. "Nothing. Only, you came as you said you would—You brought it as you said you would—" Something choked in his throat and he couldn't go ahead.

Jardine looked at him compassionately. "Once you would have taken such a thing for granted, you would have expected it of me. What has changed you, Lou? *Who* has changed you?" And softly, fiercely, through his clenched teeth, as his knotted hand came down implacably upon the table top, he exhaled: "And may God damn them for it! I hate to see a decent man dragged down into the gutter."

Durand stood there without answering.

"You know it's true, or else you wouldn't stand there and take it from me," Jardine growled. "But I'll say no more; each man's hell is his own."

(I know it's true, Durand thought wistfully; but I must follow my heart, how can I help where it leads me?) "No, don't say any more," he agreed tersely.

Jardine unstrapped and stripped open the bag. "The full amount is in here," he told him, brisk and businesslike now. "And that squares all accounts between us."

Durand nodded stonily.

"I cannot have you at my house again," Jardine told him. "For your own sake."

Durand gave a short, and somewhat ungracious, syllable of laughter. "I understand."

"No, you don't. I am trying to protect you. Auguste already suspects something, and I cannot vouch for her discretion if you return."

"Auguste hates me, doesn't she?" Durand said with detached curiosity, as though unable to account for it.

Jardine didn't answer, and by that confirmed the statement.

He gestured toward the contents of the satchel, still withholding it. "I turn this over to you under one condition, Lou. I ask it of you for your own good."

"What is it?"

"Don't turn this money over to anyone else, *no matter how close they are to you.* Keep it safe. Keep it by you. Don't let it out of your possession."

Durand laughed humorlessly. "Who am I likely to entrust it to? The very position I'm in ensures my not—"

Jardine repeated his emphasis, so that there could be no mistaking it. "I said, *no matter how close they are to you.*"

Durand looked at him hard for a minute. "I'm in good hands, I see," he said bitterly at last. "Auguste hates me, and you hate— my wife."

"Your wife," Jardine said tonelessly.

Durand tightened his hands. "I said my wife."

"Don't let's quarrel, Lou. Your word."

"The word of a murderer?"

"The word of the man who was my best friend. The word of the man who was Louis Durand," Jardine said tautly. "That's good enough for me."

"Very well, I give it."

Jardine handed him the satchel. "I'll go now."

There was a constraint between them now. Jardine offered his hand in parting. Durand saw it waiting there, allowed a full moment to go by before taking it. Then when at last they shook, it was more under compulsion of past friendship than present cordiality.

"This is probably a final goodbye, Lou. I doubt we'll ever see one another again."

Durand dropped his eyes sullenly. "Let's not linger over it, then. Good luck, and thank you for having once been my friend."

"I am still your friend, Lou."

"But I am not the man whose friend you were."

Their hands uncoupled, fell away from one another.

Jardine moved toward the door.

"You know what I would do in your place, of course? I would go to the police, surrender myself, and have it over once and for all."

"And hang," Durand said sombrely.

"Yes, even to hang is better than what lies ahead of you. You could be helped, Lou. This way, no one can help you. If I were in your place—"

"You *couldn't* be in my place," Durand cut him short. "It wouldn't have happened to you, to start with. You are not the kind such things befall. I am. You repel them. I attract them. It happened to me. To no one but me. And so I must deal with it. I must do—as I must do."

"Yes, I guess you must," Jardine conceded sadly. "None of us can talk for the other man." He opened the door, looking up along its edge with a sort of melancholy curiosity, as if he had never seen the edge of an open door before. He even palmed it, in passing, as if to feel what it was.

The last thing he said was: "Take care of yourself, Lou."

"If I don't, who else will?" Durand answered from the depths of his aloneness. "Who is there in this whole wide world who will?"

— 54 —

HE ONLY breathed freely again when the train had pulled out, and only looked freely from the window again when the last vestiges of the town had fallen behind and the dreary coastal sand flats had begun. The town that he had once loved most of all places in this world.

The train was a rickety, caterpillar-like creeper, that stopped at every crossroads shed and water tank along the way, or so it seemed, and didn't deposit him at his destination until well onto one in the morning. He found the station vicinity deserted, and all but unlighted; carriageless as well, and had to walk back to their hotel bag in hand, under a panel of brittle (and somehow satiric) stars.

And though the thought of surprising her in some act of treachery had not been the motive for his arriving a half night sooner than he'd said he would, the realization of how fatally enlightening this unheralded return could very well prove to be, slowly grew on him as he walked along, until it had taken hold of him altogether. By the time he had reached the hotel and climbed to their floor and stood before their door, he was almost afraid to take his key to it and open it. Afraid of what he would find. Not afraid of conventional faithlessness so much as her own characteristic kind of faithlessness. Not afraid of finding her in other arms so much as not finding her there at all. Finding her fled and gone in his absence, as he had once before.

He opened softly, and he held his breath back. The room

was dark, and the fragrance of violets that greeted him meant nothing, it could have been from yesterday as well as from today. Besides, it was in his heart rather than in his nostrils, so it was no true test.

He took out a little box of wax matches, that clicked and rattled with his trepidation, felt for the sandpaper tab fastened to the wall, and kindled the lamp wick. Then turned to look, as the slow-rising golden tide washed away night.

She was sleeping like a child, as innocent as one, as beautiful as one. (And only in sleep perhaps could she ever obtain such innocence any longer). And as gracefully, as artlessly disposed, as a child. Her hair flooded the pillow, as if her head were lying in the middle of a field of slanting sun-yellowed grass. One arm was hidden, the dimpled point of an elbow protruding from under the pillow all that could be seen of it. The other lay athwart her, to hang straight down over the side of the bed. Its thumb and forefinger were still touching together, making an irregular little loop that had once held something. Under it, on the carpet, lay two cards, the queen of diamonds and the knave of hearts.

The rest of the deck lay scattered about on the counterpane, some of them even on her own recumbent form.

He got down there beside her, at the bedside, on one knee, and took up her dangling hand, and found it softly, yet in a burning gratitude, with his lips. And though he didn't know it, had fallen into it without thought, his pose was that of the immemorial lover pleading his suit. Pleading his suit to a heart he cannot soften.

He swept off the cards onto the floor, replaced them with the money he had brought from New Orleans. Even raised his arms above her, holding it massed within them, letting it snow down upon her any which way it willed, in a green and orange leafy shower.

Her eyes opened, and following the undulant surface of the counterpane they were so close to, sighted at something, taking on a covetous expression with their whites uppermost, by the fact of their lying so low; but one that was perhaps closer to the truth than not.

"A hundred-dollar bill," she murmured sleepily.

"Lou's back," he whispered. "Look what he's brought you from New Orleans." And gathering up some of the fallen certificates, let them stream down all over again. One of them caught in her hair. And she reached up and felt for it there, with an expression of simpering satisfaction. Then having felt it was there, left it there, as though that was where she most wanted it to be.

She stretched out her hands to him, and traced his brows, and the turn of his face, and the point of his ear, in expression of lazy appreciation.

"What were those cards?"

"I was trying to tell our fortunes," she said. "And I fell asleep doing it. I got the queen of diamonds. The money card. And it came true. I'll never laugh at those things again."

"And what did I get?"

"The ace of spades."

He laughed. "What one's that?"

He felt her hand, which had been straying in his hair, stop for a moment. "I don't know."

He had an idea she did, but didn't want to tell him.

"What'd you do that for? Try reading them."

"I wanted to see if you were coming back or not."

"Didn't you know I would?"

"I did," she hedged. "But I wasn't sure."

"And I wasn't sure I'd find you here any longer," he confessed.

Suddenly she had one of those flashes of stark sincerity she was so capable of, and so seldom exercised. She swept her arms about his neck in a convulsive, despairing, knotted hug. "Oh, God!" she mourned bitterly. "What's wrong with the two of us anyway, Lou? Isn't it hell when you can't trust one another?"

He sighed for answer.

Presently she said, "I'm going back to sleep a little while more."

Her head came to rest against his, nestled there, in lieu of the pillow.

"Leave the money there," she purred blissfully. "It feels good lying all over me."

In a little while he could tell by her breathing she was sleeping again. Her head to his, her arms still twined collarlike about him. He could never get any closer to her than this, somehow he felt. He in her arms, she unconscious of him there.

His heart said a prayer. Not knowing to whom, but asking it of the nothingness around him, that he had plunged himself into of his own accord.

"Make her love me," he pleaded mutely, "as I love her. Open her heart to me, as mine is open to her. If she can't love me in a good way, let it be in a bad way. Only, in some way. *Any* way, at all. This is all I ask. For this I'll give up everything. For this I'll take whatever comes, even the ace of spades."

— 55 —

HE CAME upon it quite by accident. The merest chance of happening to go where he did, when he did. More than that even, of happening to do as he did, when he went where he did.

She had asked him to go out and get her some of the fledgling cigars she was addicted to, "La Favorita" was their name, while he waited about for her to catch up with him in her dressing, always a process from two to three times slower than his own. She smoked quite openly now, that is in front of him, at all times when they were alone together. Nothing he could do or say would make her desist, so it was he at last who desisted in his efforts to sway her, and let her be. And it was he, too, who emptied off and caused to disappear the ashes she recklessly left about behind her, or opened the windows to carry the aroma off, and even, once or twice when they had been intruded upon unexpectedly by a chambermaid or the like, caught up the cigar and drew upon it himself, as if it were his own, though he was a nonsmoker—all for the sake of her reputation and to keep gossip from being bruited about.

"What did you do—before?" he asked her, on the day of this present request.

He meant before she'd met him. Wondering if there'd been someone else, then, to go and fetch them for her.

"I had to go and get them for myself," she confessed.

"*You?*" he gasped. There seemed to be no end to the ways in which she could startle him.

"I usually told them it was for my brother, that he was ill and couldn't come for them himself, had sent me in his place. They always believed me implicitly, I could tell, but—" She shrugged with a nuance of aversion.

How could they have failed to, he reflected? How could anyone in his right senses have dreamed a woman would dare enter a tobacco shop on her own behalf?

"But I didn't like to do it much," she added. "Everyone always stared so. You'd think I were an ogre or something. If there were more than one in there, and there usually was, the most complete frozen silence would fall, as if I had cast a spell or something. And yet no matter how quickly it fell, it was never quickly enough to avoid my catching some word or other that I shouldn't, just as I first stepped in. Then they would stand there so guilty looking, wondering if I had heard, and if I had, if I understood its meaning." She laughed. "I could have told them that I did, and spared them their discomfort."

"Bonny!" he said in taut reproof.

"Well, I did," she insisted. "Why deny it?" Then she laughed once more, this time at the expression on his face, and pretended to fling something at him. "Oh, get along, old Prim and Proper!"

The tobacco shop he selected for the filling of her request, and his choice was quite at random, being in a resort town, sold other things as well with which to tempt its transient clientele. Picture cards on revolving panels, writing papers, glass jars of candy, souvenirs, even a few primary children's toys. There was in addition, just within the entrance where it could most readily catch the eye, an inclined wooden rack, holding newspapers from various other cities, an innovation calculated to appeal to homesick travelers.

He stopped by this as he was leaving and idly looked it over, hoping to find one from New Orleans. He had that slightly wistful feeling that the very name of the place alone was enough to cause him. Home. Word of home, in exile. Canal Street in the sunshine; Royal Street, Rampart Street, the Cabildo— He forgot where he was, and he felt lonely, and he ached somewhere so deep down inside that it must have been his very marrow. Love of another kind; the love every man has for the place he first came from, the place he first knew.

There were none to be found. He noticed one from Mobile, and withdrew that from the rack instead. It was not new; having remained unsold until now, he found it to be already dated two full weeks in the past.

Behind him meanwhile, disregarded, the storekeeper was urging helpfully: "Help you, sir? What town you from, mister? Got 'em all there. And if not, be glad to send for whichever one you want—"

He had opened it, meanwhile, casually. And from the inner page—it was only a single sheet, folded—this leaped up, searing him like a flash of gunpowder flame:

A HORRIFYING DISCOVERY IN THIS CITY.

The skeleton of a man has been unearthed in the cellar of a house on Decatur Street, in this city, within the last few days. At the time of the recent high water the occupants of the house quitted it, as did all their immediate neighbors. On their return the sunken outlines of a grave were revealed, its contents partly discernible.

It is believed the flood washed away the loosely replaced soil, for there had been no sign until then of such an unlawful burial. Adding to the belief that foul play was committed, was the finding of a lead bullet imbedded in the remains. The present house-holders, who at once reported their grim find to the authorities, are absolved of all blame, since the condition of the remains prove the grave to have been in existence well before their occupancy began.

The authorities are at present engaged in compiling a record of all former occupants in order to trace them for questioning. More developments will be given later, as they are made known to us.

She turned from her mirror to stare, as he blasted the door in minutes later, breathing heavily, greenish of face. Her own cheeks were rosy as ripe peaches with the recent application of the rabbit's foot. "What is it? You're as white as though you'd seen a ghost."

I have, he thought; face to face. The ghost of the man we thought we'd buried forever.

"It's been found out," he said tersely.

She knew at once.

She read it through.

She took it with surprising matter-of-factness, he thought. No recoil, no paling; with an almost professional objectivity, as if her whole interest were in its accuracy and not in its context. She said nothing when she'd completed it. He was the one had to speak.

"Well?"

"That was something we had to expect some day." She gestured with the paper, cast it down. "And there it is. What more is there to say?" She shrugged philosophically. "We haven't done so badly. It could have been much quicker." She began to count on her fin-gers, the way gossiping housewives do over an impending child-birth. Or rather, its antecedents. "When was it? About the tenth of June, if I remember. It's a full three months now—"

"Bonny!" he retched, his eyes closing in horror.

"They won't know any more who it is. They won't be able to tell. That's one thing in our favor."

"But they *know*, they *know*," he choked, taking swift two-paced turns this way and that, like a bear seeking its way out through cage-bars.

She rose suddenly, flinging down something with a sort of angered impatience. Angered impatience with him, seeking to calm him, seeking to reason with him, for she went to him, took him by the two facings of his coat, and shook him once, quite violently, as if for his own good, to instill some sense in him.

"Will you listen to me?" she flared. "Will you use your head? They know *what,* now. Very well. But they still don't know *who.* They don't know who caused it. And they never will." She gave a precautionary glance toward the closed door, lowered her voice. "There was no one in that room that day. No one in that house that day. No one who *saw* it happen. Never forget that. They can surmise, they can suspect, they can even feel sure, all they want, but they cannot *prove.* And the time is past, it is already too late; they will never be able to on the face of God's green earth. What was it they told you yourself when you went to them about me? You must have *proof.* And they have none. You threw the—you know what, away; it's lying rusted, buried in the sand, somewhere along the beach at Mobile, being eaten away by the salt water. Can they tell that a certain bullet comes from a certain one, and no other?" She laughed derisively. "Not in any way that's ever been found yet!"

Half heeding her, he glanced around him at the walls, and even upward at the ceiling, as though he felt them closing in upon him.

"Let's get out of here," he said in a choked voice, pulling at his collar. "I can't stand it any more."

"It's not here it's been discovered. It's in Mobile. We're as safe here as we were before it was discovered. They didn't know we were here before. They still don't know we're here now."

He wanted to put an added move, an extra lap, even if a fruit-less unneeded one, between themselves and Nemesis, looming dark like a massing cloudbank on the horizon.

She sighed, giving him a look as if she found him hopeless. "There goes our evening, I suppose," she murmured, more to herself than to him. "And I was counting on wearing the new wine-red taffeta."

She clapped him reassuringly on the arm. "Go down and get yourself a drink; make it a good stiff one. You need that now more than anything, I can see that. There's a good boy. Then come back, and we'll see how you feel by that time, and we'll figure it out then. There's a good boy." And she added, quite inconsequentially, "I'll go ahead dressing in the meantime, anyway. I *did* want to show them that wine-red taffeta."

In the end they stayed for the time being. But it was not her reasoning that kept him, so much as a fascinating horror that held him in its grip now. He was waiting for the next Mobile newspaper to arrive at the tobacco shop, and knew no other way of obtaining it than by remaining close at hand, here where they were.

It took five days, though he prodded the shopkeeper almost continuously in between.

"Sometimes they send 'em, sometimes they don't," the latter told him. "I could write and hurry them up, if you'd want me to."

"No, don't do that," Durand said rather hastily. "It's just that— I find nothing to do with myself down here. I like to get the news of the old home town."

Then when it came, he didn't have the courage to examine it there in the store, he took it back to her and they searched for it together, she holding the sheets spread, his strained face low on her shoulder.

"There it is," she said crisply, and narrowed the expanse with a sharp, crackling fold, and they read it together.

> ... Bruce Dollard, a renting agent, who has had charge of the property for the past several years, has informed the authorities of one instance in which the occupants gave abrupt notice of departure, quitting the house within the space of a single morning, with no previous indication before that day of intending to do so.
>
> The proprietor of a tool shop has identified a shovel found in the cellar of the house as one that he sold to an unidentified woman some time ago, and it is thought the purchase of this implement may well aid in fixing the approximate time of the misdeed.
>
> Other than that, there have been no further developments, but the authorities are confident of bringing to light new ...

"Now they know," he said bitterly. *"Now* there can be no denying it any longer. *Now* they know."

"No they don't," she said flatly. "Or it wouldn't be in here like this. They're guessing, as much as they ever were."

"The shovel—"

"The shovel was in the house, long after we left. Others could have used it, who came after us."

"It gets worse, all the time."

"It only seems to. They want to do the very thing to you they are doing: frighten you, cause you to blunder in some way. In actuality it's no whit worse than it was before it was found."

"How can you say that, when it stands there before you in black and white?"

She shook her head. "The barking dog can't bite you at the same time; he has to stop when he's ready to sink his teeth in. Don't you know that when they *do* know, if they do, *we* will never know they do? You are waiting for a message that will never reach us. You are looking for news that will never come. Don't you know that we're safe so long as they keep on mentioning it? When they stop, that's the time to look out. When sudden silence falls, the danger has really begun."

He wondered where she got her wisdom. From hard-won experience of her own? Or had it been born in her blood, as cats can see in the dark and avoid pitfalls?

"Couldn't it mean that they've forgotten?"

She gave him another capsule of her bitter wisdom, sugared with a hard, wearied smile.

"The police? They never forget, lovey. It's we who will have to. If we want to live at all."

He brought in three papers the next time. Three successive ones, each a day apart, but that had come in all together. They divided them up, went to work separately, hastily ruffling them over page by page, in search of what they were after.

He turned his head sharply, looked at her half frightened. "It's stopped! There's not a word about it any more."

"Nor in these either." She nodded with sage foreboding. "Now the real danger *is* beginning. Now it's under way."

He flung the sheets explosively aside, rose in instant readiness, so much under her guidance had he fallen in these things. "Shall we go?"

She considered, made their decision. "We'll wait for one more newspaper. We can give ourselves that much leeway. They may already know *who*, but I doubt that they still know *where*." Another wait. Three days more this time. Then the next one came. Again nothing. Dead silence. *Brooding* silence, it almost seemed to him, as they pored over it together.

This time they just looked at one another. It was she who rose at last, put hands to the shoulders of her cream satin dressing robe to take it off. Coolly, unhurriedly, but purposefully.

"Now's the time to go," she said quietly. "They're on to us."

He was still baffled, even this late, at the almost sixth sense she seemed to have developed. It frightened him. He knew, at least, it was something he would never attain.

"I'll begin to pack," she said. "Don't go out any more. Stay up here where you are until we're ready."

He shuddered involuntarily. He sat on there, watching her, following her movements with his eyes as she moved about. It was like—observing an animated divining rod, that walked and talked like a woman.

"You went about it wrong," she remarked presently. "It's too late to mend now, but you may have even hastened it, for all we know. Singling out just the Mobile papers each time. Word of things like that can travel more swiftly than you know."

"But how else—?" he faltered.

"Each time you bought one, you should have bought one from some other place at the same time, even if you discarded it immediately afterward. In that way you divide suspicion."

She went on into the next room.

Even that there was a wrong and a right way to go about, he reflected helplessly. Ah, the wisdom of the lawless.

She came back to the door for a moment, pausing in mid-packing.

"Where shall it be now? Where shall we go from here?"

He looked at her, haunted. He couldn't answer that.

— 56 —

THEY CAME to a halt in Pensacola, at last, for a little while, to catch their breaths. They had now followed the great, slow, curve the Gulf Coast makes as far as they could go along it, heading eastward, always eastward. By fits and starts, by frightened spurts and equally frightened stops, some long, some short, they'd followed their destiny blindly. New Orleans, then Biloxi, then Mobile, then Pensacola. With many a little hidden-away place in between.

Now Pensacola. They couldn't go any farther than that, along their self-appointed trajectory, without leaving the littoral behind, and for some reason or other, probably fear of the unknown, they clung to the familiar coastline. From there the curve dropped sharply away, past the huddle of tin-roofed shacks that was Tampa, on down to the strange, other-language foreignness of Havana. And that would have meant cutting themselves off completely, exile irrevocable beyond power to return. (Returning ships were inspected, and they had no documents.) Nor did they want to cut inland and make for Atlanta, the next obvious step. She was afraid, for reasons of her own, of the North, and though that was not the North, it was a step toward it.

So, Pensacola. They took a house again in Pensacola. Not for grandeur now, not for style, not to feel "really" married, but for the sake of simple, elementary safety.

"They spot you much easier in a hotel," she whispered, in their rain-beaten, one-night hotel. "They nose into your business quicker. People come and go more, all around you, carrying tales away with them and spreading them all around."

He nodded, bending to peer from under the lowered window shade, then starting back as a flash of lightning limned it intolerably bright.

They took the most remote, hidden, inconspicuous house they could find, on a drowsing, tree-lined street well out from the center of town. Other houses not too near, neighbors not too many; they put heavy lace curtains in the windows, to be safer still from prying eyes. They engaged a woman out of sheer compulsion, but pared her presence to a minimum; only three days a week, and she must be gone by six, not sleep under their roof. They spoke guardedly in front of her, or not at all.

They were going to be very discreet, they were going to be very prudent this time.

The first week or two, every time Bonny came or went from the house in daylight, she held her parasol tipped low as she stepped to or from the carriage, so that it shielded her face. And he, without that advantage of concealment, kept his head down all he could. So that, almost, he always seemed to be looking for something along the ground each time he entered or left.

And when a neighbor came to offer a courtesy call, as the custom was, laden with homemade jellies and the like, Bonny held her fast at the door, and made voluble explanations that they were not settled yet and the house was not in order, as an excuse for not asking her in.

The woman went away, with affronted mien and taking her gifts back with her unpresented, and when next they sighted her on the walk she made no salutation and looked the other way.

"You should not have done that," he cautioned, stepping out from where he had listened, as the frustrated visitor departed. "That looks even more suspicious, to be so skittish."

"There was no other way," she said. "If I had once admitted her, then others would have come, and I would have been expected to return their calls, and there would have been no end to it."

After that once, no others came.

"They probably think we live together," she told him, once, jeeringly. "I always leave my left glove off, now, every time I go out, and hold my hand up high, to the parasol-stick, so that they cannot fail to see the wedding band." And punctuated it: "The filthy sows!"

Mr. and Mrs. Rogers had come to Pensacola. Mr. and Mrs. Rogers had taken a house in Pensacola. Mr. and Mrs. Rogers—from nowhere. On the way to—no one knows.

— 57 —

THIS TIME he did not tell her; she guessed it by his face. She saw him standing there by the window, staring out at nothing, gnawing at his lip. And when she spoke to him, said something to him, his answer, instead of being in kind, was to turn away, thrust hands in pockets, and begin to pace the room on a long, straight course, up and down.

She understood him so well by now, she knew it could be nothing but the thing it was.

She nodded finally, after watching him closely for some moments. "Again?" she said cryptically.

"Again," he answered, and came to a halt, and flung himself into a chair.

She flung from her irritably a stocking she had been donning upward over her arm in search of rents. "Why is it always that way with us?" she complained. "We no sooner can turn around and draw our breaths, than it's gone again, and the whole thing starts over!"

"It goes, with anyone," he said sombrely. "It's the one thing you can't hold and yet use at the same time."

"With us, it seems to dash!" she exclaimed bitterly. "I never saw the like." It was now she who had sought the window, was seeking out that distant, faltering star of their fortunes, up beyond somewhere, that he had been scanning earlier. There for only the two of them, and no one else, to see. "Does that mean New Orleans again?"

They had grown so, they could understand one another almost without words, certainly without the fully explicit rounded phrase.

"There's no more New Orleans; that's done. There's nothing left there any longer to go back for."

They had even grown alike in mannerisms. It was now she who gnawed at her underlip. "How much have we?"

"Two hundred and some," he answered without lifting his head.

She came close to him and put her hand to the outside of his arm, as if she wished to attract his attention; although she had it in full already.

"There are two things can be done," she said. "We can either sit and do nothing with it, until it is all gone. Or we can take it and set it to work for us."

He simply looked up at her; this time there was a flaw in their mutual understanding, a blind spot.

"I have known many men with less than two hundred for a stake to run it up to two or three thousand."

She kept her hand on his arm, as if the thought were entering by there in some way, and not by word of mouth. It still failed to.

"Do you know any card games?" she persisted.

"There was one I used to play with Jardine in our younger days, of an evening. Bezique, I think. I scarcely remem—"

"I mean real games," she interrupted impatiently.

He understood her, then.

"You mean gamble with it? Risk it?"

She shook her head, more impatient than ever. "Only fools *gamble* with it. Only fools *risk* it. I'll show you how to play so that you're *sure* of running up your two hundred."

He saw what she really meant, then.

"Cheat," he said tonelessly.

She flung her head away from him, then brought it back again.

"Don't be so sanctimonious about it. Cheat is just a word. Why use that particular one? There are plenty of others just as good. 'Prepare' yourself. 'Insure' against losing. Why leave everything to chance? Chance is a harlot."

She stepped away, caught at the back of a chair, began dragging it temptingly after her, at a slant.

"Come, sit down. I'll teach you the game itself first."

She was a good teacher. In an hour he knew it sufficiently well.

"You now know faro," she said. "You know it as well as I or anyone else can show it to you. Now I'll teach you the really important part. I must put on some things first."

He sat there idly fingering the cards while she was gone. She came back decked with all her jewelry, as she would have worn it of any evening. It looked grotesque, overlaying the household deshabille she wore.

She sat down before him, and something made his hand shake a little. As does a hand that is about to commit something heinous.

"There are four suits, mark them well," she said briskly. "I will not be sitting in the game with you, they do not play with women, and everything depends upon the quick coordination between us, you and me. Yet on the river boats it never failed, and so it should not fail here. It is the simplest system of all, and the most easily discovered, but we must use it, for your own fingers are not yet deft enough at rigging a deal, and so you must rely on me and not yourself to see you through the tight places. We will use it sparingly, saving it each time for the moment that counts the most. Now, mark. When my hand strays to my bosom so, that's hearts. The pendant at my throat, that's diamonds. The eardrop on the left, spades. The one on the right, clubs. Then you watch my hand as it goes down again, that gives you the count. The fingers are numbered from one to ten, starting at the outside of the left hand. The little finger of the left hand is one, the little finger of the right, ten. Whichever one I fold back, or only shorten a little, gives the count."

"How does that tell me when he's holding jacks, queens or kings?"

"They follow in regular order, eleven, twelve, thirteen. A king would be a folding-back of the little finger on the left hand and of the third finger on the left hand. An ace is simply one."

"How can you hope to see every card he holds in his hand, and signal me?"

"I can't and I don't try. One or two of the top cards are all you need, and those are all I give you."

She thrust the deck toward him over the tabletop.

"Deal me a hand."

She arranged it.

"Now tell me what I am holding in my hand."

He watched her.

"Your top cards are the queen of diamonds, knave of hearts, ace of clubs."

He got no praise.

"You stared at me so, a blind man could have seen what you were about. You play this with your face, as well as with your fingers; learn that. Now again."

He told her again.

"Better, but you are too slow. They won't wait for you, while you sit there summing up in your mind. Now another."

Her only praise was a nod. "Once more."

This time, at last, she conceded: "You are not stupid, Louis." He threw the cards aside suddenly.

"I can't do this, Bonny."

She gave him a scathing look.

"Why? Are you too good? Does it soil you?"

He dropped his eyes before hers, ran desperate fingers through his hair.

"You killed a man once in Mobile, if I remember!" she accused him. "But you cannot sharpen up a card game a little. No, you're too goody-goody."

"That was different somehow—" (And why do *you* throw that up to me, anyhow? he thought.)

"If there's anything that sickens me, it's a saintly man. You should be wearing your collar back-to-front. Very well. We'll say no more about it. Sit and nurse your two hundred until it is all gone." She flung her chair angrily over to one side, while she rose from it.

He watched her stride to the door, and pluck the knob, and swing the door back to go out.

"You want me to do this very much?" he said. "*That* much?"

She stopped and turned to look at him. "It is to your advantage, not mine. I was only trying to help you. *I* gain nothing by it. I can always make out. I have before, and I can again."

Louder than all the rest, he heard in it the one word she had not spoken: *alone*.

"I'll do it for you, Bonny," he said limply. "I'll do it for you."

She dropped her eyes a moment complacently. She came back and sat down. Her face slowly smoothed out. She bent to her tutoring attentively. "Now what am I holding?"

— 58 —

How SHE found out about the place he never knew. He would never have guessed it existed. She seemed to have a nose for scenting such places from a mile off.

It was on the second floor, up a stair that occasionally someone would come down but no one was ever seen to go up. Below it was just a restaurant and wining place. They'd been there before once or twice in their nightly rounds of pleasure, and not finding it very entertaining, soon left again. If she'd detected anything then, she'd said nothing about it to him at the time.

They came there now, the two hundred secreted on his person, and first took seats below, just the two of them, close to the stairs, over two glasses of Burgundy.

"Are you sure?" he kept asking her in a doubtful undertone.

She gave him a deft little frown of affirmation. "I know. I can tell. I saw the look on one or two faces as they came down those stairs the other night. I have seen those looks on faces before. The face too white, the eyes too bright and feverish." She patted his knee below the table. "Be patient. Do as I told you when the time comes."

They sat for a while, she inscrutable, he uneasy.

"Now," she said finally.

He beckoned the waiter. "The check, please." He took out the entire two hundred dollars, allowed him to see it, while he selected a bill for payment. She, meanwhile, elaborately stifled a yawn. He turned his head to the waiter. "It's dull here. Can't you offer any-thing—a little more interesting?"

The waiter went to the manager and spoke in a corner behind the back of his hand. The manager came over in turn, leaned confi-dentially across the back of Durand's chair.

"Anything I can do, sir?"

"Can't you offer us anything a little more exciting than this?"

"If you were alone, sir, I'd suggest—"

"Suggest it anyway," Durand encouraged him.

"There are some gentlemen upstairs— You understand me?"

"Perfectly," said Durand. "I wish I had known sooner. Come, my dear."

"The lady too?" the manager asked dubiously.

"I am very well behaved," she simpered. "I will be quiet as a mouse. No one will know that I am there."

"Tell them Mr. Bradford sent you from below. We do not like too much attention called to it. It is just for the diversion of a few of our steady customers."

They went up together at a propitious moment, when no one seemed to be watching. Durand knocked at a large double door, behind which a buzz of conversation sounded. A man opened it and looked out at them, holding it so that they could not see within.

"Mr. Bradford sent us from below."

"We don't allow ladies in here, sir."

She smiled her most dazzling smile. Her eyes looked into his. Her hand even came to rest upon his forearm for a moment. "There are exceptions to every rule. Surely you are not going to keep *me* out? I should be so lonely without him."

"But the gentlemen's conversation may—"

She pinched his chin playfully. "There, there. I have heard my husband swear before; it will not shock me."

"Just a moment."

He closed the door; reopened it in a moment to offer her a black velvet eye-mask. "Perhaps you would be more comfortable with this."

She gave Durand a satiric side look, as if to say "Isn't he naive?" but put it on nevertheless.

The man stood aside, to hold back the door for them.

"Need you have been so coquettish?" Durand said to her in a rapid aside.

"It got me in, didn't it?"

Her entrance created a sensation. He had seen her attract attention wherever they went, but never anything comparable to this. The buzz of conversation stilled into a dead silence. The play even stopped short at several of the tables. One or two of the men reached falteringly behind them, as if to draw on their coats, though they did not complete the intention.

She said something behind her hand to their host, who announced in a clear voice: "The lady wishes you to forget that she is here, gentlemen. She simply enjoys watching card games."

She bowed her head demurely, in a feigned sort of modesty, and went on, her arm linked to Durand's.

Their guide introduced him at one of the tables, after having first obtained his name, and the willingness of the other players to accept him. "Mr. Castle—Mr. Anderson, Mr. Hoffman, Mr. Steeves."

Bonny was not introduced, propriety in this case dictating that she be omitted.

"Champagne for the gentlemen," Durand immediately ordered, as soon as he had taken seat.

A colored steward brought it, but she at once took over the task from him, remarking: "That shall be my pleasure, to see that the wants of the gentlemen at this table are attended to." And moved around from one to the next, filling their glasses, after the cards were already well in play. Then sat back some little distance removed, with the air of a little girl upon her best behavior, who has been allowed to sit up late in presence of her elders. If her legs did not actually dangle from her chair, that was the illusion she conveyed.

Durand took out the entire two hundred, with an indifferent gesture, as though it were simply a small fraction of what he had about him, and the game began.

Within minutes, it was no longer two hundred. And at no time after that did it ever again descend to two hundred, though sometimes it swelled and sometimes it shrank back again. It doubled itself in bulk, finally, and then when it had doubled itself again, he made two piles of it, so that he must have had a thousand dollars in winnings there on the table before him. He did not remove any of it from sight, as the etiquette of the game proscribed, the play still being in progress.

The room was warm and unaired, and the players were heated in addition by their own excitement. The champagne thoughtfully there beside them was gratefully downed in hectic gulps at every opportunity. And each time a glass fell empty, a fleeting shadow, less than a shadow, would tactfully withdraw it a short distance behind the player, in order not to interfere with his view of the table, and there refill it. With graceful, dainty, loving little gesture, hand to throat, or bosom, or toward ear, lest a drop be spilled, as the drink was returned to its place. Tapering fingers, one or the other folded shorter than the rest, clasped about its stem.

Occasionally she got an absent, murmured "Thank you," from the player, more often he was not even aware of her, so unobtrusively were his wants tended.

Once she motioned with her fan to the steward, and he brought another bottle, and when the cork popped, she gave a little start of alarm, as pretty as you please, so timorous a little thing was she, so unused to the ways of champagne corks.

But suddenly there was silence at the table. The game had halted, without a word. Each player continued to look at his cards, but no further move was made.

"Whenever you're ready, gentlemen," Durand said pleasantly.

No one answered, no one played.

"I'm waiting for the rest of you, gentlemen," Durand said.

No one looked up, even at sound of his voice. And the answer was given with the speaker's head still lowered to his cards.

"Will you ask the lady to retire, sir?" the man nearest him said.

"What do you mean?"

"Do you have to be told?" They were all looking at him now.

Durand started to his feet with a fine surge of forced indignation. "I want to know what you meant by that!"

The other man rose in turn, a little less quickly. "This." He knocked his diffuse cards into a single block against the table, and slapped Durand in the face with them twice, first on one side, then the other.

"If there's one thing lower than a man that'll cheat at cards, it's a man that'll use a woman to do his cheating for him!" Durand tried to swing at him with his fist, the circumstances forgotten now, only the provocation remaining livid on his cheeks—for he had no past history of brooked insult to habituate him to this sort of thing. But the others had leaped up by now too, and they dosed in on him and held his arms pinioned. He threshed about, trying to free himself, but all he could succeed in doing was swing their bodies a little too, along with his own; they were too many for him.

The table rocked, and one of the chairs went over. Her scream was faint and futile in the background, and tinny with horrified virtue.

The manager had appeared as if by magic. The struggle stopped, but they still held Durand fast, his marble-white face now cast limply downward as if to hide itself from their scorching stares.

"This man's a common, low-down cheat. We thought you ran a place for gentlemen. You should protect the good name of your establishment better than this."

He didn't try to deny it; at least that much he had left. That was all he had left. His shirt had come open at the chest, and his breast could be seen rising and falling hard. But scarcely from the brief physical stress just now, rather from humiliation. The whole room was crowded about them, every other game forgotten.

The manager signalled to two husky helpers. "Get him out of here. Quickly, now. I run an honest place. I won't have any of that."

He didn't struggle further. He was transferred to the paid attendants, with only the unvarying protest of the manhandled: "Take your hands off me," no more.

But then as he saw the manager clearing the disheveled table, sweeping up what was on it, he called out: "Two hundred of that money is mine, I brought it into the game."

The manager waved him on, but from a distance safely beyond his reach. "You've forfeited it to the house. That'll teach you not to try your tricks again! On your way, scoundrel!"

Her voice suddenly rang out in sharp stridency: "You robbers! Give him back his money!"

"The pot calling the kettle black," someone said, and a general laugh went up, drowning the two of them out.

He was hustled across the floor, and out through a back door, probably to avoid scandalizing the diners below at the front. There was an unpainted wooden slat-stair there, clinging sideward to the building. They threw him all the way down to the bottom, and he lay there in the muddy back-alley. Miraculously unhurt, but smarting with such shame as he'd never known before, so that he wanted to turn his face into the mud and hide it there.

His hat was flung down after him, and after doing so the thrower ostentatiously brushed his hands, as if to avoid contamination.

But that was not the full measure of humiliation, ignominy. The final degradation was to see the door reopen suddenly, and Bonny came staggering through. Impelled forth, *thrust* forth by the clumsy sweaty hands of men, like any common thing.

His wife. His love.

A knife went through his heart, and it seemed to shrivel and fold and close over upon the blade that pierced it.

Pushed forth into the night, so that she too all but overbalanced and threatened to topple down after him, but clung to the rail and managed to hold herself back just in time.

She stood there motionless for a moment, above him, but looking, not back at them but down below her at him.

Then she came on down and passed him by with a lift of her skirts to avoid him, as though he were some sort of refuse lying there.

"Get up," she said shortly. "Get up and come away. I never heard of a man that can't win either way; can't win honestly, and can't win by cheating either."

He had never known the human voice could express such corrosive contempt, before.

— 59 —

HE FORESAW the change in her that would surely follow this debacle before it had even come, so well did he know her now, so bitterly, so costly well. Know her by mood and know her by nature. And come it did, only a little less swiftly and surely than his apprehension of its coming.

The first day after, she was simply less communicative, perhaps; a shade less friendly. That was all. It was as if this was the period of germination, the seed at work but unseen as yet. Only a lover's eye could have detected it. And his was a lover's eye, though set in a husband's head.

But by that night, already, a chill was beginning. The temperature of her mood was going down steadily. Her remarks were civil, but in that alone was the gauge. Civility bespeaks distance. Husband and wife should never be civil. Sugared, or soured, but civil not.

By the second day dislike had begun to sprout like a noxious weed, overrunning everything in what was once a pleasant garden. Her eyes avoided him now. To bring them his way he had to make use of the question direct in addressing her, nothing less would do. And even then they refused to linger, as if finding it scarcely worth their while to waste their time on him.

Within but an additional day of that, the weeds had flowered into poisonous, rancid fruit. The cycle of the sowing was complete, all that was needful was the reaping; and who would the scythe wielder be? There was a sharp edge to her tongue now, the velvet was wearing thin in places. The least provocative remark of his might touch one of them, strike a flinty answer.

It was as though this had the better even of her herself; as though, at times, she tried to curb it, make an effort, at intervals, toward relenting, softening: only to find her own nature opposed to her intentions in the matter, and overcoming them in spite of the best she could do. She would smile and the blue ice in her eyes would warm, but only for fleeting minutes; the glacial cast that held her would close over her again and hide her from him.

He took refuge in long walks. They were a surcease, for when he took them he was not without her; when he took them he had her with him as she had been until only lately. He would restore, replenish the old she, until he had her whole again. Then coming back, with a smile and a lighter heart, the two would meet face to face, the old and the new, and in an instant he would have his work all for nothing, the new she had destroyed the old.

"I'll get a job, if this affects you so much," he blurted out at last. "I'm capable, there's no reason why I—"

He met with scant approval.

"I hate a man that works!" she said through tight-gripped teeth. "I could have married a dray horse if I'd wanted that. It'd be just about as dull." Then gave him a cutting look, as if he had no real wish to better their state, were purposely offering her alternatives that were useless, that were not to be seriously considered. "There must be *some* way besides that, that you could get your hands on some money for us."

He wondered uneasily what she meant by that, and yet was afraid to know, afraid to have it made any clearer.

"Only fools work," she added contemptuously. "Someone once told me that a long time ago, and I believe it now more than ever."

He wondered who, and wondered where he was now. What jail had closed around him long since, or what gallows had met him. Or perhaps he was still unscathed, his creed vindicated, waiting somewhere for word from her, in tacit admission that she had been wrong; knowing that some day, somehow, in his own good time, he would have it.

"He must have been a scalawag," was all he could think to say.

There was defiance in her cold blue eyes. "He was a scalawag," she granted, "but he was good company."

He left the room.

And now there was stone silence between them, following this; not so much as a "By your leave," not so much as a "Good night." It was hideous, it was unthinkable, but it had come about. Two mutes moving about one another, two pantomimists, two sleepless silhouettes in the dimness of their chamber. He sought to reach for her hand and clasp it, but she seemed to be asleep. Yet in her sleep she guessed his intention, and withdrew her hand before he could find it.

On the following day, coming from the back of the hall, he happened to pass by the sitting room, on his way out to take one of his restorative walks, and caught sight of her in there, sitting at the desk. He hadn't known her to be in there. She was not writing a letter, by any evidence that was to be seen. She was sitting quite aimless, quite unoccupied. The desk slab was out, but no paper was in view. Yet for what other purpose do people sit at a desk, he asked himself? There were more appropriate chairs in the room for the purpose, in itself, of sitting.

He had an unhappy feeling that some action she had been engaged in had been hastily resumed as soon as he was gone. The very cast of her countenance told him that; its resolute vacancy. Not a natural vacancy, but a studied one, carefully maintained just for so long as he was in the doorway watching. The pinkey of her hand, which rested sideward along the desk slab, rose and descended again, as he watched. The way the tip of a cat's tail twitches, when all the rest of it is stilled; betraying a leashed, lurking impatience.

There was nothing he could do. If he stopped her this time, she would find another. If he accused, she would deny. If he proved, then her smouldering resentment would burst into open flame, and he didn't want that.

A letter to the past. A letter to that other, subterranean world he thought she had left forever.

He went out and closed the door behind him, heavy hearted.

If there was an added quality to be detected in her, several hours later, on his return, it was a glint of malicious satisfaction, a sort of sneer within the eyes. The look of one who says to herself, I have not been idle. Just wait, and you shall see.

Within another two days he could stand their estrangement no longer, he had capitulated. He had capitulated in a lie; he had prostituted the truth itself to his submission, than which there can be no greater capitulation on the part of one to the desires of another. Making what is not so, so, for the sake of renewed amity.

"I lied to you, Bonny," he said without preamble.

She was stroking her hair in readiness for bed, her back was to him. Literally now, as it had been figuratively for days on end.

"There *is* more money. That was not the end of it."

She set down her brush smartly, turned to stare.

"Then why did you tell me that? What did you do it for?"

"I thought perhaps we might run through it too quickly. I thought perhaps we should put it by for a little while, for some later day."

Greed must have dulled her perceptions. He made a poor liar, at best. And now, because of the stake involved, he was at his worst. Yet she wanted to believe him, and so she wholeheartedly did. Instantly she had accepted for fact his faltering figment; that could be told by the swiftness with which she entered into argument over it. And you do not argue over something that is not a fact, you disregard it; you argue only over something that is.

"Later?" she said heatedly. "How much later? Will we be any younger when it comes, that precious day? Will a dress look as good on me then as it does now? Will my skin be as smooth, will your step be as firm?"

She picked up her brush again, but not for use; to fling it down in emphasis.

"No, I've never lived that way and I won't submit to it now! 'A rainy day.' I've heard that old fusty saying. I'll give you another, a truer one! 'Tomorrow never comes.' Let it rain tomorrow! Let it soak and drench me! If I'm dry and warm tonight, that's all I care about. Tomorrow's rain may never find me. I may be dead tomorrow, and so may you. And you can't spend money in a grave. I'll take on the bargain. I'll ask no odds. Bury me tomorrow, and welcome. In potter's field, if you want. Without even a shroud to cover me. If I can only have Tonight."

She was breathing fast with the heat and fury of her philosophy. The protest of the disinherited; the panic of the pagan, with no promise of ultramundane reward.

"How much is it?" she asked avidly. "How much, about?"

He wanted her happy. He couldn't give her heaven, so he gave her the only heaven she believed in, understood. "A great deal," he said. "A great deal."

"About?"

"A lot," was all he could keep saying. "A lot."

She had risen, ecstatic, was coming closer to him step by step. Each step a caress. Each step the promise of another caress still to come, beyond the last. She clasped hands over her bosom, as if to hold in the joy swelling it. "Oh, never mind, no need to tell me exactly. I never did like figures. A lot, that's all that matters. A bunch. A load. Where? Here, with us?"

"In New Orleans," he mumbled evasively. "But where I can put my hands on it easily." Anything to hold her. She wanted Tonight. Well, he wanted Tonight too.

She spun, suddenly, in a solo waltz step, as though unseen violins had struck a single chord. Then flung herself half onto the bed and into his waiting arms.

One again; love again. Whisperings, protestations, promises and vows: never another cold word, never another black silence, never another hurt. I forgive you, I adore you, I cannot live without you. "A new you, a new me."

Suddenly she alerted her head for a moment, almost as if an afterthought had assailed her. "Oh, I'm sorry," he heard her breathe, and whether it was to him or to herself, he could not even tell, it was so inward and subdued.

"It's over, it's forgotten," he murmured, "we've agreed on that."

Her head dropped back again, solaced.

But the belatedness of the qualm, coming as it did *after* all the pardons had been asked and given, and not in their midst, made him think her compunction might have been for something else, and not their state of alienation itself, now happily ended. Some act he'd had no inkling of at the time, now rashly completed beyond recall.

She kept asking when he was going, and when he was going, with increasing frequency and increasing insistence, until at last he was face to face with the retraction he'd dreaded so; there was nothing left for him but to tell her. So tell her he did.

"I'm not."

"But—but how else can you obtain it?"

"There isn't any there to obtain. Not a penny. It's all gone long since, all been used. The money from the sale of the St. Louis Street house, that Jardine took care of for me; my share of the business. There's nothing more coming to me." He buried hands in pockets, drew a deep breath, looked down. "Very well, I lied. Don't ask me why; you should know. To see you smile at me a little longer, perhaps." And he murmured, half-inside his throat, "It was cheap at that price."

She said, still speaking quietly, "So you hoodwinked me."

She put aside her hand mirror. She stood. She moved about, with no settled destination. She clasped her own sides, in double embrace.

The storm brewed slowly, but it brewed sulphurous strong. She paced back and forth, her chest rising and falling with quickened breath, but not a word coming from her at first.

She seized her cut-glass flask of toilet water at last, and raising arm up overhead to full height, crashed it down upon the dresser top.

"So that's what you think of me. A good joke, wasn't it? A clever trick. Tell her you have money, tell her you haven't. The fool will believe anything you say. One minute yes, the next minute no." The talcum jar came down next, shattered into crystal shrapnel, some of which jumped almost to his feet, across the room. Then the hand mirror. "It isn't enough to lie to me once, you have to lie to me twice over!"

"The first time was the truth; the only lie was when I said I did have."

"You got what you wanted, though, didn't you? That was all you cared about, that was all that mattered to you!"

"Haven't you got any modesty at all? Isn't there anything you leave unsaid?"

"You'd better make it do, I warn you! It'll be a long long time—"

"You've got a filthy mouth for such a beautiful face," he let her know sternly. "A slut's tongue in a saint's face."

She threw a scent bottle, this time directly at him. He didn't swerve; it struck the wall just past his shoulder. A piece of glass nicked his cheek, and drops of sweet jasmine spattered his shoulder. She was not play-acting in some lovers' quarrel; her face was maniacal with hate. She was beside herself. If there had been anything sharp at hand to use for weapon—

"You—" She called him a name that he'd thought only men knew. "I'm not good enough for you, am I? I'm beneath you. I'm just trash and you're a fine gentleman. Well, who told you to come after me? Who wants you?"

He took a handkerchief to the tiny spot of blood on his cheek. He held his peace, stood there steadfast against the sewage torrents of her denunciation.

"What good are you to me? You're no good to me at all. You and your romantic love. Faugh!" She wiped her hand insultingly across her mouth, as though he had just kissed her.

"No, I suppose I'm not," he said, eyes hard now, face bitter. "The wind has changed now. Now that I have nothing left. Now that you've had everything out of me that's to be had. You greedy little leech. Are you sure you haven't overlooked anything?" He was trembling now with emotion. His hands sought into his pockets, turning their linings out with the violence of their seeking. "Here." He dragged some coins out, flung them full at her face. "Here's something you missed. And here, have this too." He ripped the jeweled stickpin from his tie, cast that at her. "And that's all there is. An insurance policy among my papers somewhere, and maybe you'd like me to cut my own throat to profit you—but unfortunately it's not in force."

She was pulling things out of the drawers now, dropping more than she secured.

"I've left you once already, and I'll leave you again. And this time for good, this time goodbye. I don't ever want to see the sight of you again."

"I'm still your husband, and you're not leaving this house."

"Who's to stop me? *You?*" She threw back her head and shrieked to the ceiling with wild laughter. "You're not man enough, you haven't got the—"

They both ran suddenly for the door, from their two varying directions. He got there first, put his back to it, blocked it.

She raised diminutive fists, battered futilely at his chest, aimed the points of her shoes at his insteps.

"Get out of my way. You can't stop me."

"Get back from this door, Bonny."

The blow, when it came, was as unexpected to him as it must have been to her. It was like a man swiping at a mosquito, before he stops to think. She staggered back, turned as she fell, and toppled sideward onto the bench that sat before her dressing table, the lower part of her body trailing the floor.

They looked at each other, stunned.

His heart, wrung, wanted to cry out "Oh, darling, did I hurt you?" but his stubborn lips would not relay the plea.

The room seemed deathly still, after the clamorous discord that had just filled it. She had become noticeably subdued. Her only reproach was characteristic. It was, rather, a grudging backhand compliment. As she picked herself stiffly up, she mouthed sullenly: "It's a wonder you were man enough to do that much. I didn't think you had it in you."

She came toward the door again, but this time with all antagonism drained from her.

He eyed her under narrowed, warning lids.

"Let me get to the bathroom," she said with sulky docility. "I need to put cold water on my face."

When he came up again later from below, she had dragged her bed things out of their room and into the spare bedroom at the back of the hall up there.

— 60 —

ABOUT FOUR or five days later, he was returning toward the house from one of his walks—walks which had become habitual by now— when suddenly her figure came into view far ahead of him, some two or three road crossings in advance, but going the same way he was, down the same mottled tunnel made by the overhanging shade trees.

The distance was so great and the figure was so diminished by it, and above all the flickering effect given off by the alternating sun and shade falling over it made it so blurry in aspect, that he could not be altogether sure it was indeed she. Yet he thought he knew her gait, and when someone else had passed her he could tell by that yardstick she was small in proportion to others and not just because of the distance alone, and above all the coloring of the dress was the same as the one he had last seen her in when he'd left the house an hour before: plum serge. In short, there was too much overall similarity; he felt sure it was Bonny.

It was useless to have hailed her; she would not have heard, she was too far ahead. The separation was too great even for him to have hoped to overtake her within a worthwhile time by breaking into a run; she would have been almost back at their own door by the time he had done so. Moreover, there was no reason for undue haste, no emergency, he would see her soon enough, and besides he was somewhat fatigued from his recent walk and disinclined to run just them.

She had not been in sight only a moment before, and the point at which she had suddenly appeared was midway between two of the intervening road crossings, so he surmised she must have emerged from some doorway or establishment at approximately that location just as he caught sight of her.

When he had gained the same general vicinity himself, in due course, he turned to look sideward, out of what was at first merely superficial curiosity, as he went past, to see where it was she had come from, what it was she had been about. Always presuming that it had been she.

Superficial curiosity became outright surprise at a glance, and halted him in his tracks. The building flanking him was the post office. Immediately adjoining it, it is true, was a rather shabby-looking general-purpose store, but since there were several others of the same kind, and far more prepossessing looking, closer at hand to where they lived, it seemed hardly likely she would have put herself out to come all the way to this one. It must have been the post office she had quitted.

There was no reason for her to seek it out but one: subterfuge. There was a mailbox for the taking of their letters on the selfsame street with them; there was a carrier for the bringing of their letters who went past their very door. And what letters did they get anyway? Who knew they were here? Who knew who they were?

Uneasy now, and with the new-found sunlight dimming behind a scurrying of advance clouds, he had turned and gone in before even considering what he was about to do. And then once in, wished he hadn't, and tried to turn about and leave again. But uneasiness proved stronger than his reluctance to spy upon her, and forced him at last to approach the garter-sleeved clerk behind a wicket bearing the legend "General Delivery."

"I was looking for someone," he said shamefacedly. "I must have—missed her. Has there been a little blonde lady—oh, no higher than this—in here within the past few minutes?"

He remembered that day he had taken her to the bank with him in New Orleans. She must have had the same effect in here just now. She would be remembered, if she'd been in at all.

The clerk's eyes lit up, as with an afterglow. "Yes, sir," he said heartily. "She was at this very window just a few minutes ago." He spruced up one of his arm bands, then the other. "She was asking for a letter."

Durand's throat was dry, but he forced the obstructive question from it. "And did she— Did you have one for her?"

"Sure enough did." The clerk wagged his head in reflective admiration, made a popping sound with his tongue against some empty tooth-shell in his mouth. "Miss Mabel Greene," he reminisced. "She must be new around here, I don't recall ever—"

But Durand wasn't there anymore.

She was in the ground-floor sitting room. Bonnet and stole were gone, as if she had never had them on. She was standing before the center table frittering with some flowers that she had put there in a bowl the day before, some jonquils, withdrawing those that showed signs of wilting. There was a scorched, cindery odor in the air, as if something small had burned a few moments ago; his nostrils became aware of it the moment he entered.

"Back?" she said friendlily, turning her face over-shoulder to him, then back to the flowers once more.

He inhaled twice in rapid succession, in quite involuntary confirmation of the foreign odor.

Though she was not looking at him, she must have heard. Abruptly she quitted the flowers, went to the window, and raised it generously. "I was just smoking a cigar in here," she said, unasked. "It needs airing."

There was no trace of the remnants of one, on the usual salvers she used.

"I threw it out the window unfinished," she said. She had gone back to the flowers again. "It was quite unfit. They're making them more poorly all the time."

But the effluvia of her own cigars had never bothered her until now. And this was not the aromatic vestiges of tobacco, it was the more acrid pungency left behind, by incinerated paper.

I'll know she lies now, I'll know, he thought mournfully. She cannot evade this. Ah, why do I ask her? Why must I seek my own punishment? But the question was already out and uttered, he could not have held it back had his tongue been torn from its roots a moment later.

"Was that you I saw on the street just now?"

She took a moment to answer; though how could she be uncertain, if she had just returned? She took out one more flower. She turned it about by its stem, studying it for faults. She put it down. Then she turned about and faced him, readily enough. She saw his eyes rest for a moment on her plum-serge costume. It was only then she answered.

"Yes."

"Where were you, to the post office?"

Again she took a moment. As though visualizing the topography of the vicinity she had recently been in, reminding herself of it.

"I had an errand," she said, steadily enough. "There was something I needed to buy."

"What?" he asked.

She looked down at the flowers. "A pair of garden shears, to clip the stems of flowers."

She had chosen well. They would sell those in a general store. And there had been a general store next to the post office.

"And did you?"

"They had none on hand. They offered to send away for some, but I told them it was not worth the trouble."

He waited. She intended to say nothing more.

"You didn't go to the post office?"

But in the repetition of the question itself, in fact in its first asking, lay by indirection her answer. He realized that himself. By the very fact of asking, he apprised her that he knew she had.

"I did step into the post office," she said negligently. "It comes to me now. I had forgotten about it. To buy stamps. They are in my purse now. Do you wish to see them?" She smiled, as, one who is prepared for all eventualities.

"No," he said unhappily. "If you say you bought stamps, that ends it."

"I think I'd better show them to you." Her voice was neither injured nor hostile; rather, whimsical, amused. As one who patiently endures another's foibles, forgives them.

She opened the receptacle, took out its change purse, showed him two small crimson squares, adhering on a perforated line.

He scarcely looked. She could have bought those a half-hour ago. She could have had them for a month.

"The man said he had given you a letter."

"He did?" Her brows went up facetiously.

"I described you to him."

"He did," she said coolly.

"It was addressed to Mabel Greene."

"I know," she agreed. "That is why I returned it to him. He mistook me for somebody else. I stopped for a moment, close to his window, without noticing where I was, while I was putting the stamps away. My back was to him, you see. He suddenly called out: 'Oh, Miss Greene, I have a letter for you,' and thrust it out at me. He took me so by surprise that I took it in my hand for a moment without thinking. Then I said, 'I am not Miss Greene,' and handed it back to him. He apologized, and that ended it. Although on second thought, I don't think his mistake was an honest one. I think he was trying to—" she modulated her voice in reluctant delicacy "—flirt with me. He promptly tried to strike up a conversation with me, by starting to tell me how much I resembled this other person. I simply turned my head away and walked on."

"He didn't say you had returned it."

"But *I* say I did." There was no resentment in her voice, no emotion whatever. "And you have the choice there: which one of us to believe."

He hung his head. He'd lost the battle of wits, as he might have known he would. She was absolutely without consciousness of guilt. Which did not mean she was without guilt, but only without the fear that usually goes with it and helps unmask it. He could have brought her face to face with that clerk, and the situation would not have altered one whit. She would have flung back her denial into the very face of his affirmation, trusting that to weaken first of the two.

On her way out of the room, she let her hand trail, almost fondly, across the breadth of his back.

"You don't trust me, do you, Lou?" she said quite neutrally.

"I want to."

She shrugged, in the doorway, as she went out. "Then do so, that is all you have to do. It's simple enough."

She went up the stairs, in leisurely complacency. And though he couldn't see her face, he had never been surer of anything than that it bore on it a smile of the same leisurely complacency just then, to match her pace.

He flung himself down at a crouch before the fireplace, made rapid circling motions with his hands over its brick flooring. There was some brittle paper-ash lying on its otherwise scoured, blackened surface; very little, not enough to make a good-sized fistful. He turned up a piece that had not been consumed, perhaps because it had been held by the burner's fingers to the last. It was a lower corner, nothing more; two straight edges sheared off transversely by an undulant scorched line.

It bore a single word, in conclusion. "Billy." And even that was not wholly intact. The upper closure of the "B" had been opened, eaten into by the brown stain of flame.

— 61 —

NOTHING MORE, then, for five days. No more visits to the post office. No more idle sittings beside a desk. No more letters sent, no more letters received. Whatever had been said was said, and only the inside of a fireplace knew what that had been.

For five days after that she did not even go out, she took no more walks. She loitered about the rooms, noncommunicative, self-assured. As if waiting for something. As if waiting for an appointed length of time to pass. Five days to pass.

Then on the fifth day, suddenly, without a word, the door of her room opened after long closure and he beheld her coming down the stairs arrayed for excursion. She was carefully dressed, far more carefully, far more exquisitely, than he had seen her for a long time past. She had taken a hot curling iron to her hair; ripples of artifice indented it. Her lips were frankly red, not merely covertly so. As if to meet a different standard than his own. Rouge that did not try to look like nature but tried to look like rouge. Her floral essence was strong to the point of headiness; again a different standard than his own.

She was going out. She made that plain, over and above his own powers of observation. As if she wanted no mistake about it, no hindrance. "I'm going out," she said. "I'll be back soon."

He did not ask her where.

That was about three in the afternoon.

At five she was not back yet. At six. At seven.

It was dark, and he lit the lamps, and they burned their way toward eight. She wasn't back yet

He knew she hadn't left him; he knew she was coming back. Somehow that wasn't his fear. Something about the way she had departed, the open, ostentatious bearing she had maintained, was enough to tell him that. She would have gone off quietly, or he would not have seen her go off at all, if she were never coming back.

Once he went to her bureau drawer, and from far in the back of it took out the little case, the casket of burned wood, she kept her adornments in. Her wedding band was in there, momentarily discarded. But so was the solitaire diamond ring he had given her in New Orleans the first day of her arrival.

No, she hadn't left him; she was coming back. This was just an excursion without her wedding band.

On toward nine there was a sound at the door. Not so much an opening of it, as a fumbling incompletion of the matter of opening it.

He went out into the hall at last to see. To see why she did not finish coming in, for he knew already it was she.

She was half in, half out, and stopping there, her back sideward against the frame. Apparently resting. Or as if having given up the idea of entering the rest of the way as being too much trouble.

"Are you ill, Bonny?" he asked gravely, advancing toward her, but not hastily. Rather with a sort of reproachful dignity.

She laughed. A surreptitious, chuckling little sound, exchanged between herself and some alter ego, that excluded him. That was even at his expense.

"I knew you were going to ask me that."

He had come close to her now.

The floral essence had changed, as if from long exposure fermented; there was an alcohol base to it now.

"No, I'm not ill," she said defiantly.

"Come away from the door. Shall I help you?"

She brushed his offered arm away from her, advanced past him without it. There was a stiffness to her gait. It was even enough, but there was a self-consciousness to it. As if she were saying: "See how well I can walk." She reminded him of a mechanical doll, wound up and striking out across the floor.

"I'm not drunk, either," she said suddenly.

He closed the door, first looking out. There was no one out there. "I didn't say you were."

"No, but that's what you're thinking."

She waited for him to reply to that, and he didn't. Either answer, he could tell, would have been an equal irritant; whether he contradicted or admitted it. She wanted to quarrel with him; her mood was one of hostility. Whether implanted or native, he could not tell.

"I never get drunk," she said, turning to face him from the sitting-room door. "I've never gotten drunk in my life."

He didn't answer. She went on into the sitting room.

When he entered it in turn, she was seated in the overstuffed chair, her head back a little, resting. Her eyes were open, but not on what she was doing; they were sighted remotely upward. She was stripping off her gloves, but not with the usual attentiveness he had seen her give to this. With an air of supine frivolity, allowing their empty fingers to dangle loosely and flutter about.

He stood and watched her for a moment.

"You're late," he said at last.

"I know I'm late. You don't have to tell me that."

She flung the gloves down on the table, jerked them from her with a little wrist-recoil of anger.

"Why don't you ask me where I've been?"

"Would you tell me?" he retorted.

"Would you believe me?" she flung back at him.

She took off her hat next. Regarded it intently, and unfavorably; circling its brim, the while, about one supporting hand.

Then unexpectedly, he saw her, with her other hand, hook two fingers together and snap them open against it, striking it a little spanking blow with her nail, so to speak, of slangy depreciation. A moment later she had cast it from her, so that it fell to the floor a considerable distance across the room from her.

He made no move to get it. It was her hat, after all. He merely looked after it, to where it had fallen. "I thought you liked it. I thought it was your fondest rage."

"Hoch," she said with throaty disgust. "In New York they're wearing bigger ones this season. These little things are out."

Who told you that? He said to her in bitter silence. Who told you that you're wasting yourself, buried down here, away from the big towns you used to know? He could hear the very words, almost as though he had been there when they were spoken.

"Can I get you anything?" he offered after awhile.

"You can't get me anything." She said it almost with a sneer. And he could read the unspoken remainder of the thought: I can get anything I want without you. Without your help.

He let her be. Some influence had turned her against him. Or rather had fanned to renewed heat the antagonism that was already latent there. It wasn't the liquor. It was more than that. The liquor was merely the lubricant.

He came back in a few minutes bringing her a cup of coffee he had boiled. It was a simple operation, and the only one he was capable of in that department. He had watched her do it, and thus he knew: pour water in, dribble coffee in, and stand it over the open scuttle hole.

And yet where some others—some others he had never known—might have recognized the wistful charm there was, unconsciously, in the effort, she rebelled and was disgusted almost to the point of nausea.

"Ah, you're so damned sweet it sickens me. Why don't you be a man? Why don't you give a woman a taste of your trouser belt once in a while? It might do the two of us a lot more good."

"Is that what they used to—?" he started to say coldly. He didn't finish it.

She drank the coffee down nevertheless. Nor thanked him for the trouble.

After a period of somnolent ingestion, it had its fortifying effect. She became voluble suddenly. As if seeking to undo whatever harmful impression her lack of inhibition had at first created. The antagonism disappeared, or at least submerged itself from sight.

"I had a drink," she admitted. "And I'm afraid it was too much for me. They insisted."

She waited to see if he would ask who "they" were. He didn't.

"I had started on my way home, this was at five, hours ago, and I think my mistake was in deciding to walk the entire way, instead of taking a carriage. I may have overtaxed myself. Or I may have been laced too tightly. I don't know. At any rate, as I was going along the street, I suddenly began to feel faint and everything swam before my eyes. I don't know what would have happened, I think I should have fallen to the ground. But fortunately a refined woman happened to be just a few steps behind me, on the same walk. She caught me in her arms and she held me up, kept me from falling. As soon as I was able to use my feet again, she insisted on taking me into her home, so that I might rest before going on. She lived only a few doors from there; we were almost in front of her house when it happened.

"Her husband came soon afterward, and they wouldn't hear of my leaving until they were sure I was fit. They gave me this drink, and it must have been stronger than I realized. They were really the kindest people. Their name is Jackson, I think she said. I'll point out the house to you sometime. They have a lovely home."

Warming to her recollection, she began describing it to him. "They took me into their front parlor and had me rest on the sofa. I wish you could see it. All kinds of money, you can tell. Oh, our place is nothing like it here. Louis XV furniture, gilded, you know, with mulberry upholstery. Full-length pier glasses on either side of the mantelpiece, and gas logs in the fireplace, iron logs that you can turn on or off—"

He could see in his mind's eye, as she spoke, the shabby, secretive hotel room, hidden away in one of the byways down around the railroad station; the shade drawn against discovery from the street; the clandestine rendezvous, unwittingly prolonged beyond the bounds of prudence in forgetfulness lent by liquor. She and the man, whoever he was—

The flame of an old love rekindled, with alcohol for fuel; the renewal of old ties, the whispers and the sniggered laughter, the reminiscences shared together— He could see it all, he was all but there, looking over their shoulders.

The factor of her physical unfaithfulness wasn't what shattered him the most. It was her mental treachery that desolated him; it was the far more irremediable of the two. She had betrayed him far more grievously with her mind and her heart, than she ever could have with her body. For he had always known he was not the first man to come into her life; but what he had always wanted, hoped and prayed for was to be the last.

It was easy, in retrospect, to trace the steps that had led to it.

His lie about the money, a palliative that had only made things worse instead of bettering them. And then their bitter, brutal quarrel when he'd had to recant it at last, leaving her smarting and filled with spite and thirsting to requite the trick she felt he'd played on her. There must have been a letter North at about that time, and though he'd never seen it, he could guess what rancorous summons it contained: "Come get me; I can stand no more of this; take me out of it." And then, five days ago, the answer; the mysterious letter to "Mabel Greene."

She needn't go to the post office any more, stealthily to appropriate them. There would be no more sent. The sender was here with her now, right in the same town.

Yes, he thought with saddened understanding, I too would travel from a distance of five days away—or twenty times five days away—to be with a woman like Bonny. What man wouldn't? If the new love cannot provide for her, she has but to call back the old.

She saw by his face at last that he wasn't listening to her any more. "I'm chattering too much," she said lamely. "I'm afraid I'm palling on you."

"That you never do," he answered grimly. "You never pall on me, Bonny." And it was true.

She stifled a yawn, thrusting her elbows back. "I guess I may as well go up to bed."

"Yes," he agreed dully. "That might be best."

And as he heard her room door close upstairs, a moment after, his head sank slowly, inconsolably down into the refuge his bedded arms made for it upon the table top.

— 62 —

HE MADE no reference the following day to her liquored outing, much less the greater transgression that it had encased. He waited to see if she would attempt to repeat it (in his mind some half-formed intent of following her and killing the man when he found him), but she did not. If a succeeding appointment had been made, it was not for that next day.

She lay abed until late, leaving his needs to the tender care of the slovenly woman of all work who came in to clean and cook for them on alternate days, thrice a week. Even this disreputable malaise, which was purely and simply a "head," as they called it, the result of her over-indulgence, he did not tax her with.

When she came down at last to supper with him, she was amiable enough in all conscience. It was as if (he told himself) she had two selves. Her sober self did not know or recall the instinctive animosity her drunken self had unwittingly revealed the night before. Or, if it did, was trying to make amends.

"Did Amelia go?" she asked. It was a needless question, put for the sake of striking up conversation. The stillness in the kitchen and the fact that no one came in to wait at table, gave its own answer.

"At about six," he said. "She set our places, and left the food warming in there on the stove."

"I'll help you bring it in," she said, seeing him start out to fetch it.

"Are you up to it?" he asked.

She dropped her eyes at the rebuke, as if admitting she deserved it.

They waited on themselves. She shyly offered the bread plate to him across-table. He pretended not to see it for a moment, than relented, took a piece, grunted: "Thanks." Their eyes met.

"Are you very angry with me, Lou?" she purred.

"Have I reason to be? No one can answer that but yourself."

She gave him a startled look for a moment, as if to say "How much do you know?"

He thought to himself, What other man would sit here like this, meekly holding his peace, *knowing* what I do? Then he remembered what he himself, had told Jardine on that visit to New Orleans: I must do as I must do. I can do no other.

"I was not very admirable," she said softly.

"You did nothing so terrible," he let her know, "once you were back here. You were a little sulky, that was all."

"And I did even less," she said instantly, *"before* I was back here. It was only here that I misbehaved."

How well we understand one another, he thought. We are indeed wedded together.

She jumped up and came around behind his chair, and leaning over his shoulder, had kissed him before he could thwart her.

His heart, like gunpowder, instantly went up, a flash of flame in his breast, though there was no outward sign to show it had been set off. How cheaply I am bought off, he thought. How easily appeased. Is this love, or is this a crumbling of my very manhood?

He sat there wooden, unmoving, hands to table, keeping them resolutely off her.

His lips betrayed him, though he tried to curb them. "Again," they said.

She lowered her face to his once more, and again she kissed him.

"Again," he said.

His lips were trembling now.

Again she kissed him.

Suddenly he came to life. He had seized her with such violence, it was almost an attack rather than an embrace. He pulled her bodily downward into his lap, and buried his face against hers, hungrily devoured her lips, her throat, her shoulders.

"You don't know what you do to me. You madden me. Oh, this is no love. This is a punishment, a curse. I'll kill any man who tries to take you from me—I'll kill you yourself. And I'll go with you. There shall be nothing left."

And as his lips repeatedly returned to find her, his only words of endearment, spaced each time with a kiss, were: "Damn you! . . . Damn you! . . . Damn you! No man should ever know you!"

When he released her at last, exhausted, she lay there limp, cradled in his arms. On her face the strangest, startled look. As though his very violence had done something to her she had not counted on.

She said, speaking trancelike, and slowly drawing her hand across her brow as if to restore some memory that was necessary to her, and that he had all but seared away, "Oh, Louis, you are not too safe to know yourself. Oh, darling, you almost make me forget—"

And then the crippled, staggering thought died unfinished.

"Forget whom?" he accused her. "Forget what?"

She looked at him dazed, as though not knowing she had spoken, herself. "Forget—myself," she concluded limply.

That is not whom she meant, he told himself with melancholy wisdom. But that word is the true one, none the less. I have no real rival, but in her. It is only herself that stands in the way of allowing her to love me.

She did not go out of the house the next day. Again he waited, again he held his breath, but she remained dutifully at hand. The appointment, if there was to be another, still hung fire.

Nor the next, either. The cleaning woman came, and coming down the stairs, he caught sight of them standing close together in the hall, as if they had been secretively conferring together. He thought he saw Bonny hastily fumble with her bodice, as if concealing something she had just received.

She would have carried it off, perhaps, but the Negress made a poor conspirator, she started theatrically back from her mistress, at sight of him, and thus put the thought in his head that something had passed between them.

There are other ways of communicating than by the rendezvous direct, he reminded himself. Perhaps the appointment I have been dreading so has already been kept, right before my eyes, on a mere scrap of paper.

Toward the latter part of their evening meal, that same day, she became noticeably pensive. Again the woman, the go-between of treachery, had gone, again they were alone together.

Her casual remarks, such as any meal shared by any two people is seasoned with, grew more and more infrequent. Soon she was making none at all of her own volition, only answering the ones he made. Presently even this proportion had begun to diminish, he was carrying the entire burden of speech for the two of them. All he got now was absent nods and vague affirmatives, while her thoughts were obviously elsewhere.

Finally it even affected her eating, began to slow and diminish it, so great was her own contemplation of whatever it was that her mind saw before it. And it must have seen something, for the mind by its very nature cannot contemplate vacancy. Her fork would remain in position to detach a portion of food, yet not complete the act for several minutes. Or it would halt in air, midway to her mouth, and again remain that way.

Then, quite as insolubly as it had begun, it had ended again, this abstraction. It was over. Whatever byways her train of thought had wandered down, were now closed off; or else it had arrived at its destination.

Her eyes now saw him when they rested on him.

"Do you recall that night we quarrelled?" she said, speaking softly. "You said something then about that old insurance policy you once took out when we were living on St. Louis Street. Was that true? Do you really still have it? Or did you just make that up, as you did about there still being money left?"

"I still have it," he said inattentively. "But it has lapsed, for lack of keeping up with the payments."

She was now busily eating, as if to make up for the time she had wasted loitering over her food before. "Is it completely worthless, then?"

"No, if the back payments were made up it would come into effect again. Not too much time has passed, I think."

"How much would be required?"

"Five hundred dollars," he answered impatiently. "Have we got that much?"

"No," she said docilely, "but is there any harm in asking?"

She pushed her plate back. She dropped her eyes, as if he had rebuffed her, and allowed them to rest on her clasped hands. Then, taking one finger in the others, she began slowly to twist and turn-about the diamond ring that had once been his wedding gift to her. She shifted it this way, that, speculatively, abstractedly.

Who could say whether she saw it or not, as she did so? Who could say what she saw? Who could say what her thoughts were? It told nothing. Just a woman's restless gesture with her ring.

"How would one go about it? I mean if we did have the money. In what way is it done?"

"You simply send the money to New Orleans, to the insurance company. They credit the payments against the policy."

"And then the policy comes into force again?"

"The policy comes into force again," he said somewhat testily, annoyed by her persistence in clinging to the subject.

He had divined, of course, what her sudden interest was. She was entertaining a vague hope that they could borrow against it in some way, obtain money by that means.

"Could I see it?" she coaxed.

"Right now? It's upstairs somewhere, among my old papers. But it's of no value, I warn you; the payments have not been maintained."

She did not press him further. She sat there meditatively fingering the diamond on her finger, shifting it a little bit this way, a little bit that, so that it gave off sparks of brilliance in the lamplight.

She did not ask him for it nor about it again, but remembering that she had, he set about looking for it on his own account. This was not immediately, but some two or three days later.

He couldn't find it. He looked where he'd thought he had it, first, and it wasn't there. Then he looked elsewhere, nor could he find it in any of the other places he looked, either.

It must have been lost, during their many hurried moves from place to place, in the course of hasty packing and unpacking. Or else it would perhaps yet turn up, in some unlikely place he had not yet thought of looking for it.

He desisted finally, with no great concern; with, if anything, a mental shrug. Since it was worthless and could not have been borrowed against (which he thought had been the motive behind her asking about it), there was no great loss, in any case.

He did not even mention to her that he could not locate it. There was no reason to, for she too seemed to have forgotten her earlier interest in it, as she sat there across the table from him, idly stroking and contemplating her ringless hands.

Within the week, the cook and cleaning woman (one and the same) whom they'd had until then, was suddenly gone, and they were alone now in the house.

He asked her about this, after two successive days without her, only noting her departure, man-like, after it had already taken place. "What's become of Amelia?"

"I shipped her Tuesday," she said shortly.

"But I thought we owed her three or four weeks back wages. How were you able to pay her?"

"I didn't."

"And she agreed to go none the less?"

"She had no choice, I ordered her to. She will get her money when we have it ourselves, she knows that."

"Aren't you getting anyone else?"

"No," she said, "I can manage," and added something under her breath that he didn't hear quite clearly.

"What?" he asked in involuntary surprise. He thought she had said, "for the little time there is."

"I said, for a little time, that is," she repeated adroitly.

And manage she did, and far more successfully than in their Mobile days, when she had first tried keeping her own house, and he had had to take her back to the hotel for meals.

For one thing, she showed far more purpose than she had in those far-off, light-hearted days; there was less of frivolity in her efforts and a great deal more of determination. There was less laughter in the preparations, maybe, but there was less dismay in the results. She was not a child bride, now, playing at keeping house; she was a woman, bent on acquiring new skills, and not sparing herself in the endeavor.

For two full days she cooked, she washed the dishes, she swung a broom all up and down the stairs. Then on the second night of this apprenticeship—

He heard her scream out suddenly in the kitchen, and there was the crash of a dropped dish as it slipped her hands. She had gone in there to wash up after their meal, and he had remained behind browsing through the paper. Even the most enamored man did not offer to dry the dishes for a woman; it would have been as conventional as assisting at a childbirth.

He flung down his paper and darted in there. She was standing before the steaming washtub. "What is it, did you scald yourself?"

She was pointing, horrified.

"A rat," she choked. "It ran straight between my feet as I stood here. Into there." And with a sickened grimace, "Oh, the size of it! The horrid look!"

He took up a poker and tried to plunge it into the crevice at meeting-place of wall and floor that she had indicated. It balked. There was no depth to take it. It seemed a shallow rent in the plaster, no more.

"It could not have gone in there—"

Her fright turned to anger. "Do you call me a liar? Must it bite me and draw blood, for you to believe me?"

He dropped down now on all fours and began working the poker vigorously to and fro, in truth knocking out a hole if there had been none before.

She watched a moment. "What are you trying to do?" she said coldly.

"Why, kill it," he panted.

"That is not the way to be rid of them!" Her foot gave a clout of impatience against the floor. "You kill one, and there are a dozen left."

She flung down her apron, strode from the room and out to the front of the house. Sensing some purpose he could not divine, but disquieted by it, he put down the poker after a moment, struggled to his feet, and went after her. He found her in the hall, bonnetted and shawled, to his astonishment, in readiness to go out.

"Where are you going?"

"Since you don't know enough to, I am going to the pharmacist myself, to have him give me something that will exterminate them," she retorted ungraciously.

"*Now?* At this hour? Why, it's past nine; he'll be closed long ago."

"There is another, on the other side of town, that stays open until ten; you know that as well as I do." And she added with ill-humored decision, as though he were to blame for their presence in some way, "I will not go back into that kitchen and run the risk of being attacked. They will be running over our very bed, yet, while we sleep!"

"Very well, I'll go myself," he offered hastily. "No need for you to go, at this time of night."

She relented somewhat. She took off her shawl, though still frowning a trifle that he had not seen his duty sooner. She took him to the door.

"Don't go back in there," he cautioned, "until I come back."

"Nothing could prevail on me to," she agreed fearfully.

She closed the door after him.

She reopened it to call him back for an instant.

"Don't tell him who we are, what house it's for," she suggested in a lowered voice. "I would not like our neighbors to know we have rats in our house. It's a reflection on me, on my cleanliness as a housekeeper—"

He laughed at this typically feminine anxiety, but promised and went on.

When he came back he found that she had returned to her task in the kitchen none the less, in spite of his admonition and her own fear; a bit of conscientious courage which he could not help but secretly admire. She had, however, taken the precaution of bringing in the table lamp with her and placing it on the floor close by her feet, as a sort of blazing protection.

"Did you see any more since I was gone?"

"I thought I saw it come back to that hole, but I threw something at it, and it did not come out again."

He showed her what the druggist had given him. "This is to be spread around outside their holes and hiding places."

"Did he ask any questions?" she asked somewhat irrelevantly.

"No, only whether or not we had any children about the house."

"He did not ask which house it was?"

"No. He's rather elderly and doddering, you know; he seemed anxious to be rid of me and close for the night."

She half extended her hand.

"No, don't touch it. I'll do it for you."

He stripped off his coat, rolled up his shirt sleeves, and squatting on his haunches before the offending orifice, shook out a little powdery trail of the substance here and there. "Are there any others?"

"One over there, just a little back of the coal stove."

She watched, with housewifely approval.

"That will do. Not too much, or our feet will track it about."

"It has to be renewed every two or three days," he told her.

He put it on the shelf, at last, where the spice canisters were, but well over to the side.

"Make sure you wash your hands, now," she cautioned him. He had been about to neglect doing so, until her reminder. She held the huck-towel for him to dry them on, when he was through.

It was the following night that his illness really began. She discovered it first.

He found her looking at him intently as he closed his book at their retiring-time. It was a kindly scrutiny, but closely maintained. It seemed to have been going on for several moments before he discovered it.

"What is it?" he said cheerfully.

"Louis." She hesitated. "Are you sure you have been feeling well lately? I do not find you looking yourself. I do not like the way you—"

"I?" he exclaimed in astonishment. "Why, I never felt better in my life!"

She silenced him with tilt of hand. "That may well be, but your appearance belies it. More and more lately I have found you looking worn and haggard at times. I have not mentioned it before, because I didn't want to alarm you, but it has been on my mind for some time now to do so. It's very evident; I can see it quite plainly."

"Nonsense," he said, half laughing.

"I have an excellent remedy, if you will but let me give it to you. And I will join you in it myself, as an inducement."

"What?" he asked, amused.

She jumped up. "Starting tonight, we are to take an eggnog, the two of us, each night before retiring. It is an excellent tonic, they assure me, for fortifying the system."

"I am not an inval—" he tried to protest.

"Now, not another word, sir!" she ordered gaily. "I intend to prepare them right now, and you shall not hinder me. I have all the necessary ingredients right at hand, in there. Fresh-laid eggs, and the very best obtainable, at *twelve* cents a dozen, mind you! And the brandy we have in the house as well."

He couldn't help but smile indulgently at her, but he let her have her way. This was a new role for her; nursemaid to a nonexistent ailment. If it made her happy, why what was the harm?

Her mood was amiable, sanguine, all gentleness and contrition now. She even bent to kiss him atop the head in passing.

"Was I cross to you before? Forgive me, Lou dear. You know I wouldn't want to be. A fright like that can make one into a harridan—" She went toward the kitchen, smiling back at him.

He could hear her cracking the eggs, somewhere beyond the open doorway, and crinkled his eyes appreciatively to himself.

Presently she had even begun to hum lightly as she moved about in there, she was enjoying her self-imposed task so much.

Soon the humming gained words, had become a full song.

He had never heard her sing before. Laughter until now had always been her expression of contentment, never song. Her voice was light but true. Not very lyrical, metallic was the word that occurred to him instead, but she stayed adroitly on key.

Just a song at twilight,
When the lights are low—

Suddenly the song stopped, as if at something she were doing that required complete concentration. Measuring the brandy, perhaps. Be that as it might, it never resumed again.

She came in, holding one glass in each hand. Their contents pale gold in color, creamy in substance.

"Here. One for you, one for me." She offered them both. "Take whichever one you want." Then when he had, she tasted tentatively at the one that remained in her hand. "I hope I didn't put in too much sugar. Too much would sicken. May I try yours?"

"Of course."

She took it back from him, tasted at it in turn. It left a little white trace on her upper lip.

While she stood thus, holding both together, she turned her head toward the kitchen door.

"What was that?"

"What? I didn't hear anything."

She went back in again for a moment. She was gone a moment only. Then she returned to him.

"I thought I heard a sound in there. I wanted to make sure I had fastened the door."

She gave him back the one he had had in the first place, and which she had sampled.

"Since it has brandy in it," she said, "I suppose we should precede it with a toast." She nudged her glass to his. "To your better health."

She drained hers to the bottom.

He took a deep draught of his. He found it quite velvety and pleasurable. The liquor in it; with which she had been unsparing, gave a mellow warming effect to the stomach after it had lain there some moments.

"I wish all tonics were this palatable, don't you?" she remarked.

"It's quite satisfactory," he admitted, more to please her than because he saw any great virtue in it. It was after all, to his way of thinking, a bastard drink; neither honest liquor nor wholly medicine.

"You must drink it down to the bottom, that is the only way it will do you any good," she urged gently. "See, as I did mine."

To spare her feelings, after the trouble of having prepared it, he did so.

He tasted of his tongue, dubiously, after he had. "It is a little chalky, don't you find. A little—astringent. It puckers."

She took the glass from him. "That is because you are not used to milk. Have you never seen a baby's mouth after it feeds, all clotted and curdled?"

"No," he assured her with mock gravity, "you have not given me that pleasure."

They laughed together for a moment, in close-knit intimacy.

"I'll just rinse out the glasses," she said, "and then we can go up."

He slept soundly at first, feeling at the last the grateful glow the tonic had deposited in his stomach; albeit it seemed to confine itself to there, did not spread outward as in the case of unmixed liquor. But then after an hour or two he awakened into torment. The glow was no longer benign, it had a flaming bite to it. Sleep, once driven off, couldn't come near him again, held back by a fiery sword turning and turning in his vitals.

The rest of that night was an agony, a Calvary. He called out to her, more than once, but she was not near enough to hear him. Helpless and cut off from her, he sank his teeth into his own lip at last, and kept silent after that. In the morning there was dried blood all down his chin.

Across the room, over in the far corner, miles away, stood a chair with his clothes upon it. An ebony wood chair, with apricot-plush seat and apricot-plush back. Never heeded much before, but now a symbol.

Miles away it stood, and he looked longingly across the miles, the immeasurable distance from illness to health, from helplessness to ability, from death to life.

All the way across the room, many miles away.

He must get over there, to that chair. It was far away, but he must get over there to it somehow. He looked at it so intently, so longingly, that the rest of the room seemed to fog out, and narrowing concentric circles of clarity seemed just to focus on that chair alone, so that it stood as in the center of a bright disk, a bull's-eye, and all the rest was a blur.

He could not get out of bed legs upright, so he had to leave it head and shoulders first, in a slanting downward fall. Then there was a second, if less violent, fall as his hips and legs came down after the rest of him.

He began to sidle along the floor now, like some groveling thing, a worm or caterpillar, chin touching it at every other moment, hot striving breath stirring the nap of the carpet before him, like a wave spreading out from his face. Only, worms and caterpillars don't hope so, haven't such large hearts to agonize with.

Slowly, flowered pattern by flowered pattern. Each one like an island. And the plain-tinted background in between, each time like a channel or a chasm, leagues in width instead of inches. Some weaver somewhere, years ago, had never known his spaces would be counted so, with drops of human sweat and burning pain and tears of fortitude.

He was getting closer. The chair was no longer an entire chair; its top was too far up overhead now. The circle of vision, straight before him, level with the floor, showed its four legs, and the shoes under it, and part of the seat. The rest was lost in the blurred mists of height.

Then the seat went too, just the legs now remained, and he was getting very near. Perhaps near enough already to reach it with his arm, if he extended that full before him along the floor.

He tried it, and it just fell short. Not more than six inches remained between his straining fingertips and the one particular leg he was aiming them for. Six inches was so little to bridge.

He writhed, he wriggled. He gained an inch. The edge of the flower pattern told him that. But the chair, teasing him, tantalizing him, thefted the inch from him somehow. It still stood six inches away. He had gained one at one end, it had stolen it back at the other.

Again he gained an inch. Again the chair cheated him out of it, replaced it at the opposite end.

But this was madness, this was hallucination. It had begun to laugh at him, and chairs don't laugh.

He strained his arm down to its uttermost sinews, from finger-pad all the way back to socket. He swallowed up the six inches, at the price of years of his life. And this time it jerked back, abruptly. And there was another six inches, a new six inches, still between them.

Then through his blinding tears, he saw at last that there were one pair of shoes too many. Four instead of two. His own, under the chair, and hers, off to the side, unnoticed until now. She must have opened the door so deftly that he had not heard it.

She was arched over above him, from the side. One hand holding her skirts clear, to keep them from betraying her presence until the last possible moment. The other hand, to the back of the chair, had been keeping that from him, unnoticeably, each time he'd thought he'd reached it.

The jest must have been good. Her laughter came out, full-bodied, irrepressible, above him. Then she tried to check it, bite it back, for decency's sake, if nothing else.

"What did you want, your clothes? Why didn't you ask me?" she said mockingly. "You can have no possible use for them, my dear. You're not well enough."

And taking the chair in hand more fully this time, before his broken-hearted eyes swept it all the way back against the wall, a whole yard or two at once this time, hopeless of attainment ever.

But the trousers bedded on the seat fell off somehow, and in falling were kinder to him than she was, they fell upon his extended hand and let themselves be gripped, caught fast by it.

Now she bent to take them from him, and a brief, unequal contest of strength locked the two of them for a moment.

"They are no good to you, my dear," she said with the amusement one shows to a wilful child. "Come, let them be. What can you do with them?"

She drew them away from him little by little, plucked them from his bitterly clinging fingers by main strength at last.

Then when she had him back in bed again, she gave him a smile that burned, that seared, though it was only a sweet, harmless, solicitous thing, and the door closed after her.

Within its luminous halo the chair stood, ebony wood and apricot plush. All the way across the room, leagues away.

— 63 —

SHE CAME in later in the day and sat by him, cool and crisp of attire, pretty as a picture, a veritable Florence Nightingale, soothing, comforting him, ministering to his wants in every way. In every way but one.

"Poor Lou. Do you suffer much?"

He resolutely refused to admit it. "I'll be all right," he panted. "I've never been ill a day in my life. This will pass."

She dropped her eyes demurely. She sighed in comfortable agreement. "Yes, this will soon pass," she conceded with equanimity.

The image of a contented kitten that has just had a saucer of milk crossed his mind for a moment, for some strange reason; disappeared again into the oblivion from which it had come.

She fanned him with a palm-leaf fan. She brought a basin, and with a moist cloth gently laved and cooled his agonized brow and his heaving chest, each silken stroke lighter than a butterfly's wing. "Would you like a cup of tea?"

He turned his head sharply aside, revolted.

"Would you like me to read to you? It may take your mind off your distress."

She went below and brought up a book they had there, of poems, and in dulcet, lulling cadences read to him from Keats.

> "O what can ail thee, knight-at-arms,
>   So haggard and so woe-begone?"

And stopped to innocently inquire: "What does that mean, 'La Belle Dame Sans Merci'? The sound is beautiful but the words have no sense. Are all poems like that?"

He put hands over ears and turned his head away, excruciated. "No more," he pleaded. "I can stand no more. I beg you."

She closed the book. She looked surprised. "I was only trying to entertain you."

When water alone would no longer quench his ravening, ever-increasing thirst, she went out and with great difficulty obtained a pail of cracked ice at a fishmonger's, and bringing it back, gave it to him piece by piece to chew and crunch between his teeth.

In every way she ministered to him. In every way but one.

"Get a doctor," he besought her at last. "I cannot fight this out alone. I must have help."

She kept her seat. "Shall we not wait another day? Is this my stouthearted Lou? Tomorrow, perhaps, you will be so much better that—"

He clawed at her garments in mute appeal, until she drew back a little, to keep them from being disarranged. His face formed in weazened lines of weeping. "Tomorrow I shall be dead. Oh, Bonny, I cannot face the night. This fire in my vitals— If you love me, if you love me—a doctor."

She went at last. She was gone from the room a half-hour. She came back to it again, her shawl and bonnet on, and took them off. She was alone.

"You didn't—?" He died a little.

"He cannot come before tomorrow. He is coming then. I described to him what your symptoms were. He said there is no cause for alarm. It is a form of—of colic, and it must run its course. He prescribed what we are to do until he sees you— Come, now, be calm—"

His eyes were on her, bright with fever and despair.

He whispered at last: "I did not hear the front door close after you."

She gave him a quick look, but her answer flowed unimpeded.

"I left it ajar behind me, to save time when I returned. After all, I'd left you alone in the house. Surely—" Then she said, "You saw my bonnet on me just now, did you not?"

He didn't answer further. All his ravaged mind could keep repeating was:

I didn't hear the door close after her.
And then at last, slowly but at last, he knew.

Dawn, another dawn, a second one since this had begun, came creeping through the window, and with it a measure of tensile strength. Strength carefully hoarded a few grains at a time for this supreme effort that faced him now. Strength that was not as strength had used to be, of the body; strength that was of the spirit alone. The spirit, the will to live, to be saved; self-combustive, self-consuming, breathing purest oxygen of its own essence. And when that was gone, no more to replace it, ever.

Though nothing had moved yet but the lids of his eyes, this was the beginning of a journey. A long journey.

For a while he let his body lie inert, as it was. To begin it too soon would be to court interruption and discovery.

There; her step had sounded in the hall, she was coming out of her room. His lids dropped over his eyes, concealing them.

The door opened and he knew she was looking at him. His face wanted to cringe, but he held it steady.

What a long look. Would she never stop looking? What was she thinking? "You are such a long time dying?" Or, "My own love, are you not any better today?" Which was the true thought; which was the true she, and which his false dream of her?

She had entered the room. She was coming toward him.

She was bending over him now, in watchful attention. He could feel the warmth of her breath. He could smell the odor of the violet water she had sprinkled on herself only moments ago and which had scarcely yet dried. Above all, he could feel her eyes almost burning through his skin like a pair of sunray glasses held steady above shavings, to make them scorch and smoke and at last burst into flame. There was that concentration in their steady regard.

He must not stir, he must not flicker.

A sudden weight fell on his heart and nearly stopped it. It was her hand, coming to rest there, trying to see if it was still going. It fluttered like a bird caught under her outspread palm, and if she noted that, she must have thought it erratic and falteringly overexerted. Suddenly her hand left him and he felt her fingers go instead to his eye, to try the reflex of that, perhaps. They gave him warning of their direction, for they brushed the skin there, just below it, a moment too soon. He rolled his pupils upward in their sockets, and a moment later when she had raised one lid and peered, only the sightless white eyeball was revealed.

She took up his hand next and held it perpendicular, from elbow onward, her thumb pressed to its wrist. She was feeling his pulse.

She placed his hand back where she had drawn it from. And though she did not drop it, nor cast it down, yet to him there was somehow only too clearly expressed in the way she did it a fling of disappointment, a shortening of the gesture, as if in annoyance at finding him still alive, no matter by what test she applied.

Her garments whispered in withdrawal, fanned him softly in farewell. A moment later the door closed and she had gone from the room. The wooden stairs sounded off her descending tread, as if knuckles were lightly rapping on them step by step.

Now the flight back to life began.

Fortified by hoarded intensity, the earlier stages of it went well. He threw back the coverings, he forced his body slantingly sideward atop the bed, until it had dropped over the side.

He was now strewn prone on the floor at bedside; he had but to raise himself erect.

He rested a moment. Violent flickering pains, like low-burning log flames licking at the lining of his stomach, assailed him, went up his breathing passage as up a flue, and then died out again into the dull, aching torpor that was with him always and that was at least bearable.

He was on his feet now, and working his way alongside the bed down toward its foot. From there to the chair was an open space, with no support. He let go of the bed's footrail with a defiant backward fling, cast off into the unsupported area. Two untrammeled steps, a lurch. Two steps more, a third, he was hastening into a fall now. But if he could reach the chair first— He raced the distance to the chair against it, and the chair won. He reached it, gripped it, rocked it; but he stayed up.

He donned his coat, buttoning it over without any shirt below. That was comparatively easy. Trousers too; he managed them by sitting on the chair and drawing them from the floor up.. But the shoes were an almost insuperable difficulty. To bend down to them in the ordinary way was an impossibility; the whole length of his body would have been excruciatingly curved.

He guided them, empty, first, by means of his feet, so that they stood perfectly straight, side by side. Then aimed each foot, one at a time, into the opening of its destined shoe, and wormed it in. But they gaped open, and it was impossible to proceed with them thus without imminent danger of being thrown from one step to the next.

He lay down on the floor, on his side. He scissored his legs, brought one up until he had caught his foot with both hands. There were five buttons on each shoe, but he chose only the topmost one, the most accessible, and forced it through its matching eyelet. Then changing legs, did it with the other.

Now he was erect again, accoutred to go, and there only remained lengthwise progress, over distance, to be accomplished. Only; he said the word over to himself with wistful irony.

Like a sleepwalker, taut at every joint; or like a mariner reeling across a storm-slanted deck, he crossed from chair to room door, and leaned inert there for a moment against its frame. Then softly took the knob in his grasp, and turned it, and held it after it was turned, so that it wouldn't click in recoil.

The door was open. He stepped through.

An oval window was let into the center of the hallway's frontal crosswall, to light the stairs and to give an outlook. A curtain of net was fastened taut across its pane.

He reached there, elbowing the wall for support, and put an eye to it, peering hungrily out into life. The curtain, brought so close to the eye's retina, acted like a filter screen; it dismembered the scene outside into small detached squares, separated by thick corded frames, which were the threads of the curtain, magnified at that short distance.

One square contained a segment of the front walk below, nothing else; all evenly slate-colored it was. The one above, again the walk, but at a greater outward distance now, a triangle of the turf bordering it beginning to cut in at the top, in green. The one still above that, turf and walk in equal proportions, with the white-painted base of one of the gate posts beginning to impinge off in the upper corner. And so on, in tantalizing fragments; but never the world whole, intact.

I want to live again, his heart pleaded; I want to live again out there.

He turned, and let the makeshift be, the quicker to be down below and at the original; and the stairs lay there before him, dropping away like a chasm, a serried cliff. His courage quailed at the sight for a minute, for he knew what they were going to cost. And the distant scrape of her chair in the kitchen below just then, added point to his dismay.

But he could only go onward. To go back was death in itself, death in bed.

He'd reached their tip now, and his eye went down them, all the cascading miles to their bottom. Vertigo assailed him, but he held his ground resolutely, clutching at the newel post with double grip as though it were the staff of life itself.

He knew that he would not be able to go down them upright, as the well did. He would overbalance, topple headfirst for sheer lack of leg support. He therefore lowered his own distance from the ground, first of all. He sat down upon the top step, feet and legs over to the second. He dropped them to the third, then lowered his rump to the second, like a child who cannot walk yet.

As he descended he was drawing nearer, ever nearer to her. For she was down there where he was going.

She sounded so close to him now. Almost, he could see before his very eyes everything she was doing, by the mere sound of it alone.

A busy little tinkering, ending with a tap against a cup rim: that meant she was stirring sugar into her coffee.

A creak from the frame of a chair: that meant that she was leaning forward to drink it.

A second creak: that meant that she had settled back after taking the first swallow.

He could hear bread crust crackle, as she tore apart a roll.

Crumbs lodged in her throat and she coughed. Then leaned forward to clear it with another swallow of her coffee.

And if he could hear her so minutely, how—he asked himself—could she fail to hear him; this stealthy rustling he must be making on the stairs?

He was afraid even to breathe, and he had never needed breath so badly.

At last the bottom, and he could only lie there a minute, rumpled as an empty sack that had fallen down from above, even if it had meant she would come out upon him any instant.

From where he was now there was only a straight line to travel, to the front door. But he knew he could not gain it upright. He had exhausted himself too much by now, spent himself too much on the way. How then gain support? How get there?

Struggling upright, it came to him of its own accord. He rotated his shoulders along the wall, turning now outward, next inward, then outward again, then inward—he *rolled* himself along beside the wall, and the wall supported him, and thus he did not fall, and yet progressed.

Midway there was an obstacle, to break his alliance with the wall. It was an antlered coatrack, its lower part a seat that extended far out, its upper part a tall thin panel of wood, set with a mirror. It was unsteady by its very nature, its proportions were untrue, he was afraid he would bring it down with him.

He circled his body awkwardly out and around it, holding it steady, so to speak, and got to the other side. But letting it go in safety was harder than claiming its support had been, and for a second or two he was held in a horrid trap there, afraid to take his hands off it, lest the sudden release of weight cause it to back and sway in revealing disturbance.

He took his near hand off it first, still held it on its far side, and that equalized the removal of pressure. Then cautiously he let go of it in the remaining place, and it did nothing but waver soundlessly for a moment or two, and then stilled again.

Safely free of it, he let himself down at last into a submerged huddle, sheltered now by its projection. Out of prostration, out of sheer inability to go on one additional step, and not out of caution, and yet it was that alone that saved him.

For suddenly, without any warning whatever, she had stepped to the kitchen doorway to the hall and was peering upward along the stairs. She even came forward, clambered up a few inquiring steps until she was in a position from which she could hear better, assure herself all was quiet. Then, satisfied, she came down again, turned about rearward, and went back to where she had been.

He removed the mangled length of shirting he had crushed into his mouth to stifle the hard breath that he would otherwise have been incapable of controlling, and it came away a watery pink.

Within moments after that, his lips were pressed flat against the seam of the outer door, in what was not meant for a kiss, but surely was one just the same.

So little was left to be done now, that he felt sure, even if his heart had already stopped beating and his body were already dead and cooling about him, he would still somehow have gone ahead and done it. Not even the laws of Nature could have stopped him now, so close to his goal.

The latch-tongue sucked back softly, and he waited, head still but held forward, to see if that little sound had reached her, would bring her out again. It didn't.

He pulled, and then, with a swimmingly uncertain motion, the door came away from its frame and an opening stood waiting.

He went through. He staggered forward and fell against the porch post outside, and stayed there inert, letting it hold him.

In a moment he had stumbled down the porch steps.

In another he had lurched the length of the walk, the gate post held him, as if he had fallen athwart it and been pierced through by it.

He was saved.

He was back in life again.

A curious odor filled his nostrils: open air.

A curious balm warmed his head, the nape of his neck: sunlight.

He was out on the public walk now. Swaying there in the white sunlight, his shadow on the ground swaying in accompaniment. Teetering master, teetering shadow. He marked for his own a tree growing at the roadside, a few short yards off.

He went toward it like an infant learning to walk; a grown infant. Short, stocky steps without bending the knees; kicking each foot up, in a stuttering prance; arms straight out before him to clasp the approaching objective. And then fell against its trunk, and embraced it, and clove there.

And then from there on to another tree.

And then another.

But there were no more trees after that. He was marooned.

Two women passed, market baskets over arms, and sodden there, he raised his hand to stay them, so that they might hear him long enough to give him help.

They swerved deftly to avoid him, tilted noses disdainfully in air, and swept on.

"Disgusting, at such an early hour!" he heard one say to the other.

"Time of day' has no meaning for drunkards!" her companion replied sanctimoniously.

He fell down on one knee, but then got up again, circling about in one place like some sort of a broken-winged bird.

A man going by slowed momentarily, cast him a curious look,

and Durand trapped his attention on that one look, took a tottering step toward him, again his hand raised in appeal.

"Will you help me, sir? I'm not well."

The man's slackening became a dead halt. "What is it, friend? What ails you?"

"Is there a doctor somewhere near here? I need to see one."

"There's one two blocks down that way, that I know of. I came past there just now myself."

"Will you lend me an arm just down that far? I don't think I can manage it alone—" The man split at times into two double outlines before his eyes, and then he would cohere again into just one.

The man consulted his pocket watch dubiously. "I'm late already," he grimaced. "But I can't refuse you on such a request." He turned toward him decisively. "Put your weight against me. I'll see that you get there."

They trudged painfully along together, Durand leaning angularly against his escort.

Once, Durand peered up overhead momentarily, at what everyone else saw every day.

"How wonderful the world is!" he sighed. "The sun on everything—and yet still enough left to spare."

The man looked at him strangely, but made no remark.

Presently he stopped, and they were there.

Out of all the houses in that town, or perhaps, out of all the doctors' houses in that town, it and it alone was not entered at ground level but had its entrance up at second-floor height. A flight of steps, a stoop, ran up to this. This was a new style in dwellings, mushrooming up in all the larger cities in whole blocks at a time, all of chocolate colored stone, and with their slighted first floors no longer called that, but known as "American basements."

Otherwise he could have been safely inside within a matter of moments after arriving before it.

But the good Samaritan, having brought him this far, at the

cost of some ten minutes of his own time, drew a deep breath of private anxiety, took out his watch and scanned it once more, this time with every sign of furrowed apprehension. "I'd like to take you all the way up these," he confessed, "but I'm a quarter of an hour behind in an appointment I'm to keep, as it is. I don't suppose you can manage them by yourself— Wait, I'll run up and sound the bell a moment. Then whoever comes out can help you up the rest of the way—"

He scrambled up, dented the pushbutton, and was down again in an instant.

"Will you be all right," he said, "if I leave you now?"

"Thank you," Durand breathed heavily, clinging to the ornamental plinth at bottom of the steps. "Thank you. I'm just resting."

The man set off at a lumbering run down the street, back along the way they had just come, showing his lack of time to have been no idle excuse.

Durand, alone and helpless again, turned and looked upward toward the door. No one had yet come to open it. His eye traveled sideward to the nearest window, and in the lower corner of that was placed a placard both of them had neglected to read in its entirety.

Richard Fraser, M.D.
Consulting Hours: 11 to 1, Mornings—

The half-hour struck from some church belfry in the vicinity. The half-hour before eleven. Half-past ten.

Suddenly two white hands, two soft hands, cupped themselves gently, persuasively, to the slopes of his wasted shoulders, one on each side, from behind, and in a moment more she had insinuated herself around to the front of him, blocking him off from the house, blocking the house off from him.

"Lou! Lou, darling! What is it? What brings you here like this? What are you thinking of—I found the door standing open just now. I found you gone from your bed. I've been running through the streets—I saw you standing here, fortunately, from the block below—Lou, how could you do such a thing to me; how could you frighten me like this—?"

A door opened belatedly, somewhere near at hand, but her face was in the way, her face close to his blotted out the whole world. "Yes?" a woman's voice said. "Did you wish something?"

She turned her head scarcely at all, the merest inch, to answer: "No, nothing. It was a mistake."

The door closed sharply, and life closed with it.

"Up," he breathed. "Up there. Someone—who can help me."

"Here," she answered softly. "Here, before you—the only one who can help you."

He moved weakly to one side to gain clearance, for an ascent he could never have made anyway.

She moved as he did, she stood before him yet.

He moved back again, waveringly.

She moved back again too, she stood before him always.

The waltz resumed, the slow and terrible waltz of death, there on those steps.

"Up," he pleaded. "Let me go up. The door. Have mercy."

Her voice was all compassion, she wept with honey. "Come back with me. My love. My poor dear. My husband." Her eyes too. Her hands, staying him so gently, so gently, he scarcely knew it.

"Be content," he wept weakly. "You've done enough. Give me this one last chance— Don't take it from me—"

"Do you think I would hurt you? Do you trust a stranger more than you would me? Don't you believe I love you, at *all?* Do you really doubt it that much?"

He shook his head bewilderedly. When the body's strength is spent, the mind's discernment dulls with it. Black is white and white is black, and the last voice that spoke is the true one.

"You do love me? You do, Bonny? In spite of all?"

"Can you ask that?" Her lips found his, there in broad daylight, in open street. Never was there a tenderer kiss, breathing such abnegation. Light as the wings of moths. "Ask your heart, now," she whispered. "Ask your heart."

"I've thought such terrible things. Bad dreams they must have been. But they seemed so real at the time. I thought you wanted me out of your way."

"You thought I was the cause of—your being ill like this?" Gambler to the end. She drew a step aside, the step that he had wanted her to take before. "My arms are here. The door is there above you. Now go to whichever one of us you want the most."

He took a swaying step toward her, where she now stood. His head fell upon her breast in ineffable surrender. "I am so tired, Bonny. Take me home with you."

Her breath stirred his hair. "Bonny will take you home."

She led him down the step, the one step toward salvation that was all he had been able to achieve.

Here and there, about them, the walks, the near one and the far, were dotted with a handful of curious passersby, halted in their tracks to watch the touching little scene, without knowing what it was about.

As he and she turned their way, these, their interest palling, set about resuming their various courses. But she called to one man, the nearest among them, before he could make good his departure.

"Sir! Would you try and find us a carriage? My husband is ill, I must get him home as soon as I can."

She would have moved a heart of stone. He tipped his hat, he hastened off on his quest. In a moment or two a carriage had come spanking around the lower turn, her envoy riding upright on the outside step.

It drew up and he helped her, supporting Durand on the one side while she, strong for all her diminutive height, sustained him bravely on the other. Between them they led him gently to the carriage, saw him comfortably to rest upon its seat; the stranger having to step up and into it backward, to do this, and then descend again from its opposite side after he had relinquished his hold on him.

She, settling down beside Durand, reached out and placed her own hand briefly atop the back of her anonymous helper's in accolade of tremulous gratitude. "Thank you, sir. Thank you. I do not know what I should have done without you."

"No one could do less, madam." He looked at her compassionately. "And may God be with the two of you."

"I pray He will," she answered devoutly as the carriage rolled off.

Behind it, on those same disputed steps, as it receded, a man now stood astraddle, a black bag in his hand, gazing after it with cursory interest, no more. He shrugged in incomprehension and completed his ascent, readying his key to put it to the door.

In the carriage on their brief run homeward no one could have been more solicitous.

"Lean down. Rest your head upon my lap, love. That will ease the jarring of the springs."

And in a moment, or so it seemed, they were back again at their own door; his long Calvary was undone, gone for nothing. He felt no pang; so complete, so narcoticizing, was the illusion of her love.

The driver, now, was the one to help her getting him down. And then she left him for a moment in his charge at their gate. "Stay here a moment, dear; hold to the post, until I find money to pay him. I came out without my purse, I was in such a fright over you." She ran in alone, the doorway stood empty for a brief while—(and he missed her, for that moment, he missed her)—then she came back again, still at full run, paid off the driver, took Durand into her sole charge.

Up onto the porch floor, a last receding flicker of the white sunlight draining off their backs, and in. A sweep of her arm, and the door was closed again behind him. Forever? For the last time?

Down the long dim hall, past the antlered hatrack, to the foot of the stairs. Every inch had once cost a drop of blood.

But love enfolded him, held him in its arms, and he didn't care. Or perhaps it was death already; and at onset of death you don't care either sometimes.

Then up the stairs a dragging step at a time. Her strength was superb, her will to help him indomitable.

At the landing, as the final turn began, he panted: "Stop here a moment."

"What is it?"

"Let me look back a moment at our sitting room, before we go up higher. I may never see it again. I want to say goodbye to it." He pointed with a wavering hand, out over the slanted rail. "See, there's the table that we sat by, so many evenings, before— this came upon me. See, there's the lamp, the very same lamp, that I always knew—when I was young and not yet married— would shine upon my wife's pretty face, just across from me. And it's shone on yours, Bonny. I thank it for that. Must it never shine on you for me again, Bonny?" His fingertips traced its outline, there against the empty distance that separated it from him. "The lamps of home, the lamps of love, are going out. For me they'll never shine again. Goodbye—"

"Come," she said faintly.

Back into the room again; the bier receiving back its dedicated dead.

She helped him to the bed, and eased him back upon it. Then drew up his feet after him. Took off his shoes, his coat, but nothing else. Then brought the covers slowly up and over him, sideward, like a winding sheet.

"Are you comfortable, Lou? Is your bed smooth enough?" She put hand to his brow. "This foolish foray of yours has cost you all your strength."

His eyes were fixed on her with a strange, melting softness. Like the eyes of a wounded dog, begging its release.

She turned hers away, then irresistibly they were drawn back again. "Why are you looking at me like that, my dear? What are you trying to say?"

He motioned to her with one finger to bend closer.

She inclined her head a little the better to hear what he had to say.

He reached up falteringly and stroked the fringe, the silken blonde bangs that curved before her cool smooth forehead.

Then he struggled higher, onto an elbow, as if cast upward by the ebb tide that was leaving him behind so rapidly.

"I love you, Bonny," he whispered fiercely. "No other one, no other love. From first to last, from start to finish. And beyond. Beyond, Bonny; do you hear me? Beyond. It will not end. *I* will, but it will not."

Her face came nearer still, slowly, uncertainly; like that of one dipping toward a new experience, feeling her way. Something had happened to it, was happening to it; he had never seen it so soft before. It was as if he were seeing another face, never born, peering shyly through the mask that had stifled it all these years; the face that should have been hers, that might have been—but that never had. The face of the soul, before the blasts of the world had altered it beyond recognition.

It came close to his, falteringly, through strange new latitudes of emotion, never traveled before.

There were tears in her eyes. It was no illusion; he saw them.

"Will a little love do, Lou?"

"Any amount."

"Then there *was* a moment in which I loved you. And this is it."

And the kiss, unforced, unsolicited, had all the bitter sweetness, the unattainable yearning, of a love that might have been. And he knew, his heart knew, it was the first she had ever really given him.

"That was enough," he smiled, content. "That was all I've ever wanted."

Claiming her hand, holding it in his, he fell into an uneasy sleep, a fever oblivion, for a while.

When he awoke, the dregs of daylight were settling in the west, like a fine white ash; the day was past. Her hand was still in his, and she was sitting there, her face toward him. She seemed not to have moved in all those hours, to have endured it, this thing new to her—pain for someone else's sake—without demur; to have kept her vigil with no company other than the sight of his deathbound face—and whatever thoughts that had brought her.

He released her hand. "Bonny," he sighed, agonized. "Get me another of those tonics, now. I am ready for it. It's better—that you do, I think—"

Involuntarily, she drew her head back sharply for a moment. Held her gaze to his. Then at last inclined it again to where it had been before.

"Why do you ask for it now? I haven't offered it."

"I'm in pain," he said simply. "I can't endure much more of it." And turned a little this way, then turned a little that. "If not in kindness, then in charity—"

"Later," she said evasively. "Don't talk that way, don't say such things."

Sweat started out on his face. His breath hissed through his nostrils. "When I did not want them, you urged them on me— Now that I plead with you, you deny me—" He heaved his body upward, then allowed it to fall back again. "Now, Bonny, now; I can't bear any more. This is as good a time as any. Why wait for the night to be further advanced? Oh, spare me the night, Bonny, spare me the night! It is so long—so dark—so lonely—"

She stood slowly, absently rubbing her frozen hand. Then with even greater slowness moved toward the door. She opened it, then stopped there to look back at him. Then went out.

He heard her going down the stairs. And twice he heard her stop, as though impulse had flagged; and then go on again, as she fanned it back to life once more.

She was gone about ten minutes in all. Ten minutes of hell, while flames licked at him all over.

Then presently the door opened and she had returned. She was carrying it in her hand. She came to him and set it down upon the stand, a little to the side of him, beyond easy reach.

"Don't— Not yet—" she said in a stifled voice, when he tried to reach for it. "Let it wait a while. A little later will do."

She lit the lamp, and then went over by the fireplace to fling the match away. Then she remained there by it, looking down into it. He knew she was not looking at anything there was there before her to see; she was in a revery that saw nothing.

His revery, on its part, saw everything. Everything again. Again he waltzed with her at Antoine's on their wedding night— "A waltz in sunlight, love; in azure, white and gold." Again her playful query sounded through their marriage door— "Who knocks" "Your husband." Again she stood revealed against the lighted midnight entryway—"Come into your wife's bedroom, Louis." Again they walked the seafront promenade at Biloxi, arm in arm, and the breeze swept off his hat, and she laughed to see him chase it, herself a spinning cyclorama of windswept skirts. Again he raised his arms above her sleeping form to let hundred-dollar bills flutter down upon it. Again—

Again, again, again—for the last time.

The truly cruel part of death is not the end of the body; it is the expiration of all memories.

A bright light, like a hot, flickering, yellow star, burned through the ghostly mesh of his death dreams. He looked over and she was standing sideward to the fireplace, holding a burning brand out-thrust toward it in her hand. Yet not a stick or twig; it was a scroll of tightly furled paper. And as the flame slowly slanted upward to-ward her hand, she deftly reversed it, taking it now by the charred end that had already been consumed and allowing the other to burn.

Then threw it down at last, and thrusting out her foot, trod upon its remnants here and there and the next place with little pats of finality.

"What are you doing, Bonny?" he whispered feebly.

She did not turn her head, as if it were of no consequence to her whether or not he had seen. "Burning a paper."

"What paper?"

Her voice had no tone. "A policy of insurance—upon your life— payable for twenty thousand dollars."

"It was not worth the trouble. It lacked force, I told you that."

"It was in force again just now. I pledged my ring and made up the payments."

Suddenly he saw her cover her face with the flats of her hands as if, even after having burned it, she still could not bear the remembered aftersight of it.

He sighed, but without much emotion. "Poor Bonny. Did you want the money that badly? I would have—" He didn't finish it.

He lay there for a moment or two after that, inert.

"I'd better drink this now," he said softly, at last.

He strained until his arm could reach the glass. He clasped it, took it up.

— 64 —

SUDDENLY SHE had turned, thrown herself toward him. He hadn't known the human form could move so quickly. But she was so deft, she was so small. Her hand flashed out, a white missile before his face. The tumbler was gone from his grasp. Glass riddled on the floor somewhere offside beyond his ken.

Her face seemed to melt into shapeless weeping lines, like a face seen through rain running down a pane. She caught him to her convulsively, crushing his face against her soft breast. He hadn't known her embrace could hold that much strength. She'd never loved him enough to exert it to the full before.

"Oh, merciful God," she cried out wildly. "Look down and forgive me! Stop this terrible thing, turn it back, undo it! Lou, my Lou! Only now I see it! Oh, my eyes are open, open now at last! What have I done?"

She dropped to her knees before him, as she had that night in Biloxi when they first came together again. But how different now; how false, how studied her pleas, her posture then, how inconsolable her passion of remorse now, a veritable paroxysm of penitence, that nothing, no word of his, could assuage.

Her sobbing had the wild, panting turbulence of a child's, strangling her words, rendering her almost incoherent. Perhaps this was a child crying now, a newborn self in her, a little girl held mute for twenty years, only now belatedly finding voice.

"I must have been mad— Out of my mind— How could I have listened to such a scheme? But when I was with him, I saw only him, never you— He brought out that old bad self in me— He made wrong things seem right, or just something to snicker at—"

Her fingers, pleading, traced the outlines of his face; trembling, felt of his lips, of his lidded eyes, as if seeking to restore them to what they had been. Nothing, no voracious kisses seeking him out everywhere, no splurge of teardrops falling all over him, could bring him back.

"I've killed you! I've killed you!"

And rebel to the end, fell prone and beat upon the floor with her fist, in helpless rebellion at the trickery fate had practised on her.

Then suddenly her weeping stopped. As suddenly as though a stroke of fear had been laid across her bowed head. Her pummelling hand stilled.

Her head came up. She was bated, she was watchful, she was crafty. Of what he could not tell. She turned and looked behind her at the window, in dreadful secretive apprehension.

"Nobody shall take you from me," she said through clenched teeth. "I'll not give you up. Not for anyone. It's *not* too late, it's *not!* I'm going to get you out of here, where you'll be safe— Hurry, get your things. We'll go together. I have the strength for the two of us. You're going to live. Do you hear me, Lou? You're going to live—yet."

She sidled up beside the window, creeping along the wall until she had gained an outer edge of it; then peered narrowly out, using the slit between curtain edge and wall. He saw her nod slightly to herself, as if in confirmation of something she had expected to see.

"What is it?" he whispered. "Who's out there?"

She didn't answer. Suddenly she drew her head back sharply, as if fearful she had been detected just then from the outside.

"Shall I put out the lamp?" he asked.

"No!" She motioned to him horrified. "For God's sake, no! *I* was to have done that. It will be taken for a signal that—it's over. Our only chance is to go now, and leave it still on, as if—as if we were here yet."

She came running back to him, yet not forgetting even as she did so to throw still another backward glance of dread at the window; she settled down beside him with a billowing-out of her dress, took hold of his untended foot, raised it, while he still strove valiantly with the first.

"Quickly, your other shoe! There, that's all— No time for more."

She helped him quit his sitting position on the edge of the bed, held him upright on his feet beside her, like some sort of an inanimate mannikin or rigid toy soldier that would fall over if her hands quitted him for just an instant and left him to himself.

"Lean on me, I'll help you. There! There! Move your feet, that's it! Oh, Lou, try this one time more. Just this one time more. You did it before. This time we're *together,* we're going together. This time it's our love itself that's running away—for its very life."

He smiled at her, as the floor slowly crept by beneath their tottering feet, inch by painful inch.

"Our love," he whispered bravely. "Our love, running away. Where are we going?"

"Any train, anywhere. Only let us get out of this house—"

She struggled heroically with him, as though she were the spirit of life itself, contesting with the spirit of death that sought to possess him. Now holding him back when he inclined too far forward, now drawing him on when he swayed too far backward. Out the room door and along the upper hall. But on the stairs once she nearly lost him. For a moment there was a terrible equipoise while he hung forward, threatening to topple downward, all the way downward, head first, and she strained her small body backward to the last ounce of its strength, striving to regain the balance that had been incautiously lost.

Not a whimper came from her in that frightful moment, and surely had he gone downward to his own destruction, she would have clung to him to the end, gone down with him to her own, rather than release him. But a strength came into her arms that had never been in them before, and slowly her squeezing pull, her embrace of desperation, righted him, drew him back against her, and equilibrium was regained.

And then, as they rested half-recumbent against the rail a moment, she with her back to it, he with his head pillowed on her breast, she found time to stroke his hair back soothingly from his brow and whisper: "Courage, love. I will not let you fall. Is it very hard for you?"

"No," he murmured wanly, rolling his eyes upward toward her downturned face above him, "because you are with me."

Downward once more then, more cautiously this time, step by mincing step, like a pair of ballet dancers locked in one another's arms, pointed toe following pointed toe in a horrid, groping, blinded sort of pas de deux.

As they neared the bottom, were within one last step of it, she suddenly stopped, frozen. And in the silence, over the rise and fall of their two breaths, they both heard it.

There was a low, urgent tapping going on against the front door. Very stealthy it was, very secretive. Meant only to be caught by a single pair of ears, no other. A pair forewarned to expect it, to listen for it. Two fingers at the most, perhaps only one, kept striking at the woodwork; scratching at it, scraping at it, it might almost have been said, so softened was their impact.

A peculiar whistle sounded with it. Also modulated very low, very guardedly. Little more than a stirring of the breath against a wavering upper lip. Plaintive, melancholy, like the sound of a baby owl. Or a lost wisp of night wind trying to find its way in.

It was intermittent. It waited. Then sounded again. Waited. Sounded again.

"Sh, don't make any noise!" He could feel her arms tighten protectively about him. As if instinctively seeking to safeguard him against something. Something that she understood, knew the meaning of, he didn't. "The back way," she breathed. "We'll have to go out by there— Hold your breath, love. For the love of heaven, don't make a sound or—we'll both be dead in here where we stand."

Cautiously, straining against one another, as much now to insure their mutual silence as before now it had been to maintain his uprightness, they quitted the stairs, crept rearward on the lower floor, into the dining room. She halted him there for a preciously spared moment, to reach for a decanter of stimulant, give it a twisting shake, extract the glass stopper and moisten his lips with it, while she still continued to hold him within the curve of her other arm.

"I'm afraid to give you too much," she mourned. "You are so spent."

"My love's beside me," he promised, as if speaking to himself. "I won't fail."

They moved on into the unlighted kitchen beyond, swimming submerged in the blue tide of night, but with the curtained glass square of its door, the back way out, peering at them, distinguishable in the dimness.

He heard the bolt scrape softly back beneath her diligently groping fingers. Then the door moved inward, and the coolness of escape was grateful in their faces.

The last sound behind them, traveling through the whole length of the house from its front, was that low tapping, recommencing again after a grudging wait. A little more hurried now than before, a little more insistent. And with it the whistle, with its secretive message, that seemed to say: "Open to me. Open. You know who I am. You know me. Why do you delay?" A little sharper now, a little more importunate, as its patience shortened.

He did not ask her who it was. There were so many things in life, it was too late now to ask, too late now to know. There was only one thing he wanted to know, he needed to know, and that at long last had been told him: she loved him.

They floundered out into the backyard of their house, and out through the gate that led into it, from the lane that ran behind the backs of all these houses; down that to its mouth, and from there onto the sideward street. Then along that, and around the turn, and into the street that ran behind the one their house had faced upon.

"The station," she kept saying. "The station— Oh, try, Lou. It's just a few short streets ahead. We'll be safe, if we can only reach it. There's always someone there, day or night— There are lights there, no one can hurt us there. A train— Any train, to anywhere—"

Any train, his heart kept saying in time to its desperate pounding, to anywhere.

On and on and on, two lurching figures, breaths sobbing in their throats; reeling drunken, yes, drunken with the will to live and love, in peace. No eye to see them, no hand to help them.

It was in sight already, across the open square ahead, the station square, the hub of the town,—or so she told him, he could no longer see that far before him—when suddenly the combination of their overtaxed strengths gave out, her arms, her will, could do no more, and he fell flat there in the dust beside her.

She tried desperately to bring him up again, but she'd weakened so that his inertness could only bring her down half recumbent beside him, instead, as if he were pulling at her, not she at him. "Don't waste time," he sighed. "I can't— Not a step further."

She struggled upright again, drove fingers distractedly through her hair, looked this way, that.

"I've got to get you in out of the open! Oh, my love, my love, we may be caught yet if we stay here too long—"

Then bending to his face, to give him courage with a kiss, ran on and left him there where he was. She disappeared into a building fronting on the square, with a lighted gas bowl over its doorway and the legend: "Furnished Rooms for Travelers."

In a moment she returned to view again, beckoning to someone within to hasten out after her. She came running back toward him, without waiting, holding her skirts with both hands at once, bunched forward and aloft to give her feet the freedom they needed. Behind her appeared a shirtsleeved man, struggling into his coat as he emerged. He set out after her.

"Here," she cried. "Over this way. Here he is."

He joined her beside the loglike figure on the ground.

"Help me get him to one of your rooms."

The man, a beefy stalwart, lifted him bodily in both arms, turned with him to face toward the lodging house. She ran around him from one side to the next, trying to be of help, trying to take hold of Durand's feet.

"No, I can manage," the man said. "You go first and hold the door."

The black sky over the station square, pocked with stars, eddied about this way and that just over Durand's upturned eyes. He had a feeling of being very close to it. Then it changed to gaslight pallor on a plaster ceiling. Then this slanted off upward, gradually dimming, and he was being borne up stairs. He could hear the quick tap of her deft feet, pressing close behind them, in the spaces between his carrier's slower plod. And once he felt his dangling hand caught up swiftly for a moment by two small ones, and the fervent print of a pair of velvety lips placed on it.

"I'm sorry it's so high up," the man said, "but that's all I have."

"No matter," she answered. "Anything. Anything."

They passed through a doorway, the ceiling dark at first, then gradually brightening to tarnished silver following the soft, spongy fluff of an ignited gas flow. Their shadows swam about on it, then blended, faded.

"Shall I put him on the bed, madam?"

"No," Durand said weakly. "No more beds. Beds mean dying. Beds mean death." His eyes sought hers, as the man lowered him to a chair, and he smiled through them. "And I'm not going to die, am I, Bonny?" he whispered resolutely.

"Never!" she answered huskily. "I'll not let you!" She clenched her tiny fists, and set her jaw, and he could see sparks of defiance in her eyes, as if they were flint stones.

"Shall I get you a doctor, madam?" the man asked.

"Nothing more this minute. Leave us alone together. I'll let you know later. Here, take this for now." She thrust some money at him through the door. "I'll sign the registry book later."

She locked it, came running back to Durand. She dropped before him in an imploring attitude.

"Louis, Louis, did I once want money, did I once want fine clothes and jewels? I'd give them all at this minute to have you stand strong and upright on your legs before me. I'd give my very *looks* themselves—" she clawed at her own face, dragging its supple cheeks forward as if seeking to transfer it toward him, "—and what more have I to give?"

"Make your plea to God, dear, not to me," he said faintly, gently. "I want you as you are. I wouldn't change you even for life itself. I don't want a good woman, a noble woman. I want my vain, my selfish Bonny— It's you I love, the badness and the good alike, and not the qualities they tell us a woman should have. Be brave in this: don't change, ever. For I love you as I know you, and if God can love, then He can understand."

The tears were streaming in reckless profusion from her eyes, she who had never wept in all her life; the tears of a lifetime, stored up until now, and now splurging wildly forth all in one burst of regret.

His fingers reached tremulously to trace their course. "Don't weep any more. You've wept so much these past few minutes. I wanted to give you happiness, not tears."

She caught her breath and struggled with it, restraining it, quelling it. "I'm so new at love, Louis. It's only a half-day now. Only a half-day out of twenty-three years. Louis," she asked like a child in wonderment, "is this what it's like? Does it always hurt so?"

He remembered back along their story, spent now. "It hurts. But it's worth it. It's love."

A strange snorting sound came from the outside, somewhere near by, through the closed window, as if a great bull-like beast, hampered with clanking chains, were muzzling the ground.

"What was that?" he asked vaguely, raising his head a little.

"It's a train, out there somewhere in the dark. A train, coming into the station, or shuttling about in the yards—"

His arms stiffened on the chair rests, thrusting him higher. "Bonny, it's for us, it's ours. Any train, to anywhere— Help me. Help me get out of here. I can do it, I can reach it—"

She had lived by violence all her life; by sudden change, and swift decision. She rose to it now on the instant, she was so used to it. She was ready at a word. Instantly her spirit flared up, kindled by his.

"Anywhere. Even New York. You'll stand by me there if they—"

She thrust her arm around behind him, helped him rise from the chair. Again the endless flight was about to recommence. Tightarmed together, they took a step forward, toward the door. A single one—

He fell. And this time there was a finality to it that could not be mistaken. It was the fall to earth of the dead. He lay there flat, unresisting, supine, waiting for it. He lay face up, looking at her with despairing eyes.

Her face swiftly dipped to his.

"No time," he whispered through immobile lips. "Don't speak. Put your lips to mine. Tell me goodbye with that."

Kiss of farewell. Their very souls seemed to flow together. To try to blend forever into one. Then, despairing, failed and were separated, and one slipped down into darkness and one remained in the light.

She drew her lips from his, for sheer necessity of breathing. There was a smile of ineffable contentment left on his, there where her lips had been.

"And that was my reward," he sighed.

His eyes closed, and there was death.

A shudder ran through her, as though the throes of dying were in her herself. She shook him, trying to bring back the motion that had only just left him, but left him forever. She pressed him to her, in desperate embrace that he was no longer within, only some dead thing he had left behind. She pleaded with him, called to him. She even tried to make a bargain with death itself, win a delay.

"No, wait! Oh, just one minute more! One minute give me, and then I'll let him go! Oh, God! Oh, Someone! Anyone at all! Just one more minute! I have something I want to tell him!"

No desolation equal to that of the pagan, suddenly bereft. For to the pagan, there is no hereafter.

She flung herself downward over him, and her hair, coming unbound, flowed over him, covering his face. The golden hair that he had loved so, made a shroud for him.

Her lips sought his ear, and she tried to whisper into it, for him alone to hear. "I love you. I love you. Can't you hear me? Where are you? That is what you always wanted. Don't you want it now?"

In the background of her grief, distant, dim, unheeded, echoes seemed to rise around her. A muffled pounding on the door, clamoring voices backing it, conjured there now, at just this place, this moment, who knows how? Perhaps by long-pent suspicions of neighbors overflowing at last into denunciation; perhaps that other crime in Mobile long, long ago, overtaking them at last—too late, too late. For she had escaped, just as surely as he had.

"Open, in there! This is a police order! Open this door, do you tear?"

Their meaning could not impress, their threat could not af-fright. For she was somebody else's prisoner now. She had escaped them.

Moaning anguished into a heedless ear: "Oh, Louis, Louis! I have loved you too late. Too late I have loved you."

The knocking and the clamor and the grief faded out, and there was nothing left.

"And this is my punishment."

———

The soundless music stops. The dancing figures wilt and drop. The Waltz is done.

THE END

AMERICAN MYSTERY CLASSICS *from*

*Available now
in hardcover and paperback:*

And more!